Also by Jack Estes

A Field of Innocence

A Soldier's Son

SEARCHING for GURNEY

SEARCHING for GURNEY

JACK ESTES

O'Callahan Press  Lake Oswego, Oregon

Printed in the United States of America

ISBN 978-0-9973990-1-1

This is a work of fiction. All characters and events pertaining to the characters are works of the author's imagination. Situations pertaining to the Vietnam War and its aftermath were inspired by actual events.

Cover photo:"Marines Patrol Hills, 1969" from the U.S. Marine Corps Archives, Jonathan F. Abel Collection. Official USMC photo by Sergeant Ken Barth. Photo has been modified from the original and meets conditions under the Creative Commons Attribution 2.0 license. References to music of the era include "Eve of Destruction" by P.F. Sloan, Copyright © 1964; and "Give Peace a Chance" by John Lennon, Copyright © 1969.

Book and cover design by Pam Wells
Text and titles are set in Dante MT Std. and Strayhorn MT Std.

Published by O'Callahan Press, Lake Oswego, Oregon

To the Marines who fought in the jungles and rice paddies in Vietnam. May their sacrifice of body and soul never be forgotten.

1

JT

JT WOKE, BUT THEY WERE STILL DEAD. Seventeen dead, two wounded, two missing. The dream stuck in his mind: rice paddies, jungle, tree line exploding. He got up, head pounding, pulse racing, thinking.

Go to the baby's room.

In the hallway, he could see Marines facedown, others mangled and broken-boned. Anna's bedroom was scattered with the dead. Her crib was tucked in the corner, nightlight on the dresser, clowns and zebras dancing across her wall.

The soldiers disappeared.

He picked her up. He felt safe holding her in the darkness. Anna reminded him he was home. They sat in the rocking chair in front of the window. Soon the moon dropped below the trees, and he kept rocking her until morning.

Sunlight moved through the windows and swept across the wooden floor as he placed Anna in her crib. Quietly, he returned to Ashley's side. Rolling in her sleep, she reached instinctively, pulling him close.

Soon his mind drifted to the night Anna was born. He was in Vietnam, deep in the jungle, dug in on the side of a mountain not far from Khe Sanh. The day had been long and hard. His company was cutting and hacking through terrain so steep, ropes were needed to pull each other up. They set in to form a perimeter as the sun disappeared. He was digging his fighting hole when the radio message blew across the world, to headquarters, out to the field before passing from Marine to Marine in the dark. Finally, it reached him.

"JT," his squad leader whispered. "Red Cross radioed. Don't flip out, man, but they say your old lady had a baby."

He felt Ashley's cold feet run along his legs, his mind locked on that amazing night. He imagined her in some clean, white hospital bed, lying back, pushing life into the world. And he was in the jungle eight thousand miles away, diggin' a hole. They were both nineteen.

Back then, JT thought God ruled everything. It was simple. If he woke up in the morning, it was a bonus and everything else was meaningless. Now that he was home, the world seemed complicated, out of control. Nothing made sense.

JT rolled to his side and touched Ashley's face. He wanted to kiss her and be inside of her, but then he heard the tenant upstairs walk across the floor, pause, and flush the toilet.

They lived on the main floor of an old two-story house that had been converted into three separate apartments. Pearl, who was eighty and senile, lived in the basement with her big, brown, bugeyed cat. Duane, his wife, Megan, and their baby took the top flat. The house was fifty years old but well maintained, with green shag carpet, shiny hardwood floors, high ceilings, and an ancient furnace that clanked and chugged like an old steam engine. The front yard was small, with a couple of tall fir trees and a few red rose bushes running around the perimeter. There was a front porch with a hanging swing that looked out on the yard and street. A detached garage, leaning hard, ready to fall, stood at the end of the driveway. Duane kept some tools in there, and on nice days he'd work on his car in the driveway or fix neighbors' cars for a few extra bucks.

JT's home was just outside the Portland city limits in a quiet, blue-collar neighborhood full of big, older homes that had been deteriorating for years. It was affordable and an easy walk to a park, shopping, a couple of taverns, and churches. He could catch the bus at the end of the block. That summer it was warm; folks barbecued in backyards and hung laundry on sagging clotheslines next to gardens of corn, tomatoes, and squash. The smell of hot briquettes and hamburgers floated over fences and mixed with the sweet smell of pot drifting. It was hippies and hard hats living side by side in the summer of '69.

JT lay in bed, relishing the feel of fresh sheets, listening to the shower run upstairs. He rolled over to Ashley, kissed her awake, and lifted her nightie. Soon he was touching her breasts, then inside feeling strong. He loved her as she moaned; and when he released he was so happy he wanted to cry.

For over thirteen months in Vietnam, he'd never felt secure. Not once had he closed his eyes and drifted into a deep sleep. Maybe in the hospital, but cries from the other wounded would wake him. Now he was back in the world making love to his wife and holding his child. Thank God.

He thought he'd better get up before his neighbor used all the hot water. He slipped out of his shorts and stood by the bed looking down on Ashley. She was beautiful. Long brown hair slipped to the side of her face, lips parted, revealing the whiteness of her teeth. He loved her teeth. He thought of the old women in Vietnamese village markets, squatting, spitting, teeth blackened by betel nut, skin wrinkled. But Ashley's skin was smooth as a whisper and the color of peaches. He closed his eyes for a moment and said thank you.

He showered, leaving towels scattered on the floor. Standing in front of the bathroom mirror, he rubbed his hands up and down his stomach, feeling the balled ridges of muscles. His hair was still military short and his thick neck, face, and forearms were tanned from the harshness of the Asian sun. His body was perfect except for the slightest scar on the side of his face that cut just below his ear. For a moment, he saw his face open, blood rolling in his mouth. But he shook his head and threw a full-front, double-arm Superman pose at his reflection, forcing himself to feel good about the way he looked.

As he dropped to the floor to do fifty push-ups, Ashley asked him to bring home some milk after work. He dressed, kissed Ashley and the baby, grabbed a banana, and flew out the door. He ran to the bus stop ready to defeat the day.

The bus dropped JT off a block from his office. He charged up the sidewalk and was only a few minutes late by the time he walked through the office door.

Steve, the assistant manager of the mailroom, stopped him as he entered. Steve was the boss's son, twenty-one, in a wheelchair, both ankles broken. He told everyone in the office he did it falling off a roof, adjusting a TV antenna.

The office janitor had told JT the truth. Steve had been drafted but didn't want to go. The night before he was to report for his physical, he'd dropped acid and jumped out of the second-story window of his parents' house. He hit a wheelbarrow on the way down, and his ankles had cracked like broken baseball bats.

"You know you're late again," Steve said. "If you don't show up on time, my dad's going to make me fire you." He pulled a hankie from his pocket, took off his glasses, wiped the lenses, and looked at JT with disdain. "Do you know what I mean?"

"Sorry, man," JT said, his body tense.

Steve shook his head like JT was a lazy dumbass, then wheeled away.

Feeling the bastard's scorn, JT walked to the time clock and punched in. He was angry. Just hated this pissant job. If the dick wasn't in a chair, he could put him in one. But he wanted to do what's right. Make Ashley proud. That's all. He had it planned—work hard, make a good impression, get a raise, end up running the joint. After all, he'd led men into battle, run patrols, set ambushes, called in gunships, destroyed villages and hillsides. He'd fired rifles, machine guns, tossed grenades, and killed enemy soldiers so often that not killing felt odd. So this mailroom job was a skate. Skating for a fat man. No problem here, except the assistant manager, who needed his attitude rearranged.

At lunch, JT bought a tuna sandwich at Newberry's, then sat down to eat it on the grass in front of the post office. An emaciated, stray dog ambled up.

"Beat it," JT said. The dog didn't move, and JT saw a look of desperation in the dog's eyes. He tore off half of his sandwich, threw it on the grass, and watched it disappear in a gulp.

The post office was the same big stone and concrete building where he joined the Corps. Still had a recruiting poster out front, featuring a Marine in dress blues. He'd signed up with his friend Jerry on the buddy plan. They enlisted together so that they could be MPs and wear the same great-looking uniform. But Jerry showed up roaring drunk, his blood pressure soared, and he flunked his physical. Couple of hours later JT left for boot camp alone.

He watched the crowded sidewalk. On one corner, a couple of long-haired guys in patched blue bell-bottoms and tie-dyed tank tops were passing a joint. Next to them stood a heavyset girl in a granny dress playing a violin. At her feet was a violin case scattered with coins. Each time people would walk by, one of the guys would hide the joint behind his back and scam for spare change. If he were given money, he'd flash a peace sign, toss the money in the violin case, and thank them. Then he'd laugh behind their backs like they were stupid. Sometimes he'd ask the wrong person and get a *Fuck off, get a job.* But mostly people just walked by.

As the crowds passed, the sidewalk a circus, JT felt odd, like he'd been dropped from the sky, without roots, without connection to this world. He was happy to be alive and with Ashley, but nothing seemed real. Even eating seemed flat, unimportant. He was used to eating only when he was hungry. Food gave life, especially after humpin' all day looking for Victor Charles, but water after a fire-fight exploded the senses. Parched lips bleeding. Water—yeah!

JT had ten minutes left on his lunch break when a small group approached the post office carrying cardboard placards with hand-written slogans—

Peace Now!

Make Love Not War!

Nixon Is a War Criminal!

One in the group was carrying a North Vietnamese red flag with the gold star; another, a blown-up picture of dead Vietnamese civilians. The group marched to the top of the stone steps just in front of the entrance to the post office, next to the large recruiting poster.

The sight of the NVA flag made JT furious. He fought those bastards. Killed some.

Suddenly, a small woman dressed in blue jeans and a white T-shirt with a picture of political activist Angela Davis on it stepped from the group. She looked to her left and motioned to someone to move a sign, then held a bullhorn to her mouth.

"My name is Sashi Ji, and I am a member of the Students for a Democratic Society. We're here to protest the brutal slaughter of thousands of Vietnamese by our racist military pig government."

By now, a crowd had gathered. Two guys in blue work shirts and yellow hard hats with US flag decals were standing at the back, shouting.

"Get your ass outta here, commie!"

"Bitch!"

JT's body tingled as if he were about to go on patrol. These activists had no respect for the Marines who fought and died while they stayed home, smoking dope and dodging the draft.

His anger boiled. He wanted to join in with the hard hats, but he had rent to pay. He pushed through the shouting and shoving and stormed back to his office.

JT CAUGHT A BUS JUST AFTER 5:00 p.m., and by the time it dropped him off at his corner, any anger had long passed. When he reached the sidewalk in front of his house, Duane was working on Ashley's Volkswagen. She'd bought it just before JT came home. It had problems, and he'd asked Duane to check it out.

"Hey, car man, what's up?"

Duane drew his head out from under the rear hood. "Trying to get your darn distributor cap in place. Just cleaned the points, but it still runs like crap. I think you need new points and plugs. Maybe a new rotor."

"What's that gonna run me?"

"Ten, twelve bucks for parts, and ten bucks for my time. So how's the new job?"

"The job's OK. Can't stand the beat-off I work for. Boss's son."

"I can dig it. We got a boss's daughter who works in payroll. Every time she cuts us a check, she acts like she's doing us a favor."

JT nodded. "I appreciate you looking at the car. I'll catch up with you later. Thanks, man." He jogged up the steps past a couple of Anna's toys and pulled open the screen door.

"I'm home!"

It felt good to be home. Even though he had only been gone for the day, it seemed as if he had been away a long time. Every day felt like that. If he couldn't see them, something might have changed. Anna or Ashley might be hurt. But Anna was playing in her playpen in the middle of the front room, smiling, trying to say something. JT picked her up.

"How's my big girl doing today? Did you miss your daddy? Come on, give me a kiss! Come on now."

Ashley walked in. Her hair was tied in the ponytail that she often wore around the house. Tall and slender, she was a confident young woman, not shy of showing her emotions no matter what they were. She was artistic and still painted. She arranged their sparse furniture and her paintings perfectly, she thought. And she was insistent that everything had a place and shouldn't be disturbed. Every day the house looked like it had just been professionally cleaned.

She had met JT in biology class when they were in high school and was attracted to him immediately. He was big and strong; he could protect her. When he joined the Marines, she was afraid for him, and when he came home, he was different. He never smiled and rarely laughed, and she had a foreboding confusion about who he really was now. He had changed. He carried a sense of danger with him. Like he could explode at any time. Especially when he felt blamed for something wrong. But she was smiling when she saw JT holding Anna and moved to hug him.

"I missed you, baby man." She kissed him and moved from his embrace, brushing a hair from her mouth, and placed Anna back in the pen. "Your dad called. Wants you to call."

"He's going to croak if he doesn't stop drinking."

"Call him. He may need help. How was work?"

"Work was easy, but Stevie gave me a little heat for being late. No sweat." He pulled her tight up against him and kissed her mouth and got hard immediately.

She could sense his hunger. "Come on, honey. Not now. Did you bring the milk?"

"Oh, man, I forgot." He relaxed. "Sorry. I'll run up to the store right now."

A hint of disappointment glanced off her face as she stretched up on her toes to kiss his cheek. She pulled away with an exaggerated frown. "OK, but dinner will be ready soon, so hurry up."

JT ran out the door, jumped to the sidewalk, and sprinted off toward the Little Store.

He felt such energy. So alive. So full, like he could do anything. He jogged through the park, stopped. Three guys were shooting some hoops. They needed him. He'd kick ass quick. Two games into it, he realized he was running late.

"Gotta run." He excused himself from the court, jogged back out of the park, crossed the street, and walked into the Little Store.

The Little Store was no wider than a couple of underground bunkers. There were maybe a dozen shelves on the walls, a small center aisle, and on the aisle shelf small hand-printed signs: *Shoplifting is a crime. If we ain't got it, it ain't worth getting.* The selection was limited, though, to dented cans, boxes of cold cereal, toilet paper, detergent, and loaves of Wonder Bread. Two old red Coca-Cola coolers chilled bottles.

JT reached down through the water and ice and pulled out a bottle of milk, shook off the excess ice, and grabbed a quart of beer as an afterthought. Even though he had been in the store several times, he'd never bought beer. He turned back toward the counter tended by Charlie, the owner.

Charlie was sixty and lived in an apartment above the store. He was a friendly, rotund man with hair the color and texture of stamped-down snow. His fat face was blushed, and his bulbous nose was off center. He wore a white butcher's apron with his name embroidered in blue stitching. Although Charlie was friendly, he kept a big meat cleaver under the counter just below the cash register. He once whacked a robber in the neck and nearly split the guy in half.

"You got ID, kid?" Charlie asked in a husky, friendly tone.

JT turned the color of Charlie's nose. He was underage. Rather than argue about how he was a vet and fought and all that, he just said, "Forget it. I forgot my ID."

He paid for the milk and left, pissed off, when a slender dude with hair hanging below his shoulders walked up. The guy had an unlit joint in his mouth, no shirt or shoes, and looked like he was stoned.

"Say, Slick," the guy said. He fumbled in his jean pockets looking for a match and teetering backward, almost stumbling over the
curb. "Want to score some hash, mescaline, yellow sunshine?"

JT looked down at the milk and twisted the bag shut.

"No, thanks."

The guy smiled as if the corner of his mouth was being pinched.
"Wanta hit of this doobie I'm fixing to fire up?"

"Thanks, man," JT said, and followed him into the alley next to
the piano store.

"Name's Smoke," the guy said as he fired up the joint. He pulled
on it three times, holding the smoke deep before passing it on.

JT blew on the lit end to get it going again and took a long hit.
As he sucked in, he felt paranoid about smoking pot on the streets.
They took turns on the doobie.

"You've got some short hair, Slick. What's the deal?"

"Just got out of the Marines."

"Far out."

JT was getting a slight buzz, while Smoke's body started listing
to the side, held up by the alley wall.

"You in Vi-et-nam, Slick?"

"Yeah," JT said, not liking the question.

"Far out!"

Smoke took a roach clip out of his pants pocket and secured the
last of the joint. "This is some bad shit. Selling ounces for ten bucks.
Real clean. No shake, just buds. Can you dig it?"

JT mulled it over. Smoke's weed wasn't that good. In the Nam, he
could purchase a party pack of twelve tightly rolled joints in a plastic
baggie for ten bucks, tops. One toke would put him right on his ass.

"Sorry, man. I'm busted. Thanks for the hit. Gotta run."

"Later, Slick."

Smoke looked bum-kicked that no dope deal went down. He
took a last toke, ate the roach, then walked into the Little Store where
he talked to Charlie and ripped off a candy bar on his way out.

By the time JT got home, dinner was long over. Ashley was in the front room, steamed, Anna in her arms, exasperation in her voice.

"What happened? Where have you been? I've been worried. I waited dinner over an hour."

"Hey, lighten up," he snapped. "I shot some hoops. What's the big fucking deal? I'm hungry."

"Fix your own dinner." She walked out of the living room, down the hall into the bedroom, and slammed the door.

Ashley lay down on the bed with Anna and cried. He had changed. The gentleness he once had was missing. He frightened her. Her mom said that after WWII, Ashley's dad was a different man, too. Drank all the time. Got smashed after work, came home swearing, bouncing off walls. He'd slap Ashley, beat her mother. It went on for years before her mother had the courage to leave him. There was no way she would live through that again.

She wanted everything to be perfect. She wanted to please him by making a good dinner. She'd taken time over it, when she could have been reading a magazine on the back porch with a soda. He didn't understand, or maybe he didn't care. He looked at her as if he wanted to hurt her. That look was frightening. Unsafe. It was like her dad all over again.

In the other room, JT sat at the table, enraged. He could hear her crying in the bedroom with Anna, and he knew what she would say. *You aren't the same. You're like my dad. I'm scared you'll hurt me.* She'd said these things when he was first back. But it was like she expected that just saying this would fix him inside.

Didn't she get it? He was out of control. He couldn't stand being out of control. This wasn't who he really was—she knew that. A few weeks ago, he had power. He was a Marine with a machine gun and was feared by the enemy. He could call in artillery and napalm, make life-and-death decisions. He saw his friends shudder and die as life left their eyes. She didn't know what that was like, but damn it! She should trust he was doing his best. He'd made it home, and that was a big deal.

Give me time, he thought. *I'll get better.* He loved her, and none of this other shit mattered. He could have been shot in the face and she's worried about milk. Fuck the milk and fuck the dinner. Adrenaline surged. He stood up, punched a hole in the wall, and busted the screen door on his way out.

2

Coop

Eastern Oregon, Winter 1970

TEN O'CLOCK IN THE MORNING AND COOP was slumped on a barstool doing shots of tequila. He was home on R&R in the little town of Joseph, at the base of the soaring Wallowa Mountains in the Columbia Plateau of northeastern Oregon. The population was 1,200, and he was sitting in his favorite dive bar on his way to a good drunk. He was about half there. It wasn't that long ago he'd been in Vietnam humping the bush with JT and Hawkeye, trying to keep from getting his ass blown every which way by Victor Charles. He'd walked into an ambush and was lucky to survive, with emotional scars and memories that would never heal. It had been so stifling hot in country that he couldn't remember what being cold felt like. But in Oregon it was winter and snow covered everything.

If he could get stinking drunk, maybe he wouldn't cry or stick a gun in his mouth. His granddad, the only one who cared for or understood him, had just died. Now he had to bury him.

He leaned back from the bar and spit in the spittoon on the floor. The last stateside funeral he'd gone to was his mother's when he was a child. He remembered the snow, the crying, the long procession of cars winding through the countryside, occasional farms, closed fruit stands, and white, empty pastures. Everyone wore black, except his aunt on his father's side. She wore a flowery spring dress and didn't cry. A bitch, he recalled. After the graveside eulogy, the family had gathered at his home. His father drank shots of bourbon in a bedroom by himself while the others patted Coop on the head and said, "What a brave boy." But he wasn't brave; he was devastated and would cry in a closet when they left him alone.

Coop had been the one who'd found her. He was in a tree fort in the backyard with his friend Dennis. He'd heard a loud bang, climbed down, and ran into the kitchen, not knowing what he feared. His mother was lying on the floor. She had mouthed his father's shotgun and splattered her depression all over the wall.

"Another," Coop ordered, raising his empty shot glass. "Some gold for the bold. Double shot, damn it. I got a funeral waiting on me."

Except for the fat bartender, he was the only one there. He looked at the beer clock on the wall. In an hour, his granddad would be buried, and he'd blow this piss-ant little town and get back to the Nam. They could all kiss his ass. The alcohol had grabbed hold, and he could feel his face tighten. Soon he'd be in another long procession driving through more country snow. Tears would come.

He drank another shot. The times he spent with his grandfather bow hunting for deer every fall in the Wallowa Mountains were the best times he'd ever had. He loved the smell of fir and pine and brisk morning air filling his lungs and slapping at his face. They'd hunt for days, camping deep in the high meadows. That was where he learned how to walk quietly and sit motionless. Granddad taught him to aim just behind the shoulder for a clean kill.

Coop ordered another tequila. The bartender waddled over slowly, poured another drink.

"You keep downing those tequilas and you'll be dead before you hit the door."

"Listen, fat man, if I want any crap from you, I'll scrape it off your teeth," Coop snorted. Then he threw down the tequila and shook his head, making a face before chugging his beer. "I need a six-pack to go," he said. "A six, and I'm on the road."

Coop tucked the beer under his arm and pushed out the door with the other. The street was quiet. The few stores were closed. He had parked in front of the Joseph Saloon next to an empty hay truck with high side rails and a collie in the cab. He opened the door to his pickup, slid in, leaned out to spit, then tried twice to shut the door before successfully slamming it closed.

He looked in the rearview mirror, licked his fingers, and wet the corners of his blond mustache. He was proud of his handlebar "stash." It had been a long time coming. He picked up a round tin of chewing tobacco from the top of the dashboard, put a pinch in his cheek, opened a beer, started up the truck, and kicked up snow spinning in reverse.

Joseph was an old lumber and mill town where everyone was a member of the grange hall, and made a point of knowing everyone else's business. His father used to drink too much, his mother committed suicide, his brothers were borderline wild, and then there was Coop—berserk, off the scale, a family embarrassment.

Throughout his life, Coop had thirsted for attention and gained it through crazed behavior. He jacked off the neighbor's German shepherd to gross out his friends and got caught one night shitting in a bowl on the mayor's front porch. Sometimes his stunts were humorous. When he was in high school, he shaved half his head and wore shorts with a tuxedo coat to the prom. And there was the time he streaked bare-ass naked across the gym floor at halftime during a basketball game with *Spank Tigers* painted on his butt and a bright orange ski mask on his head. The kids roared, and everyone knew it was Coop.

Back then, as now, he was unmistakable—short, thick, with powerful shoulders and chest. He had an incessant, round-faced grin.

Most revealing, though, was an ugly eight-inch scar that ran north/south across his abdomen. When he was sixteen, he shot himself with a .22 rifle during a drunken stupor and was placed in a psychiatric ward in La Grande for six weeks. His father stopped drinking after that, but Coop continued.

Driving down a side street, Coop made a short turn and clipped a parked car before pulling into the parking lot of Apple's Funeral Home. He finished the beer, swallowed some white cross-top amphetamines, then stuffed two breath mints in his mouth. He chewed the mints like a cow and ambled across the street.

His face was rounded into a silly-ass grin that faded as he approached the rest of his family. They were standing in front of a covered breezeway. Breathing deeply, he shook his head vigorously, trying to clear his mind. But it was no use. He was stinking drunk.

He greeted his aunt, the one he hated, and noticed she was in another flowery dress. Reluctantly, he endured her crying face on his shoulder, then he pushed her away as he moved to shake hands with his brothers, Bill and Matt, absorbing their scornful stares and excusing himself to the men's room. Once through the bathroom door, he staggered to the urinal, pulled out his cock, and, peeing strongly, fell forward, banging his head on the wall and spraying his pants.

"Damn, I'm drunk! I'm so fucked up."

Just then, his brother Matt stuck his head in the door.

"Coop, hurry up—"

Matt watched his brother swaying and pissing wildly. "God, you disgust me. Hurry up! Coop, did you hear me? Hurry up. The service is about to start." The door shut and Matt was gone.

"Yeah, right. OK. Fuck you! Who gives a fuck if you're late for a funeral? You think the dead give a flying fuck?" Then in a falsetto voice, he mocked Matt as he zipped his pants. "Hurry up, Coop! Hurry up, Coop! Hurry up!"

He sat through the service thinking how great his granddad had been and how absolutely ridiculous this whole ritual was. As the minister droned, Coop's irritation grew. This was bullshit! He'd seen death. This wasn't dying. Dying was violent. His mother's brains on the kitchen walls. Arms and legs blown off. Balls and cocks cut off and stuffed into fat mouths of bloated bodies.

This wasn't death. Death was that first patrol.

This was like sleep. He loved his granddad, no question. And, by God, he'd salute him, but not like this.

The speed started kicking in, and he could feel the buzz; his body was charged again. He had to leave. He had to get out of there. *I'm going to get me some pussy, kick some ass, and stay fuckin' drunk.* He believed Granddad would understand.

The eulogy ended with an open casket, and lines of crying farmers, friends, and relatives passed by to pay their respects. Meanwhile, Coop moved cautiously toward an untended door.

"Coop! Coop, you come over here. Coop, I'm talking to you! Coop!" Matt ran over and grabbed his arm. Lowering his voice so that no one could hear, "What an asshole," Matt said. "You don't respect Granddad or anyone. What's wrong with you? Coop, are you listening to me?"

"Go fuck yourself!" He broke loose from Matt's grip and staggered to his truck.

Coop skipped the burial, reeling from bar to bar. Slowly, the funeral faded. He met a cowgirl named Lucy tending bar. She'd had a crush on him in high school. He thought he liked her—couldn't remember. But she laughed at his drunken jokes and rubbed against him when he kissed her, even if he did hit her ear instead of her mouth.

They had sex at her apartment, and in the morning she said she'd write. He did like her; he knew that now. Then he left town without saying good-bye to anyone but his boyhood friend Charlie, whose family owned the funeral home.

He paid the funeral bill and gave Charlie an extra hundred bucks to make sure fresh flowers were placed on Granddad's grave every month for the next year. Later, Charlie dropped Coop off at the airport and promised he'd take care of his truck until he got back.

"Keep your ass low, Coop."

"Keep your dick hard, Charles."

Then he was on the plane heading back to the Nam.

3

Hawkeye

Chicago, Summer 1968

ON THE DAY BEFORE HIS NINETEENTH BIRTHDAY, Jesse James Joseph "Hawkeye" Collins stood handcuffed in front of a Chicago Circuit Court judge waiting to be sentenced for assault and battery, carrying a concealed weapon (a knife), and burglary. He had on turquoise slacks, a black long-sleeve silk shirt, and white tennis shoes. A thick gold chain wrapped around his powerful neck and shined against his black skin. He had a huge Afro and looked like he should be pimping whores on the south side of town.

He had been busted twice this year. Last time in a bar on Rush Street, he was chatting up some fine-looking lady in a tight mini when her estranged boyfriend came up, called the girl a bitch, and shoved Hawkeye. A fight broke out, and Hawkeye ended up in jail for assault and carrying false ID. He did thirty days in city lockup before overcrowding pushed him back on the streets. During that thirty-day gig, about the only thing to do was read paperbacks. He dusted off eighteen books, which helped ease his frustration and anger.

This time his mother was crying openly, sitting in the front of the court next to a Marine Corps recruiting officer. Despite the cuffs and the situation, Hawkeye, as he liked to be called, had a big cocky grin on his face, as if he were about to receive a commendation for citizen of the year instead of a prison sentence.

"Mr. Collins," the judge snapped indifferently while sifting through Hawkeye's file, "wipe that smile off your face."

Hawkeye obliged, shifting his weight back and forth on the balls and heels of his feet, seeming more bored than concerned.

"Mr. Collins, this is no joke. I can have you incarcerated for years."

Hawkeye shook his head and laughed quietly at the floor. Doing time didn't bother him. What the fuck. But sensing he might be compounding his grief, he looked up at the judge real serious-like.

"Yes, Your Honor. I know I messed up."

"Mr. Collins, I have letters here from your mother and teachers at the high school from which you were expelled. They say that despite your incorrigible behavior, you are worth saving." This seemed to somewhat please the judge, as he shuffled through more papers, stacking them neatly on his desk and reading another letter.

What the letters didn't say was that school came easy for Hawkeye, and it was boring. Of course, not having a dad or siblings helped compound his feelings of being different.

He also had that other little problem—or gift, depending on how you looked at it—of a photographic memory. It came in handy when listening to classroom lectures or reading textbooks. The problem side was having total recall for events that shaped his life. Especially when they were not pretty, like seeing his cousin Clarence stabbed in the eye with a fork when he was four. They had been in a restaurant just down the block from their house eating pie and ice cream. Clarence was thirteen and was babysitting; he was also dealing heroin for his older brother. Three Chicanos walked in and up to their table. Teenagers. Wearing brown berets. The shortest one had a thin mustache. Hands in his coat pockets, he dipped his shoulders when he talked.

"Blackie, you dealin' in the wrong lo-ca-tion." Then he ripped a fork off of the table, shoved it in Clarence's eye, and they all ran out the door. There was Clarence, bent over the table, hand covering his eye, screaming. Hawkeye could remember it all. Everything. Perfectly. Even the pattern of the blood running down on Clarence's hand and into the pie.

The judge coughed, sniffed twice. "Your teacher indicates you were a gifted student before you were kicked out. She says you need focus." He reached under his desk, pulled out a Kleenex, blew his nose as he continued to study Hawkeye's file. "It says here, Mr. Collins, that you have an IQ of 152." For a moment the judge appeared a bit startled. "Why, you are very, very bright." He reviewed Hawkeye's rap sheet of mostly petty crimes like shoplifting, curfew violations, urinating in public. Once again he looked up at Hawkeye and then to his mother. The letters had touched him. Besides, jails were packed.

"Well, Mr. Collins, I am going to give you one last chance. Either you sign up with the Marine Corps today, or you're going to jail. Do you understand your options?"

Hawkeye looked back over his shoulder as the officer sat stoically next to his mother. He gulped a breath and turned back to the judge.

"Yes, Your Honor."

That afternoon Jesse James Joseph "Hawkeye" Collins walked with his mother and a police officer down the courthouse hallway to the Marine Corps recruiting office. The cuffs were removed and he was sworn into the Marines.

HAWKEYE TOOK A FLIGHT FROM CHICAGO TO San Diego and was bused from there to the Marine Corps Recruiting Depot. When the doors of the bus opened, the greeting began.

"ON THE ROAD! GET OUT OF THAT BUS AND GET YOUR SLIMY CIVILIAN ASSES ON THE ROAD! I'M TALKING TO YOU, SWEETPEA. GET YOUR FAT ASS, GET YOUR SKINNY ASS, GET YOUR DUMB ASS, GET YOUR SORRY ASS ON THE ROAD! ON THE ROAD, ON THE ROAD, ON THE FUCKING ROAD AND OUT OF THAT FUCKING BUS!"

All the recruits were instantly categorized by the drill instructors by body type or color. "You're 'bout a fat sonofabitch. Lazy, fat sonofabitch. Suckin' on mama's tit?" Or, "You some kinda Injun boy? You done sneaked off the reservation and gonna fuck up my Marine Corps?" And there were turds, white ignorant trash boys, maggots, communists, and worthless puke buckets, all tearing off the bus and lining up in a ragged row of shocked and frightened young men.

Hawkeye had seen movies about drill instructors and had even read a couple of war novels in the can, but he wasn't prepared for this. The first day they buzzed off his Afro, took his gold chain, slapped him twice on the side of the head, and punched his throat for looking the wrong way.

"You smile at me again, you little pissant," his drill instructor yelled, "and I'll put my foot up your ass."

After the third day, the drill instructors appointed Hawkeye as squad leader and put him at the head of one of the lines.

Days passed and Hawkeye did well. The drill instructors noticed that once they slapped that look off his face, Hawkeye followed orders flawlessly. During the second week of boot camp, the platoon was standing in formation outside the mess hall waiting to go in. Each recruit was dressed in fatigues, reading a hand-sized, red notebook, except for Hawkeye. The book contained general orders, information on weapons, the chain of command, and other essential military facts. It took most recruits weeks to learn it all. Some never could. Hawkeye just let his brain take pictures and memorized it instantly.

As the rest of the platoon focused on their work, Hawkeye was day tripping, thinking about how to get a craps game going that night in the shower after the DIs were racked out. He didn't notice Drill Instructor Pope walk up.

Pope was a small, powerfully built black man who had distinguished himself during two tours in Vietnam. He had been wounded and decorated for heroism and was known for his harsh but fair treatment of his troops. He noticed Hawkeye standing at attention, staring out toward the obstacle course, his book in his hand but not opened. Pope quickly jerked Hawkeye by the ear, out of formation, and brought him to face the platoon.

"I ought to run your ass in the ground, bitch." Then Pope addressed the platoon. "It appears Collins here must think he is one of them smart asswipes!" Pope announced, still tugging on Hawkeye's ear. "This fat turd here thinks he don't have to study his general orders or know who runs my Marine Corps."

As the drill instructor spoke, his agitation grew. The one thing he hated more than anything was a recruit of color falling down, not pulling his share, disgracing his race.

"It appears this worthless puke bucket thinks he's got brains on top of brains," Pope continued. Then Pope let go of his ear and got right in front of Hawkeye, his forehead pressed against Hawkeye's nose. "Why, he thinks he is so fricking smart he don't have to read no damn book. He can just divine it. Now can't you, Private Shit Bag?"

Hawkeye stood rigidly at attention, his ear hurting and Pope's foul breath and spittle all over his face. He could see the blood vessels in Pope's eyes and watched his nostrils open and flare.

"I'm asking you, private, are you trying to mess up my Marine Corps?"

By now Hawkeye realized anything he said would be turned around to make him look stupid. With great concern for his well-being, Hawkeye gulped air and spoke.

"Sir. Private Collins requests permission to speak to the drill instructor, sir."

Pope grabbed Hawkeye's Adam's apple, squeezing it so hard Hawkeye couldn't breathe, let alone speak. He put his face even closer to Hawkeye's, twisted his mouth, and snarled. "Don't you fuck with me, bitch." Then he released his grip, took a full step back. "So, you want to talk. Speak, bitch. But what comes out of your mouth better be honey, or I'm gonna rip off your head and shit in it."

For a moment it was quiet as Hawkeye gasped for breath and collected himself. Then he stood tall, and, to the amazement of Drill Instructor Pope and the rest of the platoon, repeated all twelve of his general orders perfectly. As if asked for an encore, he recited precisely the chain of command. Finally, Hawkeye, sensing their awe and amazement, continued, "The nomenclature of the US Marine Corps–issued M-14 rifle is—"

"Hold it! Hold it, Private Collins. Slow your black ass down."

Pope paced slowly back and forth in front of his troops, deep in thought, then stopped, turned, and said very slowly, sounding slightly amazed, "You do got some brain power!"

The platoon struggled to hold back smiles. Laughter was dying to come forth.

"Collins," Pope said, "maybe you can help unfuck the rest of the dumb sonofabitches that don't know their ass from a hole in the ground." Just as Hawkeye was feeling relieved and even proud, Pope was back in his face barking, "Now get your nigger ass in formation before I lose my temper. One thing I hate more than a dumb turd is a smart-ass turd."

That night after showers, Drill Instructor Pope passed the word to have Hawkeye report to the duty hut. Hawkeye arrived in skivvies and shower thongs. He stood at attention under the single light bulb that lit the room while Pope sat on a footlocker, shining a pair of boots. One hand was stuck deep in the boot, holding it upside down while the other gripped a brush and worked over the leather. Occasionally, Pope would spit on the boot or drop the brush to apply more polish. For five minutes, Hawkeye simply stood watching him, scanning the room: a Bible next to a can of shaving cream, a photo he couldn't make out. After several more minutes of silence, the drill instructor put his boot on the floor, set his brush down, stood up, and walked over to Hawkeye.

"Private Collins, I don't particularly like you, but in a few weeks you and most of the rest of these boys are going to go to Vietnam. Now, I am telling you straight up, if you mess up in Vietnam, YOU WILL BE KILLED. Even if you do everything goddamn correct, you can still get your black ass shot off."

Pope went to his wall locker, opened it, and pulled out a list of all the Marines who had died in Vietnam. It was a long list.

"Collins," Pope said, waving the list in Collins's face, "Marines are dying by the thousands in Vietnam, and now folks back home are raising hell and acting like we are the enemy. And you? You're going to a grunt unit, that's for damn sure. I read your file, Collins." He put the list away and shut his locker, and suddenly his voice softened. "I know you're bright. Your scores were outta sight. So I'm telling you to straighten out. Get your mind right. Get that slack ass, diddy-bop civilian shit out of your brain. Some of these young men can't even read or write, and most of them have about as much of a chance of surviving in combat as a gnat's ass in hell." Then the drill instructor leaned over and whispered just below Collins's chin in words barely audible. "God has chosen you, son."

Hawkeye took the words in deep. He felt them. Wanted them to be true. He felt like crying. "Sir. Yes, sir."

Then he was dismissed. As Hawkeye made his way back to his Quonset hut, he walked slowly to compose himself. No one, except for his mother, had ever talked to him like that.

4

Vuong

Hoa Binh, Vietnam, 1950

NGUYEN VUONG WAS BORN IN A BAMBOO hut with dirt floors in the village of Hoa Binh. It was spring in the year of the Tiger, and he was the first son, which was a good sign, even though his birth was difficult. His father, Diep, was a member of the Vietminh, a resistance front struggling against the French colonialists. When Vuong was born, Diep was fifty miles north in Hanoi training with troops for the revolution. On the night Vuong's spirit chose his parents and came into the world, his mother, Tuy, was in great pain. Her baby was turned slightly, nearly breach, and the baby fought to be steady. There was no doctor to tend to her, only Grandmother and another old woman from the village.

Two oil lamps lit the room, casting shadows on the family altar and the wooden bed, covered with a mat where Tuy lay. Grandmother sat on the side of the bed, wiped Tuy's forehead, and sang a quiet song as Tuy clenched her teeth and pushed down on her swollen belly. The village midwife was tending the fire in the only other room, where a pot of water boiled. When the baby finally came, it was still dark, but a cock crowed, which was a good sign, Grandmother said. The afterbirth was put in a large soup bowl beneath the bed, and at first light Grandmother buried it in the family's garden. It had been a family tradition believed to honor the earth, passed on for generations.

For the next few years, Vuong grew up never traveling far from the scattered huts and fields of his village. When he was an infant, his mother would strap him to her back and work the rice paddies or turn the garden. Other times, he'd lie happily on a blanket underneath the shade of a coconut tree, smiling toward the sun. His father would come home and bounce Vuong on his knee while Grandmother sang. Sometimes his father would play his flute while swinging from a hammock stretched between the bamboo poles that framed their doorway. But his father's time at home became less frequent as the war escalated.

In 1953 French planes began bombing close to their village, so the family built an underground bunker. When the planes came, his mother and grandmother would hurry him outside and make it a game, challenging Vuong to see how fast he could crawl down inside their bunker. Each time, his mother would say he was very fast for a small boy and give him a sweet bread or banana and pat his head gently. They had mats on the floor, a bucket of water, food in woven baskets, and a thing he did not yet understand called a rifle.

In the winter of that year, his brother Bich was born on the floor of the bunker, but his birth was not good. Vuong sat in the corner, his back against the dirt wall, the oil lamp flickering. Planes roared overhead and explosions rang as the ground shuddered. Keep your mouth open, Vuong, his grandmother warned, so the concussion would not blow out his eardrums. The bombs came again and again—*whump, whump, whump.* The explosions sent shock waves through the earth.

Finally, the planes left and the bunker was quiet. Vuong was covered with dirt; he had wet himself and he was crying. There was too much blood from his mother, and she died without a whimper. But Bich survived.

A few days later, Vuong's father came down from Hanoi. Tuy was buried in a family gravesite next to her father. There was great sadness in the family, and for a long time his grandmother did not sing.

In 1954 Vuong was working side by side with his grandmother in the rice fields. Bich was under the shade of a banana tree, lying on his back, grabbing fistfuls of air, and kicking his tiny feet. The water in the fields was brown and knee deep, touching the edge of Vuong's shorts. They were planting and she was singing again, covered from the sun by her conical hat. Their water bull strolled lazily beside them, his big head and horns swaying rhythmically as he walked. At midday, a farmer from the other field came over and told his grandmother word had come that Vuong's father was in an important battle far away. That night, Grandmother put a special offering on the family altar with the pictures of her late husband and daughter. She prayed that Diep would come home safely.

For months Vuong and his family did not see Diep. He was at Dien Bien Phu fighting the French, who had a large base surrounded by mountains and backing to the China Sea. Tens of thousands of peasants cut trails and broke artillery pieces down, carrying them through the jungle. In the mountains that surrounded the French base, they strapped pieces on their backs or on bicycles, packing them to positions to rain terror on Dien Bien Phu. Diep was wounded twice. Thousands died from malaria, French planes, and hand-to-hand combat. But the pounding continued, and in May of 1954, the French surrendered.

When Diep returned, he came home a hero and was given a higher rank in the local Communist party. Under his direction, the village and district grew and prospered. Over the next several years, a silk manufacturing plant was built in Hoa Binh, and other industries were brought in as well. Roads were constructed, as well as a new school, medical clinic, and a canal system that made it possible to flood the fields more efficiently. Soon, the family was in a new home made from concrete with a red tile roof. They had bountiful fields, pigs, chickens, and two water bulls.

Vuong and Bich enjoyed a life free of worry. They played in the fields or swam in the river that ran from the edge of the mountains toward their home. On Saturdays they would go to the market and sometimes buy ice cream or a small toy sold by vendors. They missed their mother but were guided by their grandmother's steady hand and firm direction.

"A task must be done well or there is no honor," she would say.

Diep was a self-taught man, a Confucian scholar, who often read books by candle late into the night. He instilled in his sons a love of country and discipline. Each Sunday, the boys would gather with Diep, and he would talk about the five cardinal principles of ethics: benevolence, duty, propriety, conscience, and faithfulness. To illustrate, he would tell elaborate stories of ancient Chinese heroes riding on lumbering elephants with swords drawn or tales of soldiers who fought against the French.

But it was not long before a new struggle began: the reunification of the country under Ho Chi Minh. In the summer of 1962, Diep was sent to the South as part of the Viet Cong movement to disrupt the current government and create an infrastructure for military attacks. All of this would lead to the primary goal of unification. On the night before he was to leave, he took Vuong and Bich down to the river where they sat on the bank and talked. It was nearly dusk, and a few fishermen were unloading sampans. The fields were empty, and the distant mountains seemed at peace, settling in for the evening.

"Vuong," Diep said, watching the river flow by quietly, not even a ripple, "in this world there are many struggles. We are now in a revolution fighting the American imperialists who want to divide our country. I am going away, and it may be a long time before I return. Your grandmother and our village will care for you, but you

are the head of the family. You must be a man now. You will tend
the fields and bring in workers. I have a list of instructions for what
to pay, for the price of our rice and fruit, and for consulting with
my brother Ta."

Diep turned to Bich, making sure his attention was on his words.

"Bich, you must listen to your brother."

Vuong did not like hearing that his father would leave. He felt
afraid for where his father was going and feared the American
horse-faced soldiers. But he would be strong and was honored his
father put so much trust in him.

"The spirits of your ancestors will watch over you," Diep continued. "I had a dream last night. Your mother came to me and said
that all would be good. That this journey will only strengthen us."

In the morning, Diep kissed his children good-bye, touched
Grandmother's hand, and left. Vuong acted brave, but Bich's lips
were trembling.

THE FIRST YEAR DIEP WAS AWAY WAS a good year for crops, and Vuong
felt that his ancestors and mother looked after them quite well. In
school, he learned how the American devils kept his countrymen
from the South in slavery. He learned of revolution and historical struggles for a united Vietnam. By the end of the second year,
there had been little word about Diep. That winter was hard. Monsoons became typhoons and destroyed several homes in the village.
Rice supplies were ruined and many were without food. Then his
grandmother died suddenly. She was buried next to her husband
and Vuong's mother.

The war escalated. Every day brought horror stories of brave
freedom fighters and evil Americans and puppet Southern soldiers
who supported them. Stories reached the village that American soldiers would kill and eat the dead. It was said they had great weapons
and many planes, so village bunkers were dug deeper. It was a time

of great fear. Rumors came that Americans were like giants and could fly and drop bombs that could destroy whole villages and evaporate their people and their animals. The stories of the devil soldiers made Bich cry at night. Vuong would come to his bed and wake him from his dream and hold him until he fell asleep.

Vuong and Bich stored rice and gathered weapons and helped the village dig tunnels deep underground, connecting to other homes. Soon, many of the young men sixteen or older were leaving the village and joining the National Liberation Front.

During the second month of 1967, at the beginning of the Vietnamese New Year, the year of the Goat, Vuong joined the North Vietnamese Army. For weeks, he had been visited by his ancestors in dreams telling him to seek out Diep. The last word he received of his father came from relatives in a nearby village. They said Diep was in charge of a base station near Laos along the Ho Chi Minh Trail. Vuong left his village in the morning as the first rooster crowed.

His training took place in Hanoi, just over fifty kilometers north of his home. It was the first time he had been farther than a day's walk from the rice paddies. The training camp was full of young "brothers" and "sisters" from both cities and farmland, and darker-skinned ones who came from the mountains. Many of the dark-skinned could not read or write, and often Vuong or other "literate ones" would help them with their lessons. They were taught about the Fatherland and heard stories of great patriots and ancient Vietnamese dynasties, like Hong Bang in the year 279 and the one hundred Hung Vuong kings who ruled for over two thousand years. Cadre leaders wove tales of comradeship and loyalty to the party, the cause, and freedom for the South. They would change the course of history. Vuong and his comrades soon believed they would march into the hamlets, villages, and cities and be welcomed with open arms as great liberators.

As the weeks passed, Vuong could feel his desire to be a freedom fighter growing. He nearly forgot his father was missing or that he was far away from the only sibling he had. He would be a good soldier, a patriot, and learn his lessons well. He fired weapons, studied explosives, and marched for long hours with a heavy pack on his back.

When training was over, Vuong was promoted and assigned to a three-man cell as part of an NVA squad. His battalion was operating just south of the DMZ and would help liberate the cities of Quang Tri, Dong Ha, and Hue.

Several days before he was to leave, Vuong was issued a Soviet AK-47 with a folding metal stock. He also got a pack, two uniforms— one light green and the other beige—a sweatshirt, black pajamas, sandals, a piece of plastic for cover from the rain, a square of canvas and a rope that could be used as a hammock or shelter, a small shovel, seven magazines of ammunition, one canteen, and rations for five days.

On the night before he left, Vuong was visited by the spirit of his mother in his dreams. She appeared as a vision exactly like the picture that sat on the family altar he had knelt before as a child and young man. She was dressed in a long, white, flowing ao dais, black hair dropping well below her shoulders. She had a flower in her hair and a book in her hand. She stood before a lake surrounded by cherry blossoms, singing the same song his grandmother used to sing when he was a small child. *Sweet one, sweet little one, you are my sweet one, my dear little one.* He could see her face and smile and hear the lyrical voice of love and tenderness that comforted him. It didn't matter or confuse him that his mother's voice was his grandmother's.

When he awoke, he felt rested and peaceful. He knew his mother would protect him. The next morning, Vuong and fifty-four men and twelve women left the training facility in the backs of canvas-covered trucks to begin the first stage of travel to the South along the Ho Chi Minh Trail. All of the drivers were women. They were a huge part of all military action, from pushing bicycles laden with food and ammunition, to fighting alongside their male comrades—just as they had when they helped defeat the French at the battle of Dien Bien Phu.

As Vuong sat in the back of the truck, he felt as if he belonged. He had little fear, only the abiding resolution of his soul that what he was doing was good and right and needed to be done. The truck rolled and bumped along the dirt road as Vuong listened to a senior cadre describe how in the early 1960s, movement of troops into South Vietnam had been easy.

"The Demilitarized Zone was porous," he explained between drags on a hand-rolled cigarette. His fingers were stained from the nicotine and his teeth yellowed. "The flow of Northerners was impossible to stop. However, in 1965, the Americans began bombing around the DMZ, building troop camps all along it." He tossed the last of his cigarette out the back of the truck, then rolled another and lit it.

"With thousands of barbaric Americans running patrols, crossing the DMZ is dangerous. So our troops use routes leading into Laos and Cambodia. The Americans leave us alone. Those countries are neutral, you see." He blew smoke out his nose then tossed the cigarette out the back again and sat back and closed his eyes. Vuong watched him sleep.

They traveled southwest that first day, stopping just before dusk at Station 1, close to the entrance of the trail. The station was a small compound with anti-aircraft emplacements, underground bunkers, tunnels, and thatched-roof barracks built on bamboo stilts. One hut, where they were to eat, was larger than the rest. In the evening, they ate at long wooden tables with half-log benches and watched a community musical group sing and dance to songs about national pride, the revolution, and great and heroic freedom fighters. Members from the National Liberation Front and Communist party gave long speeches and lifted glasses of wine to the revolution and Ho Chi Minh while Vuong listened carefully, vowing to himself he would be a strong and loyal comrade. This was a special occasion, going off to war, heading down the Ho Chi Minh Trail, and so it was the custom to gather in celebration of the nation and the party. The food was good and plentiful with fresh fruits and a pig strung on a pole cooking outside in a pit.

For the first time, the twelve women who were traveling with Vuong's company were introduced at the front of the room. They would be dropped in cells of three at various points along the trail to work as support staff and medical personnel. On rare occasions, they would grab arms and fire on the enemy if necessary. The women stood in a single line facing the tables and sang a song of unity. They were dressed in light green uniforms with no identifiable insignia, just like the men. They sang and clapped and all looked so youthful and pretty to Vuong. In his village, he had only spoken to a few young women, most of whom were already promised in marriage.

It was stirring and exciting to see and hear this group sing and clap. They seemed so full of promise and pride. At the end of two songs, one woman stepped forward from the group and introduced herself as Phung Thu. She was chosen by her superior to read a poem she had written. She had attended the University of Hanoi before joining the struggle, as her brothers and father had before her. Her poem praised the beauty of the country and the love of a mother for her child.

As she read, the words seemed to speak directly to Vuong's heart. When she spoke of the Red River and the sampans gently gliding and the lotus blossoms in the spring, Vuong felt transported to that time when he sat beside the river with his father and brother. Her voice was like the sound of the wind in the fields rushing past his ears just before it rained. And her face was like his mother's in the photo on the altar. When she bowed to the crowd, her hair nearly touched the floor. Vuong watched her every movement as she left the front of the hall and sat down at a table on the other side of the room. It was forbidden for the men to be with the women, but he imagined how it would be to sit with her and listen as she read. For now, it would harm no one if he just thought of her long hair and how she smiled.

The next day they traveled under the natural canopy on a well-hidden dirt road that slowly edged along forest ranges near the base of the mountains. The column stopped once when planes were spotted overhead, and most of that day they could hear bombing somewhere in the distance. On the third day, they reached the second base in the Nghe An Province on the border of Laos. A medical station was built underground where many of the severely wounded were treated. Caverns with operating tables and recovery rooms were hollowed out of the earth, with cots for fifty soldiers or more. Air tubes for ventilation and lights from gas-powered generators lit bunkers and provided enough light to perform major surgeries. The underground base was so deep and wide that more than two dozen trucks and tanks were easily hidden. That night Vuong's company stayed underground and was given a special treat—a film projected onto a sheet hanging on a dirt-packed wall. More bombing could be heard in the distant countryside as the group watched old newsreels of "Uncle Ho" and the victorious Vietminh when they crushed the French at Dien Bien Phu.

5

JT

THE DREAM AGAIN. THE PATROL. NVA COMING out of the tree line, stepping over bodies, firing. It always ended the same: rifle jammed, shot in the face.

It was still dark outside as Ashley lay next to him, sleeping peacefully, but JT was wide-eyed, sweating, and alert. His heart was pumping hard, and he could feel his pulse beat in his neck. The alarm clock flashed 4:10 a.m. He slid out of bed, pulled on a pair of running shorts and a T-shirt, then walked softly across the floor as Ashley turned beneath the covers. He moved like he was on patrol, gliding as he stepped, tuned into every shadow and sound. His face tightened as he listened to the walls move and the floor breathe.

In Anna's room, he stood over her crib watching the nightlight cast a faint glow on her round, sleeping face. He reached into the crib and adjusted her blankets, gently touching her with the back of his hand. For a moment, he thought he heard whispers. He left the room quietly.

The front of the house was cold, but the darkness was comforting. He felt in control in the dark. He dropped to the floor and did push-ups until he could no longer lift his body. This helped shove the handfuls of blood and broken teeth out of his mind. But the effort felt harder than his body remembered. In boot camp, he had done a hundred without slowing down; now he could only do fifty. He was growing soft, so he did sit-ups and forced more push-ups. He was safe, alone in the dark.

Before Vietnam, JT believed he was different from his peers because his dad was a drunk and his mother was crazy. She had two nervous breakdowns and was a joke to his friends. One friend called her Marijuana. He'd say, *how's Marijuana doing today?*— meaning did your mom flip out again? More sit-ups and he saw his mother in that hospital bed, arms outstretched, eyes rolled back in her head, screaming, "I've been through hell! I've been through hell!" And he couldn't help her.

His father was embarrassing. He'd go to work at his auto body shop fixing and painting cars and come home after work drunk. Once, he'd fallen out of the bleachers at JT's wrestling match. JT believed other kids were looking at his father disdainfully and judging him at the same time. He wanted to escape. Get away and do something important. He thought going to war might make a difference. He'd become a man. He'd know things others didn't.

But coming home from Vietnam had only magnified this feeling of being less than. Anti-war demonstrations were raging across the country, and if you dodged the draft, many thought that was cool. Few of his peers had served in the military, let alone in Vietnam. One friend told him he was stupid for going. That cut him to his core. He wanted to cry and beat the hell out of this pal that he had known for years.

He felt he hadn't done anything heroic. He'd survived and that felt a little like cheating. And the things he saw—the things he knew—they didn't give him strength. It was like all the fear he'd felt as a little kid, seeing his dad and mom out of control, had been only the first course, the appetizer to real terror. Other guys his age were exulting in their adult competence and freedom. He was further away from them than ever. He was only twenty but often felt like an old man. Killing made him age. So did pissing on dead bodies and seeing children burnt beyond belief.

His wife thought violence was when he punched a hole in the wall or broke a doorjamb. That wasn't violence.

It had been several weeks since JT busted the hole in the wall. He hid the hole with the cover of an old *Life* magazine. It showed a long procession of Negro civil rights activists marching over a bridge into Selma, Alabama. In the foreground stood rows of uniformed policemen. JT liked it because he imagined the brothers felt like he did—separated, looked down on, feared, and ostracized by society. He liked the title, "The Savage Season Begins." It described both his tour in the Nam and his coming home. In some ways, it was simple back then. He knew where he stood with his squad. It was his place to belong. The squad kept him alive. They'd die for him. Back in the world, he felt alone.

His arms were exhausted and pumped to failure, but his mind was still rushing, so he went for a run. It was dark, and he could hear the porch swing creaking in the wind. For a moment, he felt certain an ambush site had been dug in by the trees in his neighbor's front yard. He shook his head and jogged away from the house along the sidewalk. The air felt clean and smelled good. He breathed deeply as he passed under streetlights and sprinted by a big dog barking from the edge of someone's front yard. For an instant, the eyes of the dog caught a hint of streetlight and glowed like fading trip flares. He liked the dog barking, protecting his territory. He too was alert, on guard in the darkness. JT began to sweat as he ran along neat rows of parked cars, resting under elm and maple trees. A taxi drove by, then disappeared around the corner. The sidewalk was empty, and the only sounds were the barking dog and footsteps slapping.

As he ran, his mind shifted to the day he met Gurney.

THE SKY WAS EMPTY EXCEPT FOR THE chopper and blazing sun. JT and Coop sat quietly in web seats, sweating. They were the new guys going in. It was their second day in country. Kilo Company had been hit the day before, suffering many casualties. They were the replacements.

The loud whine of engines turning and wind beating through the doors seemed to numb them. Their faces were placid, eyes glazed like cattle, bodies with no brains. They wore new utilities, shiny jungle boots and flak jackets that were spotless. Their helmets had camouflaged covers that had never been worn. Packs were placed neatly at their feet, and empty rifles were clenched tightly between their knees, butts on the floor, barrels up.

Across from them was another soldier, helmet off, red hair tousled. His eyes were a startling blue. He was older, face angular, freckled. He looked like a shortstop JT once knew. He was already in the chopper when they boarded and had his helmet, pack, and rifle resting at his feet. His uniform was well worn, boots used and scuffed. When he turned his head to look out the window, he seemed to be thinking deeply.

A moment later, he looked at JT. He leaned forward, arms resting on his knees. His hands were big.

"How you doing?" he asked.

It was a simple question that someone might ask back in the world. In the chopper, though, JT thought it unusual and kind. He wanted to tell him he was frightened. That he didn't want to die. That he'd rather be anywhere else in the whole world. But he just shrugged and said, "I'm fine."

The door gunner was leaning on his machine gun, silent, flight helmet shining, dark shield covering his eyes. JT looked down as the chopper's shadow cut through rice paddies, hamlets, and huts. They flew away from the villages, toward the mountains.

"See that?" the gunner shouted, wind blowing words out the window. The chopper passed over a row of shacks and banana trees, teetering along a river. "That's Pussy Ville." He pointed out the door. "Got my first piece a' ass in that ville," he said proudly.

JT looked down but felt like puking, closed his eyes, and tried to get steady. He was thinking about Ashley and if he would ever see her again. His body was vibrating.

Coop was sitting opposite JT and the gunner, chewing mint-flavored tobacco, spitting out his window.

"Where you guys from?" the gunner shouted. The chopper took a dip, turning JT's stomach.

"We're both from Oregon," Coop yelled. "This here's my butt boy."

The gunner laughed but it was washed out by the wind. Coop turned and spat again.

The red-haired guy smiled and said, "Gurney. From Alabama."

JT felt the shudder of the blades changing speed and looked to see the ground coming up. They dropped slowly over open fields, a creek, Marines, and sandbags covering a small hill. They touched down in a landing zone of dirt no bigger than a baseball infield. The back ramp opened, and they ran off, bent over, packs and rifles in one hand, the other holding their helmets down. By the time the chopper lifted and the dust settled, the heat of the day was on them.

Gurney glanced around the perimeter. The sun was shining in his eyes as he reached out to shake JT's hand, then Coop's. For a moment, JT saw his reflection in Gurney's iris.

"Good luck," Gurney said earnestly, then turned in a hurry to leave.

"Thanks, man," JT called after him.

IT WAS SATURDAY MORNING. JT SHOWERED AND shaved after his run. There was no work to do or any place he had to be, so he thought he'd just hang out at home and get ready for the party they were throwing that night. Later he'd buy a pony keg of beer and maybe score some pot. Ashley's mom had agreed to take Anna for the evening, so he felt it was safe to get loaded.

Ashley came into the front room as JT lay on the floor and played with Anna. He was on his back, holding her above him like she was flying through the air. She would coo and giggle as little droplets of spittle rolled from her mouth onto his shirt. He needed her joy. It kept him sane and gave him purpose and meaning. With Ashley, there were always expectations for him to behave a certain way, act a certain way, and watch what he was saying. With Anna, it was pure.

"Honey, could you vacuum the front room?" Ashley asked. "I'm trying to finish the kitchen, and I've still got the bedroom, the living room, and loads of laundry to do."

He said, "OK," but kept playing with Anna. He needed a little more, another giggle.

"JT, come on, stop playing with the baby and give me a hand."

She left the room, and he could tell she was irritated. But he didn't care. He couldn't stand anyone telling him what to do. It felt just like the Marine Corps.

He changed Anna's diaper and gave her a bottle before placing her in the crib. Feeling guilty, he reluctantly dusted and was vacuuming the front room when he noticed the door opening from the corner of his eye. He turned and was surprised to see his cousin Brad sticking his head through the door.

"Turn that damn thing off," Brad shouted above the loud whine of the vacuum. He came in, shut the door, and turned back to JT as the noise subsided. "Hey, man. You look good. Real domestic-like. That's 'bout all you jarheads are good for, policing the area." He laughed and walked over and shook JT's hand, grabbed the crook of his arm, and said with real affection, "How you doing, man?"

"I'm great," JT said, giving him a playful push. "But what's your story? I thought you were still in the Nam smoking dope and playing guitar."

"Nah. Got back to the world a week ago and been doing time down at McCord. Got too horny and had to come home. Besides, I wanted to see your face. So whatta you up to?"

As an Army warrant officer, Brad flew choppers and was wearing his green flight jacket and aviator glasses. He'd arrived in Vietnam a couple months after JT, and so they used to write. One time, JT got a picture of Brad sitting on an Army cot smoking a joint and playing a guitar. This stuck in his mind. Even though he knew Brad was hauling troops and dropping supplies, to JT that was pussy. Any duty was a skate when you could slide into base each night, have hot chow, warm showers, and a dry rack. And as an officer, Brad could look forward to cold beers and skin flicks at the officer's club.

Brad was a couple of years older, so when they were in high school, he'd pick JT up in his '53 Chev and they'd tool around trying to pick up chicks. Brad's dad had been a pilot in WWII, dropping bombs on Europe, and owned a charter flight business. That's where Brad learned to fly, and eventually he joined the Army to be a chopper pilot. A few months later, JT was in the Marine Corps.

They admired each other for different reasons. Brad looked up to JT because he was big, strong, and fearless. JT admired Brad because he was bright, quick-witted, and capable. Brad used to take JT up flying in one of the small single-engine planes his father owned, and it always amazed JT how easily Brad mastered the complicated controls. But then, anything technical challenged JT.

One time they took along their girlfriends, Ashley and Mary, and flew up the Columbia River Gorge. They figured that after the flight the girls would be impressed and they could make out in the storage area of the hangar. Instead, they got caught in a wind shear. It came quickly and shook the plane hard, forcing it sideways toward the mountains along the river. The wind was severe, and they were either going to get busted up in the trees or end up floating in the river. Brad fought the controls and kept cool, even when Mary puked and Ashley nearly fainted. He pulled out, then flew back to the airport. After they landed, the girls were hardly in the mood for sex.

During the February Offensive of '69, JT's unit had been hit hard every day for a week. Many Marines had been killed or wounded. When there was a lull in the fighting, JT wrote Brad a letter. He felt he was going to die and asked him to go home with his body.

Now, as they stood trading humorous jabs, JT jumped back in time, remembering how it felt to face death. He recalled writing Brad, what he had asked him. In a way, writing that letter was like being willing to die for someone. If Brad went home with JT's body, Brad would live. He might not have to go back to Vietnam, and that would be the only good his death would bring. That's how he felt about Brad as they stood there in his front room, just being dumb and awkward and very glad to see each other again. Willing to die for him.

"Listen, I got to take off and pick up some stuff for the party. You want to go?"

"I'd like to but can't," Brad said. "Just stopped by for a minute. Have to slip by Mom's for a while, but Mary told me about the party, and we'll be there or be square." He slapped JT's hand. "Later, man."

Before JT could say more, Brad was pulling away from the curb in his Chev.

Ashley gave JT a list of things they needed for the party and told him to hurry. On his way out, he swept Anna up in his arms, giving kisses and hugs as he headed toward the door. He fired up their Volks, backed out of the driveway, and puttered down the street.

His first stop was a little market run by some Koreans who never checked ID. He bought a pony keg, some apple wine for Ashley, and a couple quart bottles of beer for Pearl.

Since he was thirsty and had time to burn, he walked into the tavern next to the store. It took a while for his eyes to adjust from sunshine to smoky dimness. He noticed all the stools were full except for one seat at the far end of the bar. As he stepped, peanut shells crunched underneath his feet. He sat down on the stool next to a heavyset guy pushing fifty. The back of the bar held beer signs, bottles, ads for cigarettes, and velvet paintings of dogs shooting pool. The counter was scattered with jars of pickled sausage, chips, and cheap bowls of full-shelled peanuts. The bartender was a tired-looking young woman, hair tangled like a mop. Even in the faint light, it was easy to tell she was wearing too much makeup.

JT ordered a beer and was relieved not to be carded. It tasted cool and went down easy. He ordered another. It was good to kick back. JT finished the second beer and had time for one more. The guy sitting next to him was wearing a plaid shirt with the arm sleeves rolled up and had a picture of a Marine bulldog tattooed on his thick forearm. His biceps were big like his dad's used to be. His fingers thick, like they'd been broken.

"Semper Fi?" JT said as the old Marine was finishing a cool one.

"Well, no shit. Semper Fucking Fi to you, son," the drunken Marine said happily, tooth missing. "How'd you guess I was a Marine?"

"Your tattoo," JT said.

"Oh, that. Got that baby on my first R&R just after that shithole in North Africa. You a Marine?"

"Yeah."

"Well then, where the fuck is your tattoo?"

"Don't have any."

The Marine finished his beer and looked at JT a little cockeyed, as if JT were from another planet. "You say you're a Marine? Sorry, bud, you ain't got a tattoo, you ain't no fucking Marine."

JT looked at the old guy. He sounded like his dad. He ought to knock him off his stool and kick his ass, but he restrained himself. The guy was a Marine.

"Listen. I just got back from the Nam, and all I was doing was trying to be friendly."

The Marine chugged another beer, spilling some of it on the front of his shirt. "Vietnam? Fuck that. You guys are getting your asses waxed. I seen every fucking thing on TV, and you're getting your asses kicked."

A flash roared through JT. Old Marine or not, he grabbed the prick by the throat, pushed him to the floor, hit him in the face, stood up quickly, looked around the bar, and walked out.

He was still angry by the time he reached the supermarket. He felt disoriented and confused as he walked down the aisles filling the cart from the list. The guy was just like his old man used to be. Drunk, berating him, kicking his mom's ass. When he was seventeen, he'd pulled his dad off his mom. *You want to hit someone, asshole, hit me!* JT had dropped his dad and hit him again and again. Looking at his father lying there on the kitchen floor with blood on his face had filled him with shame. He'd pulled his dad to his feet and looked him in the eyes. He could see how his father must feel terrible inside. It was like his father's heart was broken, and JT felt horrible.

Back then, as now, everything was going wrong. He wanted to go back to Vietnam. In the bush, they were tight. Family. He felt like going back to the bar and killing them all.

He finished the shopping and drove toward home, mind running hard. Damn drunk! Where was the guy's respect? The anger and rage were beginning to fade. He thought about the party and Brad. He looked forward to kicking back, getting ripped, and not worrying about anything.

Close to his block, he swung by the park and saw Smoke shooting hoops. By now JT was calm about the incident at the tavern, but sad. Maybe if he copped some pot from Smoke, he'd feel better. Smoke was bouncing and shooting a faded leather basketball that had been worn smooth. His shirt was off, and his skinny frame looked sickly to JT.

"Hey, Smoke."

Smoke turned to the voice, and when he saw JT, he smiled.

"Say, soldier man. Thought I recognized you in the bug. What it is?"

They walked toward each other, and Smoke pointed to the basketball tucked under his arm. "Up for some hoops?"

JT stole the ball and made a jump shot, then passed it back to Smoke.

"Wish I could, man. Just trying to score some weed for a little party we're having."

"Whoo! Soldier man wants to rearrange his brain." Smoke laughed. "You ain't narcing on me now, are you?"

JT was startled. "Of course not. Do I look like a cop?"

"Yeah, you do with that hair. Sure, you look like a cop. But I'm only messing with you. I think you're cool. Just checking it out. You gotta understand the situation. Lot of dudes gettin' busted, and I gotta be careful. Is that cool?"

"No problem."

Smoke started bouncing the basketball again, turned toward the basket, and shot before turning back toward JT. "So what you want to do? I got Cambodian Red, Thai Stick, or some cheap Mexican weed, but it will still get you all kinds of fucked up."

"How 'bout a quarter of Cambodian?"

Smoke thought about it a couple moments and decided, "I don't usually sell less than half an ounce, but I'll make an exception for the soldier man. I gotta go to North Portland, though. I'm running partners with some bloods that front me. You got a phone? I'll call when I get the shit."

"That'll work," JT said flatly. "Let me see if I have a pen in the car and I'll write down my number." He jogged over, found a broken crayon, and wrote his number on an empty french fry sack. "Now, how much for the quarter?"

"This is good shit. Thirty-five bones."

JT ran it around in his mind, imagining a tightly rolled joint and remembering how good it felt to be stoned. He'd do it.

"I'll call you tonight, soldier man, 'bout seven. We can meet here. That cool?"

"Sure, catch you later."

They shook hands and JT headed home.

He walked through the door carrying the groceries in one arm and the small keg of beer in the other. In the kitchen, Ashley was feeding Anna in her highchair. She was spooning applesauce as JT put the bag on the counter and keg in the sink.

"Hey, girls, what's going on?" He was happy to be home.

Ashley didn't look up and didn't acknowledge him. She just kept spooning the applesauce into Anna's mouth.

"Hey, what's wrong? I'm home. Aren't you happy?"

"Happy?" she said turning toward him, still holding the spoon. "While you're off doing God knows what, I had to finish cleaning the house, including the mess you left in the bathroom, do laundry, bathe the baby, fix her lunch, and call Mom to tell her we were going to be late bringing Anna because you weren't home yet. Happy? You've been gone almost three hours!"

"Come on, it's no big deal. I got what you wanted," he said, pointing to the sack of groceries. "See?"

He felt stupid even as he said it, like a kid trying to weasel out of a scolding. He hated that. How did she keep turning him into a child?

Ashley turned away and began feeding Anna again.

"Look, goddamn it! Look!" Temper exploding, he knocked the groceries off the counter onto the floor. "You make a big deal out of every fucking thing! I'm home. I'm back. Can't that be enough?"

Then the baby started crying. JT could tell that Ashley and Anna were afraid, and he felt like a freak, like a monster, inhuman, out of control, a madman.

"Listen, I'm so sorry. Here, I'll pick everything up." He bent down and picked up the apples, milk, bread, and broken eggs. As he did, Ashley gathered up Anna, who was crying loudly, and began rocking her trying to soothe her. "I'm sorry. Look. I'm sorry I'm late and I did this."

"Give me the keys to the car," Ashley demanded, her body visibly shaking. She took a deep breath and rocked and cooed Anna as the crying ebbed. "I'll take Anna and run her over to Mom's. We'll talk about this later. You act like you're insane."

JT handed her the keys, knuckles scraped and red. He saw her eyes go to the marks, but she didn't say anything. As she left the house, he noticed she was hurrying—and that once she was standing by the car, her body relaxed. She looked like the Ashley he remembered then—when she had gotten away from him.

He cleaned up the last of the broken eggs, feeling depressed. He pounded his fist on the countertop and smacked a cupboard door. The door cracked, and he felt worse. He put the groceries away and swept the floor. He finally noticed the blood on his hands, and as he washed it off in the kitchen sink, he thought of the dead and wounded in his unit. In Vietnam, blood seemed darker and thicker and much more sticky than this blood that washed so easily down the sink.

He felt lucky to be alive. He rubbed his knuckles on the side of the counter until traces of red showed, then wiped the blood across his face. It absorbed into his skin, his soul, and jarred his memory. He was ready to sob, so he grasped the sides of the sink, head bowed, and fought it. His body shook, but just as the tears welled up in his eyes, he took a deep breath. *Fuck it*, he said to himself.

"Fuck it!"

His whole body tightened more. He turned off the water, cleaned his face with a paper towel, balled it up, tossed it into the garbage, and left the kitchen.

JT called Ashley at her mom's and told her he was sorry. He was desperate for a softness in her voice, a hint of that smile that she used to give him whenever he walked in the door. He'd felt like such a man, getting married. He'd been upset about the pregnancy at first—but not for too long. Ashley was worth it, he thought.

She was still worth it. He said he was sorry and that he loved her. It used to make her whole face open, to hear those words. Now she reacted as if he were telling her a lie. So he slammed down the phone.

He started working on the keg, chugged a beer, and drew another while laying out chips for the party. Their house was sparsely furnished with an old couch his mother had given them and a used kitchen table he got from his dad. The couch was brown, and the kitchen table was chrome with a yellow Formica top and matching chairs. They were the only things his parents had given him. They didn't really have much to give.

JT's family had fractured long ago. His mother had been institutionalized twice when he was in high school and gone through shock treatments and massive doses of medication. When she became clear, she divorced his dad. His father, meanwhile, was headed toward skid row. He had a little apartment in town across from his sister's massage parlor and sometimes worked in auto body shops pounding dents out of cars. Usually his dad's sister, Evelyn, paid his bills. He had lost family, home, and business to drinking. But it didn't seem to bother his dad. He still drank half gallons of cheap white wine all day long.

JT shoved his parents out of his mind as he heard Ashley pull up. His marriage was going to be different. He greeted her on the front porch with a remorseful tone in his voice.

"I'm sorry I got so mad. But I cleaned everything up."

"I don't want to talk right now," she said, pushing by. "The party is supposed to start in a little while, so I have to get ready."

"You look great," he offered, hoping that compliments might bridge the distance. As he moved to hug and kiss her, she stiffened, pushing him away.

"Don't. I don't want to be touched right now."

People started arriving just after 7:00 p.m. JT didn't know most of them. He had lost touch with friends from high school, so those invited were Ashley's friends. And everyone seemed so young, even though they were his age. He felt odd and out of place, like he didn't belong. The music was loud, and the doorbell rang several times before Ashley shouted, "Someone's at the door."

JT got up with a pint jar of beer in his hand and pulled the door open. "Hey, Brad! Mary. Come in. Come in. You're late."

Brad took off his coat, dropping it on a black bucket car seat next to the door. "Nah. Boom-boom, mamasan!"

JT laughed as Mary elbowed Brad in the side. Raising his voice over the noise, he shouted, "Take a load off and I'll bring you a beer."

The front room was neatly packed with people sitting on the floor, bucket car seats, couch, and kitchen chairs. One group was gathered around the dining table munching on snacks, while a constant stream was spilling into the kitchen for drinks. The music was so loud it drowned out most conversations.

Duane and Megan were on the floor wrapped up in each other, sharing a bottle of apple wine. Megan had brought along an overweight girlfriend of hers who was showing off her pet ferret. The ferret was draped across the friend's shoulder like a scarf, being fed potato chips.

JT handed drinks to Brad and Mary and had just sat down next to them when he heard pounding coming from the floor.

"It's Pearl, the old lady downstairs," he said. "Whenever we make noise, she hammers on her ceiling with a broomstick. I better go take her the beers I bought. That should keep her quiet for the night."

Pearl was grateful and demonstrated her broom technique on the ceiling before JT bounded back up the stairs to the party. The ferret girl was in front of the couch. She had put a little leash around its neck and was pretending it could do tricks like a dog.

He was sitting next to the speaker when the phone started ringing. It rang many times before someone heard it above the music and yelled. Ashley got it.

"JT," Ashley called from across the room. "JT! Telephone."

But he was lost in the music and the booze.

"Hey!" she shouted. "Mr. Tambourine Man!" This brought him from his stupor. "Telephone."

He stumbled to the phone.

"Soldier man, what's happening? This is Smoke."

"Smoke!" JT said. "Did you get it?"

"Told you I would. No sweat. Meet me at the park."

"Man, I'm too messed up. Get your ass over here. I'll buy you a beer."

"You said the park."

"Fuck the park."

JT gave Smoke the address, hung up, walked over to the stereo, and got it thundering again. Then he headed for the floor next to Ashley. He felt drunk. He noticed the ferret still crawling all over. Like to snap that little son of a bitch's neck.

He picked up on a conversation Ashley was having with Duane and Megan about saving money to buy a house someday. Buying a house, what a fucking joke. Could be dead tomorrow. Buy a new car. Could do that. But owning stuff wasn't important. Getting shot in the face was. He finished his beer and asked Ashley to get him another one.

"Is your leg broke?" she replied sarcastically.

"What do you mean, is my leg broke?" Anger started to swell. "No, my leg isn't broke. Now, what kind of a smart-ass reply was that? I just asked you to get me a beer. Forget it!"

He stood up, and there was a slight stagger to his step as he headed for the kitchen, brushing by people, then pushing through the swinging door.

When he returned, the front door was open. Ashley was talking to Smoke and two black guys in cheap leather coats. He had never seen either of them before. One was about six-two with a huge Afro and wore shades. The other one was shorter and sloppy fat. Both had their hands in their coat pockets and looks of agitation on their faces. JT gulped his beer. He might have to kick some ass. He set the cup on the speaker and walked toward the door, grabbing Brad on the way.

"Get up. Bloods."

Brad hopped up holding an empty beer bottle. Meanwhile, the whole room shifted its focus to the doorway. The music turned down.

"Soldier man. What it is!" Smoke said as he reached out to shake JT's hand. "These are my partners I was telling you about."

JT noticed something odd in Smoke's face. Like a nervous kind of fear. The handshake eased the party's focus away from the door. JT watched them carefully, alert, head clearing.

"Come on in," JT said, turning to Ashley and placing his hand thoughtfully on her shoulder.

Neither Smoke nor his companions bothered to introduce themselves. They simply listened to what JT said and followed him into the kitchen.

By now the kitchen was a mess, cups and beer bottles in the sink and all over the counters. Floor sticky with beer, the air thick and musty.

"Hey, Smoke, grab a beer. Be back in a minute."

"Thanks, man," Smoke said.

JT and Brad went into the back room and shut the door. It was relatively quiet.

"What the fuck is going on?" Brad asked.

Before JT could reply, Ashley whipped open the door and walked in with a look of anger on her face.

"Who in the hell are those guys?" she demanded. "They look like a couple of thugs."

JT felt he'd made a mistake in asking Smoke to come by, but he didn't want to be shown up in front of Brad. "Look, I'll handle it. All right?"

Ashley could see he was about to explode. "Bastard!" she said under her breath and slammed the door.

"What the hell did she say?"

"Forget it, JT. Let her go. Now tell me about those pricks."

"Smoke's a connection, I guess. I just met the jerk-off a couple weeks ago. The guy says he can score some righteous dope, and I figured you'd go in on it with me. So I said what the fuck, bring it over."

"Have you tried any?"

"No. But he isn't gonna stiff us. We'll kick his ass if he even thinks about it."

Brad nodded and handed JT a twenty-dollar bill from his wallet. "But I don't like the looks of those dudes."

When they walked back into the kitchen, Megan and the ferret girl were showing Smoke ferret tricks. Smoke's friends did not look pleased.

"Look, Smoke," the tall guy said. "You drug our asses over here, and I ain't got no time for no zoo bullshit. Let's do this deal or get the fuck out ah here."

The kitchen was crowded, and tension was escalating.

"Be cool," JT said. "Let's all go on the back porch for a minute, OK?"

The big guy nodded, his fat partner grunted a noise that sounded like OK, and they eased to the back porch. The porch was small and looked out onto the yard and garage. It was dark, and the only light was from the kitchen window and door as it opened.

JT leaned up against the porch railing, "So, where is it, Smoke?"

"You got the money, soldier man?"

"Of course. Come on. Don't fuck with me."

"I ain't fucking with you, soldier man."

Smoke looked toward the fat guy who nodded and smiled stupidly. He looked like a punch-drunk fighter and had a couple of front teeth missing. He handed Smoke a clear plastic baggie, partially full of what looked like pot.

"There you go, bro. Forty bones."

Smoke handed the baggie to JT.

"Forty dollars. What's that shit?" JT asked, surprised and pissed at Smoke's words. "You told me it was gonna be thirty-five. And that's what I agreed to."

"Hey, chump. It's forty," the tall guy said, stepping across the small porch in one stride and standing menacingly in front of JT.

JT recoiled instinctively and threw a hard right hook that caught the tall guy high on the temple, knocking his sunglasses off and driving him to the railing. At the same time, the fat guy moved toward JT, but Brad caught him on the side of the head with his beer bottle and dropped him to his knees, his head bleeding profusely.

The tall guy was still stunned as JT tackled him hard, bursting through the railing and falling three feet to the ground. He got on top of the guy and started hammering him in his face.

"I'll kill you, you motherfucker. I'll kill you!"

By now the rest of the party was barreling through the kitchen, trying to find out what all the noise was about, and Smoke was running off into the darkness.

JT stood up and shouted, "Get out of here and take your asshole buddy with you!"

The fat guy struggled to his feet, holding a hand to his bloody head. He helped the big guy up, and they wobbled across the yard mumbling obscenities down the driveway and out into the night.

It was all over in a matter of seconds. It was over before Ashley reached the back porch, pushed through the crowd, and saw JT standing in the faint light, his fists clenched and his face twisted into a look that chilled her to the bone.

THE NEXT MORNING JT WOKE WITH A raging headache and a sore hand. He remembered the fight and a bad conversation he'd had with Ashley about drinking too much. Last thing he could recall was doing shots of tequila with Brad.

Flat on his back, he looked up at the ceiling and felt dizzy and sick to his stomach. It wasn't like he had slept. It was more like coming to after having been knocked out. He was exhausted. He rolled over on his side and could feel sharp pain throbbing in his right hand. He pulled it from underneath the covers and saw that it was cut and swollen.

The fight. He started to sit up but laid back down again. He was going to puke. Something was inside his head pounding its way out. His mouth was dry. He called for Ashley, but she was gone. He wondered where she was and thought maybe he had said something terrible to her. But he was too sick to really care, and so he rolled over and fell asleep.

It was noon when the phone rang and woke him. It kept ringing and wouldn't stop. His mind started to kick into the realization that it could be Ashley, so he struggled out of bed and staggered naked into the front room searching for the phone.

"Hello."

"Party, party, party!" It was Brad.

"Yeah, man. What's happening?"

"We sure hammered those punks last night," he said excitedly.

JT recalled the moment; it felt good—like being back at the Nam and blowing the shit out of tree lines full of gooks.

"Bloods talking like they're bad," JT said. "We may not be bad, but the bad don't fuck with us."

Brad laughed loud into the phone. When he stopped laughing, he told JT that Mary drove home because he was too drunk to drive and that Ashley came with them.

"You really pissed her off, man," Brad said.

"Was she mad over the fight?"

"I don't know; I was drunk, too. But she's over here. You want to talk to her?"

"No. She'll just make me feel worse than I do. Tell her I'll come pick her up in a while and then we'll go get Anna." He hung up, went into the bathroom, emptied the foulness of his poisoned system, showered, weighed himself, and got dressed.

The house was a disaster. Beer bottles, wine bottles, and half-emptied cups littered the front room and spilled onto the kitchen counter. Chairs were overturned, and overflowing ashtrays and half-eaten bowls of chips and crackers were scattered about. The room smelled of smoke and stale beer.

His head was pounding as he scoured the fridge, eating slices of baloney and draining a bottle of milk. The food settled his stomach and helped clear away the drumbeat in his temples. Reluctantly, he cleaned the kitchen and front room, leaving a window open to air out the house.

When he picked up Ashley, she wouldn't speak to him. She was furious. As she got into their Volkswagen, she slammed the door, shaking the car, and then drilled him.

"I don't want to talk to you. I don't want to kiss and make up, and most of all, I don't want to hear your excuses. Just drive, will you."

During the twenty-minute drive to Ashley's mom's house, neither said a word. On the way home, Anna fell asleep in Ashley's arms. Finally, Ashley broke the silence.

"I can't live like this," she said. "I know it wasn't easy for you in the war, but it wasn't easy for me either." As she spoke, her voice dropped and her eyes lowered until she wasn't looking at JT but rather at Anna resting in her lap. It was raining and gray. "Every day I used to wake up and wonder if you were still alive." She began to cry. "I tried not to look at newspapers or watch TV for fear of seeing you wounded or dead," she said. "And at night, I'd cry myself to sleep wondering if Anna would ever have a dad. Then you come home...and you...you seemed so different." She began to sob loudly, but her words floated in the air unattached, like a voice coming from the radio. They meant nothing to him, nothing until she said he'd changed.

"Of course I changed. Goddamn it! Who wouldn't change?" he shouted, pounding his fist on the dashboard. "And don't cry!" Then he caught himself. He knew he had frightened her. His voice flattened. "I'm sorry. I'm sorry."

When they got home, the house was still a mess. There were beer cups on the floor, kitchen chairs in the front room, and rain had soaked the stereo and records under the window that JT had left open.

"I thought you cleaned up," Ashley said, as she carried Anna and walked through the room.

"I didn't get all of it because I ran out of time," JT countered. "I'll finish tomorrow. I'm gonna watch a game on TV."

"Well, the window needs to be shut and the wall and stereo wiped dry. Could you do that while I feed the baby?" Her voice sounded beaten down.

JT felt awful about leaving the window open. It was the kind of stupid mistake that made him wrench inside. But it wasn't his fault. How was he to know it was going to rain? She seemed to blame him for everything. He put the game on hold and finished cleaning up. Later he picked up a pizza, and they sat together eating and watching TV.

That night he was startled from his sleep again. He thought he heard the sound of sandaled footsteps breaking brush. He got up and his mind cleared. He brought Anna to their bed and lay awake until morning.

6

Vuong

FOR DAYS VUONG'S UNIT WAS STUCK, HIDDEN underground at Station 2 in the Nghe An Province. Bombing from American B-52s was close by. At first the bombings could be heard as a distant *whump...whump...whump*, followed by the slightest tremor. But as they came nearer, the ground shook fiercely, some sections of tunnels caving in and concussions breaking eardrums...WHUMP! WHUMP! WHUMP! And the earth rolled and heaved, exploded and collapsed, striking such terror in Vuong's mind that his bowels gave way, his body shuddered uncontrollably. In the darkness, he was not alone. One young comrade screamed; others sobbed without restraint. Seven were buried in a collapsed section of tunnel as the bombing continued. Finally, the air was empty; the bombing ceased. The older, experienced guards sat quietly throughout the ordeal, resigned to an ancestor's corner, a place to accept death if it came. When the bombing was over, they tended to the younger ones and calmed them, explaining that the nightmare had passed.

Vuong and the rest of the soldiers remained sheltered. They cleaned weapons and wrote home. Receiving and delivering mail was difficult. A letter could take months to reach a soldier or his home. Often, couriers were killed, especially now that the

Americans knew about the Ho Chi Minh Trail. They were dropping listening and surveillance devices in trees or next to trails that could monitor sound or motion and detect human smells. At first, when the equipment was discovered, it was destroyed in place, but then the Americans began booby-trapping them, making disposal much more dangerous. Sometimes the surveillance systems floated toward villages, landing in fields or populated areas. When children found them, they would explode and maim or kill.

The time underground passed slowly for Vuong. His head hurt, his ears still rang from the bombardment, and food was not good. More wounded were brought in, and the sense of a grave battlefield slowly replaced the euphoric thoughts of marching into villages, towns, or cities as a triumphant soldier. In the following days, over twenty died from malaria and dysentery.

In these dark days, Vuong would think of his father, Diep, and his teachings about duty, propriety, conscience, benevolence, and faithfulness. His father understood these principles as a scholar or teacher might, but Vuong could only take each word and consider how it applied to him and his comrades. Benevolence was what he wanted to strive for. A state of kindness and goodwill to others is what he understood about the word. But how could he show benevolence in this jungle of war and despair? Faith he could apply, and duty was easily connected, but other principles left him wondering. He had considered the heroes who fought against the French, but now it seemed that war was less than an ideal and more of a burden than he had expected.

One night the commander of Vuong's unit addressed the company in the same cavern where they had watched the movie a week earlier. He spoke of the revolution and the high price the American dogs would pay for "enslaving our sisters and brothers." Then Vuong heard the commander say, "Comrade Commander Nguyen Diep from the village of Ho Bin was captured on the battlefield of Quang Tri. I mention his name now because his son is among you."

Nothing could have shaken Vuong more. Not even hearing that his father died would have bothered him as much.

That night as Vuong lay down to sleep, he stared at the faint overhead single bulb that cast a shadow on the cavern's bare walls. He could smell the dirt and the odor of many bodies, and he could hear the others sleeping. They had eaten monkey that night and it did not sit well on his stomach. He curled up in a ball and thought of what the enemy would do to his father, agonizing over images of him being tortured, slit open like a calf, of the Americans eating his entrails. He closed his eyes just before dawn.

Vuong and his comrades were given new liters of rice, salt, dried fish, and sugar bars from storage as they left the underground bunkers and began the marching phase of their journey. From Station 2, they walked into a forest, and before the day was half over, they were climbing into the Laotian mountains. The jungle was thick and hot with little light seeping through the canopy. But the trail was well cut with steps at the most severe inclines. In a flatter area that had been washed away by seasonal rains, thirty meters of woven bamboo, laid out like mats, stabilized the footpath. It was one of several trails and paths linking the Ho Chi Minh Trail to North Vietnam, Laos, and on into South Vietnam. It connected the next station, and because of the recent bombing, the company commander thought it to be the safest trail to travel.

As they climbed, Vuong thought of his father's words when he was a boy, the words of love for the Fatherland. He could see Diep and hear his voice as he trudged. His father was in his mind, mixed with images of the village and being tortured by Americans. They might tie him and beat him or throw him from a helicopter.

Vuong's stomach was better and his strength was good, but he was angry and felt hatred for the Americans. He would kill whoever hurt his father. He would find where his father was, then save him.

The morning wore on. Vuong began to tire. His pack straps cut into his shoulders and the small of his back ached. The heat was hard to endure and his shirt was soaked with sweat. It ran into his eyes and stung. When he licked his lips, he could taste the salt and feel them cracking. His training had prepared him for adversity, though, and so he pushed his mind through the pain. A good soldier. Push and struggle, but overcome.

At midday the company stopped along the trail, dropped packs, and prepared for the afternoon meal. Eleven soldiers stricken with malaria were sent back to the station. The enemy had not crossed the DMZ, so it was safe to be at ease, at least until the planes came. The men built a fire in such a way that most of the smoke was drafted into a hole to dissipate unseen. Each man donated a scoop of his rice ration toward the communal meal. Vuong drank from his canteen sparingly then took his entrenching tool and moved into the jungle to relieve himself. When he returned, food was ready. He took off his shirt and sat cross-legged, eating from his wooden bowl. He was tired, and his back felt like he had been bending over all day in the rice fields. The other two members of his cell, Vinh and Winh, were eating and smoking. They, too, were fatigued.

"Vuong, do you know where we are?" Vinh asked as he scooped rice from his wooden bowl with chopsticks. "Have you seen a map?"

"We could be in Laos," he proposed, lying back on his pack, legs stretching across the trail. "That is only the thought of a lowly private."

The heat was heavy, so the company rested for three hours instead of two. When it cooled somewhat, they packed up and moved out again, traversing the mountainside along the edge of a small stream. The commander said the stream was blessed by good spirits. That it originated from a natural cistern of water that appeared for the country's soldiers. Animals could drink from it, but not the enemy. Once a French pilot crashed near the cistern, unharmed, but drank of the water and was poisoned. His remains were found by Montagnards, worms crawling out of his belly.

Finally, they came to a spot the commander felt would be a good position to bivouac for the night. They were not in immediate danger, but even so, each soldier dug a fighting hole to prepare for the unexpected. As Vuong cleared an area with Vinh and Winh, he did not think about his father or the Americans. He thought how beautiful the jungle was with its shades of green and plants he had never seen before. Growing up in the village, he had never experienced the jungle, let alone slept in it. So he was pleased and felt somehow closer to the revolution just by being there. He declined a cigarette from Vinh and dug a hole next to a thick tree. Then he asked for their canteens.

"I am going to wash in the stream and fill my canteens. I'll fill yours, too."

It was nearly dusk as he picked up his rifle and the canteens and made his way down the slope. The jungle was cooler, and he thought he could hear the first cricket and the stirrings that come with night. He was tired and held on to trees and vines, slowly edging toward the sound of the water. He was quiet as he moved, practicing the skills he had learned in training.

Just before he reached the stream, he heard faint laughter and stopped. He knelt down; his heart quickened. He listened. The laughter was soft and sweet like a child's. He moved closer. It was Phung Thu! His heart raced. She was with two other female comrades, washing. She was in her black pajamas, pant legs rolled up to her knees, standing barefoot in the stream. She bent down, cupping her hands, and brought water to her mouth, then threw handfuls at the others and giggled.

Vuong felt awkward kneeling in the bush, but, after all, he had to get water, so he stood and called to them.

"Comrades," he said, and as he spoke, they were startled and reached for their weapons. Vuong immediately stepped closer into full view, waving his arms. "Comrades," he said, "I—I—I am sorry I startled you but...but I have come for water."

The three women were embarrassed and bowed their heads and looked at the ground as they slipped on sandals.

Vuong placed his rifle on the ground and stepped into the stream a few feet from Phung Thu. He felt as if he were in a dream. "I—I—oh, I just—" He started to step backward, his arms full of canteens, his feet searching for firm footing on the bank. But it was wet and slippery, and as he stepped he lost his balance and fell, splashing into the water. The three girls looked up and covered their mouths, muffling laughter. Vuong, too, tried not to laugh but did a little.

"You are quite a swimmer," Phung Thu said, smiling as she reached to grab a floating canteen. Vuong struggled to his feet, quite embarrassed.

"Thank you, sister," he said when Phung Thu handed him the canteen. Then he took a big breath and let it out quickly, talking much too fast. "I want to say that I enjoyed your poetry at the station." Then when he realized what he said, he added, "And I enjoyed the songs that my sisters sang quite well." He bent and filled the canteens. "I—I—will, I will see you, comrades." He picked up his rifle and started to leave. As he walked up the hill, Phung Thu called out.

"Comrade."

Vuong turned, startled but happy to hear her voice again.

"What is your name, great swimmer?"

A smile emerged. "I am Vuong," he said. He was shy and nearly breathless.

Then he veered away, sure she could see he was churning inside. He was feeling some kind of thing he had never felt before. It was a good feeling. Clean and powerful. A strong feeling. As big as what he felt about his Fatherland. The feeling lifted him and he raced up the mountain, smiling all the way. She was so beautiful. And the way she looked at him gave him hope.

"Brother," Vinh said to Vuong as he reached their position. "You sound like an elephant tramping your way through the jungle."

"Sorry." Vuong quickly buried his smile and apologized. "I could see it was almost dark, and, yes, I was too loud. I must be a better soldier."

"Count that, then, as your self-criticism."

"Yes. You are right. I will. Thank you, comrade."

Vuong ate precooked rice that was wrapped in leaves and a banana he had pulled from a tree the day before. Night came with no moon. It would not rain, he thought, so he tied his hammock in a tree and rested. As he closed his eyes to sleep, he could see Phung Thu standing in the middle of the stream, smiling and calling him great swimmer.

THE COMPANY CLIMBED THROUGH THE MOUNTAINOUS TERRAIN for many days, passing several stations where they could rest and gather food. Each night they would be led in classes by their superiors and hold self-criticism sessions within the squad and their own personal cell.

"My mind has wandered," Vuong said one evening. "I often think of my father and how he is being treated. And I know this is not good. I cannot allow my feelings to interfere with my direction."

Vinh and Winh and the others listened passively, squatting on their haunches, some smoking brown hand-rolled cigarettes.

What Vuong did not reveal was that even more often he'd think of Phung Thu. He thought of them together in a sampan on the Red River, floating past the riverbanks or walking along the rice dikes and small paths that wove his hamlet and the countryside together. Maybe they could ride a bicycle or listen to someone play music in the village square. They could go to the marketplace, and he would buy them sweet breads and chocolate, and every young man would turn his head when Phung Thu walked by.

But these things were selfish thoughts. His comrades would not approve. Some things he could reveal, and some things he could not. He must be careful with his dreams and thoughts and keep them to himself. He would give all his time and energy to the revolution, but not all his thoughts.

7

Hawkeye

As boot camp progressed, Hawkeye changed. Push-ups, pull-ups, and running the obstacle course had layered his body with muscle and definition. His arms and chest filled out, he gained weight and grew nearly an inch in height. He sensed his spirit and mind adjusting to the confines of training. The swagger and attitude he once projected were replaced with a walk that was tall and straight. Sergeant Pope could see the change, and after training, hundreds of recruits knew there was a stirring in Hawkeye.

Just before dawn, when dampness hung in the air and the day was opening to light, Hawkeye's platoon had begun its work. They were told to dress in their yellow sweatshirts with the red Marine Corps emblem because they were going to do the Marine Corps fitness tests again. Some of the recruits were mopping the Quonset hut and sweeping walkways; others were policing the area with silver buckets, picking up debris. In front of each billet, empty flowerbeds were being raked into straight rows, while stones were being carefully arranged to form square borders or Marine Corps emblems.

Hawkeye was pushing a broom along a narrow walkway bordered by short green crabgrass on one side and empty flowerbeds on the other. He was thinking about his life. He never really knew his father growing up. His parents were never married. He was raised an only child, his mom working two and sometimes three jobs. For years, she cleaned houses and apartments during the day, getting up before dawn and coming home late, and stuffing envelopes at night for a direct mail company that paid almost nothing. She made sure her boy was taken care of, though, most often by Aunt Lani or an old man named Damon, who was retired from the railroad and could sit with him when Lani was sick or needed a break.

By the time Hawkeye was in second grade, he was self-reliant and could stay home after school until his mother returned from work. Twice, a man called and said he was Hawkeye's daddy, but that was it, and he knew better than to talk about it. His mom was constant, gave him love, and could always be counted on.

As he swept, he recalled the way she laughed and the way she used to kiss him twice on the forehead, once for love and once for God's protection. It occurred to him that he never felt he belonged anywhere before, except maybe those moments with his mother. Boot camp always seemed loud and chaotic, Hawkeye thought. Never an opportunity for the mind to rest. But for a few brief moments, as morning light opened the day, Hawkeye relaxed and felt a sense of peace.

When Drill Instructor Pope passed the word to fall in on the road, the sun was above the horizon. Recruits quickly secured brooms, mops, rakes, and buckets in the Quonset huts and raced to gather on the road in four lines in front of their billet. The sun warmed the face of each young soldier as they stood at attention, waiting for orders from Sergeant Pope. And that morning, Hawkeye felt as if he were becoming part of something larger than himself. For one of the few times in his life, he felt as if he mattered.

Sergeant Pope faced the platoon, then walked up and down the lines of soldiers inspecting and eyeballing each in a suspicious way.

He looked in ears and at teeth, sometimes standing on his tiptoes or jerking the recruit's head down to his level. From the corner of his eye, he caught someone looking along the line toward him, not straight ahead. He spun immediately and ran down the line, stopping in front of a kid named Douchet from Kentucky.

"Dew-shit, we're five weeks into boot camp and your eyeballs are still wandering. You must think I'm a bitch. Are you eye-fuckin' me?"

"Sir. No, sir!" came the startled recruit's shouted reply.

"Do you want to get skull-fucked, boy?"

"Sir. No, sir!" By this time, Douchet was nearly pissing his pants.

"Bitch, you best keep your eyes to the front," Pope advised, his knuckles rapping Douchet on the side of the head.

Pope moved to the front of the platoon and stood at parade rest, with his hands clasped behind his back. His green fatigues were freshly starched and pressed, boots black, spit-shined to a level that no one else could attain. The round brim of his brown smoky was tilted forward hiding his eyes, showing only a neat row of white teeth.

"House mouse," Pope shouted. "Get your dumb ass up here."

The house mouse was the smallest in the platoon. His job was to clean the drill instructors' quarters, shine their boots, and basically tend to their needs. A twentieth-century slave, thought Hawkeye. The house mouse usually received extra benefits, though, like being allowed to go first in line for chow and not having to pull any extra duty. If he worked hard, he'd get PFC out of boot camp. Kool-Aid was the house mouse for Hawkeye's platoon. He was quiet, almost shy, not more than five foot four, but built like a bag of rocks. On the first day of boot camp, when all of the new recruits were stripped and their possessions collected to be shipped home, one of the drill instructors found a package of Kool-Aid in the recruit's box. The drill instructor made the recruit eat the package, paper and all.

Kool-Aid was quickly at Pope's side. "Sir, Private Kool-Aid reporting as ordered, sir!"

"House mouse. Make me a chair," Pope ordered, not smiling.

Kool-Aid dropped to all fours as he had been forced to do before, and Pope stepped carefully up on his back. If Kool-Aid moved and Pope fell, Kool-Aid would be in a world of hurt. He'd be doing PT forever or scooping shit out of the plugged-up latrine toilets with his bare hands.

"Ladies," Pope said, "we got a platoon here full of dumb-ass maggots and one smart SOB. That smart SOB is Private Collins. Private Collins is gonna help me straighten your dumb asses out." Then he barked, "Private Collins, get up here on the double."

Hawkeye burst from the formation and double-timed to Pope, where he stopped abruptly, stood at attention, and threw a perfect salute. Pope, who was still standing on the back of the weary house mouse, returned the salute.

"Sir, Private Collins reporting as ordered, sir!"

"Collins, turn your ugly ass around and face this here platoon," Pope commanded, stepping down off Kool-Aid's back and ordering him to return to the formation.

As Kool-Aid was racing back to the platoon, Hawkeye spun a tight circle and faced the group.

"Private Collins here is a certified big brain sonofabitch," Pope said, standing with his hands still clasped behind his back. Then between each thought, he would take a step and adjust his DI cover. "Private Collins has got brains on top of brains." Stepped, adjusted the cover. Looked back toward the platoon. "Maggots, I'm trying to fumigate your brains. I'm trying to unlearn all that civilian garbage that packs your young minds. You're all so full of crap you naturally are gonna fuck up." He stepped and adjusted. "Without even trying, you ruin my Marine Corps. It's natural. But Collins here is gonna help me stop you from being the worthless maggots that you are. From now on, ladies, before you eat, sleep, or take a dump, Collins here is gonna help shake that civilian slime outta your mind. We gonna create our own evolution. Is that understood, ladies?"

A huge simultaneous "Sir. Yes, sir!" thundered from the platoon.

"So forget everything. Right now consider yourselves unlearned. Readyyy? Do it. Shake your heads. Do it!" And they all shook their heads. "Shake that slime outta your brain. Readyyy?" And they all stood at attention shaking their heads until Pope said, "Stop!" And they all stopped and looked serious and somehow more ready to learn than before.

"If any of you maggots don't get what I'm talkin' about or don't get how to make your rack, or shine your shoes, or clean your rifle, or memorize your general orders, or wipe your ass, ask Private Collins, Mr. Super Brain." Then Pope walked over to Hawkeye, looked up into his face, and said with his back to the platoon, "Collins, you are my new guidon. You will help fill these empty heads. Is that understood?"

"Sir. Yes, sir!"

And from that day, Hawkeye "Super Brain" Collins was Platoon 287's guidon bearer, marching out front leading the platoon. Even though he was not the most graceful or best-stepping soldier in the platoon, he was the one up front with the honor of carrying the pole and red flag with the gold numbers 287 on it. He led the platoon to chow, to the classrooms, or marching on the big concrete parade deck where dozens of other platoons marched in choreographed precision. Whenever and wherever they stopped, Hawkeye would step out from formation, stand to the side, and ask the platoon questions like, Your first general order is? or The commandant of the Marine Corps is? And the platoon would respond in unison.

At night before they crashed, if someone had a question, they'd come to Hawkeye. He was their leader, and he would answer them thoughtfully. He would memorize everything, from general orders to the nomenclature of weapons, and share this with the slowest of the privates. He stopped thinking about himself and focused on how to make his platoon stronger, smarter, and well rounded. In this role, he changed completely.

THE PLATOON GRADUATED IN APRIL. HAWKEYE WAS honor man and promoted to private first class. Despite his high IQ, and despite being honor man, he was given a 0311 infantry M.O.S. and assigned to basic infantry school. Eight weeks later, he made lance corporal and was given a twenty-day leave before reporting back for assignment to Vietnam.

When he stepped off the plane in Chicago, his mother was waiting. She threw her arms around him and hugged him tight as if he were just leaving instead of coming home. She was crying and hugging and kissing his cheek.

"I'm so proud, and you look so handsome," she said.

He was wearing his dress blues with the red stripe down the side of his pants. The Marines were the elite defenders of the country, of his country, and he was an honor man. A Marine. Not everyone could be that. His goal now was to go to Vietnam and serve well, get promoted, and come home a corporal or even sergeant if he was lucky. Yes, he could do that. That would make his mama proud of him. Maybe he would be an officer. Maybe he would stay in the Corps and be a general someday. He could see himself leading men into battle. Maybe he would even influence history, and in doing so, help his people and his country. He knew there was a place in the Marine Corps for a smart, ambitious, hard-charging black jarhead, and it felt good to know the world was there waiting for him.

"Mama, I told you I would do well."

He gently released his mother's grip, reached down to pick up his duffel bag, and slung it over his shoulder. He felt proud and good inside. And confident that he could achieve anything he put his mind to.

Two weeks later, Hawkeye returned to the airport with his mother saying good-bye, hugging, kissing, and crying.

"Mama, I'm telling you now I set up an automatic withdrawal of my pay for you. I want half the money to be spent on your bills, and the other half goes into savings. You understand, Mama?"

"Yes, son. Just be careful."

When he bent over to embrace her, she kissed him twice. Hawkeye walked up the ramp to the plane's door, then turned to wave. He smiled a big smile of teeth so straight and white that the lights seemed to dance off them. His rich brown eyes were clear and his voice strong as he shouted, "Love you, Mama."

Then he turned and stepped through the doorway.

Hawkeye spent a week in staging at Camp Pendleton before he was issued West Pac orders and was on a plane to Vietnam. He was assigned to the 3rd Battalion, Ninth Marines, and spent three days in Okinawa getting shots and a last-minute medical checkup.

He arrived in Vietnam in a loud, prop-turning C-130 during the middle of a monsoon. When the plane set down, it slid sideways, spun 180 degrees, and skidded off the runway. A fire truck and ambulance came roaring in, and as the engines' props shut down and the loading ramp lowered, Hawkeye felt a monstrous sense of relief. He filed out with the rest of the troops into a torrential downpour, droplets the size of dimes. In a field next to the runway, a Vietnamese farmer in a conical hat, gray billowy shirt, and rolled up matching pajama-style pants stood watching. In one hand he held a small stick, in the other a length of rope leading to a big black water bull. The rope was tied to a thick ring that pierced the bull's nose. The man had a black twisted stub of a cigar in his mouth and a look of amusement on his face.

Welcome to Vietnam, Hawkeye thought as he glanced at the farmer and ran into the terminal.

Because of the storm, their plane had been diverted from Da Nang to Tan So Nuht Air Base. They'd stay there until the weather cleared. Tan So Nuht was close to the city of Saigon, and typically Marines were not assigned to that area because they were considered too crazy for the high-population cities, too violent. Rumor was they had destroyed villages by burning them to the ground with Zippo lighters. Scuttlebutt called it the Zippo incident.

The next couple of days were spent in temporary housing as the storm worked its course. The cloud cover dropped, swallowing sun and sky until the area became one unending stew of gray and darkness. Wooden billets with tin roofs were blown down, and everywhere trucks and jeeps were stuck in the crippling mud. Hawkeye's group stayed in a two-story, slapped-together wooden building, but it had bunk beds, showers, and stateside shitters. Most of the soldiers in temporary housing played cards, drank warm beer, and waited. No one left the building except for chow.

The storm raged for days before finally lifting. In the morning, as the sun edged over the horizon, the China Sea was calm and flat like a great silver and blue sheet, waves gently lapping at the sand. All of Vietnam seemed to be waking, restored, and rested.

Word was passed that the next morning they'd leave for their permanent assignments just south of the DMZ in Quang Tri. It was also announced that a military bus would be running back and forth from the base to Saigon if anyone wanted to venture into the city.

The short trip into Saigon was considered relatively safe, so weapons were not allowed. On the bus, as a safety precaution, the driver kept a rifle, and all windows were covered with wire mesh to prevent grenades from being tossed in.

Hawkeye sat next to a black kid named Ricky Flowers who was from a poor part of Georgia.

"Everybody just calls me Flowers," Ricky said, happily reaching across his body to lay five on Hawkeye.

"Yo, bro!" And Hawkeye told him his name as they slapped hands, bumped fists, and did the handshake jive.

The bus moved through the main gate, which was guarded by US Army personnel positioned in sandbagged bunkers on both sides. Sandbags were stacked three deep and nearly five feet tall around each position. Each bunker was the size of a small bedroom and came with M-60s, two soldiers, grenades, and pop-up flares. The bus turned onto the main road and passed the battalion's garbage dump. It was Monday, so the dump was full of women and children carefully picking through the weekend garbage.

"Whew. You see that shit, Hawkeye?" Flowers pointed excitedly out of the window. "Them gooks is eating garbage, man."

Hawkeye saw the peasants bent over sifting through the debris. There were mostly women with children in tow. A few of the children were barely old enough to walk. Occasionally there was a baby tied to its mother's back or cradled by another toddler. They were starving and intent on digging through the waste of an Army that had unlimited food and supplies. There were unopened or half-eaten tins of food, cigarettes, old boots, belts, blankets, and broken chairs. Newspapers and torn magazines with pictures of naked women shifted in the wind. A whole different culture lay in that dump—whatever filled the bellies or draped the backs of the American horse-faces, as some Vietnamese called the troops, was there.

"Can you believe that?" Flowers said. "Blows my mind. Whoo-wee. Nasty! And I thought I was dirt poor. Well, piss on it. When we git to town, I'm gonna git me sum ah that booty, that's for damn sure. Them girls is so small that pussy got to be tight. How 'bout you, brother?"

Hawkeye wasn't hip to that. Pope had warned him in boot camp of the danger of messing with Vietnamese whores. The DI told stories about how prostitutes lured G.I.'s off by themselves to have them killed, balls cut off and stuffed in their mouths. "Gooks think if your cock is cut off you can't go to the spirit world," Pope had said.

Stories were rampant about VC girls: razor blades stuck inside them and a venereal disease dubbed black clap that was incurable. Some said reports of Marines killed in action were really guys who died from black clap or were being kept hidden in secret, offshore US military prisons, rotting away. All of this made an impression on Hawkeye. He was on the right path now and intended to stay there.

"I don't know, man," Hawkeye said shaking his head. "I don't want no funky disease."

"Let 'em suck your dick. Might be your last chance for a long time."

"I'll think on it and let you know."

OFF BASE, THE LAND WAS FLAT AND covered with banana trees, rice paddies, and occasional pagodas and graveyards. Fields were spread out for miles, emerald green and sectioned off like Midwest farmland. The bus eased along a rugged road overflowing with motorcycles, ox carts, and three-wheeled buses jammed with people, pigs, and chickens. Red dust was everywhere. US jeeps, tanks, and Army trucks were packed with American or South Vietnamese troops in full battle gear, the howling diesel engines spewing black clouds of exhaust. Girls on bicycles dressed in traditional, brightly colored ao dais, long hair flowing over shoulders and slim hips.

The road was noisy and dirty, often littered with garbage. The pungent smell filled Hawkeye's nostrils with the stink of dirt, fish, and fuel. To him, each side of the road was the same: mile after mile of shacks made from scraps of wood, US-stamped sheets of corrugated tin, and flattened cardboard C-ration boxes. Out front in dirt walkways, mamasans and children sold fish, vegetables, rice, bananas, C-rations, warm Cokes, beer, transistor radios, dolls, or military-issued items ripped off from soldiers or traded on the black market for liquor or pot. As the bus rumbled into Saigon, the motorcycles multiplied, as did the bikes and thousands of peasants. Amputees and the deformed were on every corner grabbing, begging, or hopping away from military police. There was vendor after vendor hawking from storefronts, pulling at servicemen to "come in! Got numbah one girl! Drinks! Boom-boom!"

The bus came to a stop in front of the Rex Hotel, a beautiful but tired example of French architecture worn from years of hard sun, no care, monsoons, and bullet holes. As they filed off the bus, Hawkeye, Flowers, and the rest of the troops were surrounded by a swarm of begging children, old women, and amputees with cups outstretched pleading in broken English.

"Gimmi chow. Gimmi chow. Chop. You want a fuckie? Soul brother want boom-boom? Gimmi chow. Gimmi chow."

They crowded closer and pushed at Hawkeye. Flowers felt some-one pulling on his arm.

"Hey! Wait! What the—! Hawkeye! Hawkeye! Grab that little son of a bitch. He's got my watch." Hawkeye reached out and pulled the back of a little kid's white shirt as he was trying to run through the crowd. The shirt ripped. The kid started running down the sidewalk, his shirt flapping behind him, and disappeared.

Flowers was furious and his rage made the crowd scatter. Other soldiers started checking for missing watches and wallets as they walked into the hotel lobby, mumbling about shooting the bastards.

"That little cocksucker! If I ever see that little son of a bitch again, I'll blow his head off. Damn it!"

"Cool down, bro," Hawkeye said, putting an arm on his shoul-der. "Let's get inside."

"I can't believe that. Little pissant had my watch off my arm before I could say shit. Damn!" Flowers reached in his shirt pocket, pulled out a toothpick, and put it in his mouth. "I mean to tell ya, I'd like to fry that little pecker-head."

Hawkeye was irritated but amused; he agreed that Flowers get-ting ripped off was a bummer. "Damn rice snappers. I felt a couple hands trying to reach in my pants," Hawkeye said sympathetically. "Come on, let's get inside."

He placed his hand on Flowers's shoulder, and they moved to-ward the hotel's entrance. They walked through the huge brass and glass doorway and into the lobby, taking off their Marine Corps–is-sued baseball covers, tucking them in the back of waistbands. The walls of the hotel were covered with rich, dark hardwood harvested from deep in the jungle. The floors were marble and blanketed with worn Persian carpets. Gold-framed oil paintings were on every wall, displaying scenes of ancient Vietnamese in battle with swords and elephants and women in long, flowing regalia. Every corner had a huge lacquer vase or table covered with mother-of-pearl and tortoiseshell. Above the front desk was a painting depicting a game of lacrosse, with players running down a field carrying their sticks, surrounded by a wildly cheering crowd.

"Say, Hawkeye. What's up with these crazy muthers?" Flowers asked, talking back over his shoulder and across the lobby. He looked confused as he gestured toward the picture.

A hotel employee approached Flowers. "Chau anh. Please, sir, may I help?"

Flowers looked at the small attractive woman standing in front of him. She had startlingly beautiful dark eyes and black hair that hung straight down to the middle of her back. She was smiling as she stood between the two men. Her teeth were as white as any he had ever seen. She appeared to be no older than fifteen. She was so attractive and polite that Flowers was shaken, and as he backed up, he nearly tripped over his own feet.

"Oh, I ain't, well, I mean ... I was just, ah, lookin'." Flowers turned to Hawkeye, who was grinning and shaking his head.

"Come on, Romeo," Hawkeye called. "Come on, let's get a drink. They've got a bar upstairs." He punched the button for the elevator.

"Damn was she fine, Hawkeye. That was one fine rice burner."

"Yeah, right. Now about that picture, which has got your mind sliding sideways. Well, that's lacrosse."

"La-who?"

"Not La-who. Lacrosse! American Indians invented it. Back then, Indians were bad like a muther. Used to cut off enemy heads and use 'em like baseballs."

The doors of the elevator opened, and it took a jump start as it ascended.

"Hawkeye, how come you know all that stuff?"

Hawkeye shrugged and laughed, embarrassed. "I just read it in *National Geographic.* That's all. It's no big deal. Fact is, I read a lot whenever I got busted and jammed up for a while."

"For a fact? You was bad?"

"Damn straight, but that's history. I'm getting it together, bro. Gonna do the officer thing when my tour's over."

The elevator stopped, but the doors only opened partway, requiring Hawkeye to force them apart.

"Hawk!" Flowers said as they moved down the hall. "You shitting me, man? You, an officer? Well, kiss my ass! Damn! Ain't many colored louies!"

Hawkeye and Flowers sat at a table on the patio of the rooftop getting smashed on mai tais and 33 Beer. They ate plates of rice and fish, downed bowls of miso soup, and drank way more than they were accustomed to. They were feeling drunk and full, content to just sit and absorb the moment of being ripped in Saigon in the middle of what was supposed to be a war. Sitting in comfortable lounge chairs, waited on by beautiful women, was far from the battlefields they'd been warned of.

"This place is some kind ah pussy heaven," Flowers mumbled as he sipped on his drink complete with flower and umbrella. "The place be lookin' like Christmas or some shit."

The patio was strung with strands of colored lights, hanging slack between white wood columns carved with dragons and ancient warriors slashing swords. The light strands formed a sort of perimeter for more than twenty tables of American soldiers, assorted reporters, Vietnamese officials, and high-ranking Vietnamese military. The lights began and ended at a large covered bar, which sat just to the side of a bank of windows opening into a formal dining area. The bar had eight stools full of patrons, and behind the bar were rows of bottled liquor and two young Vietnamese women serving drinks. From the patio, Hawkeye and Flowers could see the bar and through the windows into the restaurant with its dozens of linen-covered tables and sparkling chandeliers. In each corner of the rooftop were armed Vietnamese military police.

"I'm wasted, Hawk."

"You look wasted, my man. Toasted and roasted!" Hawkeye laughed. He smiled a big toothy grin and said with wonderment, "Damn!"

They knocked down more drinks, usually Flowers's two to Hawkeye's one, and watched the silk ao dai float by. The darkly beautiful women who waited on them had stretched their imagination. Just to the side of their chairs, they could look over the low patio walls to the city and down to the square.

"Hawkeye?" Flowers slurred. There were gaps in his speech, and his head rolled around on a rubber neck as he talked. "Say . . . Hawk . . . weeee HAVE gotta git some poontang. I shit you not."

Hawkeye wasn't listening. He had realized that they were being watched carefully by MPs lurking in the corners. "Come on, bud," he said, reaching over to touch Flowers's arm and gain his attention. "We best move on down the road before one of these helmet heads busts our asses."

"What they gonna do? Send us to Vietnam?" Flowers asked.

Hawkeye shot a grin, shook his head to get some of the numbness out, stretched his mouth, then smiled. "Come on, boy, let's double-time." He helped Flowers up by the arm, grabbed his cover from the table, and guided him past the waitresses and guards to the elevator.

Out on the street, traffic had thinned and sidewalks were nearly empty. The shops were being closed as shutters were brought down and families finished their late-night meal. Soon, the last bus back to camp would come, and curfew would go into effect, shutting down most of the city. What would remain open were the backroom bars and whorehouses that catered to drunken journalists and soldiers.

As they stood on the corner, a boy of about eight or ten walked up, leading a middle-aged woman whose eyes looked as if they had been gouged out, then healed over with flaps of brown scar tissue. The woman had high cheekbones and dark French features combining into a soft and gentle face. She was dressed in a clean, white, pressed blouse and loose black slacks. Her hair was long and gathered in a smooth ponytail. One hand rested on the shoulder of the young boy. She tilted her head slightly and smiled pleasantly as if she had closed her eyes and was thinking of another time.

Flowers, whose mind was wandering and sloshing from the alcohol, did not notice them. He was braced against a wall, fumbling through his pockets looking for a cigarette. Hawkeye had become transfixed by this woman, captured by her beauty and stunned by her deformity.

"Soul brother, souvenir me one, souvenir me one," the boy said to Hawkeye, holding his small hand out.

Hawkeye didn't quite register the words. "What'd you say, little man?"

"Souvenir me one."

"Souvenir you one? One what?"

"Soul brother, souvenir me one chop-chop."

"So the little brother wants some chow?" Hawkeye's face lit up, reveling in this new understanding. He had bridged the language barrier, but just as quickly he realized he had nothing for the child and woman to eat.

"Little bro, I ain't got no chop-chop. Sorry."

Flowers, meanwhile, had given up on finding cigarettes and staggered away from the wall, curious as to what Hawkeye was doing. He moved close to Hawkeye, then bumped into him before being steadied by Hawk.

"Say, what's the little gooker want? Does he want to rip off my watch?" he said angrily. "Well, tell 'im he is too damn late."

The boy appeared to be leery of Flowers, so he motioned Hawkeye to bend down as if he had a secret to tell him. "Soul brother, you want boom-boom?"

"Say what?" Hawkeye said, blown away by the boy's offer.

"Boom-boom. Numbah one. Me mamasan boom-boom you five dollah. Numbah one."

The boy smiled a huge kind of smile that children take on when they are pleased with themselves.

The words shook Hawkeye to his core. "Boy pimping his mom," he said out loud. "Jesus! Boy pimping his blind mom. Damn!" Then he stared at the woman again and saw her beauty and her tragedy and imagined the pain she'd gone through. And he could see past the slits in her lids to the faint hint of white that held no pupil.

"Take this money and just get the hell outta here and don't be talking 'bout no boom-boom, or I'll kick your ass."

He shoved ten dollars in the kid's hand and stood there a moment watching the boy and his mother walk down the sidewalk dodging motorbikes as they crossed the street. Hawkeye grabbed Flowers by the arm angrily and said, "We're outta here."

They caught the last bus leaving town. It was full of drunken soldiers laughing in the darkness.

8

Vuong

VUONG'S COMPANY CAME OUT OF THE MOUNTAINS and marched through
sparsely populated countryside resembling the village where Vuong
had been raised. And more comrades fell from malaria and were left
dying, unattended. By now, all knew they were in Laos. It looked
like the North, which made Vuong feel more at ease. Rice paddies
and occasional clusters of thatched roof and bamboo-walled huts
and even a pagoda and graveyard looked similar to his family's. But
it was forbidden to talk to the few peasants working in the fields.
One day, they came to a river where boats were waiting; and they
traveled down river for most of the day before landing and hiking
through flooded paddies and back into the mountains.

The company had been moving almost every day for weeks
since leaving Hanoi and for the last ten days had been traveling
inside and along the Laotian border. On November 10 they reached
Station 21 near an area called Tchepone, the last point before crossing back into Vietnam below the DMZ. The company was tired and
needed rest. At Station 21 they would receive additional training
and preparation for the push into Vietnam, where they planned
to meet with other elements of the 325B of the NVA. The camp
was primarily aboveground, with huts and staging areas for classes,

sleeping, eating, and storage. Because they were still in Laos, the threat of American bombardment was diminished.

For the next two weeks, Vuong was in training, learning skills to survive and elements of combat in both large- and small-team engagements. Each morning, discussions were held on liberation, historical revolution, and sometimes Marxist theories on communism. The afternoons were spent learning how Americans fought and where they were most vulnerable. The closer to the enemy the better, to avoid air strikes. The tunneling could not be seen and often led to an area or home close to the Americans. The horse-face soldiers did not fight well in the dark, and that was a clear advantage. All of this touched Vuong's senses and made him more confident.

Evenings meant more classes and self-criticism. Twice, singers and actors came through to share songs and plays with themes of national pride and unification, but it was boring for Vuong.

"Americans are cowards and will not die gladly for their country," a comrade in charge lectured. "They will bring in aircraft and drop bombs and napalm. But the closer we attack their lines, the more it gives them fear of destroying their forces. And at night they cannot see us with their weak eyes."

Vuong absorbed the words. His mind was strong, but it still wandered to thoughts of his father and home and, more often, Phung Thu.

It was difficult for him not to think about her, especially when he saw her almost daily. One afternoon, Vuong's squad and several women including Phung Thu went to a demonstration on how to build an underground bunker. They cleared the ground, then began picking and shoveling a hole deep enough and wide enough for three to stand in. The sun was barely seeping through the canopy, but Vuong was sweating profusely as he swung the pick, kicking loose the ground. He stopped and took off his shirt. He felt strong as he lifted the pick overhead and brought it down forcefully, tearing more earth, bringing it down again and again. When he rested, Phung Thu approached with a canteen. They didn't speak; their eyes met for just a moment. It was only a brief glance, and she quickly turned away.

The squad dug and hollowed the earth, framing the inside with freshly cut timbers designed like an A-frame. More timbers were lowered and used to cover the floor and form a roof. The timbers would help absorb the shock waves from the B-52s. They covered the roof with four feet of dirt, then camouflaged it with brush. Finally, they dug trenches leading from the bunker's entrance, which would connect with smaller fighting positions.

As they worked, Vuong felt gratified to have time with Phung Thu. He didn't worry about protocol or the future; he only thought of her eyes, so brown and rich. When the work was done, he felt a sense of completion. Pleased they had shared a common goal.

One evening when rain was heavy, everyone gathered in a large meeting hall made of bamboo and thatch. Dressed in black pajamas, they discussed their failings. Vuong was surprised when Phung Thu stood to address those gathered on the matted floor around her.

"Comrades," she said, her head bowed. "I have found that I have become vain. Each day I take time to brush and tend my hair and find that I think of it often. I want to not separate myself with vanity, so I have decided to cut off my hair."

When she sat down, no one spoke. It was quiet until the commander came forward and said, "Goodnight, comrades."

Vuong was not sure what had happened. He wondered if it was her idea or a superior's. How would she look? There was no mention of Phung Thu by Vinh or Winh or the others. They ate or smoked and then slept. When the new moon passed, his company was prepared to move on.

ON THE MORNING OF DECEMBER 3, 1968, Vuong took out his notebook and wrote a poem about the Red River. He wrote of peasant farmers fishing on the red clay banks in early morning light and how just before night, the sun dove toward the horizon, deep into Hia Phong Bay. He wrote about a father, son, and mother who depended upon the river for survival. And the poem ended with, *It happened a long time ago.* When he finished, he closed his book, wrapped it in clear plastic, tucked it in his pack between his black pants and matching shirt, and moved to the small cooking fire. He joined his squad and ate balls of rice, drank tea, and picked over a small portion of dried fish that was too salty for his liking.

"Pass me the nuoc, Vinh," Vuong said. "This fish is not good. We had better food at the last station. Don't you think?"

Vinh was squatting with the others, back on his haunches, smoking a cigarette rolled from his tobacco pouch. It looked like a gnarled root, and the smoke was harsh. He took Vuong's cup, pulled the pot from the edge of the fire, poured the tea, and returned it to the hot rocks.

A handful of birds scattered in the trees. No one looked up.

"I never did like dry fish," Vinh finally replied, as if he were considering Vuong's question in a contemplative way. "I lived in Hanoi, and we always had good food, plenty of fresh fish, meat, vegetables. Especially at market on Sundays."

Vuong sipped at his tea, ate the last bit of rice, hungered for Vinh's market, and wondered if he would see Phung Thu soon. The sun was seeping through the trees, and he could feel the warmth on the back of his neck and was content.

Word came that they were to move out immediately—douse fires, scatter ashes, bury garbage, and sweep the area with branches to minimize detection. Vuong thought it a waste of time to sweep dirt. Who will ever know we are here? Not the Americans. They never come to Laos. But he wanted to do his share, or even more than his share, to demonstrate willingness.

"I'll clean up," Vuong offered.

When he was done, he gathered up his gear, packed his pack carefully, wiped down his AK-47 rifle, and prepared to move out.

Sixty-one North Vietnamese Army soldiers, including seven women comrades and three joy girls, boarded canvas-covered German trucks and left the "safe haven" of Tchepone and Station 21. The joy girls would be dropped off to tend to the sexual needs of higher-ranked cadre. They had been "borrowed" from villages in the South months ago and were told they would be returned when things were better. No one was allowed to speak to the girls, and relations were forbidden. Vuong was surprised to see them and thought it was unfair to bring them against their will. The three carried packs and were dressed in black pajamas and soft brown jungle covers. They looked tired. When they boarded the truck, they sat in the cab isolated from the troops.

The trucks traveled east through Laotian countryside toward South Vietnam. Their destination was Station 22 in Quang Tri Province, just below the demilitarized zone. There they would link up with other elements of the 325B and launch coordinated attacks against Quang Tri City, adjacent enemy bases, and Hue City to the south. This operation would be a part of a nationwide offensive involving over three hundred thousand NVA and their Viet Cong counterparts. The mission was to defeat and demoralize the enemy, giving North Vietnam and the National Liberation Front a stronger bargaining position at the peace talks in Paris. Attacks were planned to take place during the celebration of the Vietnamese Lunar New Year. Movement would be difficult, though; monsoon rains were still hammering the roads, flooding some areas and making travel almost impossible. In addition, the Laotian border was under constant patrol by enemy troops, which mean that once they entered Vietnam, they would be much more susceptible to attack.

Despite the grave reality, Vuong felt a special excitement as their convoy crawled along the rain-soaked road. The truck heaved and rolled, and it was hot and jarring. But it was a victory for him just to have made it this far, to have survived the long march, the leeches, the bombings, and jungles with malaria. He was proud of himself.

Proud and determined to live up to the soldier's oath and, in doing so, honor his family, his ancestors, his nation. He sat in the back of the truck on a hard wooden bench crowded with twenty other comrades and their rifles, ammunition, and packs. There was a mortar tube on the floor with its heavy base plate, boxes of Chinese mortar rounds, and a German machine gun. Their uniforms were new, clean, and in assorted colors of light brown and soft green. Only two soldiers wore pith helmets. The rest had soft brown or green covers. Vuong felt an overwhelming sense of unity as they talked or clapped hands and sang patriotic songs about liberty and freedom. Several of the soldiers had tattooed "Born in the North, Die in the South" on their arms as a sign of commitment to the cause. One soldier wrote on his cover, "Die for your brother."

Vuong felt these comrades were his family, that he was destined to be here. After weeks and months of travel and training, he was finally about to help liberate his people. The trucks labored through the downpour, sometimes sliding off the road into irrigation ditches next to rice paddies, only to be pushed back on the road, moving on. There were no towns, only hamlets and small villages with adjoining paddies or open spaces of brush, fields of elephant grass, scattered plants, bamboo, and banana trees.

By the end of the second day, the trucks left the main route and traveled on a narrow road concealed and covered by trees, passing undetected into Vietnam. It was nearly dusk when the trucks stopped in a small clearing. His back aching, Vuong climbed down with his squad. They were led away from the trucks by a woman in brown uniform, up a hidden path that climbed into the mountains. Hungry and fatigued, they trudged along four hundred meters before coming to a row of small thatched huts, where they would stay until morning.

Vuong slept restlessly on the dirt floot, his dreams filled with his father and Phung Thu. In one dream, he flew above the jungle and through an American base camp, landing in a small lake that turned into snakes. This woke him in fear, but his mind eased as he heard muffled snoring from someone in the dark.

In the morning, a meeting was held in Vuong's shelter, and his new platoon leader, Hein, was introduced. He informed them they were below the DMZ, linking up with additional troops in a huge base at the foothills of the Truong Son Mountains. Hein was nearly forty, but strong and sinewy. He had a black patch over his left eye, lost from a Montagnard arrow. The story that whispered among the men was that Hein was in the mountains along the Cambodian and Vietnamese border training a group of reluctant Montagnards when wounded. Some said it was an accident, but the guilty Montagnard's head was cut off and stuck on a pole. Thereafter, the Montagnards had much higher morale. Hein's eye, however, became infected; and with no medication, it festered. Soon it was grotesquely swollen, the pain unbearable. He was near madness when the medic held him down and lanced it. By then the infection had destroyed the iris and pupil, blinding him. What remained was the yellow color of a boiled egg yolk.

Hein led them from where the trucks first stopped, showing Vuong's squad every footpath, bunker, and fighting position. The base meandered up the side of the mountain under a thick, woven canopy. As they negotiated along the footsteps and pathways, Hein often stopped to address them with long explanations, as if he were a tour guide.

"This base is the major staging area for the surrounding provinces," said Hein. "It was carefully designed to be within striking distance of Route 9, which winds past US military bases at Khe Sahn, the Rockpile, Camp Carroll, and on to Quang Tri City."

Hein explained how the camp sprawled upward with elaborate trenches, bunkers, underground rooms, and tunnels. A hospital with gas-driven electrical generators held an operating room, beds, and supplies. Bunkers, including the hospital, were dug deep and reinforced with timbers to survive B-52 bombardments. Even so, if there was a direct hit, the concussions alone could still kill or drive one mad.

"We have an armory built above ground and a smaller one below ground," said Hein.

The surface armory was constructed on bamboo stilts and full of hundreds of neatly stacked rifles, banana clip magazines, grenade launchers, bandoleer torpedoes, plastic and box mines, and hundreds of cases of grenades and ammunition supplies donated by the Soviet Union, China, Czechoslovakia, East Germany, and North Korea.

The supply depot was overflowing with uniforms, sandals, boots, bush covers, pouches, packs, shovels, belts, canteens, and several boxes stamped SHIPPED FROM THE USA, YALE UNIVERSITY. The boxes contained white shirts emblazoned with "Students for a Democratic Society" in red print on one side and a big black clenched fist on the other. There was a reading area stocked with books in Vietnamese, such as General Vo Nguyen Giap's *People's War, People's Army*, and French and English titles including Mark Twain's *Tom Sawyer* and *The Complete Book of Shakespeare*.

One section of the camp housed a squad of Chinese soldiers in a bamboo hut built on stilts, two feet off the ground. They were sent as observers, but they carried weapons and often ran ambushes and patrols. Next to their hut was a smaller hut, which four Russians occupied. They served as camp radiomen and advisors, monitoring American radio transmissions.

Five hidden artillery gun emplacements set on rolling platforms were dug into the side of the mountain. When not firing, they rolled back inside the safety of the cave to be cleaned and cared for, undetected. Three anti-aircraft guns scanned the sky, camouflaged by trees tied with rope and pulled down across them. The rope could be released in a moment and guns fired in deadly volumes overhead. In the last two weeks they had shot down four helicopters and a spotter plane.

In other locations, bamboo ramps were erected to launch 122-millimeter rockets toward Khe Sanh and Route 9 or US Marine and ARVN patrols.

They walked for several hours, Hein halting the group constantly. To Vuong, Hein seemed out of place, like a tired old man, ready to fall. As if the years in the jungle had eaten him away, drained him physically, and left him with no passion or emotion.

The camp had two lines of trenches that snaked and stretched like a dragon's tail nearly one thousand meters in one direction. The first line had machine-gun emplacements every hundred meters, usually dug close to a tree for concealment. Behind this trench was the second trench at a slightly higher elevation where troops could fall back in case they were overrun.

A stream ran down from a clear lake, passing through portions of the camp and providing constant water supply. At the center of the camp, near the widest portion of the stream, was an outdoor area with bleacher seating for one hundred men that encircled a 20 x 20-foot-square sandbox and large standing chalkboard. Trees were woven together with vines to help conceal it from the sky.

The sandbox and chalkboard were used to diagram and rehearse battle plans. Miniature buildings and enemy bases were constructed from scouting reports, and assaults were planned and practiced for weeks or months at a time. Often a planned attack involving months of preparation had to be called off at the last minute. Sometimes it was called because of information received from agents working on or around the American bases, and sometimes from radio transmission picked up by Soviet personnel.

Hein led Vuong and the rest of the soldiers back to a central staging area for deployment around the base, stopping at a small footbridge crossing a stream. He rubbed his bad eye as he stood next to the bridge. Vuong watched and listened with heightened interest. As Hein spoke, his words began to resonate with Vuong, sounding like words his father might have spoken.

"In 1943, when I was thirteen, I joined the resistance against the Japanese. They killed my mother and father and two sisters. When the French took over, I fought again. Many of my friends died in these same jungles. Now we face the Americans, who are big and strong like water bulls. But we will drive them from our country as we have the others. I know you have all traveled a long way. You have left friends and families. You have faced many adversities. I, too, left home as a young man, and even though I am older than you, I still remember the laughter of children playing in my village. I remember how it was to wake up in the morning with no worries other than, have I prepared well for school? Or, will that girl I like smile at me today? I salute your courage for leaving all this behind. You have left your youth, your innocence. But now there is a larger purpose in your life: to see your country free again. There will be times of hardship and terror. Many of you will pass to your ancestors. But in the end, we will prevail. In the end, we will have all served in a great and noble cause that will be remembered until the end of time."

9

JT

"I DON'T NEED THIS CRAP!" JT SHOUTED. "I spent nine months in the bush and another six months ordered around by lifers. If I wanted someone to tell me what to do, I'd still be in the Marine Corps." He slammed the front door and bounded down the steps into the early evening light.

So what if he forgot to deposit his check in the bank and the rent check bounced? It was no big deal. But he hated to be called on his mistakes. It felt terrible to be wrong. Like the time he threw a smoke grenade in a bunker, and only children came out, choking. Or fell asleep for a few minutes on guard duty.

By the time JT finished mentally abusing himself over Ashley, the check, and their fight, he had crossed over the river and was thirty blocks from his house. He passed the Union Mission Gospel Inn, where lines of low-life drunks, drug addicts, the homeless, and two-bit chumps leaned against an old brick wall waiting for a meal. A doorway up, a guy lay in his own shit and piss, passed out, two empty wine bottles by his side. Both sides of the street had wild nightclubs that rocked all night.

JT was thirsty. He wanted a cold beer and something to distract him. He heard music in the next block, past a tattoo parlor and blacked-out storefront where gypsy fortunetellers worked and lived. He walked to the Family Zoo. It was a notorious late-night joint, punched out of a rundown building that rented rooms by the hour upstairs. He pushed through the door.

The place was packed and drunk. Jammed to the rafters with every cross-section of street life—pimps, queers, and big-titted hookers dressed in tight miniskirts stretched over butts as round and tight as volleyballs. A great place if you wanted to be licked, laid, sucked, or score drugs. Everyone was on the prowl—bumping, grinding, sticking tongues in ears and down the throats of darkly attractive women or transvestites in big wigs and campy gowns.

Two hip business-types were leaning on the bar, tossing back shots of Jack Daniel's. One wore a three-piece suit, the other a trendy tweed. They were both looking for a way to blow their rocks cheaply. In one corner, a couple of bull dykes with slicked-back hair were shooting pool. On the other side of the table, two underaged girls with short hair and long necks, wearing too much makeup and smoking Kools, looked on.

The music shook the walls, and bodies danced where they stood. Across the room, a half-dozen college boys pushed, shoved, and shouted as they spilled beer in sloppy states of inebriation. Smoke was thick and lay over the crowd in a gray, milky haze.

JT stood in the middle of it all, his mind rushing. It felt wild, dangerous. It primed him, and he was pumped with adrenaline, ready to explode. As he shoved his way through the crowd, he bumped the back of a big, black, muscled transvestite dressed in a short, slinky red cocktail dress, spilling the guy's drink. The guy spun around angrily.

"What the fuck!" He had diamond studs in both ears, one gold front tooth, and a tattoo of a Marine Corps Bulldog on his forearm. The drink had spilled down the front of his dress. He was enraged and shoved JT with one arm. JT tried to respond, but by now the crowd surged between them.

"Listen, asswipe," Red Dress threatened. "Either yer shovin' me 'cause you want your dick sucked or your ass kicked, and either one is fine by me."

The crowd was so thick that there was no way for JT to fire a punch, and after seeing the tattoo, he shook his head, laughing. This infuriated Red Dress, and he pushed closer to JT.

"Listen, fuckstick. What are you laughing at?"

"Whoa! Whoa!" JT said, still laughing and lifting his hands up palms out. "Semper Fi. Semper Fi!" he added, trying not to horse-laugh in the guy's face.

"Sember what, mutherfuck? What'd you say?"

"I said Semper Fi." JT repeated, shouting over the noise. "The bulldog on your arm," he said, pointing to his own arm to illustrate. "Your tattoo. You're a Marine."

This enraged the guy more, and he screamed angrily back. "Bitch! I ain't no Marine. So forget that shit!" Then he snorted, "I'll bet you're the fucking Marine. And this bulldog got your dick hard. Am I right flat head? You hep, flat head?"

JT thought Red Dress was no longer funny and needed his ass kicked. He thought of breaking the guy's nose, but he turned away and pushed through the crowd, shaking his head, knowing he could kill him.

Red Dress screamed out. "Hey, bitch! You better run."

JT eased his way through the crowded room, sometimes stepping on feet. The smoke was irritating his eyes as he squeezed through a group of young ladies and tried to draw the attention of a female bartender. She was working furiously at the end of the bar, pouring, shaking, blending. The bartender was petite and dressed in a white shirt with a black bow tie that matched her short-cropped black hair, black lipstick, and fake black mole just above her lip. The crowd was becoming increasingly louder and more intoxicated, so it took a full ten minutes before the bartender acknowledged JT, took his order, and without checking ID brought him a beer.

As he drank, the college boys and a couple of girls were crowded together doing shots of tequila. One wobbling gal, her hair up in a bun, brought her hand to her mouth, bent over, and puked. This cleared the group and a path to the bar. A moment later, another coed helped guide the puking girl toward the restroom.

JT got another drink from the bartender and noticed that the mole above her lip had become smeared and looked like a small smudge of soot. This amused him as he crossed the room and pushed though to a foosball table next to the pool tables. He watched a couple of suits play for a while, thinking about the guy in the red dress. The more he thought about it, the more upset he got for not rearranging his face. The jerk probably wasn't a Marine anyway. In fact, the more he thought about it, the more he realized that the guy was just some twisted, tattooed faggot making fun of the Marines.

A waitress came up in a tight miniskirt with a matching tube top that allowed her tits to bounce as she walked.

"Would you like a drink?"

"A Singapore Sling with a beer back."

His mind tripped for a minute on the last Singapore Sling he had on his way back from Vietnam in Okinawa. That night after several Singapore Slings, he and another Marine ended up in a dark row of clapboard whorehouses. A young woman with sad eyes took his hand and led him past her parents, who were eating, and into her bedroom. There was a mattress on the floor, a pan of water, a chair in the corner, and two candles on a stand.

Feeling like shit, he put a quarter on the foosball table and leaned against a brick wall underneath a beer sign waiting his turn to play. He tried not to think about Okinawa, how he had wronged God, and Ashley, but his mind slipped into more sadness. His dad used to drink, and JT feared becoming like his father, drunk and broke. God would damn him. He remembered how his father used to stumble into his high school wrestling matches reeking of alcohol, drunk and disheveled. He could see him now, dressed in greasy white overalls from the auto body shop, yelling louder than anyone else. A drunken yell that made JT want to disappear into the mat. All his friends knew his father was a drunk, and he hated that.

The family lived in a small house in a lower-class neighborhood. Every morning for years his dad got up and walked down the hall to the bathroom across from his room. His dad would leave the door open and piss. Every morning his dad would piss, and JT could hear it, and then his dad would walk in the kitchen and pull open the cupboard that always stuck and get out his bottle of vodka. JT would listen to his dad twist off the cap, pour a shot into a drinking glass, drink it, turn on the faucet, drink a glass of water and spit in the sink. Every morning it was the same pissing and drinking and spitting in the sink.

It was a long time before the waitress came back. JT paid for the drinks and told the waitress to hang on while he chugged the beer and then set the empty glass jar on her tray. He worked on his drink and waited for his turn on the table. He thought about his dad and Red Dress. He could feel the alcohol and needed to pee. Weaving his way through the crush, he found the men's room and pushed open the door. The restroom was dimly lit and smelled like urine and marijuana. The floor was wet. Next to the sink, a guy with a shaved head was standing with his back to the wall while another guy was on his knees blowing him. A third guy who was nearly a midget was leaning on a pair of crutches. The guy being sucked was smoking a joint, banging the back of his head on the wall wailing, "Come on, baby man. Come on, baby man."

He pissed and left, the sound of the guy's voice still violating his senses. He forced his way through the bar and burst out of the door into the night. The street was quiet and the sidewalks empty. He felt drunk—not sloppy, falling-down drunk—just drunk enough to realize he should be home. He gathered himself for a moment, collecting his bearings, preparing for a long walk home.

"Say, mutherfucker," came a voice from behind him.

JT recognized it, and chills raced up his spine. It was Red Dress standing next to two long-haired guys in white, sleeveless T-shirts. Their faces were shadowed, but in the weak street light, he could see their muscular, tattooed arms. They each had a bottle of beer and were laughing. JT could feel the adrenaline coming on when a cop car cruised up, stopping in front of them. There were two officers in the front seat. Everyone on the sidewalk froze, except for Red Dress.

"Candy ass," Red Dress said, moving toward JT with a twisted scowl on his face. "You're about a lucky mutherfucker."

Just as the words left his mouth, the cops were out of the patrol car and on the sidewalk, grabbing Red Dress and slamming him face first up against a wall. One cop with a bulging belly and glasses had his gun drawn and was backing away from the police car, shouting and acting as if he were afraid.

"UP AGAINST THE WALL, FAGGOTS!" he screamed. "I said get your face up against that DAAAAMMMN WALL!"

The T-shirts dropped their beers and joined Red Dress kissing brick.

"You too, faggot," the cop with the gun said, aiming at JT, who was no longer angry but amused and not moving. He thought this cop was nuts and looked silly with two hands on his pistol, legs spread.

"I'm talking to you!" the cop with the gun growled at JT, as the other cop handcuffed a pissed-off Red Dress.

JT turned and faced the wall.

"You gonna feel my butt, cop sucker?" Red Dress asked.

"Shut up, fag! And you," the cop said, motioning to JT, "you're under arrest."

"Arrest? For what?"

"I'll show you for what," barked the cop without the gun. He rushed JT, baton drawn, shoving it lengthwise toward his back, ramming him up against the wall next to the handcuffed Red Dress. As he did, the two T-shirts busted away, running down the street around the corner, melting into the night.

The cop was outraged. "Listen, queer boys. You're both goin' to jail. Either of you make a move, my partner will put his gun up your ass. Now, I'm going to back up. Get your faces down on the sidewalk. Nice and easy."

JT and Red Dress got on the pavement facedown while JT was handcuffed behind the back. They were both jerked to their feet and shoved into the back of the police car. As they drove toward the station house, JT's rage was building. He wanted to scream and head-butt Red Dress, bite off his nose, kick the windows out, break his cuffs, and kill the cops. Show them the horror he was capable of. Kill them both. Kill them all.

The fat cop was driving and turned his head toward the back of the car. "I'm kind of curious. Which one of you faggots takes it in the butt?"

Both cops laughed out loud.

"Listen, pigs," JT said slowly, deliberately. "Take these cuffs off and I will hurt you." His voice was dead and came from a place so violent and mad that the cop turned back and reached for his gun.

"Yeah, right," the other cop said, not seeing JT's look. "And I'll stick this Smith and Wesson so far up your punked-out ass your brain will pop."

When the patrol car entered the parking garage in the basement of the jail, JT felt like he was in a trance, or a movie, with no control. Like in the middle of the rice paddies with Coop and Hawkeye, and everyone around him dying.

Red Dress roared, "Wait 'til I get my lawyer on your sorry ass. I'll get you for discrimination, motherfuckers!"

They exited the car and walked to the elevator that would take them to booking and fingerprinting. In the elevator, the fat cop gave Red Dress the billy club chokehold and that stopped the noise for the ride upstairs.

"Used to be we busted black boys and queers," he said. "Now it's queer black boys."

The other cop held his hand on his holster, eyes fixed on JT.

The elevator doors slid open. JT and Red Dress were split up. Red Dress was manhandled by two guards who fought him down another corridor. The last thing JT saw was the hairy, bare ass of Red Dress peeking out his skirt as he flailed and screamed for his lawyer.

JT was fingerprinted and placed in a cell that smelled like puke, piss, and alcohol. There was a steel cot, a plugged-up steel toilet with turds in it, a sink, and a pay phone. Two guys shared the cell with him. One was older, looked like his dad, and was passed out on the concrete floor. The other guy had long scraggly brown hair and ragged jeans; he was on the pay phone talking dirty when all of a sudden he slammed down the receiver.

He turned angrily away and plopped on the cot.

JT read the small handwritten sign that explained the phone was for collect calls only. In the margins and on the wall, there were handwritten messages that said you could get a blow job if you called Debby or big black cocks if you called another number. He stared at the phone and the messages and worried about calling home. Ashley would be asleep. If she came to bail him out, she'd have to bring the baby. He ran numerous scenarios on what to do, and they were all bad. He was ashamed and felt horrible. He stared at the phone and thought how stupid he was.

A great sense of guilt rushed through him. He could feel this dread in his body, this overwhelming sense of remorse and shame. It weighed him down. He loved Ashley and felt God had protected him so he could come home and take care of his family. Now he slighted God by not being thankful, and his behavior was destroying his family. When other Marines had died, God had spared him, and he believed when he came home he would be a good man, be important. His wife would love and admire him. Now he was in jail, like some street rat. He felt worthless. It was like he had no soul, or it had been destroyed.

"Say, man, you gonna use the phone or stare at it? I gotta call my bitch, you dig?"

Startled, JT's mind shifted to the longhair. He lifted the phone and waited for the operator to place the call. He took a deep breath.

Ashley answered. She was not asleep.

"Honey, sorry to wake you."

"Where are you? Are you OK?"

"I'm . . . I'm in jail."

"Don't tell me that. That's not even funny. Where are you and why aren't you home?"

"I'm sorry. I'm sorry, Ashley. I'm really downtown in jail. I got arrested and—"

"Don't tell me." There was a long silence. "What am I supposed to do?" More silence. "Get up in the middle of the night and take the baby with me to jail? To jail?" She began to cry.

"Honey. Honey. I'm sorry, but—"

"I don't want to hear it. We don't have any money. How do you expect me to get you out, huh?" Her crying was inconsolable.

"Honey. Honey. Listen, I hid fifty bucks in my tennis shoes in the closet. Get it, call Brad, and tell him to come by, pick up the money, and get me out."

Ashley hung up the phone without saying good-bye.

There was no use calling back. If she didn't get Brad, he'd just hang in there until he was arraigned in the morning. He found a clean place on the floor in the corner just a few feet away from the alkie. The drunk was lying on his side in a fetal position, comatose, pants wet with urine. What a loser, JT thought. What a bunch of crap.

Maybe he could call his brother to get him out, or his dad. Son of a bitch owed him one anyway. JT had gotten him out of jail a couple times a few years ago. Last time his old man was blitzed and got into a fight at the Keyhole. Mom sitting on some guy's lap, no doubt. Dad tore up the place and the cops threw him in jail. Same jail. How fucking great.

"I'm as fucked up as my dad," JT said below a whisper.

He remembered driving his old man home, just as the sun was coming up, and the only thing his dad said was, "You'd be a good soldier, son."

A good soldier? How the hell would he know? His old man didn't know shit about war. War was dudes blown into the air and coming down in pieces. War was stepping over bodies so rancid and decomposed that they looked like rotting trees with rags wrapped around them. And war was sitting in night ambushes sick with malaria and the shits and having it rain so long and so hard that you just wanted to shoot your own goddamned self.

JT closed his eyes, leaned back against the cold, concrete wall, and hit the back of his head. The pain reminded him he was alive.

He was dug in on the side of a hill, and he could see Coop with him, rain hammering at their backside. LZ Winchester, deep in the jungle, no food for days. Two choppers shot down. The night was a black pit pouring on them, wind roaring like a typhoon. And he was sick. Weak. His bowels erupted, and there was nothing to do but crawl out of the hole and rinse off in the rain.

He banged the back of his head again and again as the war came back to him.

Coop didn't say a word that night. Didn't embarrass him. He helped JT out of the hole they dug, poncho flapping in the wind, then cleaned him off with just his hands and carried him back to the hole.

JT banged his head again then stopped. He loved Coop. With his eyes shut, the cell disappeared, and he felt like he was invisible.

HOURS LATER, BRAD BAILED JT OUT. By the time he got home, it was after 8:00 a.m.

"Thanks, man," he said in an exhausted voice as he got out of Brad's car in front of his house.

"Don't sweat it. I'll call you later."

JT swung the door shut and watched Brad drive away. His heart was pounding hard as he stepped on the porch and saw a note posted on the door—

I've gone to my mom's.

Shit. How could she leave? Now everyone would know he got thrown in jail.

"Shit!"

He stomped around the house cussing, shoving kitchen chairs, then snapped open the refrigerator door. He foraged for a few moments and pulled out an old bowl of spaghetti and carton of milk and sat down at the kitchen table.

As he ate, and drank from the carton, his anger waned, then suddenly turned to panic. He was supposed to be at work by eight. He gulped the milk and quickly jumped in the shower, dressed, and sprinted out of the house for the bus stop.

He missed the 8:45 and waited twenty minutes. By the time he arrived at the office and made it to the mailroom to punch in, it was 9:40 a.m. He was an hour and forty minutes late.

His boss wheeled up as he turned from the time clock.

"Gosh, I'm sorry," JT said. "Something came up and I missed the bus. I'm sorry. It won't happen again."

"You're right. It won't. You're fired."

"What do you mean, I'm fired?"

"This is the fourth time you've been late for work this month, and you didn't even bother to call. We have a business to run here, and we need someone we can depend on. Now please get your stuff out of here, and we will send you your check."

JT looked at his boss and imagined sticking a .45 in his mouth and blowing his brains out, just killing him and then killing everybody in the whole goddamn office. His face was in a rage, and his boss could see it. He spun his chair and backed quickly from the room.

"I'm calling security if you're not out of here in ten minutes."

JT stood alone in the room surrounded by walls of brochures and the hum of an automatic collator separating flyers. His rage turned to self-pity. As he walked out the door and waited for the elevator, he wanted to stick a gun in his own mouth and blow away the pain.

10

Coop

COOP'S PLANE LEFT PORTLAND IN THE RAIN and landed in Okinawa during a thunderous morning shower. After recovering from his wounds in '69, he'd elected to stay in the crotch and was assigned to 3rd Force Recon. The war in Vietnam was winding down for the United States. Thousands of troops were being withdrawn. The 3rd Force Recon would become a casualty of this withdrawal, but for now, some of its 142 men were on temporary duty station, going through jump school and additional training. The training phase was drawing to an end, and elements of the battalion were preparing to go back to Vietnam.

When Coop reported in at headquarters, he was already two days late, AWOL as far as the Marine Corps was concerned. After straightening things out, he reported to his area and checked in with the noncommissioned officer on duty. The office pogue looked at him as if he were the biggest screwup he had ever seen. He took Coop's file into First Sergeant Blue Thunder's office, returned, and then promptly showed Coop to the sergeant's doorway.

Coop banged on the doorjamb with his fist three times and shouted, "Sir, Corporal Cooper requests permission to enter the first sergeant's office, sir."

He adjusted his trousers, then stood at attention waiting for a response.

"Enter, bitch," came a growl from inside the office.

Coop entered in strict military countenance, stepping smartly, as if he were marching on the parade deck back at the Marine Corps Recruiting Depot. Coop did a quarter pivot and stood in front of Sergeant Blue Thunder's desk. He threw a perfect salute and said in his best Marine Corps voice, "Sir, Corporal Cooper reporting as ordered, sir."

Tall and slender with blond hair and blue eyes, Blue Thunder looked little like his Indian heritage. He glanced up to see Coop standing rigidly in freshly starched and pressed fatigues, spit-shined boots, with his cock and balls hanging out from the fly of his pants. Blue Thunder hardly seemed surprised as he sat back in his chair and fastened his hands behind his head.

"Coop, you're about eight kinds of fucked up. Now, how the hell are yah?"

Coop smiled a ridiculously big grin and put his privates back in his pants. "Sarge, I got a hard-on a yard long, and I'm looking for somethin' ta start on!"

Blue Thunder laughed, shook his head, then leaned forward with his arms folded on his desk. "Well, sit down and let me see what the green machine has in store for your sorry ass."

He reached across his desk for Coop's file and shook his head again as he thumbed through it. He made mental references to the awards, commendations, promotions, and demotions Coop had earned in his two years in the Corps: September '68, meritorious promotion to corporal for digging a string of connecting bunkers by hand on LZ Winchester; November '68, busted to private first class for being drunk and naked in the enlisted men's club, dancing on the bar with a pair of girls' panties on his head, and urinating on an MP; meritorious promotion to corporal for carrying a critically wounded Marine to an area of safety.

Blue Thunder closed the file. He was that "critically wounded" Marine. Coop had saved his life on patrol near the DMZ.

"It looks like you're going to go with the battalion when they ship out at the end of the week. You'll be back in country where you belong."

"It's where I want to be," Coop replied. "Pissing them gooks off and getting me some slant-eyed pussy."

The first sergeant's face tightened and his voice became stern. "You gotta stay away from the civilians. You get drippy dick again and you'll be busted outta the Corps. I shit you not. You're a great warrior, a hard-charger with brass balls the size of Geronimo's, but you're a fuckup! And you best straighten the fuck out! You got it?"

"Got it."

"Good. Now get out of here. You can pick up your issues at supplies. Oh, and this order is coming down from the top. No more gook ears. And that means you. This ain't just pissing in the wind, Coop. There's been too much of that BS going on. Got it?"

"Got it."

"Good."

Coop left the first sergeant's office, strutting right and proper, down the hall and out of the headquarters building.

THE US BASE WAS A MASSIVE, SPRAWLING collection of metal Quonset huts, tents, and stucco buildings crammed with pencil-pushing support personnel. There was a huge PX, enlisted and officers' clubs, mess halls, a gym, even a church and movie theater. The US presence on Okinawa was strong and committed from the days of WWII. The local economy was the military. Everywhere, Okinawans were working for the US government, from the PX to cleaning toilets.

Off base, the serviceman's dollar was honey to the hive. All day long, soldiers caught beat-up taxis at the front gate and would ride into town to sightsee, shop, barhop, or hang out at skivvy houses and get laid for four bucks. Coop, though, thought Okinawa was fucked up. The bloods were running in packs at night, robbing and sometimes killing white soldiers. Anti-war shitheads were in the streets, and morale sucked. The war sucked.

"Should have been over a long time ago, if you ask me," Coop said to anyone who would listen. "And it would have if we just got on line and swept the Nam." Everyone wanted to get out, so discipline waned. Because of all the trouble, warnings were issued: do not be out at night alone. Soldiers alone at night, white or black, were easy prey for drunken white thugs or gangs of angry blacks.

Coop checked in at supplies, was issued gear, then reported to the duty shack where he was assigned a place to bunk with the rest of the 3rd Recon. Over the next week, he and his platoon were restricted to base in order to ready themselves for rotation back to Vietnam.

The mornings were spent on physical training, including long runs around the base with full packs. Nights were spent in the enlisted men's club or Quonset huts getting gear ready, writing letters home, and making personal wills. Coop wrote a letter to his grandmother apologizing for not staying at the funeral and promised to go see her when he got home. Then he crumpled it up and threw it away.

On the last night before leaving, soldiers gathered in their Quonset hut talking quietly about girls back home, family, cars, or sports. They'd slip in and out of conversations like moving through doorways. They lay on bunks or packed gear, trading nervous talk. Two soldiers just back from the showers, still wrapped in towels and shuffling along in flapping thongs, were talking future.

"When I get back, I'm gonna get me one of those new GTOs, four on the floor, power to burn, big-eight 352 with chrome mags. Now that'll be some wheels, Jack."

"Piss on the chrome mags. I'm going after some hippie chicks for some ah that free love. Hell, this war is winding down anyway. Guy in stateside supply told me they're cutting troops every day. Gotta keep Tricky Dick in office."

Coop was lying on his bunk, reading a skin magazine and smoking a cigar. His gear was packed in a duffel bag at the foot of his bed, jungle boots underneath his bunk. War was not on his mind. Most soldiers felt tight inside and showed their fear in stiff gestures, averted eyes, and false bravado. But unlike the others, Coop wanted war and didn't care if he died. It was only when he felt at risk that he felt alive.

Eventually the room grew quiet and letter-writing began again. Dip Shit, a kid from Alabama with two front teeth missing, showed Coop a picture of his overweight girlfriend standing naked in front of a fireplace. He was proud of the picture. Dip Shit had a low IQ and could barely read or write. He got into the Corps because a crooked recruiter wanted to satisfy his quota. If he hadn't had constant help along the way, he never would have made it through boot camp, let alone recon school. He was stupid but busted ass on all-night runs and succeeded in anything else physical, which endeared him to the others.

The bay was quiet for a long time, and fear was back, feeding on the imagination of each soldier. They worried about not knowing where they were going and what it would be like. Some worried about never seeing their wives or lovers again. Others thought about how it would feel to be gut-shot or have your body blown in half by a land mine. They worried about dying cowardly with shit in their pants.

Then Coop broke the silence. "Well, you guys can sit around here pulling your pud or crying about home. I'm skying into skivvy town," he said, tossing a magazine on the floor, then picking up his boots. "Anybody else up for a little pussy run?"

No one replied.

"Yer crazy, Coop," PFC Fruitcake said, bending to pick up the tossed magazine. "We're restricted. There ain't no way they'll let your ass off the base."

"Listen, brain cramp. Not only can I get off this base, but I can get me a piece of sugar and bring it back here and lick it right in front of your ugly face."

"Right," Fruitcake said sitting on Coop's bunk. "I got ten big ones you can't even get off the base. And ten bucks more says if you do you're sure as hell not coming back with no pussy."

By now the whole squad was laughing, making side bets, forgetting tomorrow they'd be headed back to a place where death ruled.

Coop put on his boots, dumped his cigar, stood up, and walked confidently toward the billet doorway, stopped, and turned back to shout, "RECON! . . . ERRRUU-GA!!" And an echo of ERRRUU-GAs and cheers bounced off the walls and barreled through the bay.

In the morning, 3rd Recon flew out of Okinawa back to the Nam in the bellies of two C-130s.

Coop had failed his mission.

He did get off the base by hot-wiring a colonel's jeep and impersonating an MP, complete with white helmet and black baton "requisitioned" from the back of the guard shack. But when he got into town, he just went to a bar and sat by himself and drank. Finally thrown out of the bar, he drove off, weaving his way back to the base. He ran the main gate with MPs shouting, "Stop!" and firing weapons in the air. He crashed the colonel's jeep into a row of garbage cans next to the mess hall.

The MPs caught him and dragged him in front of the sergeant of the guard. Coop was incoherent, could barely stand, but when the MPs let go of his arms, he lurched across the sergeant's desk, threw a punch and broke his nose.

Just before dawn, First Sergeant Blue Thunder came to the brig and arranged for Coop to be released.

"You're burning it hard," Blue Thunder said, his voice laced with sadness as he walked Coop across the grounds and back to his billet. "You're a private again. The papers will be in the mail." Then he stood in front of Coop and addressed him as a therapist might a client. "You're trying to kill yourself, and I don't know what to do. I just hope you don't end up putting a bullet in your head before someone else does."

Coop watched Blue Thunder leave and wanted to laugh. *I'd never just kill myself. Was he crazy?*

ON THE PLANE, 3RD RECON TROOPS SAT quietly in dim light on web seats. They wore combat fatigues with packs and seabags scattered around them. Each had a weapon. Some had M-16s, others sawed-off shotguns or short-stock M-18s at their side. Conversations were brief and disjointed. Some slept and others relieved themselves in piss tubes and ate cold C-rats or wrote simple, sad letters home. The flight was long, boring, crowded, and uncomfortable. The drone of the engines reverberated inside each soul as the plane moved into darkness.

There ain't no frills on this bitch, Coop thought, musing on the smell of passed gas, body odor, and freshly oiled weapons. His mouth was tight and dry as he gulped water from a canteen. He still had some dry puke on the side of his shirt, and his head throbbed from an angry hangover. He lay back on his seabag and twisted the end of his mustache.

"Ain't it about time you cut that son of a bitch off?" Fruitcake joked, referring to Coop's stache. Fruitcake was in the seat next to Coop. He liked Coop and respected his ability as a soldier but thought he was insane. Last night only proved it. There was no telling what Coop was going to do, even in the bush, and this tended to make people anxious and on guard.

"I'll cut this off right after you French-kiss my butt," Coop said with a bite in his voice.

No one laughed. No one joked. The only sounds were the four engine props turning.

The C-130 made its approach toward the corrugated steel landing strip at 3rd Marine Headquarters. The 3rd Marines were located near Quang Tri, a few miles south of Dong Ha and the DMZ. On the approach, the plane passed over rice paddies and thatched-roof villages that spread out to the mountains and jungles.

About two miles from the landing strip, an old woman in black pajama pants and a conical hat crawled out of a tunnel and crouched in a thicket of banana trees. She tipped her hat back so it was held by a string, then fired an AK-47 skyward. Most of the rounds danced by the plane, but several raked the underbelly. One round entered the fuselage, ricocheted around before lodging in someone's seabag. A second round followed a similar route until finally resting deep in the temple of a kid from Nebraska. It was so quick and sudden that the plane had landed, the ramp had opened, and troops were deplaning before the captain in charge screamed, "Good God! Get off this plane. We got a troop wounded."

Feet started shuffling quicker, and seabags and backpacks were flying as the rest of the troops double-timed down the ramp, under the tail, spreading out on the tarmac.

The plane's props were shutting down when someone said, "In the head, man. Some dude got it in the head."

The wounded troop was carried off the plane and stretched out on the runway. A stream of red ran down the side of his face and neck. Head back, mouth open. His dog tags were glistening in the sun. Frantically, a corpsman blew into his slack lips, but it was no use. Nebraska was dead.

"Newbie," Coop said to no one in particular. "Talked to the dude in the shower," he added, shaking his head, more disgusted than afraid.

The body was bagged up, put on the back of a jeep, and moved out of the area.

COOP THREW ON HIS WEB GEAR OVER his jungle utilities and fastened the suspenders in front. He jumped up and down to see if there was sound or movement in his canteens and ammo pouches. For this mission, he'd carry a PRC-77 radio and a sawed-off .12-gauge. He felt it was more dependable than an M-16. He borrowed it from a guy in supply. In return, he promised him a gook ear, never thinking twice about the warning he'd received from Blue Thunder back on Okinawa. Besides, who'd know he copped an ear except the guys with him? He knew they wouldn't say diddly. He carried four grenades in his ammo pouches and a specially loaded double-aught buckshot that enhanced the beehive blast of a short barrel. He tied a dog tag in his boot and stuck it under the tongue, then grabbed his ruck and carefully packed. He had a mix of long rats, enough for eight days. He also toted an extra battery for the radio, a claymore mine, listening sensors, a Snoopy, a pair of socks, insect repellent, and a picture of his granddad cutting wood, swinging a double-edged ax.

The 3rd Force Recon consisted of one hundred and fifty men broken into six-man teams. Each member was required to pack their packs the same and dress their gear the same. The only things Coop carried different from other troopers were the picture, a can of chewing tobacco, a small vial of mustache wax, and his bone-handled hunting knife. He'd had run-ins with the brass about the wax, but as long as it didn't compromise his team, they'd let it slide. He also knew they didn't like him to chew in the bush because the spittle had an odor and texture that the enemy might pick up. He called it his "stateside betel nut." But Coop was good in the field; some said the best. He was careful about making noise when he spit and made sure to cover it. So they let that slide, too.

Fruitcake was on the other side of the hootch sitting on the edge of his cot, rubbing shaving cream on his feet. This was a daily ritual to keep them from cracking. He was pissed about going out.

"Damn! Seems like they's always sendin' us out on hairy-ass details. A chopper goes down, and we're supposed to find the son of a bitch in the middle of nowhere? Come on. I'm Semper Fi all the way, but fuck this shit. This should be a platoon-sized gig, not six men."

Coop lifted his head as he packed. "Quit crying. They say go. We go. Maybe they had some pussy on board."

Jenkins, Lats, and Weldon laughed. Lieutenant Klimp ignored Coop and reminded them they were about to saddle up. "Men, we're due at the helipad at 0500."

Their plywood hootch was home for two teams. Team Big Daddy was out near the DMZ, monitoring enemy movement. Team Bad Boys, Coop's team, had the digs all to themselves. The chopper had gone down in the mountainous A Shau Valley, west of the city Hue, where one of the biggest and longest battles of the war was fought. It was a key infiltration route for North Vietnamese forces where there was fierce fighting. There was supposed to be a bigwig on board, and the mission was to find the chopper, pull out survivors, evacuate them, and get the hell out. During the mission, they'd plant seismic and acoustical sensors to eavesdrop on the enemy. The mission was extremely high risk. While the United States was reducing troop strength, the NVA was not. Recent intelligence reports indicated NVA counter-reconnaissance forces were operating in the A Shau, and they wanted to destroy them. The 3rd Force was now a special target.

Coop's team was a cross-section of highly skilled Marines. Each had been trained and conditioned in recon school stateside or in country. They were the elite of the elite and took great pride in their individual abilities. Typically, before each mission, they'd practice and go over insertion, movement, specific duties, contingency plans, and extraction. But this was an emergency, with little advance preparation.

Corporal Jenkins was an albino-looking twenty-year-old from Colorado. An expert in mountain climbing, he had climbed everything worth climbing in Oregon, Washington, and Montana long before he dropped out of college and joined the Corps. He just returned from Subic Bay in the Philippines, where he completed jump school. He was proud of his jump wings and would surely be selected for Officer's Candidate School. His head had been turned in boot camp; he was definitely lifer material. Jenkins would walk point and carry an M-14. For most soldiers walking point, a 14 would be a little big, but Jenkins was strong and could handle the added weight. He liked the firepower and reliability the 14 brought.

When the team was inserted, Lats would follow Jenkins. Lats was Jenkins's good buddy, though they were from entirely different backgrounds. Lats hated the Corps, hated the Nam, and couldn't wait to get back to the world and his life as a surfer bum. He was a stud, physically. He loved to do push-ups and pull-ups and had the battalion record of forty-six dead stop pull-ups. His real name was Oscar, which he hated. He picked up the name Lats because of his powerful V-shape and lateral muscles. Lats would follow Jenkins, carry the primary radio and an M-16.

The team leader was Lieutenant Klimp. Barely twenty-three, he had only one other mission under his belt. He had the least experience in the Nam of anyone but had a quiet confidence and attention to detail that all respected. The LT would follow Lats and humped an M-79 grenade launcher and a .45. He liked the simple nature of the 79. He had never been good with a rifle and almost didn't qualify in boot camp, so the "blooper" compensated for his lack of accuracy.

The LT put Coop behind him because he knew from reputation that Coop was all business in the bush. He was fearless, intelligent, and trustworthy. It was just back in camp or in the world that Coop had problems. It wasn't that Coop loved combat or killing or even the Corps. It was that out in the jungle where fear could eat you alive, he had come to a place of peace. He loved being silent, stalking. It always reminded him of bow hunting with Granddad and how he would lead him in silence with simple hand signals, up steep and beautiful switchbacks, down gullies, and along the pristine lakes. They'd go off trail into areas so remote the elk and deer felt safe. They'd break camp early, when fog still covered the ridges, and the sun had barely brought morning. Then edge along the rocky knobs, tracking doe or bucks and sometimes elk. At night they'd return to camp or build a lean-to on a slope above a meadow or lake and never make a fire.

"Fire scares them away," Granddad would say.

And in that darkness, they'd lie on flattened earth and look at stars. Then his granddad would tell stories about family pioneers who settled in those very mountains. Or draw Coop in with tales of Chief Joseph and the band of Nez Perce Indians who roamed those same mountains.

Being in the jungle, alone with his team, was the next best thing to those memories. Coop would protect the LT, like he would protect his granddad.

Weldon Hollar from Homedale, Idaho, followed Coop. He came over with the rest of the 3rd Force from Okinawa. He had a troubled life and ended up in the Corps to get away from an overbearing mother and a stepfather who thought he was a sissy. When he got to boot camp, he thought he was trapped in hell. He was a bright, sensitive kid, not quite all there. In high school, he had been considered strange for thinking too much and reading poetry.

Weldon first got to the Nam with the 3rd Marine Division. A month into his tour, the division began to rotate back to Okinawa. Through an accidental paper shuffle, Weldon was transferred to 3rd Force. A couple of months later, he was a skilled member of the silent and the deadly. He carried an M-16, along with a new attitude. Devoutly Catholic, he never cursed and carried a rosary with him wherever he went. Before each patrol, he'd bend to his knees to pray, then stand in front of the small mirror attached to a post in the middle of their hootch and look at his reflection as if it were someone else. When he marked his face with the green and black camouflage stick, it reminded him of how the priest used to mark his forehead on Ash Wednesday. He also carried a wallet-sized laminated picture of Jesus tucked neatly out of sight in the side of the boot.

Fruitcake was walking tail-end Charlie, carrying the Starlight Night Scope. He wasn't a big or imposing presence, like Jenkins or Lats. He wasn't fearless and wild like Coop. He was not really special, except in the way he moved through the jungle. He was a blue-collar, everyday kind of soldier, carrying a slight grudge against the world. But he worked hard in the bush and was dependable. He had walked tail-end Charlie many times before.

"When Fruitcake be walking tail-end Charlie," a black Marine once remarked, "he be gliding." The team felt good knowing Fruitcake was watching their rear.

Coop threw his pack over his shoulder, picked up his rifle, and slipped his bush cover on so it hung on the back of his neck. He pushed through the swinging door of the hootch and stepped into the darkness of a new morning. A slight breeze carried the stench from the dump, mixed with diesel exhaust and the smell of burning shitters.

Fruitcake followed Coop. "This is bullshit! I'm just about ready to tell those lame bastards back in the rear—"

"Cut the crap!" Coop snapped. "If your chopper was shot down and yer ass was puckering, you wouldn't care who was rolling out."

"Ladies," Lieutenant Klimp said, joining them. "Let's focus. Get our minds clear. This is going to be textbook and tight ship all the way. I don't want any pissing and moaning to interfere with this mission."

As he spoke, the rest of the men gathered outside, illuminated by a white quarter-moon hanging sideways in the night. In the faint light, each uniform was the same, each pack the same, each bush cover and each face marked with the same green and black camouflage stick. There was a looseness to the way they stood, like confident athletes, yet each felt tight in the chest and dry in the mouth.

"Last chance to drain your lizard or take a dump," Klimp warned.

"Right, LT," Coop said. "I'm gonna take a bull wiz. You want to hold it for me, Weldon?" This brought a couple of snickers.

In those last moments, Klimp checked out each man's equipment and had Jenkins recheck it again. He examined both radios
and took out his map and made sure coordinates for the insertion
and extraction were clear in his mind. Because of the distance, they
would not receive artillery support from the howitzers on base or at
Dong Ha, nor would they have offshore naval support. They'd have
air support in the form of fixed-wing Phantoms or Huey and Cobra
gunships, and maybe Spooky with its mini guns blazing, but they'd
have to wait in line. They were not a priority. Empty canteens were
filled from the heavy canvas water bag that sat in the middle of the
hootches. Rifles were checked, and once again troops jumped up
and down listening for noise and loose gear.

Coop was sitting on the steps of the hootch, a chew going in
the side of his mouth. He was sharpening the edge of the large,
bone-handled knife his granddad gave him. As he ran the blade back
and forth across a whetstone, he thought about how he'd skinned
and gutted his first deer with the same knife.

Granddad had taken him up into the mountains in the middle of
late September, during a hot Indian summer. The kind of summer
that makes kids sweat in classrooms and hope they can bust outside
and run wild. His granddad picked him up at school in his truck and
drove to the base of the mountains. They hid it off an old logging
road and humped in.

"I can smell the rain, boy," his granddad said, which amazed Coop.

That night it rained. It blew so cold and wet that Granddad started
a fire next to their lean-to. The next morning, the sun burned away
the moisture, but the forest was softer and quieter. They moved along
a hog's back, eating candy bars, when two deer darted from a tree
line then stopped, as if alerted, in a clearing just opposite the ridge.

It happened quick. Coop's granddad swung his bow, drew, and
released. The arrow passed through the doe's neck but brought
her down. Coop remembered she was still kicking, her brown eyes
opened wide.

"Put her down, son," Granddad said gently, his hand resting on Coop's shoulder. "You got to put her down now, so she don't suffer." Then Granddad handed him the bone-handled knife and showed him where to cut her throat. There were tears in his eyes, but when Coop was through, his granddad said, "You done good, son."

The knife was Coop's from then on.

When he was done sharpening, Coop stuck the knife in a scabbard attached to the suspenders of his web gear. Soon, an open-bed, deuce-and-a-half with wooden side rails and bench seats pulled up. Its motor thumped in the silence, and there were no lights on. At 0455, they loaded up and left the small courtyard of tents and plywood hootches, heading for the helipad.

"Guys," Klimp instructed, "when we reach the chopper, we're in silence. So if you have any questions or concerns, get them out now. Focus. Be clear. Jenkins, load them and make sure we tie into a circle when we land. OK?"

"Cool, LT," Jenkins replied.

"Grab hands," Klimp said in a voice that was almost a whisper. In the back of the truck, they joined hands. Jenkins, Lats, the LT, Coop, Weldon, and Fruitcake. No one spoke as the truck bumped through the darkness.

When they arrived at the helipad at the far end of Quang Tri Combat Base, the chopper was waiting. Its rotors were turning as they jumped from the truck and shoved through the side door of the Huey. They sat on web seating, snapped magazines in, and put rounds in their chambers. There would be one other chopper following, touching down as a decoy a few clicks away, then repeating the touch down again farther away to conceal the real insert.

Coop could feel his pulse in his temples and his mouth parch as he played with his mustache. Then he pulled his bush cover tight on his head with the strap hanging loosely around his neck. As they choppered through the early morning sky, everyone was thinking about not wanting to die.

The Huey lifted, banked, its shadow gliding over rice paddies and rivers, then lifting again up into the mountains. It cut a sweeping path through the fading night, passing beneath the sideways moon, then disappearing into the A Shau. This was a valley snarled in double and triple canopy so thick that trucks were easily hidden from the air. It was a nightmare, overflowing with hardcore NVA soldiers—battle-tested soldiers who had walked the length of the Ho Chi Minh Trail charged up with liberation, hoping to kill Marines.

Their chopper touched down in a green meadow of elephant grass just as the sun peeked over the horizon. The tip of the valley and the meadow was a brief respite in an otherwise miserable and dense jungle. Around them on all sides were knots of tangled vines, broadleaf plants, trees, and vegetation mixed so thick the enemy could conceal its location from only a few feet away.

Jenkins led the squad out quickly from the side of the Huey, almost disappearing into waist-high grass. In a few moments, the team had formed a circle and was lying flat, their weapons pointing outward. The sun was coming up, and they looked like hunters in a duck blind. A moment later they were on their feet, with Jenkins leading them into the walls of the valley. By the time the chopper was high and out of sight, the A Shau had swallowed the Bad Boys deep into its belly.

After a few minutes Lieutenant Klimp signaled to stop. He knelt down on one knee, triggering Lats, who signaled Jenkins. The LT brought out his compass and map and studied them in the morning light. He had marked his map carefully, showing the reconnaissance zone where the chopper was reported to have gone down and possible extraction LZs. While the LT was not a great marksman, he was an expert with map and compass. In jungle warfare school, the map course had hardly been a challenge to him. His ability to recognize site locations was extraordinary. He could run his fingers over the wavy shades of green on his map and almost feel the changes in topography. He found their approximate position on the map, shot an azimuth with his compass, and recorded it in pencil on the border of his map. They would work their way along the side of the valley floor for two one-thousand-yard clicks, then climb. By late day, they'd be in the area where the chopper was thought to have gone down.

Coop was feeling at ease as he waited for a sign from Klimp to move forward. He knew the day would be long and difficult. There were reports of roads dug out of the jungle wide enough for trucks. It stoked him. Fixed up an adrenaline rush. From the air, it was hard to believe trucks were here; from the ground, it was inconceivable. How could Victor Charles possibly cut through this shit!

In a moment they were moving again. They pushed and glided silently. The terrain steepened and became more difficult. The Bad Boys climbed and snaked their way up the side of the mountain, pushing through foliage so dense it seemed like night had fallen. Occasionally, Klimp would stop and check his compass and map to confirm his bearings. At midday, they rallied into a circle and took turns eating—three eating, three watching. Then they rested—three dozing, three watching.

By late afternoon Coop had relieved Jenkins on point. He led the team differently. Jenkins moved like an elk, Coop like a mountain lion, stronger, closer to the ground. His vision was better, more peripheral. His hearing tuned to a greater sensitivity. They climbed through a tangled thicket, and the jungle thinned. There were gaps between trees and sunlight seeped through. From their position, Coop could see through the canopy to blue sky and white whispers of clouds floating beneath a brass sun.

He stopped the team to one knee and rested, listening to a lizard's squawk that sounded like *fuck you, fuck you*. He drank a swill from his canteen and felt the temperature climb. Sweat soaked his shirt, and his pack felt heavy. Birds skipped and fluttered from tree to tree. Coop took in the jungle smells in deep inhales. His lungs filled; he was happy.

Just before dusk, they crossed a narrow stream and refilled canteens, dropping in halazone tablets to purify the water. Ten minutes later, Coop reached an opening half the size of a football field. His adrenaline surged. There were a few craters, the result of recent B-52 strikes, which meant that at one time the place was probably crawling with the enemy. Some of the trees close to the craters had been mangled and blown away. He stopped the team at the entrance to the clearing and moved back to Klimp.

"Big space, LT," he whispered. "Definitely Injun country. Could be uncool trying to cross."

Klimp, propped on one knee, took off his jungle cover, wiped sweat from the corner of his eye with the back of his wrist, then slipped off his pack and sat on it. He looked tired, as if wanting an excuse to stop for the day.

"This could have been the spot the helicopter was trying to reach when it got hit," Klimp said quietly. "How long would it take us to cross, and what's the downside?"

Coop considered Klimp's question and how stupid it was. The downside was obvious; they could get caught out in the open and get scorched. After all, every slope-eye this side of the DMZ would love to catch six Marines waltzing by in the middle of nowhere.

"This is it, LT." Coop knew they were close. He could feel it. "I think we got gooks all around us. But they're probably dug in closer to water. A lot of them were killed here, so they're gonna think it's bad luck. I say let's do it. Piss on it. We can cross quickly, scoot into the bush, then set in for the night."

"OK, Coop. Let's go for it."

Coop and Lats slid out of their cover under a fading light and crossed into the field. Twenty-five yards into the opening, Coop turned and signaled, and the other team members followed. Approaching the edge of a bomb crater, Coop glanced down and saw a pool of water in the crater holding two bloated bodies, splitting at their midsection. Stench rolled from the crater. He knew they'd been wasted for days, but he also knew their buddies usually came back to bury them. He dropped to one knee, looked back toward Lats, flashed two fingers like a peace sign to indicate two enemy, then drew a line with his finger across his neck to show they were dead. Lats passed the same sign back to the team.

Coop crouched and moved on. The area felt wrong to him as he reached another crater, this time empty. And as he walked, he could see the flattened grass where gooks had rested. There were burnt impressions in the ground where cooking fires had been. Another empty crater and another, then one that stopped him cold. On the crater's wall, he saw what appeared to be a naked woman with long hair lying on her back. She had an arm missing at the shoulder; a chunk of her stomach was torn out. The last bit of sunlight was bouncing off her swollen face. Beside her was a green US Army metal ammunition box, lying open on its side.

At the end of the clearing, there was another opening leading to two well-worn trails. Coop had seen this kind of thing before. They were in an enemy base camp. A camp that had been hit hard just days ago. They were moving into the dragon's den. But where were the gooks? Had they skied? His heart pounded, and he could hear it beating in his ears. One path led straight, probably to command positions or bunkers strung together. The other branched off to the right. Both had been well traveled. He chose the path to the right, turned back toward Lats and caught his eye. Without speaking, Coop motioned that he'd look for the tripwires, and Lats should scan the jungle.

After ten minutes, Coop decided to leave the path and find a night harbor site. But before he could get another dozen yards, he came upon a small clearing, not more than twenty feet wide and ten feet deep. There was a shrine built on a stand made of bamboo poles tied together with thin strands of bamboo. A platform supported a bowl holding a couple of shriveled, rotten bananas. Behind the bowl was a picture of an older Asian man dressed in a soldier's uniform. He was standing alone with a pith helmet on, which cast a shadow on his face and a wisp of a beard. To the side of the picture was a bamboo flute. On the ground, a few feet away, an NVA soldier was lying on his belly with half of his head blown away. He'd died instantly, Coop figured. The soldier had missed the pain and rattle of a slow death by catching a large piece of shrapnel when the bomb came.

It would be bad luck to hang out here. Sort of like putting on a dead Marine's boots because yours were worn out. He checked the body for booby traps and decided to harbor just a short way from the shrine. That way, if all hell came, they could quickly rally at the opening for air evacuation. It was trouble, but time was short. They had to take risks.

Soon the rest of the team was on-site, dropping packs, eyeballing the shrine.

"Check it out," Lats whispered excitedly as he stood in front of the shrine. "Check it out. This is Ho Chi Fuckin' Minh," he said, picking up the photo and turning toward Jenkins and others.

"Bullshit," spouted Jenkins.

"I shit you not. This is the dude," Lats pleaded quietly but emphatically. "This is Uncle Ho."

"You're full of—" Jenkins started to reply when Lieutenant Klimp walked up, his face twisted in anger.

"Cut the noise," he whispered. "Let's set in. It's damn near dark. Jenkins, you, Lats, and Fruitcake buddy up. Take it about twenty-five yards into the tangle, and we'll follow. I want to be able to view this area. I got the feeling there're slopes all over this joint. Coop, after you square away your position, you and Weldon plant some permanent acoustical devices. Then string out the claymore mines. Fruitcake, you help. Stay focused. Got it?"

Heads nodded in reply.

The team was in total darkness. Coop hit the release on his shoulder harness and dropped his pack and radio quietly. He set his shotgun on his pack and spread out his Snoopy blanket. Then he and Weldon placed listening devices and command-detonated claymores, running the claymore wires back to the harbor site. When they were done, they told each member of the team the location of the mines, how they were directed, and gave out the hell boxes that fired them.

By 2000 hours the jungle had disappeared, devoured by a moonless night. Even the stars were dead. Without the stars, the Starlight scope brought for night vision was useless. If the team was in the middle of an active enemy base, the only thing to do on a night like this was hide and hope.

Coop slept for two hours, then was awakened by a tug on his boot. He sat up quickly and was immediately alert.

"Your watch," Klimp whispered. Klimp lay back on his Snoopy next to Coop's. They were separated only by the radio.

Coop took the handset and checked the dial on his luminous watch. Every thirty minutes they would contact 3rd Recon's rear with a signal from the handset. If everything was secure, the person on watch would squeeze the handset twice, sending a sit rep that all was clear.

The night crawled along. An hour into his watch, a breeze came up, mixing the leaves and vines into tangles. Dry brush, shifted by the wind, cracked and slapped. The slightest sound of leaves shuttering was terrifyingly loud. Coop was tired and wanted to close his eyes, just for a moment, but he would not. He grabbed a chew from his tin and rolled it around in his mouth as the night wore on. He checked his watch again. Then the calls came.

The radio was turned as low as a whisper. But Coop could still hear the enemy jamming the team's radio with Vietnamese propaganda and the high twang of their music. They knew the team was out there. Somewhere. It was unsettling, but Coop had experienced their games before. A Vietnamese voice came on in clear, choppy English, talking to them directly.

"Recon Marine. You tired. The war is long. You miss your back home. Do not be fool. Put weapon on ground. Go home."

But Coop thought he *was* home. Being here with a buzz pumping was the only real place left on earth. In this hole, it was simple. Either you're gonna live or you're gonna die. No rules. No crap from family or lifers. Out here, you made it happen. Out here, you were in control.

Lats replaced Coop at 2400 hours. Radio watch was switched again and again until the night grew cold but passed. When the gray dawn approached, the team had already eaten, buried their debris, and reapplied more camouflage. Weapons were cleaned and checked, and they moved out before sunrise. Coop was up front, and as he passed the shrine, he snatched the picture of Uncle Ho and stuffed it in the side pocket of his camouflaged pants.

They were quickly back on the main trail working silently through the wet mist of a heavy fog. It was a huge risk to travel on the trail, but time was critical. They needed to find the chopper and crew and do it quickly.

Morning light slipped through the fog during breaks in the canopy. Along the trail, sticks had been stuck in the ground, placed there by the enemy as trail markings. Off to the side, sections of jungle looked as if they had been stomped and torn out by the hand of God.

They had humped for twenty minutes when Coop noticed something unusual on his left flank. Recognizing subtle changes in the way bushes and background meshed together was a skill he'd brought to the Nam with him. He noticed the jungle's canopy had been disturbed—more light than usual was being cast along the jungle's floor. He followed the light down the steep slope, and his eyes caught something different. A subtle change in the thickness of vegetation.

The chopper was approximately seventy-five yards off trail. The tail section was barely visible, supported by a cluster of trees. It appeared to Coop that the chopper nearly landed where they were stopped, then skimmed the top of the trees before diving, nose down.

He moved back along the trail to Klimp and motioned the team off into cover. By the side of the trail, they lay flat, on full alert. Coop and Klimp were on one knee as Coop pulled out his canteen and took a long pull. Then he poured a little water on his head and the front of his shirt.

"LT, the gooks know we're here."

As he spoke, he could see in the lieutenant's eyes, beneath the green and black grease, that fear was setting in. Coop had seen it before, and he could feel fear washing through his own body.

"We both know what the situation is," Klimp said. His breath was shallow and rushed. "They could be waiting for us. Or maybe they moved out of the area. They did receive a lot of incoming," he added hopefully. But the lieutenant's response was weak and hardly reassuring.

"Piss on it! That's what we're here for, LT. Let's not sweat the small stuff. I'll go in and check it out. Why don't you get on the horn and let the fat boys in the rear know we found her. Have them call in some artillery a click or so away to fuck with the gooks' heads."

Suddenly the leadership shifted to Coop. He was the man, and Klimp was just the rank. They agreed that Coop and Lats would move cautiously toward the craft, then radio back for the rest of the team. Lieutenant Klimp called in artillery strikes that banged around the chopper's perimeter and farther out. For thirty minutes, it screeched and rang exploding as they lay flat, hugging the earth.

Then it was quiet.

The team knew that hell could be just minutes away, and that all the NVA in the world could be out there. They knew that the short distance between them and the chopper was a lifetime.

Moving down the steep embankment, Coop broke bush carefully, bent over, pushing the jungle aside with one hand, his shotgun in the other. Lats followed by twenty feet. Whenever he stepped heavily and made a slight noise, Coop would turn and point his shotgun to the left flank.

Coop took nearly twenty minutes to navigate thirty yards until he could see the chopper caught in the trees, half turned, rotor snapped, hanging like a big, bloated pheasant. The nose of the Huey had been punched in from the impact, and the glass was shattered. The pilot's door was open, as was the threshold on the sides where troops enter.

He flashed Lats a hand signal, motioning him to sit down, and then he nestled into a mangled gnarl of vines and thin trees to look for those subtle differences his granddad spoke about. Coop had reached a heightened awareness. He could see, hear, feel, and smell things with an electric acuity that transcended normal human ability. Like an animal. What Lieutenant Klimp called hyperfocused. He felt the wind adjust slightly, and the fog began to lift. He could smell faint fumes of fuel from the gunship, and he could see that the jungle surrounding the ship had been shaken, matted down, and walked over many times. Not once did his eyes leave the area. He pulled out a chew and stuck it in his mouth, savoring the mint and tobacco like never before. He looked for broken trees, disturbed brush, and signs that the enemy was waiting. For thirty minutes he simply sat, watched, chewed, and listened. His eyes kept drawing back to the tail section and shades of color that did not fit. His mind searched for understanding, and his eyes for evidence, until finally he knew what he was seeing. The section of tail and rear rotor caught up in the trees had something hanging from it. It reminded him of walking back to camp with his granddad when he was a boy and seeing a deer strung up and being skinned for the first time. Ten minutes more passed before he moved from his cover and approached the chopper.

By the time he reached the chopper, the fog had dissipated, and the change in the sunlight where the canopy was destroyed was clearly evident. It was like the difference between dusk and day. A sweeping bolt of light now formed a spotlight through the jungle onto the chopper. Coop could see an American soldier hanging by his feet from the broken tail section. A crude rope made from vines supported his weight. His jungle pants were on; his shirt was not. His hands were tied behind his back, and his belly had been slit, exposing his entrails. His throat was cut, and there were dozens of stabs and slashes, like a bull might have from a picador. The body had swollen, and flies had found it.

As Coop looked at the hanging soldier, he felt sick for an instant, then his emotions flattened like a wave smoothed out by the sea. He was sad but not angry or afraid. He was in control. He motioned Lats forward, then moved closer and circled the chopper, passing under the tail section, almost touching the soldier. By the time he made it back around, he was confident no enemy troops were there.

Lats signaled to Klimp. Soon, the rest of the team had traversed the distance and were at the chopper. Coop directed Jenkins to watch a trail leading away from the chopper. When the lieutenant saw the hanging body, he turned his head, bent over, and puked.

Weldon turned away and muffled a howl. "Jesus," Weldon sobbed. "Jesus. God!" He thrashed about, shaking his head, muttering and shaking until Coop grabbed him.

"Get ahold of yourself, boy," Coop scolded him, grabbing him by the shirt. "Get your shit together. Get ahold of yourself," he snapped again, and as he did, Weldon calmed, and Klimp wiped the puke from his mouth.

There were no more dead this time and no enemy. The chopper had been stripped of everything. They cut the body down, and Klimp regained his composure and had Fruitcake and Lats take the dog tag from the soldier's boot and wrap the body in a Snoopy blanket he carried.

By the time the area was scouted and considered secure, it was approaching dark. Headquarters radioed orders to move up and scout the main trail, and they received instructions from a colonel in the rear to leave the body. Another team would be sent in to recover it.

Coop knew that would never happen. He knew the poor bastard would just lie there and rot because some fuck in the rear didn't give a rat's ass about the dead unless it was enemy body counts. That boy would be just another dog tag lying on the desk of some asshole who probably never set foot in the boonies. Nothing changes. Nothing.

That night they sat in a circle two hundred feet from the chopper for one hour, then mobbed again about fifty yards away. This time they strung claymores. They all popped amphetamines to stay alert. The moon drifted behind clouds, mixed with a few stars. With the Starlight scope, Coop suddenly caught movement around their harbor site: silhouettes thirty yards away, bent over and carrying rifles. The night crawled, and fear consumed them. Toward morning, they could hear voices and whistles and more radio propaganda.

There was no fog in the morning. Just as the sun edged its way toward light, they got hit.

Jenkins blew the first claymore. Small arms cracked. Weldon was killed a moment later, head shot by a sniper. Coop popped another claymore and threw two frags. AK-47s and B-40s slammed into their position. Lats fired two more claymores, and Klimp was hit in the face. The round spun him sideways like a left hook and tore a sizeable hole in his jaw, shattering his teeth, knocking him flat. Coop wrapped his face with a battle dressing and forced a tube of morphine into his thigh. They moved back toward the open space near the craters, which was the only possible LZ close enough to be extracted. Lats and Fruitcake dragged Weldon. They set up another defense position. Coop stuck another tube of morphine in Klimp's thigh and fixed the tube to the LT's shirt so the rear would know how much morphine he'd been given. Then he wrapped Klimp's jaw with another dressing. Klimp moaned, spit blood, and choked. The VC started dropping mortars. Fruitcake took some shrapnel in his leg, wrapped it, and kept laying fire over Weldon's body with his rifle and then with the LT's 79.

The sun was up as Jenkins glided toward the opening then turned back to help with Weldon. He went back to the opening, heard a chopper overhead, tossed a green smoke, and was killed while looking up. A single round entered the back of his head.

Coop worked the radio and explained the situation to the two Cobras escorting the evac chopper. Then he switched frequencies and tied into the medevac.

For some reason, a giant CH-46 was brought in for the extraction. It was a much bigger target. But the Cobras were working over the jungle with suppressing guns and rockets, and enemy fire was waning. Just before the chopper set down in the clearing, a B-40 burst close to the team as they struggled toward the opening. The blast knocked Coop and Klimp to the ground, sending shrapnel into Klimp's body and shattering his leg. At the same time, mortars started popping and dropping again. *Thunk! Thunk! Thunk!*

The medevac flew down into the opening as Cobras continued to blast away all around them. The chopper settled in the smoke, and the ramp opened. Coop carried Klimp, who was near death, under the loud prop wash, up the ramp, and on board. He returned to the field to pick up Jenkins. In life, Jenkins was nearly a head taller than Coop. In death, he seemed even bigger. Coop was strong, but it was hard to lift Jenkins. On his first effort, he fell and tore a muscle in his shoulder. He finally picked Jenkins up by the back of his arms and dragged him backward to the chopper and up the ramp. The door gunner raked the jungle with his M-60 as the crew chief helped pull Jenkins aboard.

Lats and Fruitcake emerged from the edge of the jungle carrying Weldon by the arms and legs. As they approached the chopper, more small arms fire ripped through the area, raking the chopper.

The sniper who killed Weldon and Jenkins drew Coop in his sight. He squeezed the trigger as the chopper shuddered slightly. The round hit Coop just above the ankle, bringing him down on the ramp. Fruitcake and Lats fell to the ground a few feet away.

"Let's get the fuck out of here," the crew chief yelled to the pilot above the sound of rotors turning, ramp closing, and gunner firing. "Another bird's on the way."

"Fuck you, asshole!" Coop screamed. "We're not leaving without—" But it didn't matter. The chopper lifted. Fruitcake, Lats, and Weldon were left behind.

11

Hawkeye

Hawkeye and Flowers choppered out of Quang Tri on a cloudy day, sky more gray than blue. With them were Quick and Sleepy, also in Kilo Company's 3rd Platoon, and Steve Bittner, a Navy corpsman. They were headed toward a section of mountains close to the A Shau Valley known as Mutter's Ridge. There had been heavy contact over the last eight days, and the scuttlebutt was that an entire gook regiment was in the area. No one was looking forward to going to the bush, especially Quick and Sleepy.

Quick had a month left in country. Sleepy was four months into his tour. Both were discipline problems. Quick had risen to the rank of lance corporal but was busted back to private for an assortment of screwups, including insubordination and disobeying direct orders. He had refused to burn shitters and do night patrols. He never thought the war was his problem.

"This is Whitey's war," he'd say. "They be runnin' everything. If you're a black man in the Corps, you're shit outta luck. They don't care how many black men die. The man thinks ain't nothing worse than a black man—'cept a black man with a machine gun." His first platoon commander who wrote him up thought he was "one of those lazy, black-power Brillo heads, agitating and stirring up trouble."

Sleepy, on the other hand, was deemed "a poor, dumb son of a bitch" by the same platoon commander. He only got into the Corps because IQ standards had been lowered to fill a need for more men. His platoon commander once told the company commander that Sleepy was "a malingering moron. Dumber than Cassius Clay."

Sleepy was still a private because he always screwed up or tried to get out of work. More times than not, Sleepy just forgot what he was supposed to do or didn't think things through—like leaving his ammo back in the rear when they went on patrol or bringing a flashlight on a night ambush, "'cause I can see lots better." Most people thought he was bad luck to be around, especially in the bush.

The Navy corpsman was even newer to the Nam than Hawkeye and Flowers. Bittner had been in country only four days. He'd attended the University of Oregon and played some football before getting booted off the team midseason. Apparently, he had been caught naked in the closet of a girl's room by the dorm mother. Normally, that would be a minor offense, but the girl just happened to be the football coach's daughter. With football over for him, Bittner lost interest in school, dropped out, and was about to be drafted when he joined the Navy. The recruiter had promised he'd see the world, get laid a lot, and when he got out, he could look up his sweetie back home. "Son, there's no way you'll see Vietnam," the recruiter had said.

He became a corpsman and was shooting for an assignment in Hawaii but wound up transferred to the Marine Corps. Irritated at first, he even wrote his congressman but finally figured he'd just tough it out. He wasn't overly afraid of combat, but he felt tricked by the government, forcing him to fight in a war he believed was senseless.

The big, double-rotored Chinook also carried a belly full of cardboard cases of C-rations, wooden ammo crates packed with rifle and machine-gun ammunition, sixty-millimeter mortar rounds, and two red sacks crammed with letters and packages from home.

Wind blew through the gunner's open doorway, slapping at his pant legs as the chopper cut through the sky like an enormous amusement ride, climbing and dropping with the mountain's topography. The chopper blades cranked and roared as each soldier worried about getting shot down or his balls blown off. Finally it leveled and flew on a straight, descending line toward Firebase Stubblefield. The small outpost was carved on the top of a mountain in the middle of Vietnam's thickest jungle. From the air, it looked like a figure eight, where one half of the eight held troops, bunkers, and artillery, and the other half a small landing zone. Firebase Stubblefield was named after a Marine gunny who led the charge securing the position. The battle to take the mountaintop turned into hand-to-hand combat, and gunny Stubblefield was honored posthumously for killing six enemy soldiers with his E-tool.

The firebase was manned by the three platoons of Kilo Company, a couple of mortar teams, and two 105s. Daily patrols were run off the mountain, and artillery support was provided for the other companies in the area. India, Mike, and Lima companies occupied mountaintops in the battalion's tactical area of operation. They networked with Kilo and supported each other, often acting as blocking forces for each other when needed. During the previous weeks, there had been constant contact on patrols, and the lines were probed at night. Reconnaissance reports and captured enemy documents indicated a serious buildup of troops, as if a major enemy offensive were coming.

As the chopper made its final approach, Hawkeye thought the base seemed to drop from the sky. It reminded him of WWII concentration camps he'd seen photos of in his high school world history class. It was entirely encircled with concertina wire and fighting holes or sandbagged bunkers. The artillery pieces and mortars were at one end of the firebase along with a green, car-length water tank called the water bull. After the hill was taken, satchel charges were set against trees, and LZ was blown. More troops were dropped in, parapets dug, and artillery was flown in hanging in giant slings from the underside of the Chinooks. The entire first stage took less than a day.

As the green giant drew closer to the ground, Hawkeye's body surged with excitement. It reminded him of how he felt as a kid back in Chi-Town, trying to ditch cops by running down some alley. The chopper settled smoothly. The ramp opened, and troops hurried off under the loud, spinning force of the rotors. They carried rucksacks in one hand and M-16s in the other. Just off the ramp, Sleepy tripped. Bittner reached down to help him up and hand him his helmet. At the same time, several soldiers in jungle utilities, flak jackets, and the dirt of the field rushed on to unload supplies. One other soldier who had stepped in a hole and broken his ankle was carried aboard, while two other Marines hurried on, both heading for R&R in Bangkok. The chopper lifted, banked hard toward the horizon, then disappeared. The firebase was quiet.

"I'll tell you straight up," Quick said to no one in particular, "I hate the jungle. It's some funky shit. Bugs and leeches. But once I'm in the rear, I want to come back. Can you believe that shit? Crazy, huh?"

Flowers nodded, not having any clue as to why someone would rather be in this hellhole when he could be in the rear. Neither could Bittner, but Hawkeye thought he understood. The bush and the squad were a place to belong. Growing up, Hawkeye never felt like he belonged. Maybe it was because his dad was gone, or maybe it was because he was brighter than all his friends and believed he could have a better, safer life. He chuckled to himself over that thought. Imagine leaving Chicago because it felt unsafe and ending up in Vietnam? The irony was almost funny.

Quick's chatter and Hawkeye's thoughts were interrupted by Captain Clancy, the company commander. He was a small man in his early thirties with a huge, bulbous nose. Behind his back he was called Snozz, even though he was well liked. Clancy was a career soldier but wasn't about to get his men killed just to further his ambition, so he protected his troops and made sure they had the best of everything whenever possible. He welcomed Hawkeye, Flowers, and Bittner to Kilo Company and told Quick and Sleepy their vacation was over.

"Quick and Sleepy..." Clancy shook his head with a look of exasperation on his face. "You buzzards remind me of a couple of draft-dodging civilians," he joked, which drew a grin from Hawkeye.

They shrugged their shoulders.

"Doc," he said to Bittner, "I don't want these guys sick, understand? We got enough to worry about without having troops malingering."

"Yes, sir."

"Good. Now carry on."

Hawkeye, Flowers, and Bittner were assigned to Second Platoon with Quick and Sleepy and were introduced to Lieutenant Marlentas, their platoon commander. They also met their squad leader, Skidosski. Ski was tall, blond, and slight, with an angelic face that looked emaciated. He had a cigarette tucked behind his ear and a self-made scrawl of Jesus tattooed on his forearm. When he spoke, he never made eye contact. His eyes would just flit around like a liar.

"This is my first week as a squad leader," Ski advised. "Took over for a guy named Luke," he said. "Dude got hit by a phosphorus grenade."

He took the cigarette from behind his ear and lit it as everyone waited for him to continue. His hands were small, his fingers stained yellow from nicotine. He blew smoke.

"We were taking rounds. One hit his grenade and blew up. Face just melted. Now I don't know where you're coming from," Ski continued, "but we're tight here. Black or white don't mean a thing. We're just gonna get along. That cool by you, Quick?"

"Cool."

"Sleepy?"

"Huh?"

"Is that cool by you?"

"Is what cool?"

"Jeez. Listen up! I said I want us all to get along. Is that cool?"

"Yeah, cool."

"All right, so let's roll," Ski ordered. "Pick up your gear, and I'll show you where we're setting in."

They left the barren LZ, heading toward the command post bunker past fighting holes, piss tubes, and slit trenches. The command post was little more than a dug-out hole three feet deep, six feet wide, and ten feet long, surrounded by sandbags. A crude roof was constructed out of blown-down timbers and corrugated tin, topped with more sandbags. It would never survive a direct hit by heavy artillery or rockets, but it kept out the rain and gave comfort from the sun.

They passed soldiers cleaning weapons, writing letters, or sleeping under the shade of a stretched-out poncho, then moved down the hill toward the perimeter. It was a gradual drop of two hundred feet in elevation before they reached their position of fighting holes, bunkers, and pitched ponchos. A row of concertina wire was strung thirty feet on their front. Brush and small trees had been cleared on the other side of the wire to provide a clear field of vision to the jungle. Hawkeye quickly scanned the perimeter and recalled his training about fields of vision and killing zones. He was a newbie to be sure but had absorbed everything in infantry school and knew the position was fundamentally secure.

Ski stopped at the side of two plastic ponchos snapped together stretched out over some rope like a tent and told the group to drop their gear.

"Moose. Little Mike. Wake up! Get out here," he yelled. "You guys aren't going queer on me now?" he asked playfully as two Marines crawled from their hootch.

Ski explained that Moose carried the 60 and Little Mike humped the ammo. Moose was big and broad, and his partner was about half his size. They were buds, inseparable. They'd gone through boot camp and infantry school together and had arrived in the Nam three months earlier.

"OK, guys," Ski directed, hands deep in his pockets scratching vigorously at crotch rot. "Moose and Little Mike, you got Sleepy in your hole. Quick, you and Hawkeye and, ah ... what do they call you now? Wait. Don't tell me. Flowers. Right? You three guys set in together. Now there's some black power," he joked.

Quick rolled his eyes and Hawkeye shook his head, acknowledging Quick's glance.

"Doc and I will team up," Ski went on. "Quick, you take your guys down past my hole to set in. That way I'll be in the middle. Doc and I will keep the radio at our hole so we can all split watch. How's that sound?"

Everyone agreed, although it was clear from the look on Moose's face that he and Little Mike wanted Sleepy with them about as much as a kick in the balls.

Black clouds, gathered in rolling waves, smashed against the gray as Hawkeye and Flowers followed Quick down the line, past Ski's fighting hole and stretched out poncho, to a spot where they would dig in.

"This is it, cherries," Quick grinned. "Dig in d-e-e-e-p! I'm going to slide on down line and check in with some brothers. Scope out the situation. Maybe score some Mary Jane."

Hawkeye felt unnerved setting in without any real direction. He wanted to understand how it all worked. What to do. How to do it. He was feeling unsure.

"Flowers, it's you and me, bud," he said.

"You believe this crap," Flowers griped, ready to roll into a litany of complaints. "How the hell they 'spect us to set in? Damn! I mean, I'll dig me a hole. Big ass hole! But what we 'spose to do here, blood? I mean, like, where the hell are we? And what we 'spose to do? You know what I'm saying, Hawk? 'Sides, I'm hungry."

"Flowers, let's just dig a hole. It's simple. There's three holes and Doc's in the middle. Tell you what. I'll start digging; you lay out the gear and fix us some chow."

Hawkeye took the E-tool off the back of his pack and started picking and shoveling the ground. It was peaceful in a way, digging and turning the earth. The ground wasn't rocky and the dirt shoveled easily. He scooped and tossed, and as he began to sweat, he thought about his home and mother and how she used to read magazines to him when he was very young. She kept old magazines tied in bundles, stacked neatly in her bedroom. There were bundles of *Time* and *Life* and *Reader's Digest*. He could remember the covers: JFK shot dead, astronauts, Cassius Clay, and then his mind flashed on a picture he saw in *Look* magazine—a farmer in a wheat field cutting hay with a scythe. The farmer was home from the war, his mother explained. The wheat was representative of young soldiers cut down in war. He remembered it all so clearly, and he was only five. He even recalled how her voice sounded and that they were sitting at the kitchen table eating cereal for dinner. But he liked those old magazines and his mama reading.

He turned from his work toward Flowers, who was squatting, shirt off, fumbling with a couple of brown C-ration cans.

"How's that chow coming?" Hawkeye asked.

"What you think this is, McDonald's or some shit?" Flowers struck a match to a heat tab in a can that he cut away and was using as his stove. The tab burst into a blue flame, and the smell of sulfur caught his nose. "I'm firin' up your spaghetti and meatballs, but these tabs smell nasty. Phew!" He placed an open can of spaghetti on top of the little stove. "This is stinky, man. You smell these tabs, Hawk?"

Just then, Ski walked up, scratching and itching, shirt sleeves rolled down over Jesus. "'Course it stinks. See me later. I got some C-4 you can use."

"I ain't gonna blow my ass up with no C-4."

"Flowers." Ski's hand jumped out of his pocket, outstretched in protest. "We use C-4 to blow down trees and blow up gook bunkers and ammo. But take just a pinch, and it fires up real quick and hot and don't smell. I'll get you some."

Ski stepped over to the hole Hawkeye was standing in, sat down, and dangled his feet, gazing out on the perimeter, past the wire and down the mountainside. "Some pretty country, huh?" he said, as Hawkeye leaned against the side of the hole, half propped up by his shovel.

They looked out past the concertina wire toward the jungle. It was every shade of green and looked pure and wild and full of life.

"I never got too far out of Chicago," Hawkeye said, "so anything is better than concrete, I suppose. Although I did bus it down south to Carbondale, Illinois, one time with my mama. Had to go to a funeral. I kinda dug the pastures outside of town, with cows and horses and big old red barns. Made my mind relax. Know what I mean?"

"You bet! I'm from Nebraska. Used to live on a farm. Cows, pigs, chickens, the whole nine yards. Dad grew corn mostly, but then we had a couple bad years and lost it all. Had to move into town. One stoplight, two bars, couple churches." Ski stopped for a minute and reached in his pocket, scratching.

"I'm sick of this jungle rot. That's one thing. Don't wear under-wear. It'll rub you raw when you're humping and give you jock itch for a son of a bitch. Anyways, Dad and Mom rented a small house, me and my two brothers crammed in a room. Dad got hired on with the state, drivin' trucks. We didn't have any money, so I couldn't go to college." Ski grabbed a cigarette from his pocket. "Didn't want to anyway." Lit it. "So I got drafted. Kind of like the Corps, though. They don't mess with you in the bush, and I kind of like looking at the jungle. And the sky, most of the time it's double blue. Not like today. Today looks and smells like rain."

Flowers carried over Hawkeye's cans of spaghetti and meatballs and hot chocolate by the corners of the lids, handed them to Hawkeye, and sat down next to the hole. Hawk pulled a white plastic spoon from the side pocket of his jungle pants and ate as Ski talked.

"For now, we're stuck manning lines. But I'll tell you, there're gooks up the ass. The A Shau is full of 'em. Gooks dug in all over the mountains. Couple days ago, First Platoon was two clicks out, ran into a VC patrol. They killed the first two sons-of-bitches and the others took off running. Later they found six gook packs, soaked with sweat. Fact is, I just heard from the top that Charlie rocketed the hell out of Da Nang Air Base. Blew up some planes. Had gooks in the wire. It's like an offensive."

Hawkeye and Flowers were on edge, taking everything in, feeling waves of fear rush over them. "I understand it's the Vietnamese Lunar New Year. They call it Tet," Hawkeye said.

"Yeah? Well, so what we got here is another Tet offensive. I think that's what the top said. Another goddamn Tet offensive!"

Ski pulled on his cigarette, blew some rings that drifted and disappeared, telling them how they would split up and watch between the three holes. He'd make sure they got the early duty 'cause they were cherries. "Cherries always fuck up and have a hard time staying awake."

He left, came back, told them how the watch would go, and gave them each a claymore to string out and an M-72 LAW to tote.

"Now, don't try and fire this sonuvabitch if we get hit 'cause I know you forgot everything you learned in basic," Ski said. "Besides, they misfire all the time. When the sons-of-bitches work, they kick booty, but when they don't, it's dangerous as hell. And if you can't get 'em recocked or fired, you have to blow up the sonuvabitch so the gooks don't use 'em for booby traps. So—do—not—try—to—fire—the—sonuvabitch. OK?" Ski wasn't angry, just firm.

They finished their hole as it got dark. Hawkeye moved down the hill in front of their position and set in his claymore. He was sweating profusely and breathing hard from the tension he felt placing his first claymore. He worried that gooks would shoot him or maim him. He remembered to carry the charger in his pocket and made sure the mine was faced the correct direction before he pushed the metal prongs into the ground to hold it in place. He knew the mine couldn't explode without the charge connected and pushed, but he still worried. He moved back up the hill trailing wire, worried about snipers with nightscopes, until he reached their hole and connected the box. He laid out his frags and extra ammo, speaking quietly to Flowers as the night thickened and swallowed the perimeter. They sat on the edge of their hole eating chocolate bars and talking until Hawkeye checked his luminous watch and suggested they get some shut-eye. They moved to the hootch Flowers had made from stretched-out ponchos.

Despite the fear of being in the bush for the first time, they both fell asleep quickly. At ten o'clock, Ski woke up Flowers, which woke Hawkeye. Ski led Flowers back down the line to the middle bunker. Hawkeye's watch was midnight to 2:00 a.m., but at 11:00, unable to go back to sleep, he moved to the middle bunker to sit with Flowers.

"It's black as my ass," Flowers whispered. "Hawk, I can't see a damn thing."

Just then a slight breeze came up, bringing a swath of cold and jiggling the tin cans tied to the perimeter's concertina wire. The cans' slight noise put them both on alert, hearts racing like hummingbirds.

"It's cool, bro," Hawkeye said exhaling. "Just the wind. It ain't nothing," he said, not totally convinced.

Flowers left the bunker a little before midnight and Hawkeye was alone. There was no moon, no stars, only darkness. It was as if the mountainside and everything around it had been sucked away. Only the wind moved with its soft whispers of cool air. He rolled the sleeves of his jungle shirt down and put his hands in his pockets as he stood in the hole. He could feel his eyes straining, and his jaw ached from the strain of listening. After what seemed like a long time, he checked his watch. It was only 12:23. Then 12:40. His mind wandered. He listened hard, but it was quieter than the quietest moment he had ever known.

At 1:14 he heard the sound of a chopper in the distance. It hummed, and he could also hear the faint sound of rifles popping. Both sounds were new and frightening. It seemed like a long way away, though, and that helped ease the apprehension. In the distance, he could see illumination flares being dropped from an invisible plane, strings of red tracers streaking from the ship to the earth, like a dotted line. First the line, then the sound of the rounds. He played with the calculations of the speed of light versus the sound. He wondered who was dying.

By 2:00 a.m. the show was over. He crawled a few short yards to where Moose and Little Mike slept, got up, and stepped carefully over their feet. He heard Moose snoring, or at least he thought it was Moose, but it was too dark to tell.

The last time Hawkeye looked at his watch, it was 2:30.

OVER THE NEXT FEW DAYS, SKI INFORMED his squad that the North Vietnamese Army and Viet Cong were launching an offensive that was running the length of the country. "They're blowin' smoke out their ass, everywhere," he said. Rumors were that Firebase Stubblefield would be hit hard and that Kilo Company was going to Khe Sanh, a Marine base under siege. Forty thousand enemy were said to be massing outside the US base of only six thousand Marines. Each rumor carried dread in the telling. It was more easily believed if it was bad, because most rumors were. It was the good rumors that no one believed. Like ice cream being choppered in or milk or beer. Everyone knew it would never happen. But rumors came and went. One day a story circulated about a company of NVA soldiers being led by a couple of Marines. The next day, the Marines were CIA. Rumors.

Hawkeye and Flowers never left the firebase. They spent their time digging slit trenches, stringing wire, filling sandbags, or just BS-ing. Sometimes Hawkeye would play chess with a guy from 1st Platoon or read, but the books passed around, westerns mainly, bored him.

On the night of February 13 there was an enemy probe on 2nd Platoon's position down by the LZ. One Marine was wounded. The next morning the area was searched for blood trails, but none were found. Hawkeye could feel a different kind of tension in the air and heard some of the old-timers talking about "getting short and getting out" because something bad was gonna happen.

The next afternoon, as they were cleaning their weapons, Ski said, "Well, cherries, Hawkeye and Flowers, you guys got the LP tonight."

Hawkeye's body tensed. "Quick, you'll be fire team leader and take Sleepy as your radio man."

No one complained because there was no room to complain.

"Slip out of the wire just after dark. Move down the hill about a hundred yards into the tree line. Set in and shut up. Take a claymore and frags. Every twenty minutes, squeeze the handset on the radio to let us know you're not dead."

The word *dead* resonated in Hawkeye's ears.

"I'll get it from the LT," Ski said. "Are you hip? Any questions?"

They shook their heads.

The sky was solid gray, empty, and endless. The air didn't move. As the afternoon waned, Hawkeye, Flowers, and Quick sat on empty, green chow vat cans, broke down their rifles again to clean them, and lightly oiled their magazines, so the rounds pushed into the chamber smoothly.

Soon Sleepy joined them. They ate, gathered their gear, and agreed Quick would string out the claymore and trip flares once they set in. Flowers would carry the Starlight and Sleepy the radio.

As night fell, they saddled up. They carried 16s except Quick, who was using Ski's short-barreled shotgun. Each brought one bandolier of magazines and two frags. They wore flak jackets and helmets and carried one canteen and their Snoopys, rolled up and tied to the backs of their flak jackets. They spread bug juice on, took one last pull on canteens, and one last piss in the tube in front of their hole. A half-moon shed light as Quick led them down the slope to the break in the wire. Flowers followed Quick, sweating through his shirt even though the night was cool. Hawkeye behind Flowers. Sleepy took the rear. As they moved through the wire, stepping carefully over tanglefoot, Sleepy caught his fatigues, tearing them, and scratched his leg deep, drawing blood.

"Shit!" he said, clenching his teeth. Everyone froze.

Sleepy had revealed their position. They stood in the wire as Quick came back to the end of the group, checked Sleepy, wrapped a battle dressing over the cut, then went to the front and moved forward. Thirty yards on the other side of the wire, Quick led them slowly downhill, into the jungle. He pushed the brush quietly, moving the broadleaves and vines with one hand, holding the shotgun with the other. The jungle was thickly vined, with a canopy overhead that blocked most of the moon. In daylight, the jungle could swallow someone quickly. At night, it was inevitable. About seventy steps in, Quick stopped. When Flowers approached, he touched his shoulder to stop him. Then came Hawk and finally Sleepy who caught his foot, tripped, but did not fall. Hawkeye steadied him.

They settled in a half circle, close enough to touch. The walk from the perimeter was a short distance, but it took nearly forty minutes. Quick rested for a while before crawling out to string his claymore. With the natural slope of the land and the length of the cord, he could set the mine closer than usual. He set one trip flare a few feet to each side of the claymore. By the time he crawled back to their position, he was exhausted. Hawkeye and Sleepy would take the first watch.

Hawkeye sat up holding the Starlight like a telescope and looked out on the jungle. It was dark, and the moon was hidden, so images washed together with little distinction. The wind was still. The jungle asleep. He checked his watch. It was 11:07. He squeezed the radio's handset. At 11:30, he squeezed it again. Sleepy dozed off. At 1:00 a.m., Hawkeye reached over and shook Quick and Flowers. He pushed Sleepy awake, whispering for him to move so he could lie down.

Hawkeye lay back on his Snoopy but couldn't sleep. He kept listening to the silence, finally sitting up to drink from his canteen. He lay back again and thought of his mama and how firm she was with him. He remembered in grade school when he left to catch the bus without his hat. It was snowing, and she'd come running down the sidewalk shouting, "You best get your hat on, boy. And don't think I'm too old to whip your butt." He smiled at that memory and remembered how she always used to hug him. He missed being hugged. Being read to. The magazines. He focused on better things. Good things, like five-cent snow cones in the summer on West Taylor or walking down by the lake in spring. That's where he learned how to play chess, on granite boards next to the park.

Suddenly, Quick grabbed his leg. Hawkeye sat up and his heart surged. Quick shook Sleepy, covering his mouth. Brush cracked. Hawkeye could hear jungle being shoved aside. *This is it,* he thought. *This is it!*

A trip flare burst in a fireball, opening the night; at the same time, Quick blew the claymore, sending hundreds of steel balls tearing into the jungle. In the flash of light Hawkeye could see silhouettes. Six enemy or more with rifles and pith helmets, scattering. Immediately, streams of green tracers splashed the jungle. Hawkeye threw a frag then laid flat. *Boom!* Then Quick, Flowers, and finally Sleepy tossed grenades. *Boom! Boom! Boom!* But Sleepy's throw was short, and he was still on one knee when some of the shrapnel came back, slashing his face, taking out an eye, and blowing him back.

"Oh, Jesus! I'm hit. I'm hit," Sleepy cried, holding his head and rocking back and forth on his back.

Rounds sprayed from both sides as Hawkeye pulled a bandage from his side pocket, tore off the plastic and shoved it into what was left of Sleepy's face. A B-40 shot by, slamming twenty yards from their position, sending a spray of shrapnel overhead. Hawkeye fired and threw another frag as Quick lay flat, screaming into the radio, "We're coming in! We're coming in!" In that crazy moment of terror, Hawkeye feared being killed by his own men when they approached the lines.

Quick stood, grabbed the radio, and yelled, "Let's get the fuck out of here," running ahead, leading the team through the maze and tangle of vines, rounds stinging all around.

Hawkeye pulled a moaning Sleepy, who flailed loose, spinning madly, screaming, "No! No!" Sleepy ran back into the bush, back toward the enemy. Quick and Flowers were out of Hawkeye's sight, racing toward the perimeter. Sleepy tripped and fell. Hawkeye, consumed with fear, crawled on his belly, searching frantically for him.

The firing waned. Hawkeye called for Sleepy, which brought an explosion near him. He was out of grenades and could hear a whistle blow and movement all around him. In that instant, two figures appeared. He opened up on them, scrambled to his feet, and ran toward the firebase. White tracers slashed by him as he ran, until he broke through the jungle screaming, "Don't shoot! Don't shoot! Don't shoot!" He scrambled up the hill to the wire with flares popping overhead lighting his way, stepped over tanglefoot, then passed through the concertina. He stumbled to the edge of Ski's bunker, tumbling in as Ski popped a hand flare on a row of sandbags, illuminating their front.

"Where the fuck is Sleepy?" Ski demanded. Above the range of rounds smashing into their position, Ski was calm as he asked again, "Where's Sleepy. What happened?"

"He was wounded and—"

The night opened up as Ski, Hawkeye, Doc, and Flowers returned fire. Mortars popped in the dark and exploded behind, in front, and all over the firebase. Another B-40 rocketed just above the ground, destroying the wire. More whistles blew and a group of ten, then twenty, enemy pushed up the hill firing. The Marines along the line returned fire in full automatic bursts, mixed in with heavy machine guns and M-79s. Another explosion blew more space in the lines. Four enemy carrying satchel charges dove into the wire, blowing themselves up. More enemy dove on the wire, comrades stepping on their backs and rushing the slope toward Hawkeye's position.

Moose worked the gun as Little Mike fed belt after belt, barrel sizzling. Quick and Flowers were taking intense fire when Flowers yelled, "Doc! Doc! Doc!"

The illumination died as Bittner grabbed his bag and left the safety of the hole. He was just steps from the side of Moose's hole when a blast knocked him to the ground. He got up shaking, his left shoulder dislocated in the fall. He stopped at Moose's gun, then moved toward Flowers's voice.

The night lit up again and Bittner dove toward the hole. He crawled the last few feet and saw Quick lying back with Flowers's hand on his throat, blood gushing. Rounds impacting all around. Bittner opened his medic's pouch and pulled out a compress. The illumination faded. He had worked on wounded in hospitals before, but never blind or under fire. As Bittner placed the compress on Quick's throat, he could feel his blood and the slackness in his neck and knew that he was dead.

A second group of enemy dashed over the wire. Three were cut down instantly by Moose's gun. Two others raced toward Flowers's hole. One died from Flowers's grenade; the other made it to the hole, spraying them with AK-47 fire, tearing off the top of Bittner's helmet and almost killing him. Flowers spun the Viet Cong around with a short blast, then emptied his magazine into his small body. More claymores exploded, and more illumination lit the sky, floating on small parachutes like children's toys. A new wave crossed the wire as mortars fell. The firebase was overrun.

Choppers came blowing through the night, dropping light and raining the perimeter with thousands of rounds of red tracers. Explosions and more fire inside and outside the perimeter. Then it slowed. A magazine emptied, and it was quiet. Two more rounds, then one, then the jungle was quiet. The chopper ceased fire.

Bittner was badly wounded. A round clipped Flowers's ear; another hit his rifle, shattering the stock. A bullet slashed Little Mike's arm. The others were unhurt, except for Sleepy.

Hawkeye was stunned and fell back in his hole. What had he done? He'd lost Sleepy. He felt like a coward.

Ski moved from hole to hole, telling everyone to be cool. His voice was lower but still confident. Then Ski stopped, touched Hawkeye's shoulder, and moved on.

12

JT

It had been three weeks since Ashley slipped out the door. JT, meanwhile, clung to the thought that God meant them to be together. Why else would he have survived Vietnam? But this time away from her was eroding his belief.

"Ashley, I can't sleep. I need you. I miss you."

"No...I can't come home," her voice cracked, and she began to sob. "I'm afraid of you."

That triggered him. He squeezed the phone, trembling with rage. He wanted to reach through the phone and grab the bitch.

All I ever thought of was you. All I ever dreamed of was coming home. You were my life. I went through fucking hell! I'd die for you! Now you pull this shit? I ought to kick your ungrateful ass. But he composed himself, inhaled deeply.

"Ashley...please...come on. Give me a chance."

"I've given you chances." By then, she was crying, but protected by the distance between them, she let her anger seep out. "Remember last week? You were supposed to pick up Anna and take her overnight, but you never showed up. Didn't call for hours. Probably running around, messing with Brad. I can't trust you. My mom's right. You don't care about anyone but yourself!"

It was hard for JT to maintain. He wanted to rip the phone out of the wall. He could feel himself shaking. He wanted to go over there and kick the door off its hinges. She didn't understand shit. She didn't give a damn about him. If only she knew what he was feeling, if she'd just understand that he was crazy right now, and all he needed was some time to get his mind right, she'd forgive him and come back. *Stay calm, JT. Suck in the air. Don't lose it.*

He spoke slowly, enunciating each word as if they were separate ideas. He was trying to coerce her gently, making sure not to raise his voice or attack his mother-in-law.

"I told you. The car broke down. By the time I got it running and came by, you were gone."

"That's a lie!" She was yelling at him. "Of course I was gone! Mom took me to Mary's. Give me a break. The car never broke down. While I'm crying, you're screwing off with Brad."

JT could feel the conversation going out of control. Once she was upset, no matter what he said, he'd be wrong. He'd tried and tried. He could never manage to say the right thing. It was hopeless. He took a fork off the counter and drove it hard into his forearm until it bled. Maybe she'd understand this.

His voice was flat. "Who said I was with Brad?"

"Mary. You're such a liar."

He was with Brad. So fucking what? He felt numb inside.

"I've got to go. Anna's crying."

"Can I call later?"

"Whatever."

"I love you, Ashley." But he didn't feel it, and she didn't respond.

JT sat staring out the kitchen window, watching Pearl work in her garden. He began to feel sorry for lying, for being late. He took the fork out of his arm and drove it into his thigh. See, bitch, this is pain.

After carrying wounded and dead soldiers with shattered arms and faces, physical pain was all he could relate to, the only kind of pain he could understand. In the war, he developed an emotional numbness, a way of shutting down how he felt so the next guy who died wouldn't have an impact on him. He could place his hand over a Marine's bloody face and be calm as he wrapped a compress. She didn't understand. Maybe if she saw him wounded, she would understand how bad he felt.

As he watched Pearl work her hoe, his breathing eased. He pulled the fork from his leg. It was nothing.

He imagined Pearl in Vietnam. The old mamasans used to work in their gardens like that, bent over, hair pulled back, shoveling, sifting. Pearl was covering plants for winter; but back in the village, there were no seasons. No winter. No autumn. Here, the wind came howling down the Columbia River Gorge, blowing cold rain and snow. Leaves turned color, dropped, and blew into gardens like Pearl's.

He rested his head on the table, feeling the throb in his arm and thigh, while his mind rolled back to Ashley and how they met.

SHE WORKED AT A BURGER JOINT SERVING Cokes and fries. She had a look, a way of tilting her head when she smiled. He was shy, even when his friends were shoving and being loud.

"JT's got a boner for the Arctic Circle girl," they teased, punching him in the arm.

That first summer he came by just to see her smile or walk across the room. Each time she was friendly, ringing up checks, taking orders.

"Can I help you?" she asked, wiping the counter, her eyes a startling blue, teeth straight and white.

Whenever she spoke, his heart raced. Words felt like they were stumbling from his mouth. "Well, I . . . uh. Well, I guess I'll have a, uh, Green River. I guess."

"Good choice," she'd say.

One evening after a baseball game when he was still in uniform, he stopped at the drive-in alone. He walked up to the counter, his cleats clicking across the floor. Ashley was standing with her back to him working the milkshake machine, her white uniform snug across her backside. She looked over her shoulder at him. Her eyes flashed, and her mouth eased into a smile.

"Did you win?" she asked bringing two chocolate shakes to the little girls standing at the counter.

"Yeah. Yeah, we did." A jolt of confidence shot through him. His back straightened slightly. "You like baseball?" He grinned, looking toward the floor, then to her face.

"My mom says I was baseball crazy when I was little. Granddad used to take me to games at Beaver Stadium."

"I used to go there, too, when I was a kid," he said, laying a dollar on the counter for a burger, fries, and a Green River. JT sucked on his straw and felt someone edge in behind him, pushing toward the counter. "You ought to come see us play," he said hopefully, taking off his cap, running his hand through his hair.

"I'd like that."

"We're playing a doubleheader Friday night at Lents Park. I mean...well, uh...if you're not doing anything." The people behind squeezed in front and JT began to blush. "Anyway, uh...I better go."

"See you," Ashley said, moving back to the cash register.

JT walked to his car feeling stupid but happy and hopeful.

She showed up at the second game, walking her red setter. When he saw her from the dugout, he tried harder. He dove for third on a triple, bounced up on an overthrow, and slid into home, dirt flying and a handful of fans screaming.

Ashley watched, and when he took the field again, she walked the dog around the cyclone fence behind center field.

"Nice hit," she yelled, dog nosing at the hem of her cutoffs.

"Thanks," he shouted back, a little full of himself. Just then a fly ball came streaking toward center, and he went roaring to his left and dove as it floated beyond his glove. By the time he got up and threw home, a guy on second scored, and the game was over. The guys ribbed him as they picked up helmets, bats, and loose balls.

"Hey, see that Arctic Circle girl hanging out in center?" joked the catcher. "Looks like JT's pussy-whipped. Divin' for a ball with a big stiffer in his pocket."

Everyone laughed. JT ditched his friends and walked over to the duck pond, showered in field lights. Ashley was standing at the edge, her dog focused on a mallard.

"I'm glad you came," he said, hitching at his pants nervously, pulling up his socks then reaching over to pet the dog.

"I like baseball."

"Well...uh. I blew that catch in center. But, uh...you know I'm...well, do you want to go get something to eat?" he asked, drum beating in his chest.

"I'd like that."

"How'd you get here?" JT asked, hitching at his pants again, adjusting his cap.

"I just walked over. I live close by."

They sat in the parking lot in his beat-up '55 Chev, right front fender coated with gray primer. The Arctic Circle sign flashed, casting a blue neon glow through the windshield. In the car next to them, a young couple necked as three kids stopped to look. The dog's head stuck out the rear window, tongue lapping at the air.

"I was glad you came to the game," he said. "So...uh, what do you like to do?"

"I don't have time for much, what with all the work I'm doing. How 'bout you?"

"I work at my dad's auto body shop, and, well, I play a lot of baseball."

JT and Ashley worked in and out of awkward talk. He felt embarrassed, unworthy. He was afraid she would find out his family was lousy. Dad a drunk, mother crazy.

She came to two or more games, and they parked in a lot or in front of her house and talked but didn't touch. As the long summer days passed, JT sanded cars and thought about Ashley. At night he'd drop by her work for a Green River.

Finally he made up his mind to kiss her. He drove with her along the river and pulled off a side road, parking in a strawberry field. Stars, a half-moon, and a pole light in front of a barn cast light on the berries. The windows were rolled down to catch a breeze. The radio was broken, and it was almost 11:00. They had their backs against opposite doors with a mile of car seat between them. JT felt a rush of anticipation sweep over him. Sweat ran down his back. He wanted to kiss her. They were both seventeen.

"I really should go," she said nervously. "My mom's strict about curfew."

Occasionally a car drove down the road near the field, the headlights robbing his momentum.

"Yeah. OK . . .". His whole body a tremor. Her hair, caught in the light, fell across her shoulders. He reached for the nape of her neck and pulled her to him. The first kiss was short, awkward, teeth clipping. The second was longer, better.

"I can't," she said, leaning away. "My mom will kill me if I'm late."

A couple of days later, after a ball game, just before the sun went down, they walked around the empty field holding hands.

"I hate living with my stepdad," she told him as they moved toward a section of bleachers and sat down. "He acts as if I'm invisible. Never smiles or jokes. Just sits in his chair reading the paper or glued to the tube."

It was quiet. The sun dipped into right field.

"My real dad was a drunk," Ashley sighed, her voice dropping, mixing in with the breeze. "When I was little, he'd leave me in the car and go into bars and come out hours later smelling like beer and smoke. Then he and my mom would fight. They divorced when I was in third grade. Then one night a couple years later, dad was killed in a car wreck, drunk."

JT understood that kind of pain. He put his arm around her. The night air was cool and the moon was climbing.

"Sounds like my family," he said. "My parents are getting divorced. My dad's a drunk. They used to fight all the time. One night they were out partying and got into a big argument about her dancing and sitting on some guy's lap. I guess they were screaming at each other in the parking lot of this bar, and my mom grabbed the keys to the truck and tried to run over him. She got his foot and tore some ligaments. I was pretty small then, but I remember going to the hospital."

For a few moments they sat quietly, moonlight playing across the field and the faint sound of a train clacking over tracks, blocks away. JT's memory flared.

"My mom's nuts. Always yelling and screaming. She used to hit me all the time when I was little. She still calls me names or says she hates me and wishes I was never born. She's been having shock treatments. First time she came home, her eyes were empty, like a chunk of memory was missing. Her voice was real flat like she was doped up. Sometimes she acts so crazy I push my dresser against my door at night. I'm afraid she'll try to kill me."

JT LIFTED HIS HEAD FROM THE TABLE, absorbed in memories. He stared vacantly at Pearl working and wondered where his love for Ashley had gone. He stared at the wound in his arm as if it belonged to someone else. Eyes closed again, he recalled making love the first time. His mother had been in the hospital, his dad was working, and his brother at school. He and Ashley had skipped class. It was like they both understood this was the day. At first they watched TV lying on the front room floor, rolling over to neck. Then he was on top, grinding. Not speaking, they went to his bedroom. There were bats and balls on the floor and posters of Mickey Mantle and Willie Mays. It smelled of tennis shoes. Both were frightened as they stood in the middle of the room looking at each other, kissing. She took off her bra and slipped her long legs out of her panties, then crawled under the covers in his bunk bed and called to him. He was so ready it hurt. He kissed her and touched her with a sense of discovery.

He remembered it all. But it was gone now.

JT pushed from the table, moved to the front room, flipped on the stereo, lay on the couch, and masturbated. He took off his shirt and wiped himself, then threw it on the floor. The house was a mess. There were half-eaten apples and empty TV dinners and dirty clothes. It smelled sour, like stale beer and rotten food. It was a weekday morning. He should be out looking for work, but he felt detached from himself. He thumbed through an old *Sports Illustrated* and wondered if he'd ever be with Ashley again.

He thought of those nights when he'd climb to the roof of her house and sneak in her bedroom window. Or making love in the back seat of his cousin's car, while Brad and Mary got it on in the front. Or at her beach house on her parents' bed when they'd gone fishing. Even at high school one night after wrestling practice after everyone on the team had gone home. He'd stayed in the whirlpool. Ashley was working late on a school paper. When she came downstairs to wait for him, everyone had gone home. She waited. When he came out of the locker room, he kissed her. No one was around. He took her hand and led her into the dark wrestling room. Down on the mat, sweating, hurrying, deep inside of her, so full of love for her. Then he heard the janitor come, pushing his bucket and mop.

Sex was so great back then, so exciting and pure and kind. Now it seemed like all she wanted was to be done and have him off of her. He hated his life. No job. No future. Ashley gone.

JT rolled to the floor and started doing push-ups. He ripped off fifty, felt a flush on his face, his arms tightened. He was about to take a shower when he heard a song he recognized but had never really listened to. Remembering the dope Brad left the night before, he grabbed the silver Zippo and fired up a joint. The song bounced off the walls, the words echoing in his head, and he shouted along with the refrain—

"Ah, you don't believe, we're on the eve of destruction!"

This was his song, he thought, brought by some force at this particular moment. Like God letting him live when Gurney and Ski and—it was his deal with God: be faithful to Ashley, he lives. Simple. And he did, and he came home. But what the fuck was happening now? He wanted to kill.

"Jesus Christ!" he screamed, pounding the floor. "Jesus. Jesus!"

JT STAYED INSIDE FOR THREE DAYS, NOT answering the phone and rarely sleeping. He listened to music, drank beer, ate cross-tops, and smoked the entire lid. He brooded about his wife and baby and felt scared at night because they were not with him. Scared because without her and Anna, he had no one to protect and could see his own vulnerability. He had lost her, and now he felt like a loser.

His mind flipped over and over, until it landed on his best friend, Coop, and the first patrol. Land mines. *Boom!* Shattered legs. *Boom!* Bodies blown in half! Firing down the line! Blood swimming. Mind fucking. *Oh God! 105s IN THE TREE!* Face mangled, spurting. And the screaming, *EVERYONE'S DEAD! DOC! DOC!* He crawled under the bodies. Choppers in the air. All gone. Fourteen. Gone. *Fuck it. Fuck them. It's over. It's history. Fuck it.* He fell to the floor and did push-ups and sit-ups as tears burned his cheeks. *Incoming! Incoming!* Ski, legs twisted like a rag doll. Blood. Colors, so bright. Red splashed on white. Green sock holding an arm together. More sit-ups. Jungle and mountains, waves of green. Rice paddies, hamlets, and villagers picking stinking garbage. Shit and mud and trucks and tanks and artillery. The pounding and pounding. Blowing up hamlets and water bulls and every-damn-thing-else that got in the way. Kids in gaggles like geese. *Gimme chow! Gimme chow!* Clips emptied into enemy heads. And the Marines who died, split open like cords of wood and stacked on flatbed trucks. And in that last minute, last second—just before they died—they had a look in their eyes. It wasn't terror they felt in that last goddamn minute. They looked more like they were sorry. Ski lookin' up at JT like he's sorry. Head back, eyes open—sorry.

JT curled on the floor, exhausted. Mind drained. Empty.

THE MORNING AFTER ASHLEY LEFT HIM, JT showered, ate a bowl of cornflakes, and decided to turn his life around. He was ashamed of himself. He had to buckle down, as his dad used to say. He was broke and the rent was due. He had to find a job right away. Maybe if he got a job, Ashley would come back.

He dressed and jogged down to Charlie's for a newspaper and carton of chocolate milk. He shot the breeze as Charlie boned a chicken for his tiny meat department, asking if he knew anybody who was hiring. Charlie shrugged his big round shoulders, wiped his hands on his apron.

"Try the docks. Or maybe the warehouses over on produce row."

JT didn't want to do manual labor if he could avoid it. He'd had two years of busting butt in the Corps. He'd shoot for an inside job where he could use his brain.

Back home he sat down at the kitchen table, had another bowl of cornflakes, this time with chocolate milk, and read the paper. He glanced briefly at the headlines—new peace talks and more anti-war demonstrations; in the sports section, "Packers Roll." Finally he took a pen and began circling help wanted ads.

He didn't have a degree and couldn't say he'd worked in a mailroom because he'd been fired. His only real experience was helping paint cars with his dad, which he hated. Or carrying a machine gun.

He snickered. Maybe he could be a mercenary in Africa. No. He could re-enlist. Forget it. He'd miss Anna too much. Probably die in the process. He finally found some ads that looked promising, all of them downtown. He didn't have a suit or tie, so JT put on his best shirt and slacks, got in his Volks, and headed for the city.

REMINGTON'S SPORTS WAS LOOKING FOR A COMBINATION warehouse-retail trainee. JT plugged the meter and walked a few short blocks to the warehouse. Twenty other guys were lined up against a wall or sitting on benches outside a door marked *Private*.

He surveyed the competition and decided he had a good chance of landing the job, since he used to be an athlete in high school. They'd probably give him bonus points for being a Marine and fighting in Vietnam, he figured. They'd recognize his leadership abilities. He grabbed an application and stood against the wall. When he was done, he placed it into a tray and got in line.

After two hours, a pimply-faced girl in her early twenties led him into the interview room. She wore red lipstick the color of a ten-dollar whore, his dad might say, and tight clothes. The girl left, smiling at JT. The room was cluttered with shelves overflowing with books, manuals, hand tools, and a couple of car racing trophies.

Behind an old oak desk was a small man with a tiny head, cheap glasses, and a mustache that reminded JT of a Mexican drill instructor he had in boot camp. His desk was perfectly clean except for JT's application, a phone, and a sign that read *Shit rolls downhill*.

"Sit down, sit down, sit down," the man said to JT impatiently, gesturing toward a folding metal chair that looked out of place on the carpeted floor. His voice was nasal. "So, so, so. Tell me about yourself, young man. It says here you're married and have a child. Aren't you a bit young to be married?"

The question startled JT, and at the same time made him think that if he didn't get a job, he might not be married for long.

"Well, yes. I am young to be married, but my parents married young, and they have been happily married for over twenty-five years," JT lied.

"Yes, yes, yes," the man said, surveying the application, then looking at JT, and back to the application. "OK. OK." The constant repetition was annoying. "So you were a Marine in Vietnam?"

"Yes."

"Good, good. I never was in the service, but I was a National Scout Leader for years. Did a lot of camping. Not like you, I'll bet. Nope, Marines are tough. Vietnam is bad. So can you drive a forklift?"

"Yes, some." Again, a lie. The only time JT ever really drove a forklift was during a summer job, but he got fired for running the thing down a ramp too fast and tipping it over.

"Good, good, good. Well . . . I like you. Check back with us in thirty days."

"In thirty days?"

"Yes. The position isn't open for thirty days, but I like to get people lined up early. I can tell you right now you're in the top ten." He grinned and showed his yellow teeth.

"But I can't wait thirty days. I need to go to work right away."

"Sorry. Check back in thirty days for a final interview. Could you tell Mindy to call in the next person?"

JT got up, incensed that he'd waited over two hours to talk for five minutes to a moron about a job that wouldn't even be available for thirty days!

He stopped at five other places that either said they had filled the position or hung up signs in the window indicating the same. The next place was closed for lunch, so he wandered around town, up Broadway, and by the building he used to work in.

He heard some noise coming from up the street, next to the post office. As he approached, he saw a group of six bald-headed Hare Krishna chanting, singing, and banging tambourines. He watched them jump up and down in long saffron robes with a single white streak of paint on their foreheads. Like Buddhist monks on acid, he imagined. Just then an attractive young woman in her late teens walked up, smiling.

"You're so handsome," she said, handing him a white carnation. She sounded like she meant it.

Then, like a sledgehammer to the forehead, she asked, "Do you know Hare Krishna?"

The question brought him to his senses. She wasn't interested in him. She didn't think he was handsome. He was just another knucklehead she was trying to recruit or get money out of. He looked at her closer and could see that she had a wig on and was bald to the bone, just like her buddies doing the two-step. He felt stupid.

He found his car with two parking tickets and a towing warning on the windshield. He tossed them on the ground and drove off. At home, he showered in the dark, feeling dejected, yet resolved to look for a job again the next day. He called Ashley and asked her to come home, but she wouldn't, so he talked baby talk to Anna, ate hot dogs, and crashed.

The next days were more of the same.

"Job's been filled. Sorry."

"You're too young for this position. We need someone with experience."

Experience, my ass; he could call in artillery and gunships or have million-dollar jets rain hell. What kind of experience do you need to drive a Pepsi truck or sweep floors and pick up boxes?

"Nope. Been filled."

"Sorry. Have you signed up for unemployment? Veterans get unemployment, you know."

But he wouldn't do that, take a handout. So every morning before first light, he would do push-ups, sit-ups, and run, look all day for work, and every night call Ashley. Hoping.

13

Coop

Coop was medevacked to Da Nang, and within an hour of being wounded, he was x-rayed and in surgery. The round had cracked both the tibia and fibula in his lower left leg. Doctors were content with cleaning the wound, setting the fractures, and suturing as needed. He spent two days in Da Nang heavily medicated on morphine.

On the third day, he woke up to the sound of someone screaming, "I killed Jesus! I killed Jesus!"

He was still groggy from the morphine but could see two soldiers grabbing a naked patient who was standing in the middle of the ward screaming as they wrestled him to the ground. The sudden noise pushed aside his sleepiness. A third soldier rushed down the corridor dividing rows of beds and helped overpower the madman.

"I killed Jesus! I'll fucking kill you all!" he yelled as they carried him kicking and screaming out of the ward.

By the time the noise faded, Coop and the entire ward were alert, adrenaline surging.

The ward was an inflatable building formed like a tunnel or Quonset hut, forty beds lined up in two long rows. All of them occupied with head wounds and sucking chest wounds and patients missing arms or legs. Sometimes both. Close to Coop was a Marine whose face was bandaged, a feeding tube running out of the bandages. He had IVs in both arms. He'd been accidentally shot in the face on patrol by his best friend.

Coop felt deep throbbing in his leg. The morphine was wearing off and the pain was taking over. He stared at the ceiling and could hear an occasional, "Doc. Doc. I need some meds." He lifted his head from his pillow and gazed at his leg, propped up by pillows, splinted and wrapped in clean bandages, with a spot of blood easing through. The throbbing grew, and he remembered the pain as being much like what he had felt when he had been wounded before.

His bed was in the middle of the ward, four away from the corpsman's station. He lifted himself up on his elbows and looked for a corpsman. There were none. From his elbows, he could see the length of the ward in both directions. At one end was a door marked *EXIT*; at the opposite end was a set of swinging doors. The corpsman's station had a counter with a water jug and a tray with pills placed in small paper cups for those who could walk to the station, roll up in wheelchairs, or hobble on crutches. Behind the counter were a chair and a locked aluminum cabinet that held medication.

He fell back into bed, feeling like his leg was imploding. The pain in his leg was searing when he heard the sound of the swinging doors open and a chorus of "Doc! Doc! Listen, Doc, I need some help here."

Coop didn't want to cry out for the corpsman. He wanted to be strong and fight through the pain. He wanted to be like his granddad, who used to get his teeth worked on without Novocain. Once he broke his wrist falling in the barn and just wrapped it with duct tape and finished the day bucking hay.

He closed his eyes and forced his mind to remember his granddad and the mountains, with fields full of wild huckleberries and the sweet smell of green clover. But the pain was too much. It racked him and blew him back to the chopper leaving Lats, Jenkins,

Weldon. He was sick with grief. His mind jumped to last year's wounds, firefights, and clear back to that first patrol with Hawkeye, JT, and Gurney . . .

"Hey, guy. How you hangin'?" the corpsman asked as he walked up to Coop's bed, pushing a cart with medications and dressings.

"Screwed," he responded weakly, sweat beaded on his forehead, memories still in his eyes. "I need something, Doc. My leg hurts like hell."

The corpsman looked at the chart hanging at the end of the bed, checked his watch, then wrote the time down.

"Here you go, bud," he said, moving toward the side of Coop's bed and handing him a white paper cup with pills in it. Then a cup of water. "I'm going to give you a shot of morphine that should put you on another planet." He took a syringe from a tray on the cart. "Now try rolling to your side."

Coop felt the slight prick of the needle and a striking pain shooting through his leg when his weight shifted. Shot done, he rolled back flat, watching the corpsman adjust the IVs. He felt weak, but the pain was ebbing.

"Later, bud." The corpsman pushed his cart to the next bed.

In a few moments, Coop's throbbing subsided, and he drifted into a haze of disconnected thought. Soon he was dreaming about his legs being blown off, then Lucy on top of him in a motel room back in the world. When he woke, the room was dark. He had lost his bearings. For a moment he was disoriented, dismayed. Then he recalled being shot, medevacked, and brought to the ward. He felt dizzy, mouth dry, and the pain was on him again, moving up and down his leg, lingering where the wound was. He needed more morphine.

"Doc. Doc." Coop pushed himself up to his elbows and could see the corpsman station with a reading light on, but no one was there. He lay back, trying to relax into his injury, forcing his leg not to hurt. If he could just kick pain's ass—but it was no use. He wanted more morphine or anything that would work.

"Doc. DOC!" This time he shouted.

"Shut the fuck up," someone said in the dark several beds away.

"Bite my ass," Coop responded. "I need some morphine."

"We all need morphine, brother," came an anonymous voice.

A small light went on from where the voice had come. A few minutes later, a guy in a wheelchair pulled to the side of Coop's bed. His hair was longer than the typical Marine, and he had a mustache that drooped slightly over the corners of his mouth. He wore small wirerim glasses that definitely were not military issue. His right foot was in a cast.

"Here, man. Fire in the hole," the guy said, handing a lit joint to Coop. "This will straighten your shit out until the corpsman gets off his ass and makes it back here."

"Thanks, man." Coop took the weed in the dim light and sucked it deep. The pain dulled. The leg was not imploding. He took another long hit and felt his head floating.

"Name's Jarvis. Tommy Jarvis. From Philly. Where you from, man?"

"Whew! That's good, man. Thanks." He handed back the roach. Jarvis took a drag, bringing it down to almost nothing, then ate the tip. "Call me Coop. From Oregon. Joseph, Oregon."

Just then the swinging doors at the end of the ward bounced open and the corpsman walked in. He flipped the light switch on, blasting the room with artificial light, startling Coop and Jarvis.

"All right. All right! Whoever's smoking pot can cease and desist right now," he ordered. He walked briskly to his med station, sorting through some papers on the counter. He stacked the papers neatly, placed them back on the counter, then turned in the direction of Coop and Jarvis. "I told you, Jarvis, that I didn't want to see any dope smoking in my ward."

Jarvis grinned like he had heard the same shallow warning many times before. "Well, Doc, where do you want to see it then?" Jarvis asked, breaking into a grin.

"You're funny, Jarvis. So funny I forgot to laugh."

"Now that's original," Jarvis said sarcastically, smirking as he rolled his chair toward the med station, stopping just a couple feet short of the corpsman. "You oughta write dialogue for TV shows. You know, like, like *Gunsmoke!*"

The corpsman shook his head, "I'm not BS-ing. No more dope in my ward. I don't give a damn what you do outside my ward, but no reefer in my house or I'll write your ass up. Got it?"

"OK. OK. I'll be cool. It's just my man here." Jarvis wheeled his chair toward Coop. "He's hurting. Can you fix him up?"

"Yeah, yeah. I'll be right down. Now, why don't you make yourself useful and go hang off the ceiling."

"You're cruel, man. Stone cold," Jarvis said, heading toward the swinging doors. He turned back toward Coop. "Oregon, I'll check in with you after chow," he said, pushing himself through the doors.

The corpsman shot up Coop and lifted him so he could empty his bowels into a pan and took it away. Soon breakfast was brought in, and the ward was alive again with patients eating, talking, or shouting complaints.

"Doc. I need something to clean up this mess. Doc, Doc, hey, Doc."

The voices seemed to blend together as Coop floated high on morphine and reefer. He didn't eat. He faded away to a series of wild dreams.

When he woke, it was lunchtime. A physician was standing at the end of his bed reading his chart and making notes. He was dressed in a surgical gown that had bloodstains near the waist and more red on the sleeves. Fatigue was on his face.

"Well, young man, we'll be sending you home. They got you ticketed for Japan, then stateside. Back to the world. How's that sound?"

Coop was too tired to be thankful or acknowledge the doctor with enthusiasm. His mouth was dry, so he just nodded his head and asked for water. For the next of couple days, he slept twenty hours a day, drifting in and out of consciousness. He'd dream himself into the jungle then back home hunting with Granddad. Once he imagined flying through the small town, past stores, shooting up a restaurant with his 16. In another dream, his mother appeared and said she was sorry she died.

The next night he saw the corpsman pull the tube from the face in the bed next to him. Then two guys came in with a stretcher and covered him with a sheet and took him away.

Jarvis rolled in one morning and shook Coop awake. "Wake your ass up, boy. We're goin' home!"

Coop opened his eyes and tried to focus.

"C'mon, Oregon. We're gettin' outta here!"

"Get real!"

"Straight scoop. We slide to Jap-land for a week or two, then to the world, bud."

That afternoon Coop, Jarvis, and twenty other wounded Marines were loaded onto military buses equipped with gurneys and brought to the airport, then carefully transferred to a medically equipped C-130 for their flight to Yokosuka, Japan. As Coop was lifted aboard, he could see, farther down the busy tarmac, another C-130 being filled. Filled with aluminum caskets, headed home.

The wounded lay on stretchers, strapped down, or they sat on web seats attended by a corpsman. Coop felt guilty leaving. And helpless. But the pain was so profound, and at times he wondered what would happen to him.

He spent nine days in Japan before his leg was operated on. The fibula was not healing correctly, so it was re-broken and prepared for a future bone graft.

During his stay, his dependence on morphine grew. Jarvis had been able to smuggle in several party packs of reefer, along with a dozen bottles of Darvon he purchased from a corpsman at 3rd Med in Da Nang. When the morphine high dissipated, they ate Darvon and smoked weed. The hospital was overwhelmed with the influx of wounded, and getting high went undetected.

A new guy in the bed next to Coop had hit a powerful land mine and was blown in half. His legs were gone below the knee, and both hands and forearms were missing. He was blind, and his face was rearranged, a gaping hole where the cheekbone used to be. Coop wanted to cry for the poor son of a bitch. It made his heart sick. He smelled like he was rotting away, and most nights he would hear him gurgle or whimper. Coop wished the guy would just die. Who would want to live like that?

One evening when the ward was dark and sleeping, Jarvis came by Coop's rack. He was on crutches and had a joint in his robe pocket, four Darvon, and a warm can of beer. He pulled a chair up and put his crutches on the floor. Another Marine on the other side of Coop was recovering from a brain operation. A piece of shrapnel the size of a dime had lodged just inside the left temple where the skull is soft. The operation had gone well, although the soldier was partially paralyzed on his right side. He was breathing unlabored, as if he were only in a deep sleep. Before the operation, he had gone into cardiac arrest, which brought a fury of corpsman and doctors thumping on his chest and banging him back to life.

"Say, man, I brought a party," Jarvis said, firing up the joint. "Time to get wasted."

"What about the squid on duty?" Coop asked, referring to the corpsman who was alone at the med station asleep in his chair.

"He's toasted. Heard from a dude at lunch today that the guy's shooting heroin. Anyway, screw it. Fire in the hole," Jarvis said as he toked up.

"Hey, bogart," Coop protested. "Give me some ah that shit."

Jarvis blew smoke in a loud exhale that honked out his nose, then sighed, heavy-eyed. "Whew! That some good blow, Billy Bob." He handed Coop the joint and fished in his robe pocket for the Darvon.

"Speaking of blow, why don't you speak into this microphone," Coop joked, grabbing his cock beneath his robe. They both launched belly laughs.

"Yo, Billy Bob." Jarvis popped the beer can open and took a healthy drink.

"Where'd you get this Billy Bob BS?" Coop asked between deep hits on the joint.

"Be cool, bro. You just seem like a Billy Bob to me with that mustache hanging down, looking weird and stuff. You mind if I call you Billy Bob?"

"You can kiss my Billy Bob," Coop said, and they both broke out in laughter, which woke the corpsman and a couple other beds.

"So tomorrow we outta Dodge," Jarvis said. "We're busting out of Jap-land. Flyin' stateside, my man. And when I get back I'm gonna get me some round eye." He passed the beer to Coop and took back the joint. He licked his fingers, pinched the end of it, and put it in the shirt pocket of his pajamas. "What about you, bro? What's your plan besides lying on your ass and waiting for your leg to heal?"

"Beats me." There was a sudden sadness in Coop's reply. A vacant kind of gap. Tomorrow? He had been on his back for months. He felt anxious and afraid—not of the pain, but the boredom. When he was wounded before, he could still get up and move around, but now he was worried and felt more helpless than before. "Maybe I'll go back to school. I don't know. Maybe I'll try to stay in the Corps. Anyway, give me my meds."

Jarvis laid two Darvon in Coop's hand. He stood up and looked down the ward at the corpsman, sleeping soundly again under the glare of his nightlight. "I'm gonna go back to my rack and pull on my pud for a while. Hang in there, bro."

Coop lay back in the dark and took out two more pills from his shirt pocket that he'd been saving and swallowed them down. He had a shot of morphine an hour before, so with the pills, pot, and beer, his mind and body sank in numbness. His brain was flat and vacant like an endless desert road. He felt no pain and was easing into sleep. The guy with the small hole in his head was quiet, and the Marine who was blown in half wheezed. There were a few coughs in the dark and a sigh of relief from Jarvis's rack. The corpsman snored, his head on his desk, as Coop faded into black. Just as the curtain dropped, he thought he heard someone mumbling.

In the middle of the night, the guy blown in half awoke. He had been in and out of drug-induced sleep and was again aware of where he was. He knew he was a lump. A fucked-up body with no arms or legs. He wanted to die. He tried talking, but his words were little more than a mouth full of spittle. He used all of his strength to scoot to the side of his bed, then roll and tumble, tearing out IVs and tubes, smashing his head on the cement floor.

The thud woke Coop, who turned his head slowly to the noise and looked down. He could see in the dim light the half body of the Marine, lying facedown, moving.

Coop screamed and screamed at the corpsman.

"WAKE UP, YOU MOTHERFUCKER! WAKE UP!"

The corpsman came to and rushed to flip the wall switch. The glare of light destroyed the darkness, and the entire ward was shaken like a barrage of incoming.

The corpsman ran toward Coop, who was still screaming. Jarvis scrambled to his feet, grabbing his crutches. When the corpsman reached Coop and the broken soldier on the floor, blood was pooling at his head. He looked like he was swimming, barely moving the stumps of his arms and legs. The corpsman flew out the doors.

Coop screamed, "You fuck. You fuck!"

Moments later a doctor and male nurse were at the bedside gathering up the half Marine, carrying him in their arms, rushing him out of the ward.

Meanwhile, the Marine with a tiny hole in his head quietly hemorrhaged and died.

14

JT

ALL JT HAD LEFT TO EAT IN the house were two cans of corn and some cranberries. The landlord was complaining about the rent being late, and his car had transmission trouble. It wouldn't go into reverse, and he was too embarrassed to ask Duane if he would take a few minutes and look at it.

After a week of no luck in his job search, he stopped by his dad's apartment. He wanted to borrow a few bucks to pay part of the rent. His dad had been fired from a succession of jobs for drinking and was getting unemployment and help from his sister, Evelyn. His sister gave him money for fixing things at a massage parlor she owned across the street. Dad said the parlor was legitimate, but JT never went into the place and avoided the subject. If Evelyn was running whores, he didn't want to know. Didn't need any more shame to deal with.

The doors were locked. He knocked. No answer. He left a note and got back in his car.

It was a wet and nasty morning with rain coming down sideways when JT got off a downtown bus and headed for the offices of the *Oregon Journal*. They were hiring drivers to deliver advertising proofs to businesses around the area.

The rain and wind felt good lapping at his face. It reminded him of monsoons in the village. The enemy didn't move during heavy rain, and the countryside was at peace. Just before the *Journal* building, he passed a wino, covered with plastic garbage bags, sleeping in a doorway. He had a shopping cart full of clothes and beer bottles tied with a rope to his foot. If it wasn't for Aunt Evelyn, that's where his dad would be.

Approaching the *Journal* building, JT was anxious, unsure, hoping he'd get the job. He pushed through revolving doors into the busy lobby, brushing water from his hair and Navy peacoat. On one side was a long counter with stations for Classified Ads, Archives, Billing, Yesterday's Paper, and Information. On the other side was a guard's desk. A tiny woman with a pushcart of cleaning supplies moved by, stopping to empty a cylinder ashtray. He followed the *Restroom* sign down a side hallway. Inside, it was empty and smelled like lemons. He peed, stood in front of the mirror, and looked at himself, but he didn't look like who he thought he was. He wanted to feel confident, but the rain had soaked his coat and left him cold, disheveled, and doubtful.

"It'll be all right," he said to himself. He rubbed color back into his face, took a deep breath, and shoved through the door.

At the Information counter, a pinched-faced woman in glasses directed him to take the elevator to the fifth floor. As the elevator doors closed, he stood alone, feeling gravity suck at his feet. When the elevator slid open, he stepped into a large room full of reporters, secretaries, desks, and phones ringing. Against the far wall was a desk with a sign taped onto the front of it:

Interviews

He filled out an application and waited in a chair next to the elevator. Soon a middle-aged woman with graying hair pulled back in a bun walked up.

"JT Hadley?" she asked. "Hello, I'm Claire O'Callaghan."

JT stood up nervously and shook her hand. "Hi," he said.

She smiled. "You want to give me that or just crush it?"

JT looked at the crumpled application in his hand. "Oh—sorry," he said. "Yes."

"Come on over and sit down."

Her desk was at the back of the office and had an unobstructed view of most of the activity. Behind her was a wall full of news clippings and a big wooden door, covered with newspaper cartoons and anti-war slogans.

JT sat at the side of Claire's tidy desk. Her lips were the color of plums, and he could smell her perfume. As she read his application, he scoured the room, from the bank of windows that looked out on the street to walls full of maps, awards, and a green chalkboard. Stacks of newspapers sat on gray and chrome-colored desks and long black tables. As people hurried, telephones kept ringing, typewriters banged, and a teletype hummed. Doing something important, JT assumed. Big stories, interesting stuff. Just seeing others working made him feel inferior.

Claire read through his application. She looked as if she had had a long morning and was tired of interviewing. Her back was stiff, shoulders squared, and there was a pallor to her skin that gave evidence of her years.

"You were in Vietnam?" she asked cautiously, looking up from his application. For the slightest moment, her eyes changed, and JT sensed compassion.

"Yes. I came home a few months ago." He watched her closely and could see sadness had turned the corners of her mouth.

"My nephew was in Vietnam," she explained. Claire seemed to get lost in her thoughts as if she were recalling something both she and JT understood. "Can you wait a minute?" she asked.

He could feel his stomach tighten, preparing to be let down.

Getting up from her desk, Claire crossed the room and conferred with an older, heavyset man who was standing next to a window, smoking a thick cigar. As she talked, the man looked toward JT. A few minutes later she was back, sitting down.

"This job isn't much," she said, drifting off. "Did I tell you it was less than full-time?"

"Yes, but I really need this job. I'll work hard. I'll always be here. I just need some work. I'm broke, and any work right now would be great." He felt like he was begging, and it made him feel like a coward.

She looked at his application one more time then smiled weakly. "I'm going to give you a chance. Don't let me down. If you want the job, it's yours. You start tomorrow."

BACK HOME, HE CALLED ASHLEY, EXCITED, AND asked if he could come over.

"I'm glad you got a job," she answered cautiously, "but the baby's not feeling well. She kept me up most of last night."

"Look. Could I watch her while you nap?"

"Not tonight. Maybe you can see Anna this weekend."

In the bathroom JT turned off the light and took a long shower in the dark. He liked the warmth and rhythm of the water. When he was a little boy and his parents would get drunk and fight, he'd shower in the dark. It was his closet, his place to hide. When his mom had her first breakdown, he showered in the dark. And the night before he left for Vietnam, he did the same. The warm water soothed him, helped him feel safe, like his bunker on the side of a hill.

JT woke early, ate a can of cold corn, and caught the 7:30 bus for downtown.

Claire started him unloading trucks in the warehouse, next to where reporters and staff parked their cars. The trucks brought in yesterday's newspapers, which were later picked up by recyclers to be ground up and used again. Loading and unloading the trucks was slow and boring, but the weight and repetition provided him a sense of peace.

Claire came down at lunchtime with additional paperwork for him to sign and to introduce Leif.

"Had lunch yet?" she asked.

"No. But I'm not hungry. Ate a huge breakfast," he lied.

"Leif will get you headed in the right direction, explain the routes, and show you what we expect. I'll talk to you at the end of the day."

She left quickly, leaving JT and Leif standing awkwardly looking at each other.

Leif was tall, thin, with a big head dropped on a long, skinny neck. He wore round, rimless glasses and had a short, bad haircut. He was eating an apple, and a tiny fleck of red lingered on his chin. He had on a white T-shirt with *Boycott Grapes* slapped on the front, hanging just above a picture of Cesar Chavez. When he spoke, he smiled, lips nibbling at each word.

"How you doin'?" Leif asked, extending his hand. JT shook and could tell he had no power.

"Fine," JT said. "I'm glad to be working."

"Well, you may change your mind after you've been here for a while."

Leif's mouth edged toward a good-sized grin, as if he knew some secret that no new guy could hope to understand. His voice was soft, though, and presented no sense of authority, which JT liked.

"I'm just part-time here myself," Leif said. "Going to Reed. Dodging the draft." He laughed. "Know what I mean?"

JT instantly thought he was a dickhead but didn't want to cause problems, so he nodded and gnashed his teeth.

"I'm actually getting sick of school," Leif said chomping on his apple, wiping his mouth with the back of his hand. "We're saving whales on one floor and disarming nukes on the next. And that's just on the weekends." Leif laughed again and tossed the apple in a garbage can placed under a fire alarm.

"Well, I see you're gettin' 'er down," Leif remarked as JT went back to loading the remaining bundles onto the back of the truck. "Learning the fine art of truck loading." Leif laughed.

"Yep," JT tossed the last bundle. "I figure in about ten years I ought to know which end of the truck to throw the papers in." This seemed to please both of them.

"I'm gonna take a whiz, then we'll fly outta here," Leif said.

They got in the company's beat-up yellow Toyota Corolla, Leif driving. Surging down streets past cars parked to the curb in front of retail and office buildings.

"I'm not bragging, now. But I'm about their best driver. Or at least one of the few who doesn't drop acid on day shift. So they let me drive this fine vehicle."

Leif patted the cracked dashboard. There was the smell of old food in the car and a hint of gasoline coming from the floorboards. JT rolled down the passenger-side window.

"This is the only car with a radio," Leif said proudly. "I call her Tweety."

"Yeah. Right."

JT furled his brow, a little annoyed with the humor as Leif shifted uneasily in his seat. They crossed the Morrison Bridge over the Willamette River, a few boats floating below. JT felt like he didn't belong. Wrong country, wrong time. Should be back in the Nam, sitting on the banks of the Da Nang River. Sampans gliding, swimming with Coop, tossing grenades, kids diving for stunned fish. Smoking reefer. Poppin' caps, shootin' up the other side of the river.

They scooted down backstreets, through parking lots and alleys, dropping off advertising proofs at the sprawling United Grocers' Building.

"So you're from Portland?" JT asked, making mental notes of the circuit they were traveling.

"Sort of. Actually, I graduated from Lake Oswego, and now I'm a junior at Reed. You from around here?"

JT knew Lake Oswego was just outside of Portland. The homes were like mansions, and the kids were pricks. He wrestled there once; guy was a fish, just flopped on his back.

"I graduated from Parkrose. Spent time at Mt. Hood Community College before joining the Marines. Just got back from the Nam."

Leif was suddenly quiet. His face stolid. His jaw tightened as if he had swallowed something unpalatable. The joking died. They turned down Milwaukie Street, passing cheap taverns where rednecks and barflies came for eye-openers and sat 'til closing.

Crossing back over the Hawthorne Bridge, they entered the heart of the city and stopped at a red light, when Leif finally spoke.

"Man. I don't mean to give you any heat. I'm sure you went through hell. But I hate this war. Makes me sick to think about all those who died. We never should have gone into Vietnam in the first place."

Leif's words hung there in the air for a moment like a slow curveball that JT wanted to smack. Leif drove along, his face tight and determined, waiting for a reply. But JT had stopped listening. Leif's words struck him. Confused him. Maybe it wasn't all bullshit.

Finally, Leif pulled to the curb and parked in a truck loading zone.

"Hey, man. I know I got it dicked. I'll never go to Vietnam. I also know the war is wrong. Sorry, man, but that's the way I feel."

JT kept his feelings to himself and stared out the side window. He could kill him.

They delivered advertising proofs to sporting goods stores and department stores and office buildings with names and businesses JT had never heard of. By the end of the afternoon, they were back pushing through five o'clock traffic, heading for the warehouse. As they drove along, there was a heavy silence.

THE APARTMENT WAS DARK, COLD, AND EMPTY as JT stepped inside after his first day of work. He went to the light switch and flipped it, but there was nothing. He tried the kitchen lights, more of the same. No electricity. Damn! How was he going to see? Was a breaker or fuse out? He found a candle and some matches and melted wax so the candle would stand up inside a tuna fish can. He checked the fuse box on the back porch, but everything looked OK. He could see Duane upstairs had a light on and he heard Pearl's TV crackling in the basement.

He sorted through the mail that he had ignored for days, dreading he would find a bill not paid. Damn! A cutoff notice from the electric company. It was only twelve dollars. *The bastards! What the hell was wrong with them? You'd think they would've called and given a warning or something. Jesus!* He was furious and wanted to go down there and kick somebody's ass. *Those rich bastards sit up there in their air-conditioned little boxes like officers or some shit, and a guy is late with a bill, and they don't give a damn where he's been or what he's been through.*

Now what was he going to do? No TV, no radio, and no way to cook anything. He was hungry, so he ate another can of corn, called Ashley, but no one was home. Tired, he crashed early. He lay back and thought about the day. He had a new job, and that was good, but he was broke and his wife must hate him. He wanted to hold Anna. She loved him. Just as his eyes closed, he could hear Duane yelling upstairs and the sound of breaking glass.

The next morning the bus was late, and JT worried that he wouldn't make it to work on time. When it finally came, it was nearly empty.

The driver greeted him with a big, "Happy Thanksgiving."

"What did you say?"

"I said, 'Happy Thanksgiving'."

"Oh. Yeah...thanks."

Shocked, JT walked down the aisle to a seat in the back of the bus. He hadn't realized it was Thanksgiving and hadn't talked to anyone in days, except for Leif and Claire. Maybe he wasn't supposed to work. With Mom and Dad divorced, Mom was probably over at Grandma's, and Dad had to be at Aunt Evelyn's. It'd been years since he'd celebrated with them. Last Thanksgiving, Kilo got rocketed.

The bus left him a few blocks from the *Journal* building. It was cold as rain slapped his backside. When he got to work and started to punch in, the guard stopped him.

"Hey, buddy. Ad Service is closed for the day. Didn't Claire tell you?"

JT mumbled and walked out of the building feeling foolish and wanting to cry. He didn't think his life would be like this. As a boy, he was going to be a great baseball player. Play center field for the New York Yankees, like his hero Mickey Mantle. He even slept with his bat and glove as a kid.

When Ashley came along, his dreams got bigger. Someday they would marry, and he'd be throwing fastballs in the bigs. He went to a junior college to play ball and thought his dream would happen. Then life changed. Ashley got pregnant. He dropped out of college. With no job and no one to turn to, he joined the Corps. He thought he would buy time and come back better than when he left. But now he had nothing, not even Ashley. He walked seven miles in the rain to a dark, empty house.

JT cashed his paycheck on Friday at Charlie's, even though Charlie had signs all over the place declaring *No Checks Period!* Bought a package of hot dogs, buns, and toilet paper and thanked Charlie, who snorted back in a friendly way. He stopped at the drugstore, paid his utility bill, but was told the electricity couldn't be turned on until tomorrow. He roasted dogs by candlelight, then called Ashley and asked if he could see Anna. It felt more strained each time he heard her voice. Like they were both dying from an incurable disease. She was distant.

"OK. You can come by and pick her up tomorrow." Click.

Well, at least he could see his little girl and hold her. Maybe he could talk Ashley into joining them for ice cream. With a few bucks left in his pocket, JT felt confident again and decided to call Brad. Maybe they could go downtown and hang out or catch a flick. But Brad was busy with Mary, going over to her mother's to talk about buying a house.

He was lonely and didn't feel like sitting alone in the dark or trying to sneak into a tavern, so he shoved his car out of the driveway and headed to his dad's.

He walked through the back door, screen banging, into the tiny kitchen, bumping a small table as he passed.

"Da-a-ad. You home?" he shouted. But no answer.

Dishes were stacked neatly on the counter, next to empty wine bottles and an angel food cake covered with clear wrap. He lifted the wrap and pinched off a piece then opened the refrigerator. On one shelf were two cans of beer and a bottle of white wine in a green half-gallon jug. On the other shelf were a soda, lunch meat, carrots, and a plate of meatloaf, uncovered, grease whitened like paste. He shook his head, grabbed a beer, and pinched off another piece of cake.

The front room was empty, cold, TV quiet, coffee table full of papers, curtains drawn. There was a small crack in the window, and the wind was whistling through. He sat in the overstuffed rocker, wooden lever on the side, and pulled it to kick up his feet. The room was clean except for hunting magazines scattered on the floor. Took a hit off the beer, set it on the coffee table, and picked up a handful of loose papers. *What's this?* Pink past-due notices on rent and electricity, a yellow ticket for drunk driving, and a tattered picture of his uncle Chuck in his uniform standing next to an Army tank.

He looked at the photo and turned it over. On the back were the words *Jack's tank.*

He barely remembered his dad talking about the war, or anything, really.

He tossed the papers on the table. Only thing he could recall was how his dad used to go away on Veterans Day and come home drunker than before. But his dad's brother, Chuck, was the big asshole. Tormented JT as a boy. Stuck him in a freezer one time when they were alone. Twisted his arm, kicked him in the butt.

"You little pussy. What are you crying about, boy?"

He was always drunk and mean. He'd come into JT's dad's auto body shop, loud and intoxicated. Always picking on JT.

"I'll make the little fucker tough."

JT finished his beer, pulled another from the fridge, flopped back on the couch, fixated on Chuck. Used to have a monkey he'd carry on his shoulder and bring it around all the time. Monkey wore a stupid little hat and chewed sunflower seeds. It bit kids, too. Chuck thought it was hilarious.

Chuck was a certifiable prick. And that Christmas when JT was only five, he had been hanging out at his dad's shop, sitting on some tires in the back room, looking at baseball cards that he carried in a shoebox. The light was dim and the room was smoky. One end was full of shelves packed with auto parts; the other was where his dad and Chuck and a couple of other men were drinking and telling dirty jokes. On the walls were calendars of naked women lying on the hoods of shiny cars or half-dressed in work overalls, teeth flashing, their perfect breasts showing.

"So this big-titted bitch was walking in front of the shop," Chuck explained, a monkey on his shoulder munching seeds. "When all of a sudden, she slips and falls on her ass in the snow."

He took a drink from the bottle and passed it around. "I'm watching and she's moaning and can't get outta the snow."

"So what'd you do?"

"Humped her like a dog before she got cold."

They all laughed. Then Chuck was coming at him.

"Speaking of pussy, lookit here. Look at this little pussy," Chuck said, grabbing JT's arm. He bent down, his foul breath in JT's face. "Come on, boy, hit your Uncle Chuck in the gut. Come on, show me what ya got." Chuck's big hand cuffed him on the side of the head and punched him in the arm. "You ever see an Indian rope burn, boy?" He grabbed JT's bare wrist and squeezed and twisted until it turned red. "Come on and cry, you sissy."

Still furious at the memory, JT kicked the table and got up. His dad had done nothing to stop him. Fuck 'em both.

Down the hall, the bedroom was dark and smelled musty and wet, like cigarettes and old socks. The bed was unmade, clothes on a chair in the corner. A picture of his grandmother hung on the wall, and beer bottles gathered on a stand next to the bed. An ashtray overflowed. His eyes were surveying, framing, figuring out how his dad lived. Never really went into his bedroom before. It was depressing. He walked into the bathroom and started to piss, but there was blood in the toilet. What the hell? He noticed prescription bottles on the sink from the Veterans Hospital for pain and constipation. And more blood on a towel.

JT stood in the bathroom, looking at the blood on the towel. Shaken, he left slowly through the kitchen, screen door slapping.

As HE CLIMBED THE STAIRS BACK TO his apartment, he was thinking about his dad, the blood, Vietnam. He stopped quietly at his door, listening. Slowly eased into the kitchen. It was dark as he crossed the floor to the table with the candle. But he didn't light it. He stood in the middle of the kitchen perfectly still. For over ten minutes, he stood not moving, trying to recall what it was like to be in the jungle. His senses heightened. He could hear the refrigerator hum. Duane walked across the floor above. Outside a car splashed. His eyes could see clearly, and he listened and listened until he heard their voices crying, his own heart beating.

Saturday morning, JT grabbed the hot dogs and buns and pushed his Volkswagen out of the driveway. It was a pain in the ass not to have reverse, but now that he was making money, he'd get it fixed.

He drove toward Ashley's, stopping to put two bucks in the tank. He was nervous as he parked in front of the house, making sure he could leave without backing up. Ashley met him at the door but was cool as she passed Anna, the stroller, and a diaper bag over to him.

"Can you come, Ashley? It would be fun. I'll buy you a Green River just like the old days."

"No, I need a break. I've got Anna twenty-four hours a day. You're just the Saturday dad. Be back by five."

Saturday dad? All she ever did was guilt-trip him and screw with his mind. *Bitch!* He drove to Laurelhurst Park with Anna in the back, snuggled safe in her car seat, gurgling at her dad's banter. It was one of those rare winter days, when the sun is warm and the sky incredibly blue. Most of the trees had cast their leaves, sprinkling them on lawns and sidewalks in wet blankets of gold, brown, and shades of magenta.

The air was cool and crisp as he pushed the stroller over gentle hills and down paved pathways. They rolled past basketball courts where guys in shorts and stocking caps shot baskets under leafless trees. People strolling by smiled as JT and Anna worked their way along the edge of the duck pond, toward a picnic table with benches. They stopped to feed the ducks.

JT softened when he was with Anna. He felt calm, good, and proud to be a father. He held her in his arms, tossing bread in the water as ducks splashed, quacked, scurried, and snapped. Teetering on tiny legs, Anna stood by the pond, giggling, eyes full of amazement.

He bought ice cream and hot chocolate from a vending truck and laughed when Anna plopped her cone on her head. He cleaned her and kissed her, then they played on the swings. He held Anna in his lap and changed her diaper on a small blanket near the pond, watching ducks feed and fuss.

When the day was done, he returned her to Ashley. JT stood just inside the threshold of the front door, memories flooding. He looked around the room. It was the same. The same chairs and tables, pictures on the walls. The same couch where he once made love to Ashley as her parents slept in the next room.

"We had a great time today. I wish you would have come," he said, placing the last of Anna's things on the floor next to Ashley. "It was fun, but we missed you."

Ashley was smiling but silent.

"What did you do on Thanksgiving?" he asked, wondering if he'd been missed.

"Not much. Woody took us to North's Chuck Wagon for the buffet. It's his favorite. With you gone and Mom not wanting to cook, it was all right. How about you? Did you see your mom?"

"No. And I had a terrible Thanksgiving. Can't you just come home?"

She didn't reply.

"I'm sick of this. I miss you. I love you. Don't you care?" As he spoke, his body tightened. "Jesus Christ, can't you answer me!"

In that instant, he knew he had blown it again. He could see her back away, frightened, holding Anna tightly, and all of the apologies in the world would not erase her fear.

Ashley's mom rushed in. "Is everything all right?"

This just seemed to trigger him more. He was raging inside. Didn't either of them understand? He loved Ashley. He'd die for her.

"No!" he said. "Nothing's right." He turned and walked out of the house feeling defeated. Hopeless.

On the way home, he stopped at a tavern and drank beer after beer until his brain was numb and his body was numb. *I ought to kill her mom*, he thought. At home, he puked and passed out on the front room floor.

WORK WENT WELL. CLAIRE CHECKED IN ON him from time to time, but he was pretty much on his own, which suited him fine. Some days there would be big ad inserts, and he would work with a crew in an assembly line stuffing papers and stacking them. Afterward he'd go home to an empty house and drink beer or smoke pot. He was always at work on time and always did push-ups and sit-ups and almost every day he would run. Sometimes he'd hang out with Duane, and sometimes Brad would stop by and they'd get loaded and cruise downtown.

The days and weeks passed, and Ashley would talk to him only briefly on the phone. Some days he'd pick up Anna and stop by his mom's or dad's. But when he went to his dad's, he could see sickness in his eyes and his body shrinking.

A FEW DAYS BEFORE CHRISTMAS, ASHLEY AGREED to go with him to his mother's house for Christmas Eve. She told him she was glad he was working but knew he was still getting loaded with Brad and drinking all the time. JT, though, was overwhelmed with hope and promised he'd quit if she'd only come home. They were going to be together again, just like he had envisioned for all those months while he was in the Nam. It seemed so simple. They were going to be together like before, a family, and be happy just like he planned.

On Christmas Eve, he got off early, cashed his check, and went shopping. With only a little time and less money, he went from store to store, running up escalators and across crowded department store floors, looking for gifts. It was hard to find something nice that he could afford. What would Ashley like? And Anna?

He crowded by last-minute shoppers, past bell-ringing Santa Clauses and dancing bears. Carolers sang, and the lights and music all felt overwhelming. He finally bought Anna a dress and a wagon. He bought Ashley a bowl to replace the one he broke when he tossed groceries across the kitchen. A note in the bowl explained that he loved her and was sorry, but as he drove toward their home, he worried that it was all wrong.

JT picked Ashley and Anna up on time and drove to his mom's. He really hated being around his mom because she was always negative, saying bad things about his father. When he got there, the only ones around were his mom and his younger brother, Jim, who was obviously ripped, eyes glassed, head bobbing. But since Jim was Mom's good son, it was overlooked. They exchanged presents and his mom played with Anna.

"You better not grow up lookin' like your daddy," she said, bouncing Anna on her knee. "You want to look like your mama. She's got the looks in your family." Her comment cut JT, reminding him of all the times she said his brother Jimmy was her handsome boy.

"So have you seen your drunk of a dad?" his mom asked.

"No. And I wish you'd quit calling him a drunk."

"Well, he is a drunk."

"I know. But do we have to talk about it now?"

"Now's as good a time as any."

"Well, I don't want to talk about it. OK?"

"Suits me. So are you going to stay married or not?" his mom asked, handing Anna back to Ashley. "I told you both you were too young."

"Mom. Forget it. We got to go."

They packed up and said their good-byes at the door. As JT was cutting across the grass to his car, his mom called out, "If you see that old drunk, tell him to send me some money."

It was quiet as they drove away, Anna bundled up in her car seat in the back and Ashley stiff and uneasy.

"God, I hate going over there," JT said. "She thinks Jim is perfect. Her handsome boy. Her good boy. Wouldn't she flip out if she knew he was zonked on acid?"

"I just want to go home now," Ashley said. "Just take us back to Mom's."

When he heard her words, he snapped inside. Not with anger or an adrenaline surge. It was more like he couldn't believe her words. A desperate unwillingness settled inside.

"We're going to our house! We're a family. We're going to our house," he said. And as he spoke, the weeks without his family felt crushing. Tears welled in his eyes. "Don't you love me? Don't you love me?"

She was silent. Afraid.

"Ashley . . . don't you love me anymore?"

She was quiet for a long time. Anna asleep in the back. A light shower of sleet pelted the windshield. The sound of the engine filled the darkness.

"No, JT. I'm sorry. I don't love you anymore."

In the war, he had learned not to be close to others. He had learned how to shut off feeling so that he could go on. But when he heard her voice say those words, he was destroyed.

"No! No! No! That's not true." He shook his head, sobbing. "You love me, and we're a family. We're going home, and things are gonna work out. And don't ever say that again. You love me. We're a family. We're going home."

Ashley didn't answer as they drove past homes lit up for Christmas Eve.

This would not happen. He would not lose his family. He had the strongest will to survive. He could survive with Doc laying on him being shot again and again. He could survive with Coop in the middle of the rice field. He had survived his own wounds, being shot, stabbed, and a bout with malaria so bad he almost died. Surely he could survive this. He could force his will on Ashley, and his marriage would survive just as he had. He would have his family. He would save his dream.

They pulled up in front of their apartment. He could see Duane's Christmas tree in the window upstairs. Even Pearl had lights in her basement window. He had cleaned the house, set up a small tree, and made it perfect for his family. He went up the steps to the porch and opened the door. Then he went back to help Ashley.

"I'll take Anna inside. You get her things," Ashley said, heading for the porch.

"OK. I'll do that."

He felt a sudden sense of joy. It was working. She wasn't arguing. She was coming home. He gathered the presents and quickly took them inside, then went out to the car for the baby's things. But when he went back to the house, shut the door, and called for Ashley, the house was empty, and she was gone.

15

Hawkeye

24 January 1969

To: Private First Class Jesse James Joseph Collins
*   3/9, Kilo Company, 3rd Platoon*

Re: Meritorious Promotion and Award of Bronze Star

Private First Class Jesse James Joseph Collins is herein meritoriously
promoted to Lance Corporal and awarded the Bronze Star with
Combat V for valor under fire, during an engagement with numerically
superior enemy soldiers in the Quang Tri Province, Republic of
Vietnam, on 3 January 1969.

During this engagement, Private First Class Collins showed
initiative and courage under extremely hostile conditions. Confronted
by heavy small arms and mortar fire, Private First Class Collins rallied
his fellow troops, moving them to a safe location and at the same time
delivered rifle fire that did effectively suppress the enemy's assault.

His bravery under this most difficult situation resulted in several
enemy kills and saved Marine lives. His dedication and unflinching
devotion to duty reflect proudly on the Marine Corps tradition.

Commanding General W.T. Walt
3rd Marine Division
Headquarters

HAWKEYE READ THE AWARD LETTER, RECALLING EVERY sight, sound, and movement of that night. He could see Sleepy thrashing through the bush and hear his voice crying. He remembered the sound and the smell of gunfire and explosions and how his heart nearly burst through his chest. Words like courage and bravery did not seem appropriate. That night he'd felt fear and shame for Sleepy's death. He was ashamed he didn't save him. It didn't matter that all those around him believed he had been heroic.

He folded the commendation carefully and slipped it into an envelope and mailed it with a note to his mother. She'd be proud of him. With his promotion came extra pay. He was taking home a base salary of $138 a month with an additional $60 for combat pay, so the extra stripe would add about thirty bucks. Of that, $50 went to her. Maybe it would help. At least he was headed in the right direction. He was going to make a success out of this opportunity, no matter what.

Kilo Company was at LZ Stud, a firebase near Route 9, a major road running out of Dong Ha. They were resting and recuperating, manning lines but no patrols. Doc Bittner was back from 3rd Med, twenty-four stitches in his head, insisting he was all right. Flowers was back, too. His wounded ear was not as serious as Doc's injury. Moose and Little Mike were on R&R in Bangkok screwing anything that walked, and so the squad was reduced to Ski, Doc, Flowers, Hawkeye, and Andy from New York, a cherry to the Nam. Andy was quiet, kept to himself. Hawkeye thought he looked like a hamster: pointed nose, beady eyes, no lips. He even ate hunched over, eyes darting from side to side.

The sun was an orange fireball stamped on blue, beating down on Hawkeye's tent made from a stretched-out poncho. Flowers was crashed inside next to him. He just got back from doing a couple of jays with some brothers from 2nd Platoon. Every afternoon and evening, a group got together inside a black-power bunker next to the tank destroyer, the M-50 Ontos with six 106 cannons. They were firing up joints and listening to jams on a car battery rigged up reel-to-reel. They'd wear sunglasses and rant on about oppression, pigs, and Whitey's war. It was BS as far as Hawkeye was concerned, so he steered clear, stayed straight. But Flowers would come back stoned, calling Hawk a "fucking Oreo." Then pass out like a big dog.

At first light, Kilo Company was saddled up and waiting at the helipad. Fog layered across the mountains, and a light mist licked the air. There was the smell of the jungle and a clean sort of wetness to it all. Everything looked gray. It was quiet throughout the company. A heavy feeling of doom sat in each soldier's belly.

Rumors ran wild. "There's hardcore NVA battalions with tanks and planes," and "you best write that last letter home 'cause we're goin' into hell, brother."

As the platoon waited for the choppers, Ski passed out machine-gun ammo to the squad, and Doc Bittner gave Moose another shot of penicillin. Andy was spitting sunflower seeds, which didn't escape Hawkeye's observation.

"Check it out, Flowers," Hawkeye suggested, cutting through the profound stillness. He was standing a few feet away from Andy, who was lying back on his pack. "Andy-man is consuming rabbit food like it's goin' outta style."

"What's the deal, Andy? Your old lady send you that?" Hawkeye asked.

Andy finished the last few seeds, shoveling them in his mouth like a hamster, and said quietly, "Yep. Mom sent 'em."

"Well, you tell yer mama she best stop sendin' that funky bullshit and send us cookies or candy or sumpin' decent, dude," Flowers interjected, adjusting his shades, walking over to Andy. "Ain't nobody I ever knowed, 'cept you, A-man, likes that bullshit. You hear what I'm sayin', Hawk?"

They laughed out loud and tapped hands.

The fog melted and Hueys started rolling in, *whap-whap-whapping*, descending to the tarmac. Kilo's troops boarded through side doors, passed the gunner, and sat on web benches. The choppers lifted, base dissolved, and all they saw was jungle below, a washed-out, pewter sky, and wind whapping at the soldiers.

They circled a field of dry rice paddies a hundred meters from the Perfume River. A thousand meters away was a large village, and past it was the backside of Hue and the walls of the Citadel. Hawkeye's squad was the third chopper going in, and like the first two, caught a few rounds of small arms fire.

"Hot LZ!" Ski yelled across the chopper and over the whine of wind and rotors rushing. "Hawk, bust out fifty meters when we land. Set your team in."

Hawkeye leaned forward in his seat, the butt of his rifle on the floor, barrel up, magazine snapped in place, safety on.

"Right! Got it!"

Their birds landed as rounds cracked. Choppers emptied, lifted, and the firing stopped.

Hawkeye ran his team out and set them down in a half circle, with the bipod 60 in the center. Andy was carrying the radio and dropped to his belly, awkward as a calf stumbling. He was trembling. Pee ran down his leg. Doc landed next to him, followed by Moose, Little Mike, and Flowers.

"Fuck this shit," Flowers blurted out to no one in particular.

No more fire as the squad spread out on their bellies. Ski, meanwhile, walked the perimeter making sure all was well. Behind the squad, more Marines landed with no resistance until the rest of the company was in place.

Kilo quickly formed a perimeter. Each fighting position had rifles, machine guns, or grenade launchers. Some soldiers carried LAWs or M-79s; others brought belts and green metal boxes of machine-gun ammo, and each toted a sixty-pound pack and wore a flak jacket and helmet.

The company was ordered to dig in and be available for support as needed. Within an hour, they formed a solid perimeter made up of fighting holes and machine-gun emplacements, with a command post in the middle of it all. In the direction of Hue, they could hear sporadic rifle fire and see gunships working. When the choppers disappeared, planes roared overhead, passing over the village and dropping a load of napalm on the base of the mountains west of the city. There was no noise, but Hawkeye could see smoke rising. An hour later they were told to fill their holes and move closer to the ville.

They dug in again, and just as they settled, orders came to pick up and move. This time the company was sent back toward the Perfume, where they set up in one staggered stretch along the banks of the river.

"I'm sick ah this bullshit," Flowers snarled. "Move. Bust yer ass diggin' then fuckin' movin' again. You can bet yer sweet ass sum lifer son of a bitch thought up this cocksucker. You know what I'm sayin', Hawk?"

Hawkeye nodded with understanding and said, "One thing you can always count on is you can't count on anything." He was pleased with his observation. "You see the brass is just lookin' at maps and stickin' pins and moving 'em around. So they set up a tentative objective and plan and forecast all day long. They pop a pin wherever they please and think they're brilliant. What they're really doing is reacting to the enemy's intention. So I'd say the NVA must be choreographing this war."

Flowers shook his head in disbelief. "You're a smart muther."

Kilo Company finished digging in, ate C-rats, and waited for night to fall. There was a tension in the air that dried throats and made soldiers talk nervously. Andy, though, kept to himself. His pants had dried but the smell hung around and increased his embarrassment. Moose was still fired up, complaining to Doc about the clap. Ski was figuring radio watch. Flowers and Hawkeye were sitting on a poncho playing spades with Banger and Cueball from 1st Platoon.

Banger, a black hillbilly from Arkansas, was shuffling cards. Cueball was from Detroit. They were part of the black-power gig back in the rear. Cueball was kind of the leader because he was big, angry, and intelligent—what Flowers called a bad motherfucker.

"What I wouldn't do for sum righteous pussy 'bout now," Flowers said, dropping a trump on Banger's ace.

"Pussy?" Cueball snorted. "We're 'bout to go toe to toe with Luke the Gook and the blood's talkin' pussy. Flowers, you ain't had no pussy since pussy had you."

The group exploded with laughter. They played cards as daylight turned and shimmered toward darkness.

"Hawkeye," Cueball asked, "how is it you an' yer boy here always be kickin' our ass?"

Before Hawkeye could answer, Flowers butted in. "Because he's got one of them photograph minds. Like his brain be takin' pictures."

"You tellin' me this here dude be cheating on me?"

Cueball's face twisted into a scowl.

"No, asswipe," Flowers replied. "He's just rememberin' every damn card your silly ass be playin'. That's all."

"Bullshit," Cueball said as he gathered up the cards and wrapped a rubber band around them. "Hawkeye, what's this fool talkin' 'bout?"

"I just remember things, that's all," Hawkeye said. "It's no big deal."

"See, boy," Cueball snapped at Flowers. "You're full ah bullshit."

"Come on, Hawk," Flowers said. "Show this monkey sum brain power."

Flowers grabbed Hawkeye's pack and started going through it.

"What ya doing, boy?" Cueball asked.

"Here. Here. Look at this shit." Flowers waved a copy of Moby Dick, as if its contents held some secret inside. Hawkeye shrugged, bemused.

Cueball failed to see the significance. "I know all about that Moby Dick, but his dick ain't half as big as mine."

Banger and Cueball started laughing.

"You fools. You don't know shit," Flowers said, pounding the book in his hand. "This here's all about this big old whale and—"

"I know. I know. It's in the Bible, and some guy gets swallowed," Banger interjected excitedly.

Flowers was getting frustrated and irritated. He banged the book in his hand. "You're both dumber than snot. This is about this big fuckin' whale and this one-legged guy tryin' to catch the bastard."

"So what, limp dick," Cueball said.

"The point, my man, is Hawkeye done read the whole damn thing!" Flowers held the thick, tattered paperback high above his head like a Baptist minister preaching fire and brimstone.

"Big fuckin' deal," Cueball said. "Any fool can read a book. Even Banger here can read a book if he gits his mind to it." He reached across the poncho and slapped Banger's leg with the back of his hand. Darkness was coming quick. "My point is, Hawk done read the book and remembers every damn thing he read. Every single damn word!"

Hawkeye sat shaking his head, embarrassed.

Cueball, meanwhile, looked at Flowers. A big grin lit up his face. He reached in his pant pocket, pulled out a wad of military money. "I got five bucks says you're bullshitting. Gimme that book. Now, you said every word? I'll turn a page, read a little, then you tell me what comes next. OK, Hawk?"

"I'm not going to do some mental jerk-off," Hawkeye protested. "I'm racing out. Flowers, keep your yap shut."

"See! I told ya!" Cueball said, grin busting out his mouth. "He's got 'bout as much happenin' upstairs as the rest of you burr heads."

Hawkeye wanted to let it slide, but he couldn't. He began quoting favorite passages.

"'Call me Ishmael... Whenever I find myself growing—'"

"Growing tits!" Banger said under his breath.

"'—growing grim about the mouth; whenever it is a damp, drizzly November in my soul—'" Hawkeye stopped and said, "I like

'damp, drizzly November in my soul.' And I like Melville's description of the sea: 'waves rolled by like scrolls of silver.' That's in the
middle of the book. I liked Captain Ahab and Starbuck and Stubb
and Flask. But I sure don't remember every word."

Cueball sat bug-eyed. Banger was amazed.

"Despite what Flowers says," Hawkeye continued, "I don't remember every word. I just remember the phrases and passages that
caught my attention."

"Well, damn it. Hawkeye, you're one smart dude." Cueball's eyes
gleamed. "With a brain like that, we ought to be able to make some
money somehow. You ought to be on one of them game shows
where they asks questions and shit. You know what I'm sayin'? You
can win big money or a boat or a trip somewheres."

"Yep, he already won an all-expense-paid trip to this puke
bucket," Flowers cracked.

That night a drizzle started, and an hour later there was firing
all around. The listening post got fragged, and a guy from Missouri
was killed. By 3:00 a.m. the company was on full alert. At 3:20 the
sound of shooting came from the village to their front, followed by
a series of explosions. More firing. It went on for twenty minutes.

About 4:00 a.m. a squad of NVA stumbled in front of Hawkeye's position. Flares shot overhead, and for three minutes his squad
erupted—Moose and Little Mike rattling the gun, Flowers, Hawkeye, Ski, and Andy firing and throwing frags. When it was over, six
enemy lay dead, caught in the floating light not fifty meters away.

"We kicked ass big time, bro," Flowers said, joy in his voice,
a smile on his mouth. He was standing in a hole with Hawkeye,
pointing his 16 toward the sky, flares popping overhead. "Those
fuckin' gooks. We're gonna roast 'em 'n' toast 'em. We're the mean
machine. We're bad motherfuckers!"

Hawkeye was excited but outwardly calm as he watched the last
parachute flare drift lazily away, landing in the river. Dark again.
Hawkeye's mind raced, wondering what kind of lives had just ended.

A half hour later, an RPG smashed into the end of Kilo, farthest from Hawkeye, down toward the river—one killed, three wounded, medics frantic, night choppers taking bodies away.

Just before dawn, a light was noticed coming from the village. Then another, followed by AK-47s cracking. It went on for six minutes. Steady. Then a salvo of small arms fire erupted all along Kilo's line, green and red tracers trading back and forth. Soon mortars dropped on their position, tail fins scattered, shrapnel spraying. Across the river, three 122 rockets were launched and passed overhead, exploding on the other side of the platoon's position.

Then it was quiet again.

"GEEZ! What's happenin', Hawk?" Flowers blurted out nervously, his voice not as confident as it was an hour before. Flares shot up and popped, and chutes danced. In the flickering light, the six bodies out front were just stacks of debris, hardly human.

"This is Tet," Hawkeye said firmly. "Charles is runnin' wild with peace talks goin' on in Paris, trying to influence all that negotiating goin' down."

"I don't give a rat's ass 'bout no peace talks, Hawk. I jus' wanna get my young butt home in one piece." Moose fired up the gun again, Little Mike feeding it with the belt.

"CEASE FIRE! CEASE FUCKIN' FIRE!" Ski yelled from a couple holes over. Then he ran in a crouch toward Moose's hole. "WHO IN THE HELL SAID TO FIRE?"

Moose shrugged his big shoulders as light from another flare made his sweat glow. "No one, Ski. I just thought I saw—"

"Listen, dumb shit, you know better than that. Every time the gun opens up, it gives away our position. Don't fucking fire until I tell you to, and if you do, there had better be bodies, or you're going to get your balls cut off. Is that clear?" Moose grunted and nodded. Ski eased up. "Show some discipline, dickhead. Shit."

Morning came full of haze and drizzle. Across the paddies, a plume of smoke drifted from the village. The air was heavy and wet and smelled foul. There was no wind. Hawkeye, Ski, Flowers, and Doc searched the bodies, checking for weapons, booby traps, and papers. Andy stood by, radio on his back, not wanting to look. Six NVA in new uniforms, sandals, and packs were nourishing the morning flies. Rigor mortis and bloating could wait for the sun. At one body, a rancid smell festered, bowels shot open. Flowers kicked an arm, then a leg.

"Cool it!" Hawkeye demanded. "They're dead."

"Fuck 'em!" Flowers said, but moved on, stopping to look carefully at a blown-open head.

One body had a small grappling hook stuck in his pack with a rope attached, as though someone was trying to pull him from the battlefield.

"That's some freaky shit," Flowers noted, motioning toward the hook and twenty feet of rope.

Doc Bittner hesitated at one soldier who looked as if he had crawled off and was twenty yards from the others. He bent down. The soldier was lying on his belly, blood caked on the side of his head. There was a stain of red, still fresh, at his back and a small hole in his green shirt where a bullet had entered. His calf had also been shot but was wrapped with a yellow cloth and knotted like a tourniquet.

"Hold it. Hold it." Doc froze. "Ski. We've got a live one!"

Ski, Hawk, Flowers, and Andy were startled.

"Let me cap 'em," said Flowers, racing over.

"Bullshit!" Doc jumped up, his mouth twisted in anger. He was in Flowers's face, threatening. "Nobody's going to shoot this man. Back off, Flowers. Back the fuck off."

"Settle down, Doc," Ski said pushing between them. "Check him for booby traps then let's roll him over and take a look. See what we got."

The soldier was facedown, arms extended as if he were floating in water, drifting, legs slack, barefoot. Carefully, Doc turned him over. The man was barely breathing, an exit wound in his chest.

Dirt had been rubbed in the wound as if to cauterize it. The combination helped control the chest wound. The cool weather kept his body temperature down. Doc touched his fingertips to the man's throat to feel a pulse and check his watch.

"The guy's a tough son-of-a-gun," Doc said. "We can save him, but he's lost a lot of blood and needs to be medevacked."

"Doc, I ain't requesting a bird for no fuckin' gook so you can forget it!" Ski asserted, shaking his head. "No fucking way."

"We can't just leave him here and let him die."

"Why the fuck not? He's just a gook," Flowers said.

"And you're a dickwad, but we're gonna let that slide," Hawkeye interrupted. "His war's over. Let him skate."

"I still say we pop the little cocksucker," Flowers said excitedly. "Put 'im outta his misery. Come on, Ski, you're head honcho. Let's waste this little fuck." Flowers hopped in place, psyching himself up like he was some boxer bouncing in the corner, ready to come out.

Ski was quiet for a moment, probably figuring the guy was gonna kick it anyway, no matter what happened.

"Listen. Maybe the dude's got some info. Let the LT decide," Hawkeye suggested.

"Hawk's right," Ski said. "Flowers, go fuck yourself. You got plenty of killin' to look forward to. The gook slides. Doc, you work on the bastard, and I'll check with the LT to see if we can get a bird. We'll call the little fart a prisoner of war. That ought to be worth a couple extra beers, maybe two days at China Beach."

Ski got on the radio, receiver to his ear, while Andy stood stolidly by taking everything in. His face was placid; his eyes were flat. The bodies and the packs were searched as Doc cleared the wounded soldier's mouth and stuck a tube of morphine in his leg.

The 3rd Platoon's commander, Lieutenant Neal, came up to supervise.

"Good work, gentlemen," Neal said, surveying the dead and wounded. He took the best-looking enemy rifle, had his radioman carry it, and called in five kills, five weapons, eight chi-coms, and a POW.

"LT?"

"What is it, Ski?"

"Any chance we can score some extra beer for the dinks we got? And maybe a little skate time?"

"I'll get you beer on the next drop, but the CO says no extra R&Rs. We're up to our ass in alligators. NVA runnin' all over the country. This is a big push. They're trying to take Hue. Right now there's enemy in the Citadel. So the answer is no. But I'm going to write you guys up for a citation."

"Fuck the citation. Just get me outta here," Flowers mumbled louder than a whisper.

Hawkeye jabbed him with his elbow.

Neal's mouth tightened and eyes narrowed. "What was that, soldier?" he asked.

"Nothin', LT," Hawkeye said. "Flowers is just copping an attitude. He's hoping he can find the girl Moose's been bangin'."

That loosened the group up. Everybody laughed.

"Ski, get your squad ready to move out," the LT ordered. "Fill in your holes. Third Platoon's going to sweep that ville at 0730. I want your squad on point. We'll play it by ear. Any questions? I've got the grid coordinates zeroed in. If we need to, we can blow the ville."

The LT and his radioman left, as did Ski and Andy, while a group from 2nd Platoon came to haul off the bodies. Doc cleaned the wound on the NVA soldier's chest a bit and put the plastic bag from the battle dressing over the hole and secured it with medical tape. He cut off the wounded soldier's shirt and worked an IV into his slender arm. Hawkeye held the bag of plasma above the wounded enemy as they waited for a chopper. The soldier's head wound was superficial but needed stitches; a bandage would have to do. The leg wound was clean and through the calf and easily bandaged. The chest wound was by far the worst, causing him to gurgle and wheeze as he struggled for air. The plastic helped.

The medevac chopper was six minutes out when the LT came back with the company's Kit Carson Scout, a former enemy now working with the Marines. The wounded soldier's eyes were closed.

"How's he doing, Doc?" the LT asked, scout standing by.

The Kit Carson was a tiny man, less than five feet, bug-eyed, face weathered and scarred like a beat-up baseball caught in a lawn-mower. He had an ear shot off. His small fingers looked like gnarled roots from digging tunnels, and his arms were like short lengths of gathered rope. He had surrendered to the Marines as part of the Chieu Hoi program, where enemy soldiers could switch allegiance and be trained to scout.

"Is he gonna make it, Doc?"

The LT was impatient, hovering over them.

"He's hangin' in there, LT."

The scout bent down and said something that made the wounded soldier's eyes struggle to open. Blood bubbled in his mouth, his lips moving a little. Hawkeye pulled out a canteen, took a swallow then patted a little on the soldier's face and lips. The soldier's eyes slit open, focused slightly, and landed on Hawkeye.

"What'd he say?" Doc asked the scout.

The scout bent closer and said something again and listened, but the soldier was weak, his voice less than a whisper. Finally, his lips trembled. A word fluttered.

"Goddamn it!" the LT snapped. "I heard something. What'd the little bugger say?"

The scout stood up as the soldier's eyes closed. He turned to the LT.

"He say name Vuong."

16

Vuong

ONE NIGHT VUONG DREAMED OF HIS FATHER. In the dream, his father was in a sampan drifting on a river. Vuong was in the water, holding on to the side of the boat. Then the river turned to blood, and his father became Phung Thu. Her hair was long again, and she smiled at him and sang a song his mother used to sing. Then she stood up and dove into the river of blood. But when his eyes opened, he was lying in a strange place he had never seen before. A light hurt his eyes. His chest throbbed and his mind was not focused. Maybe he was still in a dream, he thought, as he squinted at the ceiling.

It was hard to breathe. Tubes ran from jars that hooked to his body. Were they trying to poison him? He was too weary to pull out the tubes. He was lying on a bed of cloth that felt cool and good. His leg hurt, and he could feel something around his ankle. He lifted his head just enough to see that his foot was chained to the metal frame of the bed. He knew then he was not dreaming.

He lay back and stared at the stucco ceiling. A single light bulb hung down in stark brightness. His eyes strained against the light then wandered the small room. A gecko raced across the ceiling. Two more on the bare walls. There were no pictures, no wall coverings, no altar to offer prayers to his ancestors. Window spaces were covered with wood, and only a crack of light seeped between the boards. A door was shut. He was alone. Too tired to be frightened, he fell back asleep.

"Well. Well. Well. We got us a sleepy little zipper head, wrapped up all neat and tidy here. Just layin' back enjoying the hospitality of the United States Government."

Vuong's eyes opened to the noise of language he didn't understand. At the side of his bed was Captain Shore from intelligence, a medic from 3rd Med, and the same Kit Carson who questioned Vuong days earlier as he lay half-dead in Hue.

Vuong looked at the horse-faces of the Americans and worried they would bite him. He remembered stories of Americans eating their enemy.

"Well, you little fucker. It's about time you woke your ass up," Captain Shore said.

"OK, Kit. See if you can get any information out of this prick. Find out who he is, what unit he's in, and whatever else he'll cop to. I'm gonna go to chow. Comprendo, amigo? I'll check back in an hour."

As Captain Shore left, the medic adjusted the IV tubing, changed the dressing on Vuong's leg, cleaned off the stitches on his head wound, and cleaned the chest wound. The alcohol stung but felt cool running down his cheek and chest. He was thirsty and motioned with his hand toward his lips. The medic reached under the rolling metal table and produced a pitcher. He poured water in a paper cup, lifted Vuong's head slightly, and gave him some.

"*Cam on ban,*" Vuong said weakly.

"He say thank you."

"You're welcome," the medic replied. "Kit, tell this guy that if he needs to take a piss or a dump to use this." He held out a plastic bedpan. "If he needs help, yell, and the guard outside will help him. And tell him not to sweat it. We're not going to hurt him."

This horse-face was softer, Vuong thought. Maybe he would not be eaten.

"Ask him if he wants some food. Some chop-chop."

Kit told Vuong he would bring rice, pork, and tea, but first he needed information. Kit spoke slowly in Vietnamese, making sure his dialect was clear and understood.

"You were wounded in Hue and are now in a prisoner-of-war compound outside of Da Nang. This compound is located next to American bases, and you will be here until you are well enough to be transferred in with the rest of the prisoner population. Do you understand?"

Vuong nodded, frightened, his brown eyes floating in tears.

"You were shot crossing a field. Do you remember?"

A nod again. His face gaunt, clammy, sweat resting on his lip.

"Good. Now you told me your name is Vuong. And by the newness of your uniform and rifle, it appears your unit just moved into the area. Is that correct?"

Vuong felt weary and afraid. Afraid that if he said anything, it would betray his comrades and afraid if he did not cooperate he would be killed. He imagined being tortured, cut, choked, beaten.

"I hate to break up the party, Kit," the medic said, "but I think you should go with me to the chow hall and see if we can find him some grub. Let him eat before you break out the whips and canes, OK?"

"You go. I come soon."

"OK, Kit, but hurry up."

The door opened, and a shot of sunlight poured through then disappeared in the closing.

"Vuong, listen to me carefully. I will only ask you this one time. Are you a true patriot of the North?"

Vuong heard the words and was puzzled. He looked at the man's eyes and could sense his urgency.

"Yes," he answered.

"Good. Now I will tell you I have not abandoned my comrades. You must be strong. Someone will come to you."

Kit left the room.

Vuong was alone again, puzzled by the small Vietnamese man. Who was he? What did he mean? Who would contact him? But he was too tired to consider more. As he closed his eyes, he thought of the villagers who had died.

OVER THE NEXT TEN DAYS VUONG WAS given good care and food, and soon the tubes were taken from his arms. Kit came to see him every day, asked questions, and gathered information to satisfy Captain Shore. The information Vuong gave was mostly useless, with numbers and names of units that didn't exist. Kit never mentioned again that someone would contact him.

One afternoon Captain Shore walked in and listened as Kit gradually, then angrily, questioned Vuong. "You're doin' a damn fine job here, Kit. Getting this little cocksucker to squawk. Hell, he's probably been living on bugs and dirt for the last six months. But he'll do anything to keep from goin' back out there and havin' us kick his skinny little ass again. Ain't that right, amigo?"

"I think him not a strong communist."

"All right! Well, you keep pumping him and see what you come up with and report back to me as soon as you find out anything else. Comprendo? Understand?"

"Yes. *Dai uy.*"

The days and the nights were slow for Vuong. He slept deeply, only to be startled awake by a dream of his face peeled off by the Americans. Or he dreamed of the village by Hue and all the Southerners there who had been killed. When fears and dreams were too troubling, he'd remember Phung Thu.

In the days before the massacre, his unit had been attacking Southern troops and meeting with great resistance. It was not what he had understood the war would be. In the beginning, he'd expected the villagers to greet them with open arms and share their food and water willingly. That did not happen. Villagers resisted with force, and many of his comrades had been killed or wounded. Brother Vinh had been shot in the stomach and died slowly during the night, holding his entrails.

During the day, Vuong's unit had to dig holes and hide most of the time for fear of American planes and napalm. Twice he had seen it dropped, turning the ground into waves of fire. The flames couldn't be put out, and all the oxygen was sucked from the air. Many of his comrades had been burnt beyond belief. When Vuong walked through the area with his platoon, soldiers were like ash. Touch a corpse, and it would splinter into hunks of seared flesh. And the smell was something he had never known—burning oil and honey. Some soldiers were caught fleeing, tangled in wire fences, crouched in holes, cowering, arms still covering their heads. One soldier fried and smoked at a well. Half his body was charred, the other half untouched, hanging inside the well, tangled in rope like a puppet. And the helicopters could rain death down nonstop. Earth exploded and a dozen comrades were torn apart in an instant.

The burying. Usually at night, he'd been assigned burial detail, crawling out in open fields, with ropes and hooks, and everything so black. Sometimes the hooks would embed into bodies, ripping chunks of flesh and bone. And blood would run through his hands and stick between his fingers. But the burned ones were the worst. Bloating and exploding or tearing apart, the smell so revolting he would gag and vomit. The smell could not be washed away.

In the short time he was in battle, it had been a succession of terror as comrades died all around him. Finally, when he was sent on a scouting party, he was wounded. The others in the scouting party had died without firing a shot. He remembered lying there, shot in the leg and chest, hearing a burial party creep out to retrieve him. Someone had tossed a hook that hit him in the head, and when Vuong swore, the party had fled.

Vuong was transferred into a POW camp and was soon helping in the compound's garden. The camp was about twice the size of a football field and consisted of a mess hall made from plywood, with sheets of tin for a roof, and four other buildings. Two were built like the mess hall and designed to hold twenty prisoners to a floor. Often they were crammed with as many as fifty. The third building was for women and children suspected of aiding the enemy. The last building was the Command Center, made from reinforced concrete, surrounded with sandbags. It contained an underground bunker where Marines slept, a radio room, shower, and toilet. Prisoners were interrogated and tortured there. If the camp was attacked, windows on each wall became fighting positions. On a covered porch at the front of the building, Marines stood guard.

Four South Vietnam Army personnel walked the yard during the day armed with black batons. They were harsh and treated the prisoners badly, sometimes beating them for little reason.

The camp was surrounded with razor-sharp concertina, tangle-foot barbed wire, and an eight-foot cyclone fence. Inside the wire, at all four corners, were guard towers made of reinforced concrete and sandbagged. Each tower was manned by two Marines and two ARVNs. Each position had an M-60, M-79, ammo, claymores, flares, and a radio. Because the entire tower was concrete, guards could climb up the stairwell under fire and not be hit.

In the middle of one section of wire was the only entrance to the camp. It had a moveable gate and a sandbagged guard position with a small guard shack where ARVN slept.

Marines would often bribe the guards and sneak out the gate at night to screw whores in a row of shacks about a quarter mile away, called Dogpatch. There they could be with prostitutes, smoke pot or opium, and be back before dawn.

Next to the prisoners' sleeping quarters were three wooden out-houses and two metal barrels set on supports that held water for showering and drinking. By the outhouses were tiger cages: pits dug deep with a dozen four-foot-square cages dropped in. The cages opened from the top and were padlocked when closed. If a prisoner got out of hand or wasn't cooperating, he'd be given a bucket to piss in and be locked in a cage. They would spend weeks at a time in the worst of weather, come out disoriented, unable to walk, skin blistered, ulcerating, nearly blind, smelling of sickness, and willing to behave or talk.

The camp was six hundred yards from the tarmac of the Da Nang airport serving US forces. It was surrounded by empty fields, so that a ground attack would require enemy crossing large open spaces with no chance of concealment.

Every morning food, purchased by the military, was brought in on carts pulled by villagers. The carts were checked at the gate by the guards, given an OK, then dropped at the mess hall where the food was unloaded by prisoners. The carts carried rice and fish, sometimes chicken. One holiday brought rice cakes. But there was never enough. The prisoners would not starve unless they were in the tiger cages, but they were kept undernourished to keep their resistance down. The garden was allowed but not encouraged, and only visits by the press allowed them that much.

Vuong had been interviewed repeatedly by the original Kit and interrogated by both American and ARVN officers. He was put in a tiger cage with no food or water for two days. This was "orientation." Eventually, the ARVN officer in charge filed a report to his superiors confirming he was a lowly private, fresh from Hanoi with no intelligence value. He was, however, suggested as a candidate for the Kit Carson program. Even though he had limited battle experience, he knew how the NVA operated, was cooperative, and at worst could walk point and trigger a booby trap meant for a Marine.

Vuong was satisfied to hoe the garden and enjoyed the company of his comrades but was anxious about his next mission. He was afraid to discuss it because everyone was guarded and suspicious. Some felt great depression, as if they had failed as a soldier. Most, though, were confused, as Vuong was.

Vuong showered under the barrel in the early morning light as American planes and choppers flew overhead. Their loud roar was startling and reminded him of days and nights dug deep in the ground, earth rolling and trembling.

He wiped the water from his skin and put on the same gray shirt, shorts, and plastic sandals each prisoner was issued. It was his turn to unload the food cart. The sky was overcast as he walked across the dirt courtyard to the entrance of the mess hall and waited.

Two carts came through the gate pulled by women in loose white clothing and wearing conical hats, an ARVN guard by their side. The women stopped, cartloads tilting back, resting, guard watching.

Vuong unloaded a bag of rice, then a basket of dried fish. No one spoke. He could see both women were young. They reminded him of Phung Thu. Their skin was unblemished, and their eyes full of light. One of the girls smiled. It was a shy look, full of innocence and promise. The kind of look that could keep a young man up all night or cause him to spend a whole day thinking about it.

She pushed her hat back, and Vuong could see her face clearly. She looked familiar. His mind searched for the connection. Then it came to him! She was a comrade! Friend of Phung Thu. His heart raced! She was at the creek that day he fell. He remembered her now. But was it possible? She looked at him, and there was a moment of recognition. Then her smile flattened. As she turned away, he reached and touched her arm and started to speak. Instantly, an ARVN guard hit him on the shoulder and swore. Quickly the guard pulled him from the small group and berated him angrily. When Vuong tried to speak, the guard struck him again, and another guard came running up, laughing at Vuong bending over gasping for breath. The one laughing slapped him on the head like a naughty child, then shoved him to the ground.

The guards dragged him to the bamboo tiger cages, threw him in, and spat on him. The cover on top slammed shut; the lock snapped. He could hear footsteps, then quiet. How stupid he had been. How wrong. But he was sure it was one of his comrades. In a cage next to him, an old man was naked, brown skin wrinkled and cracked like that of a lizard. He had sores all over his body and bones were pushing through his diseased skin. He had a wisp of white hair and swollen lips. Eyes bulged at the sockets. He stared at Vuong vacantly.

That night the rain came, and with it a storm. Soon the camp was flooded. Water seeped into Vuong's cage, covering his legs and backside. It was cold and the wind raked the cage as Vuong shook and trembled. He prayed to his mother to come and comfort him. Sing to him. But the cold was too much and brought great thoughts of bitterness toward his enemies.

On the second night, he was sure the old man had died, but Vuong's shouts brought no one. What it brought was a stronger hate for the horse-faces. He imagined freeing himself and secretly killing the Marines and the Vietnamese guards. He'd put them in the cage and feed them rats. He'd torture them with sharp sticks and poke their eyes out. He'd attack the Marines as they slept with explosions and rifle fire and set their tents on fire.

By the morning of the third day, the sky was clear, the sun warm, and all the water had drained through the cage floor.

Hawkeye was in the area and wanted to see for himself the enemy they captured. He was carrying a canvas bag of food he would take back to his buds. Soon he found the prisoners and bull-shitted his way passed a couple of Marine guards.

At first, he was startled at the sight of humans treated like animals. Even though his Marine brothers had been killed or wounded too, he felt guilt and despair.

Hawkeye found Vuong and stood at the edge of the enclosure, saying something Vuong did not understand. Hawk was shaking his head as if he were sorry, and dropped a banana and bar of wrapped chocolate into Vuong's cage. He noticed the old man curled in a fetal position, not moving. He left quickly, and soon more Marines were back, opening the cages, lifting the prisoners.

As Vuong walked back to his billet, shaking, he saw Hawkeye yelling at two of the ARVN guards and was pleased.

Some nights later Vuong was awakened. "Comrade Vuong," the voice in the darkness said, shoving a note in his hand. "Your new mission."

The voice disappeared among the others sleeping.

There was no light to read, so Vuong lay there in the dark, clutching the paper, worried and excited. At first light, he rushed to the bathroom, slipped inside, and in the dim light unfolded the note.

> *My dear Vuong. I know your thoughts. Be strong and brave.*
> *Work with the Americans. Soon we will see each other.*
> *—Phung Thu*

Vuong was overjoyed and filled with hope. Hope for the end of the war and hope that he would soon see Phung Thu.

Later that week, Kit brought him in front of the ARVN commander. Vuong requested to join the Americans. He wanted to be a Kit Carson Scout.

17

JT

"I can't believe Nixon. What an asshole," Leif said, shaking his head as he helped JT load a truck with bundles of newspapers, banner headlines declaring FOUR STUDENTS KILLED AT KENT STATE. The front page photo showed a girl kneeling next to a student lying facedown, arms tucked under his belly, legs slack, shot by the National Guard. Her arms were outstretched, pleading, her face twisted in anguish. In the background, students were crossing a grassy knoll, frozen in midstride. JT could tell by the legs the boy was dead.

It was warm in the warehouse, late afternoon, as sunshine and shouting rolled through the loading dock doors. Sidewalks were packed with chanting anti-war protesters, TV crews, and those stopping to stare—

"NO MORE WAR! NO MORE WAR! NO MORE WAR!"

A couple of hard hats stood across the street holding lunch pails, yelling, "Get a job! Get a job, you filthy little pissants!"

Inside, the noise of the trucks and protesters mixed with the drone of the press in the basement. Its plates slapping, paper whapping, and big cylinder drums rolling out a special afternoon edition.

"This country is going to hell," Leif continued, more riled than JT had ever seen. "Nixon's a pathological liar. Tells us he's winding the war down, bringing troops home. Feeds us this pablum about honorable peace, then last year bombs the hell out of Cambodia. Come on, does that make any sense? Now this crap. Military killing civilians. Just like Vietnam."

JT didn't reply. He picked up the pace, tossing bundles faster, working harder, sweating.

"At Reed and Portland State, we're mobilizing. JT, you could help us end this damn war. I'm helping put this march together. We're getting our own troops together, JT, and there's going to be a back-lash across campuses and across this country like no one's ever seen."

JT listened, burning inside. He wanted to rip Leif's head off. He didn't know a goddamn thing about the war. Bombing Cambodia was a great idea. Save soldiers' lives. Should have been done years ago. Kick their asses or get out. And he never killed civilians. Never saw anyone do it either. What a bunch of garbage. Students dying at Kent State was tough luck. But it was nothing. Try hundreds a week. Or hell, try seventeen. Just a goddamned platoon. Nobody's crying about that.

"JT, you got to be pissed with all this. I know this has got you upset."

JT suddenly stopped working and looked at Leif in the same way he had frightened Ashley. His eyes were punishing. Jaw tightened, teeth biting down. Voice full of hate, the kind of hate Leif had never seen or imagined.

"You—don't—know—ANYTHING."

He started up again like a machine, tossing papers, slamming them onto the truck. They were heavy like crates of ammo. His body remembered . . . the firebase, loading crates of ammo, sun pounding at his back, T-shirt soaked, heat waves dancing from the ground. Sweat in his eyes burning, rope handles cutting. Choppers overhead. The smell of oil and gasoline. Coop next to him.

"Hey, jerk-offs," Flowers called, walking up, no shirt, shades, rifle in one hand, can of beer in the other. "Grab your shit. We're goin' on patrol."

Hawkeye stood there bigger than life, carrying the 60. Arms hung out of his flak jacket, long and strong. Back straight, mouth tight. Waiting. Gurney laughing, teeth like Chiclets. A dozen others grabbing rifles, flak jackets, filling canteens, bitching, pissing . . .

JT flung the last bundle of newspapers in the back of the truck and told the driver he was done. He washed up and tossed the paper towel in the wastebasket like shooting a basketball. A line at the time clock. Leif was in front. They punched out, not speaking.

Outside, the crowd had grown, spilling from the sidewalk out into the street, taking on a life of its own. Like a mob, JT thought, something he hadn't seen before except on TV. The hard hats were gone. Dozens of police were on every corner, standing next to cop cars, or sitting on motorcycles forming lines to clear intersections, where cars were backed up trying to leave the city. Across the street Leif was already passing out fliers, pushing his way toward a guy dressed like Uncle Sam—red, white, and blue. The guy was built like a barrel with a top hat and fake beard. He was carrying a pole with a string of naked baby dolls hanging from it. The dolls were covered with red paint to look like blood. At the top of the pole was a sign: *Stop the Killing!*

Leif and Uncle Sam were arguing. JT felt angry, as if the guy with the pole was toting a lie about him, about his friends. *We never killed babies or villagers intentionally.* Some did, he was sure. But not him or his platoon. It hurt to be thought of like that. *We had rules of engagement. We weren't bloodthirsty.* He looked up at the rooftops and imagined he could set up machine guns and grenade launchers and kill them all. A perfect ambush. Just fire down into the crowd and watch them blow up.

The crowd kept chanting—

"NO MORE WAR! NO MORE WAR! NO MORE WAR!"

An ambulance pulled up, lights flashing, crowd parting, siren sounding. For a moment, he thought he saw Gurney standing underneath a clock on the side of a bank building. It couldn't be! He pushed through the protesters, but by the time he reached the other side of the street, the guy's face had changed. Gurney was gone.

Soon the crowd multiplied to several hundred, crude cardboard signs waving, Viet Cong flags sticking up over it all. The smell of pot permeated the air. A couple guys in camouflage utility shirts, jeans, and long hair were hanging with someone wearing a Nixon mask. The mask had an exaggerated ski jump nose, and the face was wrinkled and frowning. Now and then Nixon would raise both arms and flash peace signs, tip back his mask and sip from a can of beer.

For a while, the demonstration concentrated on the block around the *Journal* building, gradually moving in a swarm up Broadway, toward Portland State University. It grew to the point where JT couldn't see the front or the guy shouting on a bullhorn, but it sounded like Leif.

"Stay together. Stay together. We're going to march on the university. Stay together!"

PSU fronted Broadway five blocks away. As the demonstration gathered steam, chants turned to—

"PEACE NOW! PEACE NOW! PEACE NOW! PEACE NOW!"

Suddenly, a fight broke out between someone trying to get into his car and Uncle Sam, who had been standing on the driver's fender waving his pole. It was short-lived, and Uncle Sam melted back into the gathering, dead babies swinging in the breeze. Soon the mass turned west on Montgomery and moved south again, up through the park blocks like a football crowd rushing the exits. JT followed, keeping his distance. He felt like the enemy.

The park ran along the backside of the university for several
blocks. On the other side of the park were old brick apartment
buildings, big run-down houses, and the school library. A paved path
wound through the park beneath elm and maple trees that had yet
unfolded. Along the path were benches and garbage cans and a huge
concrete statue of a general on his horse, hooves pawing the air, as

"PEACE NOW! PEACE NOW! PEACE NOW! PEACE NOW!"

echoed off the buildings like artillery in a valley.

A small stage, microphone, and speakers were being set up in the
middle of the park facing Smith Memorial Student Union.

At intersections that led to the park blocks and campus buildings, barricades were being erected out of chairs and scraps of
wood or benches scavenged from the park. Other groups had set up
crude booths, like The Freaks (Fuck Recruiting and End American
Killing) and the Yippies, calling for a Festival of Life. In the center
was a table stocked with information on the Black Panthers. Next
to it hung *Free Bobby Seale* posters and tables of buttons and articles
about the Weathermen and recipes for making Molotov cocktails.
The campus priest manned another table, giving instructions on
avoiding the draft, as well as information on living in Canada.

A small girl with big, ratted hair stepped on stage and started
the crowd singing—

All we are saying . . . is give peace a chance.

People began swaying, a guitar playing, JT thinking, *Flash Charlie
a peace sign and he'll blow your head off.*

The singing slowed and dogs began barking, chasing Frisbees.
Soon, music played from speakers placed in trees as Yippies dressed
in brilliant-colored attire formed circles, spinning, dancing in the
park. Meanwhile, JT cruised the perimeter, checking out girls in

shorts and tube tops or long spring dresses, stopping with curiosity to watch a group erect a large white tent.

"I want everyone to pay attention," Leif shouted from the stage.

JT moved through the crowd and situated himself so he could see the stage. The music stopped. Leif was holding a microphone, wearing a black armband, addressing the crowd.

"Listen, I'm a student at Reed, and right now we're working with the Student Mobilization Committee to End the War in Vietnam. We're demanding that Reed and PSU be closed down with a general strike beginning tomorrow."

"Right on!" someone shouted. "Power to the people!"

The noise and excitement surged.

"FUCK THE PIGS!
FREE BOBBY!
STRIKE NOW!"

"OK, OK," Leif said, his voice rising above the crowd, hands in the air. "We're going to let others have their time on stage today, but right now, if we stand together, maybe we can stop the shit that's goin' down!"

A big cheer erupted, then chanting—

"STOP THE WAR! STOP THE WAR! STOP THE WAR!"

"OK, now!" Leif raised his hands to lower the noise. "Hear me. The four issues are—number one, the students killed at Kent State." He shouted through more cheers and chanting.

"The second issue is Nixon's reescalation of the war." He paused as the crowd erupted.

"Third, the imprisonment of Black Panther Bobby Seale." Leif let the crowd's emotions rise for a moment, then could hardly hear himself as he shouted over them.

"And the fourth issue is the shipment of nerve gas into Oregon."

A deafening roar. Yippies spinning, dancing.

Four members of the Freaks rushed on stage. Leif looked a little stunned as a girl in a *Free Bobby* shirt grabbed the microphone and started screaming—

"Strike now! Strike now! Strike now!"

As Leif stepped off the stage, a black guy with a huge Afro took the microphone from the girl and shouted, "Brothers and sisters, listen to me now." His voice was deep and full of conviction. "Make no mistake, this is a revolution! Whitey be putting down brothers for two hundred years! They got Bobby locked up 'cause he's black!"

Students began pouring out of the buildings and apartments, pulled to the crowd and the noise.

"Listen to me, my brothers and sisters. They killed Dr. King 'cause he's a black man. They even killed Bobby Kennedy because he liked black people. Now you can talk about peace, and you can talk about strikes, and you can talk about Kent, but I'm tellin' you now, we are in a revolution! And this week don't spend your money on booze. No, don't do that. And don't spend your money on dope. No, don't do that. Go out and get yourself a weapon!"

The crowd was half-frenzied.

JT wished they were dead.

"This administration don't give a damn about no Vietnam and soldiers shootin' everybody. Or no Kent State. All they care about is sitting on their fat asses collecting their fat checks making sure they're keeping us quiet, behaved, puttin' us all down." He was evangelical, clenched fist shaking at the crowd, pacing back and forth across the stage, rage on his face, anger in his voice. "Ain't nobody gettin' no free lunch 'cept them fat cats. What I'm saying is we need to show the pigs they can't keep us down no more. I'm sayin' forget the bullshit negotiations. We're tired of negotiations. Let's take it now. Strike now! Strike now! Strike now! Take the school, brothers and sisters! Take the school!"

The crowd was feeding off each other, getting louder and louder. The black guy jumped off the stage, scattering bodies, and ran across the park, busting into the Smith Memorial Student Union cafeteria with a dozen others in pursuit.

JT followed, wanting to smoke 'em all. Revolution? Hell. He caught a glimpse of the black dude as he dodged tables and jumped on the lunch counter yelling, "Free food! Free food!" while tossing hamburgers and sandwiches to students as stunned employees watched on. The cafeteria was under attack. Coke dispensers opened up, nozzles shooting Coke and 7 Up at students and workers. Slabs of pie flying, exploding on the walls. Ten more stormed the counter. Apples, oranges, french fries, and donuts ripped off or were cannon fodder for the hysterical. One student flying out the door with a tray of dozens of wrapped burgers, flinging them to the eager.

JT caught a cheeseburger in one hand, and a blast of orange juice splattered his back. No one was in control. Two uniforms from campus security turned and fled. The cafeteria was taken, as were the lounge and classrooms. A core group took over the president's office. A sit-in.

JT wandered through the bedlam, comfortable in the chaos. He went upstairs to the lounge with the huge bank of windows overlooking the park and could see the mob as it poured into Smith. Teachers and students were pleading for order as chairs overturned, paper flew, and the last calls for free food climbed the stairwell.

Leif made his way upstairs through another entrance and was standing at the opposite end of the lounge, looking out the windows, wiping ice cream off his shirt, cleaning his glasses with a napkin. Two girls stood next to him talking. He dodged a piece of cake. One of the girls was short, and JT thought he recognized her but couldn't place the face. He walked up next to Leif.

"Can you believe this?" Leif said, glancing at JT, then back to the window. He had a look of exasperation. "We didn't want this to happen. Now all we'll get is a bunch of bad press. Of course, we didn't plan on the National Guard murdering students either. What do you think?"

"I'd say there's a party going down."

"I didn't want this to be a party," Leif replied, solemn, looking out at Yippies spinning in the park. "It's stupid and it's sad."

As they stood there, no one spoke and the noise and confusion waned. Leif turned back to the girls and JT.

"Sorry, I should have introduced you," he said, putting his glasses on, a speck of vanilla ice cream still at the bridge. "JT, this is Kendal and Sasha Ji."

JT nodded. He remembered Sasha now, but she looked different wearing a black beret and seemed smaller than he recalled. She had a book bag slung over her shoulder with a *Free Bobby* button attached.

Kendal was tall and slender like Ashley, blonde hair hanging nearly to her waist. Her face looked kind, JT thought. She wore jeans, a white blouse, and held books in both arms, close to her. She smiled when Leif said his name and that pleased JT.

"So, you're JT?" Kendal said, her voice soft, her mouth tender. "Leif mentioned you were in Vietnam."

The words hung there. Something felt wrong and right about being known as a soldier.

"I was there. Now I'm back, and well...I don't know what to say." He felt embarrassed and wondered what Leif had told her.

"Well, Sasha and I have to go up to the president's office to see what's coming off with the strike committee," Leif said, "and maybe help straighten this mess out." He looked tired, his shoulders rounded forward, as if he had been carrying something on his back all day. "JT, I know you were furious with me today and I'm not sure why, but this isn't against veterans. We just want the war over. We're not looking for a revolution, just to stop the killing. Hope you understand. Anyway, I gotta run. See you guys later."

JT didn't much care for Leif, and he was feeling disoriented and irritated. This whole thing, these demonstrations and protesters were spewing the same lies he was seeing on TV or reading about—soldiers killing innocent women and children, acting like animals, raping, burning villages. Like they had no soul. It wasn't true. He wasn't like that.

The campus was like a firebase getting overrun, JT imagined. Only he was the enemy whom everyone wanted to kill.

The lounge had thinned out. The food attack had ended. A few student employees were cleaning up, and some homeless people drawn by the demonstration were scavenging for food.

The sun was dropping behind the West Hills as JT and Kendal sat on the floor, looking out on the park blocks. As they watched through the window, JT felt like he did on his first date with Ashley. He imagined his arm around Kendal, her head on his shoulder.

"I've got to get going," Kendal said, standing up, trying to slip her foot in her sandal. She picked up her books, brushed her hair from her face. "It's getting late. I'll miss my bus."

JT stood, his eyes averted not to look at her tight jeans too hard. He wanted her to stay. "Where do you live?" He felt a catch in his throat. He liked her face. He wanted to be with her. He didn't care if they closed the campus or blew it up. He wanted to hang out with Kendal, have a beer, get to know her. "I can take you home if you don't mind riding in my beater," he offered. She accepted.

They stopped for a burger and split a warm beer JT had in the back of his car. Kendal was a little younger, came from a Catholic family with ten kids, and lived in an exclusive area full of sprawling brick and Tudor homes with big lawns and wide driveways.

"That must have been horrible. Vietnam, I mean," Kendal said.

As she spoke, JT felt that stirring again. She was beautiful and smart and seemed different than anyone he had ever met. She didn't judge him.

It was almost dark when they pulled in front of her house. He wanted to kiss her and hold her and feel her arms around him. He felt like she knew him.

"There's supposed to be a dance later," he said. "It might be a kick to go." He needed to be around her.

"I can't. Sorry. I've got to babysit my little brothers, but I really would like to go with you." Another awkward moment of silence separated them. Finally she said, "Thanks for the ride."

She got out and was in the house before he had a chance to get her phone number. He didn't even know her last name.

When JT got home, he talked Brad into picking him up and going back to PSU.

"It'll be cool. We'll get loaded. Fuck up some hippies."

"OK. But only for a couple hours. I'll tell Mary you need a ride."

By the time they got back to campus, there were burning barrel fires at each barricade, watched over by hippies. Some short-haired, big-shouldered football players were hassling them.

"What the hell are you doing? You commies are tearing up our school."

"Fuck you, man. It's our school, too."

"I'll kick your scrawny little ass."

The longhair picked up a two-by-four. "Yeah, come on, muscle head."

JT liked the tension. Jocks against hippies, clean and simple. Right against wrong was what he figured. The longhairs were draft dodgers, vilifying the ones who had the courage to go. He thought of Marines wounded or dying and thought of the demonstrators so safe in their world. It was sickening.

"Put it down or I'll stick that board up your ass," JT said , stepping out of the shadow, looking for an opportunity to unload. Ashley, the divorce, Leif—he could take care of it all in the next five minutes.

Brad stepped in, grabbing his arm. "Come on, let's go check out the pussy. You can kick ass later."

Across the park, the stage was empty, booths closed, tables vacant, music coming from Smith. A stream of people entered and exited the hospital tent, lights inside, hum of a generator. The night smelled of cannabis. Three guys sat underneath a maple tree. One was playing a guitar quietly; another crashed on a blanket, and the third was smoking a bowl.

"Hey, buddy," the guy with the hash pipe called. "Hash, mescaline, yellow sunshine? Got some righteous windowpane, dude. Five bucks a hit."

Brad turned to JT. "Wanna get loaded?"

"What about Mary?"

"Screw Mary."

"I don't want to be up all night," JT said.

"No sweat, dude," the dealer said. "Buy some windowpane, and I'll throw in a couple of 'ludes. Bring you right down."

They scored and took a freebie off his bong, then cruised toward Smith, JT's senses fine-tuned.

The place was crawling, music coming from the ballroom upstairs, jug band banging away. Cafeteria was a tomb though, metal gates drawn down, doors closed. A few kids crashed outside the gates, lying on the floor. Student lounge overflowing, people lying on couches and the floor. A couple of chairs were broken, and beer and wine spilled everywhere.

Students were sitting in the halls, smoking dope, necking, one couple lying down dry humping. Holes had been punched in the walls, and lights were dim or broken. JT and Brad made it to the ballroom. The place was hot and packed, almost dark. The jug band was playing a bad rendition of "Mr. Tambourine Man." The singer raked a washboard. Another played harmonica and another the guitar. The acid kicked in as JT eyed a girl dancing by herself. A moment later another girl danced up and started laying lippers on her, arms around her, riding her leg, dancing like they were doing it standing up.

"Shit!" JT laughed.

He began hallucinating. He thought the black light over the band changed the shape of each member's head. The floor had deep holes in it. Every time he stepped, the floor would rearrange itself.

"I'm ripped," JT said to no one. Brad was gone, in a corner piss-ing on the wall. JT edged back toward the door and leaned against the wall, hands in his pockets, head feeling heavy, light from the doorway framing him. He felt unsafe, worried that he would be too stoned to protect himself if the wrong person came through the door. He didn't like the feeling of being out of control. As he fought his mind for control, a girl came up. She was short with big hair, like a country western singer, and was wearing snug white bell-bottoms. She had a matching tube top with a roach clip on a chain dangling around her neck. She was drunk and smoking a joint.

"Hi. How you doing?" she asked, looking up at JT with lonely, big, round eyes. "Wanna . . . wanna hit?" Her voice barely made it over the bands rocking.

JT thought she was cute but stupid. He'd rather be with Kendal. As the floor shifted again, he lost his balance, staggered, steadied himself on the wall. He took her joint, thought about her naked, and drew hard.

"Thanks," he said, and handed it back. "Man, I'm so wasted. I got to sit down." The floor was giving way, his legs melting as he slid down the wall. The girl sat beside him.

Brad wandered back with two beers drawn from a keg set up next to the band. He handed JT one and spilled some of the other on the girl's foot. She looked up, vaguely aware, but said nothing. JT passed the cup to the girl while she worked the roach, holding it with her clip. She took a last long drag. The tiny orange glow captured JT's attention. He watched the tip with amazement as it grew out of her mouth like a firefly, flickered, and died.

The music changed and so did the band. The new group was louder. Its members loaded. No use trying to shout over the guitars or the screaming vocals. The girl leaned against JT, his back braced by the wall. He turned to her, reached down her top, cupped a full breast and kissed her mouth. Later they spent thirty minutes in the custodian's office having sex on the desk, floor, and up against the wall. When she was done, she ditched him. Later he got a ride home with Brad.

IT WAS LATE WHEN HE TOOK HIS quaaludes. When he woke, his pants were down to his ankles and it was noon. He crawled out of bed, called into work, saying he was very sick and very sorry. He ate some canned chili and went back to sleep. When he woke again, he wondered what happened to Brad. He remembered leaving PSU but not coming home. He also recalled the girl and wanted her again. He ate another quaalude, drank a beer, and watched TV.

Then he remembered a letter from Ashley's lawyer was unopened, waiting on the table. Reluctantly he opened it.

A court appearance was scheduled in two weeks, after which the marriage would be over.

He crumpled the letter, punched a hole in the wall next to the cover of *Life*, and called Ashley.

"Ashley, I want to talk to you."

"So talk."

"I want to talk to you in person, not on the damn phone!" Anger rising.

"There's nothing to talk about."

"I'm going to contest the divorce," JT said.

"Don't. Can you get it through your head that I don't love you anymore?"

"You bitch!" And he slammed down the phone. He felt worthless. Like he was a lowlife with no future or accomplishments except living through hell.

It was almost dark when he went outside and started running. He could feel the aftereffect of the drugs and alcohol, but he pushed and punished himself. She hurt him so bad he felt like dying. Maybe that's what he should do. Die when Anna was small, so she wouldn't miss him.

He ran toward North Portland, breathing heavily, sweat dripping in his eyes, cutting through front yards and across sidewalks, his feet stamping at the pavement. He was nearing exhaustion as the sun dipped into the horizon. He slowed and walked. The rage was gone as he turned onto Union Ave., where high-heeled hookers turned tricks in run-down motels or gave blow jobs in the front seats of parked cars. Storefronts were boarded up, and drunks, drug dealers, and strung-out addicts hung on every other corner. He passed the boarded-up McDonald's blown up by the Black Panthers and an alley with two addicts shooting up, needles in their arms, eyes rolling back, mouths full of spittle.

As he walked past low-life bars and second-rate used car lots, he began feeling strong again. Alert. Like on patrol. He hoped someone would mess with him.

It was dark, streetlights on. Rich white guys with fancy cars were on the street, looking for pussy and cocaine. JT came up on a skinny white guy—a pimp, he figured—and his whore in spiked heels and nothing for a dress. They were standing next to a pickup camper parked in a vacant lot. Back door of the camper was open. Two blacks were playing cards. The pimp had a fistful of money and was angry.

"You best get off your ass, girl, and git out there and make your man some money. You hear me, cunt?"

JT walked toward them, sweating profusely. His body was tight. Pimp yelling, girl cowering. With the moon and the streetlight, he could see she was frightened. The pimp was gripping her arm, not noticing JT.

"Are you listening to me, cunt?"

JT dropped him with a punch to the side of the head. He bent over, took the money, gave it to the girl, and started running toward home. He ran along side streets lined with elm trees and no streetlights. There was a sense of excitement pumping through him that was familiar, and he liked it. The pickup camper was following, gaining on him. He turned down a dark street running hard, look-ing back over his shoulder. The truck screeched around the corner, camper swaying.

"We're gonna kill you, motherfucker!" a voice screamed at him through the pickup window.

He ducked into a yard, hopped two fences, bolted past a barking dog, and lost them as he crossed through the parking lot of a tire shop.

Back home, the flush on his face and sweat were exhilarating. Laughing, he opened the fridge and pulled out a couple of beers. He cranked up the stereo and sat on the floor. As he drank, his mood changed. He thought of how he had cheated death so many times. And he thought about Ashley leaving him and not caring about what he went through. He smoked a joint. A heavy depression was setting in. He felt stupid and useless again. No good, like his mom used to say. His life was over. He wanted to hate Ashley, but he couldn't. He thought about Anna and fell asleep on the floor.

JT SHOWED UP AT WORK LATE AGAIN and argued with a truck driver. He did his route, stopping to buy a beer and a sandwich for lunch. When he got back to the warehouse, Claire called him into her office. He sat in the chair next to her desk.

"You've been missing work and have been late on your pickups. We have a business to run and need to know that the people who work here can be counted on. I know you've had a difficult time in your life, but your job performance has to improve."

He'd dropped his head. He was ashamed. She was right.

"Let's see a better attitude."

In the elevator on the way down, he stared at a deliveryman. "What are you looking at?"

He caught a bus home. Walking up to the house, he could tell from the ruts in the front lawn that a truck had been there.

The house was empty. No furniture, nothing! He called Ashley, and she talked to him like he was nothing. She had taken everything except the bed, his clothes, and a few dishes. Depressed and furious, he started drinking and called Brad, but no one was home.

Coop! He'd find Coop. He called information, then dialed Coop's brother Bill and found out Coop had been wounded and was in the naval hospital in Bremerton. He called the hospital. Coop was still there, and would be for a while, but it was too late to talk to him.

Speed kept JT up until four in the morning, and it took a lot of beer to finally knock himself out. He missed loading the morning trucks.

Claire came down. She handed him an envelope. "I'm sorry," she said.

By now JT was numb. He cashed his check at a downtown bank and felt better with a pocketful of money. He bought some papers at the little store across from PSU and rolled a joint. Another demonstration was going down.

The park blocks were jammed, and motorcycle cops were back on all the corners, gathering at the far end. The air was charged with hostility. JT could feel it. People were yelling at those on the barricades, exchanging insults and accusations. On the east end of the park blocks, a garbage truck rammed one of the barricades, sending chairs, couches, cardboard, and an effigy of Nixon flying. When the truck stalled, a half a dozen football players got behind it, leaned their broad shoulders into it, pushing the truck away.

Picket signs soared above the heads of the crowd, and the booths and tables were gone. The stage had been flattened and was being hauled away by campus security.

Hundreds of chanting students were between the hospital tent at one end of the park blocks and the police and their tactical squad at the other. Dressed in black leathers, boots, white helmets, guns and black batons at the ready, the TAC squad looked ominous. Reporters and TV crews were interviewing demonstrators and positioning for the best crowd shots.

JT loved it. Like anticipating napalm.

He stood on the retaining wall in front of an old apartment building and could see the TAC squad, squaring, ready to sweep the ville. By the time the TAC squad had pushed through the park and through the trees, only twenty-five protesters were still in the trenches, arms linked in front of the tent, awaiting the assault. Batons swung indiscriminately into the picket line and the tent, splintering it into pieces of white canvas and broken poles. Some protesters were dragged out by the police, screaming; others ran away.

JT watched them crumble, detached, wondering only about Leif. In the end, the park was cleared. No more tent or demonstrators. Only a few cops and the TV crews remained, carefully stepping over the human debris.

Back home, he felt the real pain of being fired. And unloved or disrespected. He was a fool. And as he lay in bed, he thought of getting a bike tomorrow and taking Anna to the park.

THE PHONE KEPT RINGING AND RINGING. JT fell off the bed, stumbled over tennis shoes in the dark. Grabbed the phone off the kitchen counter. *Who in the hell would be calling at this hour?*

He opened the refrigerator for light, lifted the receiver.

"Hello."

It was Aunt Evelyn, his father's sister.

"Your dad is dying," she said. "You need to take care of him."

18

Coop

COOP WAS MOVED AND SPENT THREE MONTHS on his back in Bremerton Naval Hospital, pins in his fibula, traction pulling at his leg, bone grafts from both hips. By the fourth month, he was in physical therapy, walking in parallel bars, doing leg lifts, stretching, stepping gingerly in the therapy pool. Jarvis was long gone, promising to write. Mrs. Ford, the head nurse on his floor, had grown tired of his crazy behavior and wouldn't talk to him anymore. The war had slowed. President Nixon had ordered troop reductions, and soldiers were being brought home.

Outside his window, Coop could see the bay and streets of the small, gray town. Occasionally a group of anti-war protesters would gather on the front lawn waving placards or shouting from a bullhorn.

But usually every day was the same. Fewer soldiers rotated in and out of his ward, and the routine of hospital life tapped into his fear of boredom. He had to destroy monotony in order to bury memory. The only way to do that was by using drugs or being crazy, and crazy was easy. He'd light farts in the dark for roommates or orderlies, smuggle in beer and wine, and throw late-night parties he called Gimp Nights. He watched TV and went to movies in the gym on Saturday nights when Gold Star mothers who'd lost their sons or widows brought trays of cookies. He'd behave, but later he'd sneak into the dental clinic and snort laughing gas with a night guard. Everything he did was calculated to keep his mind from the first patrol, the last ambush, and everything else in between.

One evening Coop "borrowed" a wheelchair from Phil, a double amputee sharing his room. Phil had both feet blown off a couple of years earlier when he was walking point for the First Marines. He was back being treated for circulation problems and was scheduled for more surgery to pare down the stumps of his diminished legs. He'd taken downers and was out cold when Coop swiped his chair and rolled out of the ward. He pushed down empty halls full of artificial light where wounded soldiers slept in darkened rooms smelling of ammonia and infection. His first stop was the smoking area. No windows but tables, lamps, chairs, magazines, and ashtrays. The years of smoke had yellowed the white ceiling tiles and permeated the walls with a biting stench.

A thin man with glasses and a huge Adam's apple sat alone, legs crossed, ashtray full of butts balanced on his knee. Nicotine had stained his fingers; his face sagged and was ashen. He sucked, exhaled, and stared at the floor, talking to himself.

"Say, nutcase. What it is?" Coop joked, wheeling up, his chair positioned directly in front of the man. "Your problem is you haven't been laid. Get your testosterone back up. You in there, partner?"

The guy lifted his head, face in anguish, trembling, and started to cry. Coop left the room, shaken. He caught the elevator up two floors to Mental Health, and by the time the doors opened, he was feeling good again. He popped a wheelie and flew up to the night desk. A patient Coop knew, called Jesus, was standing next to the orderly on duty, quoting scripture.

"Say, Jesus. How's it hangin', big fella?" Coop asked. "Any miracles tonight? Heal the lame? Raise the dead? How 'bout turning some water into wine? Cook me up some Mad Dog 20/20. Can you do it?"

Jesus was six-foot-four, two hundred and forty pounds, with burnt brown hair and beard, scars across his forehead he claimed were made from the crown of thorns, and scars on his palms where "they nailed me to the cross. My father had forsaken me." He wore a brown peasant robe, carried a Bible, and a plain wooden cross hung around his neck. He looked at Coop as if he were a curiosity. "The hell-yuns and harlots and demonizers of God are facing everlasting damnation," Jesus said. He turned back to the night clerk, ignoring Coop. "And his sword will cut and cleanse the earth with his power and his fury."

Coop smirked. He had heard from an orderly that Jesus had spent eighty-eight days in a bunker during the siege of Khe Sanh. On the eighty-ninth day, his bunker took a direct hit and killed everyone but Jesus. Before the bunker was hit, he was just Todd Cartwright from Wyoming. After they'd dug him out, he was Jesus.

"Jesus, settle down, brother. I'm just trying to get my mind right, hoping to score a little Mary-j-wanna."

"Thy rod and thy staff will cleanse the earth of fornicators and evildoers, like you."

"Right. And I'm Ho Chi Frickin' Minh."

Coop pushed on and found the recreational therapist who sold him a couple of joints and a hit of yellow sunshine. At the canteen, Coop bought a drink from the Coke machine. The halls were empty at 1:00 a.m. He pushed up a ramp to a small alcove leading to the canteen. He dropped the acid, smoked the reefer, and drank his Coke. Soon the Coke was gone and the acid was tending to his mind. He was climbing over slash, pushing through the brush, past fir trees three hundred years old and one hundred feet tall, following deer trails that meandered up slopes and around switchbacks. The lake cold, breathtaking, flat and calm. Throwing rocks. Splashing and ripples rounded almost to the shore. The woods near Joseph were home to brown bear. Granddad called one of the bears Chester because he walked with a limp like the guy on *Gunsmoke*.

"Seen him twice before," Granddad said. "Down by the lake, chompin' fish, getting fat. Getting ready for winter."

The acid kicked in hard, Granddad was gone, and suddenly he felt like he'd been spinning in his chair. He rolled down the ramp laughing and smacked into the Coke machine. Stars were in his brain like clusters of cameras flashing. His face itched, and the canteen sign on the wall started moving and dripping. He pulled his cock out, peeing on a wall while laughing maniacally. Done, he raced around the barren cafeteria, bumping into tables then running up to a pay phone. A janitor walked in, keys dangling, gray uniform, white paint splashed on his trousers, the smell of lacquer trailing.

"What's goin' on, boy? Don't you know this area is off-limits after ten?"

Coop laughed, his red eyes glazed, face looking stupid, blond stache drooping. "Just calling home, good brother." He took a deep breath, exhaled, and thought about calling Charlie Apple or his brother, then settled on JT.

"You finish up, boy. Or security will come down here wondering what all the racket is. Hurry up now."

Coop snickered as he shoved coins into the phone, pleased, listening to them clang, drop, dial tone empty and far off. He called information and asked to be connected, imagining the operator sitting in a chair in a room by herself, lonely, wanting him.

The phone rang and went to message. Coop was agitated.

"JT! Wake your sorry ass up, you son of a bitch! Do you know who in the hell you're talking to? I'm a red, white, and blue all-American boy. I love Mom, home, apple pie, and Kentucky Fried Chicken on Sunday. I'm a lover, a fighter, a wild bull rider, I got a hard-on a yard long, and I'm lookin' for somethin' to start on. Are you there, man? I'm coming to Oregon to see your sorry ass. We'll get drunk and get some pussy. Are you there, man?"

Mrs. Ford found Coop outside the next morning, passed out in a flowerbed, wheelchair covering his head.

Coop was discharged from the hospital a week later. He'd been caught in the therapy pool late one evening with a nurse from the medical school. They were naked, drinking Johnnie Walker Red. By 11:00 a.m. the next day, he was dressed in wrinkled khakis on a bus heading for Joseph. He had his duffel bag, three hundred dollars, and a heavy metal leg brace. Final discharge papers were on the way.

"You're going to have to watch it," the doctor warned him before he left. "With no feeling and circulation problems, you have to be extremely careful. You don't want us to have to remove the foot now, do you?"

"No, Doc."

But he really didn't give a damn. Either way, he was gonna be half-crippled. He figured if they took the foot at least he'd get a bigger disability check.

THE BUS CHEWED ALONG THE HIGHWAY MOST of the day, stopping in cowboy and logger towns before it finally arrived in Joseph. It was spring, and when he got off the bus, he could smell hay and cherry blossoms. The town had not changed since his granddad's funeral. It was still small and dusty, an IGA grocery store, Hank's Hardware, Texaco gas—big red-winged horse flying from a pole—old Country Court House, and Apple's Funeral Home. Outside town, fields were coming into their own, as farmers sat on tractors turning earth and logging trucks rolled toward the mill.

Near the Wallowa Mountains six miles away, construction crews were just laying the groundwork for a ski lift with the thought of attracting tourists to the area. Coop's brother Matt was now the town mayor and had pushed hard for the project. He got it approved and financed with local bond money. He was most folks' favorite son.

Coop limped across the street, leg dragging, and stepped up on the wooden boardwalk that fronted the Joseph Saloon. Inside, the fat bartender had been replaced by a woman who looked familiar.

He dropped his bag, plopped on a green leather barstool, and watched her draw a mug and slide it down the counter. At the other end, catching the beer, was a skinny, sickly looking guy wearing a Harlton Trucking baseball hat. The place smelled like peanuts and beer sausage. There were tables, chairs, a jukebox, and walls covered with deer heads, ducks, bobcats, and beer signs. In the back was a pool table, green felt stained, light dangling. Next to the crooked cues on the wall was a poster of two well-stacked country girls sitting back on bales of hay. Big smiles, cowboy hats, tight jeans, halter tops, breasts aching to come out. Peanut shells covered the floors, and two brass spittoons sat at opposite ends of the bar. When the bartender came back, she started to speak but stopped at midsentence.

"Can I—" Her eyes squinted, and her face showed astonishment, mouth turning into a wide smile. A front tooth overlapped and was a little crooked, but she was pretty, and her eyes lit up like she had just found twenty bucks in her pocket. It was Lucy. "Coop. Why, you dog. I thought you were never coming home." Then her smile evaporated, mouth tightened, eyes narrowed, and she drew her head back quickly. "You son of a bitch. Why didn't you write? You told me you'd write. I wrote you six times, and you didn't answer one of my letters. Even Charlie Apple said he got a letter from you."

Coop was glad to see Lucy and flashed briefly on that night in the motel, sweat rolling on her belly. "Gosh . . . I meant to write . . . but, well . . . I didn't have much to say. And I got wounded again and—"

"Wounded?" Her face changed. She reached across the bar and touched his arm. "Are you OK? What happened?" Both hands were on his forearm, touching his sleeve.

"Just my leg. No biggy." He spun slowly on the stool, kicking his bad foot in the air and showing how the metal brace slapped over his boot.

"Does it hurt?"

"Only when I dance."

They both laughed.

"Oh, it's good to see you," Lucy said. "And I'm so glad you're OK. Well, here, here. Let me buy you a drink. In fact, let me buy you a lot of drinks. Coming home is a big deal. That Vietnam." She shook her head, wiping the bar. "I read two boys over in Jefferson County was killed just last week. One boy's daddy used to come in here all the time. Makes me sick." She went back to wiping. "Well, enough of that. Guys will be getting off work soon, and the steady drinkers will all be here. You know some of them." Lucy put the towel under the bar and emptied an ashtray. "Well, anyway, what can I get ya?"

"Double shot of Johnnie Red and a beer back." Coop felt good seeing Lucy.

"So are you home for good now? Or are you going back?" Lucy set his drinks in front of him, reached under the bar, and brought out a bowl of peanuts.

"See you got a new moose head over the bar," Coop replied, not answering.

"Yeah. Bill, the owner. You know Bill? Anyway, he hit the damn thing with his truck when he was up in Alaska. Tells everybody that comes through town he shot it, makes him feel like a big man. But forget that. Are you staying or what?"

Coop finished his beer and started cracking a peanut.

"Don't know. Half the reason I came back here was to see you," he winked. "I thought about you a lot." He wanted her going down on him, crooked tooth raking the side of his cock. "Wanted to see you again."

Lucy blushed, tossed her hair, turned to pick up a bottle, poured another drink. "Well, you should'a wrote," she said, putting the bottle back and drawing another beer. Then her voice became firm as if she were a mother scolding her child. "You blew a yellow light, buster. You best not run a red one."

Coop shrugged, looked at his beer glass as if it held some sort of provocative response, but all he could think of was, "Sorry." He got up off his stool. "Look. I'm goin' across the street to use the pay phone and call Charlie. See if my truck's still in one piece. Will you watch my bag? Be back in a few minutes."

"Sure."

"Can I see ya when you get off work?"

"I'm here 'til closing. But let's talk when you get back."

Farmers and loggers were pulling in, parking their trucks as Coop clumped up the block to use the pay phone at the Texaco. His leg muscles had atrophied from all those months of lying in bed. His leg brace seemed heavy and awkward. By the time he got to the station, he was tired, back full of sweat. He noticed the red-winged horse flying above the station.

"If I had a chopper," he said to himself, "I'd blow the shit out of it."

He looked up Charlie's number in the tattered phone directory, which was no thicker than a comic book, fumbling for a dime. But Charlie was gone.

"Out of town," his dad said. "Pendleton maybe, chasing some long-legged gal he met at the roundup. Yep. Got your truck all right."

Coop hung up, took a piss, then wandered back to Lucy.

At the bar, no one recognized him. Or at least no one said they did. Which he found hard to figure because he'd only been gone a couple years. And, hell, he had his uniform on. You'd think someone would say something.

The night wore on as he shot pool, plugged the jukebox, and got drunker by the minute. By 11:00 p.m., most folks had gone home, and Coop was sloppy drunk, passed out in a chair underneath a stuffed bobcat. Lucy, meanwhile, swept up peanut shells and sang along with Patsy Cline.

When he woke up, his head hurt, and his mouth felt like he'd been chewing cotton balls and sawdust. He was lying next to Lucy and vaguely remembered walking upstairs.

Once he got his truck back from Charlie, he rented a trailer out-side of town and bought some furniture from a flea market in Baker. Disability checks started coming in that paid rent, but he got tired of sitting around, drinking, and having raging hangovers. He tried humping the Wallowas, Granddad hanging in his dreams, but the foot wasn't strong enough to handle the terrain. So he talked to his brother, whom he called Mayor Matt, and got hooked up with the crew working on the ski lift. Every day or so he'd run into Mayor Matt, but it didn't go well. They were both awkward and annoyed with each other, as if they were never really brothers but old acquain-tances from high school who had nothing in common anymore.

Work on the ski lift and tram was easy, compared with beating the bush. The days went fast. But at night, his foot kept swelling and looked as if it had been in water too long. When he washed, skin along the bottom would tear like wet wall paper. Nerve damage never improved, and there was no feeling. The foot was dead. One afternoon he was helping lay the forms for a foundation when he stepped on a nail. It drove deep into his foot, but he felt nothing. He finished the day, then stopped to see Lucy at the tavern.

They were an item, comfortable with each other but not expect-ing much. If he got tired of drinking, he'd usually go up the back stairway to her apartment, lie on the couch, and watch TV until she got off work. But this time he wasn't feeling good. He grabbed a grilled steak sandwich, headed home, neck sore, head pounding, brow slick with sweat.

Not touching his sandwich, Coop lay down and was out. He woke up in the middle of the night shaking, shirt soaked. He pulled off his boots, slipped out of his clothes, lay back in the dark. Head spinning, fever on him, he fell asleep again.

JT was carrying the radio when the patrol left that first morning. Hawkeye was in front of JT, and the Kit Carson was leading the patrol. They walked along a well-traveled path, hugging the tree line on one side, paddies on the other.

When the machine guns and explosions started, Coop sat up, and the dream was over.

He turned on the lamp next to his bed and was startled by a strong smell. At first he thought he'd messed his sheets, but the smell was more sour than that. It was something he had smelled before in piles of the dead. He looked at his foot; it was twice the size of normal. It had turned the color of plums and rotten pears, with pus and traces of blood oozing from the bottom. He called Lucy.

She drove him to the veterans hospital across the Washington border in Walla Walla and stayed in a roadside motel. Doctors stuck IVs in his arms and legs as the fever rose. He was in and out of delirium.

"We aren't set up for amputations here. We may need to send him to Portland to take it off," the doctor told Lucy. "There's so much nerve damage and infection in the bone. The next twelve hours will tell."

By late afternoon the following day, color had come back to his foot. The fever broke, and he was awake and clear-thinking. He felt relieved and a great sense of indebtedness to Lucy. He could count on her to come through. After eighteen more days in the hospital, bombarded with antibiotics, he was finally discharged, using crutches.

"You'll need to take care of that foot," the doctor advised. "Next time you could lose your leg. Or worse."

That afternoon Coop was in a cast and Lucy was driving his truck. The sun was shining, a flock of geese cutting through the sky. He was glad to be alive, glad to have his foot, and glad to be with Lucy. They pulled out of the parking lot, kicking up gravel, and headed for Reno, where they were married in a twenty-four-hour chapel and spent the night in a budget motel.

19

JT

JT MOVED INTO HIS FATHER'S APARTMENT A few days after Evelyn called.

"Your prodigal son has returned," he joked, dropping a big cardboard box in the middle of the front room. The box held most of what he owned, the rest sold or left behind. Jack was resting on the couch reading a western, smoking Camel straights, feet covered with a blanket.

"Hungry?" Jack asked, setting the book on his distended belly. His arms and face were sallow, shrunken.

"No, thanks. Just ate." JT sat in the chair facing the couch. He leaned forward, elbows on his knees. "See you're still smoking."

"Why not? It's already killed me."

JT felt like he'd just been punched in the face or had a heavy flu and was trying to recover. He looked around the room.

"Your window's still cracked. Why don't you get the manager to fix it?"

"He's dead on his ass, tryin' to screw all his tenants," Jack said, coughing up phlegm. He turned his head and spit in a coffee can sitting on the floor. Traces of spittle and blood marked his shirt, and the carpet was soiled.

"I'll talk to the manager and straighten this shit out. The son of a bitch can fix the goddamn window. That's what you pay rent for."

"Don't make a fuss. Evelyn talked to him." Jack coughed again. "Can you bring me some water?"

JT grabbed a glass from the cupboard. There were no wine bottles on the counter, just cans of chili and a pie Evelyn must have bought at Safeway. No bottles in the fridge either. Strange. He ran the tap until the water was cold, took a drink, and filled the glass back up again.

"You quit boozin'?" JT asked, handing the glass to his dad.

"Set it on the table, will ya?"

"Didn't see any bottles. You stop drinking?"

"Now don't start on me. I'm tryin'. 'Sides, Evelyn won't get it for me anymore. And Lizzy run off with some damn cab driver." Jack placed the book on the table, slowly sat up, and put his feet on the floor. It was an effort. He kicked around for slippers then willed himself up, arms shaking, legs unsteady. "Gotta piss," he said, catching his breath. "Little tired today. Had chemo this morning."

JT tried to hide the realization from his face.

"You can put your stuff in the bedroom," Jack said. "I'll sleep on the couch." He wavered a bit as though a strong wind was forcing him off balance, then painfully shuffled across the room, bent over, pants sagging to the crack in his ass. His clothes were wrinkled, and his body looked feeble. He stopped and leaned on a wall to catch his breath, muttering to the floor. "I feel like I'm a hundred goddamn years old."

"Dad, let me take the couch. You need to rest."

"No, dammit."

JT watched him round the corner and disappear into the bathroom. He wanted to kick the shit out of the manager, make him fix the window.

That night Evelyn came over with a bucket of fried chicken, and the three of them sat in the front room eating and watching TV.

Evelyn was older than JT's father, squat and determined. She ruled
the girls at the massage parlor with a firm hand but always helped
them out when they needed food or rent money. She mothered JT's
dad, called him "honey," except when he drank; then she would well
up into a fury, knock things on the floor, and barrel out the door
screaming, "That's it! That's it! You're not getting no more help
from me you lousy son of a bitch!" They'd make up a few days later,
and he'd be back over at her place, fixing a steam cabinet extension
cord or a broken leg on a massage table.

They finished the chicken and were eating the chocolate pie JT
bought at Piggly Wiggly. Evelyn, always blunt and to the point, told
him he should take Jack to get welfare.

"Wouldn't hurt and I sure can't keep paying all his rent," Evelyn
said. Dad was asleep on the couch deep in a codeine dream as Evelyn folded her TV tray and stacked it in the corner.

"I guess I could take him down tomorrow. If he'll go."

"He'll go, all right," Evelyn said. "Or he won't have rent money.
And believe me, they'll kick his butt out the door, cancer or no cancer."

THE NEXT MORNING, JT GOT UP BEFORE first light, did push-ups, and
ran. There were more hills around his father's place, and the run
was not easy. The sun was rising as he ran by a high-rise, concrete
retirement center that had a fountain and wishing pond out front.
A large mass of fake rock with water tumbling down reminded him
of the first patrol.

The waterfall. Gurney. Trees exploding.

He crossed the street and ran back toward the apartment. On his
way, he jimmied a news rack and ripped off a paper.

Out in front of the complex, he saw a small girl in a dress riding
a tricycle and thought of Anna. Suddenly the tricycle tipped, and the
girl fell and banged her knee. By the time JT reached the little girl,
she was crying and her knee was bleeding. He took off his white

T-shirt and wrapped her knee and kept saying, "You're going to be OK. It's OK, sweetheart." JT picked her up in his arms. "Now show me where you live, sweetie." He felt like he was carrying Anna.

The girl had stopped crying and pointed to a red door in the apartment complex. As he walked toward it, the screen door opened and a man shuffled out.

"Oh my God, honey. What happened?"

JT handed the girl to her concerned dad and explained.

"Thank you, man. I just came in to answer the phone. Thank you so much." They shook hands. JT felt good.

After being outside, the apartment smelled foul and unnatural. Jack was still sleeping. He picked up the coffee can and washed it out in the sink and put a paper sack full of used Kleenex outside in the garbage. Each apartment had a back door and small porch with three steps down to a sidewalk. The sidewalk was cracked and uneven and cut through the complex like a Parcheesi board winding to each tired building. The neighbor next door had set out a cat box, and a stray dog was nosing in the litter box as JT stuffed the trash.

Sitting on the porch steps, he looked out across the fresh-cut grass to similar red, two-story buildings. A crew of roofers had just arrived and were busy setting up ladders, buckets, and tarps and mixing a bin full of hot tar. The smell of tar reminded him of LZ Stud, trucks and tanks rumbling by, gas, oil, and creosote. The smell didn't bother him, but just as he got up to go inside, he saw a roofer with his shirt off climbing a ladder. He had red hair, like Gurney. He shook it off and went inside.

His dad was sitting up, smoking. He looked a little better.

"How 'bout some corned beef hash?" Jack asked.

"Sure," JT replied, opening the fridge. "That chemo kicks your ass. I'll cook."

Dad crossed the room dragging his leg slightly, determined. "Outta my kitchen," Jack said, pulling out a skillet, potatoes, and reaching for his favorite butcher knife.

JT relinquished, grabbed the paper, pushed through the screen door, and sat down on the porch. Skipped over the headline *More Troop Reductions* and settled on the sports page.

"You like green pepper?" Dad asked through the screen door.

"Yeah." He could smell potatoes frying and hear bacon popping.

After breakfast, he drove Jack's old station wagon to the welfare office. It had dented fenders, torn seats, a driver's window that wouldn't roll down. Always thought it was odd that his dad never had a decent car. After all, his father was a body and fender man. As they crossed town, JT remembered being taken to school as a little boy in junkers: missing fenders, broken windshields, car always needing paint. It embarrassed him, almost as much as when his dad was drunk at his baseball games or wrestling matches.

Lot of folks at the welfare office, mostly women. Long lines, paperwork to fill out. When JT took his dad home, it was late and Jack was tired. Didn't want to eat. JT helped him lie down on the couch and take off his shoes, made sure he had water and a clean coffee can.

EACH WEEK JT DROVE HIS DAD TO chemo and radiation at the VA hospital. He'd pull up in front of the building, thirty steep steps to get inside.

"Want me to help you, Dad? Or I can take you around the side to get a wheelchair and you can take the elevator."

"No. Get the hell out of here. I ain't dead yet." And Jack would hold on to the rail and climb the steps slowly.

Treatments were hard. His hair fell out, and each day his body became more frail and thin, except for his bloated stomach.

JT would wait in the lobby all day with the older vets and their wives or the few young veterans like him. Later he would take him home to the couch. One day, JT walked around the hospital and counted all the arms and legs missing or men blind. He quit counting because it was a morbid curiosity and only made him grieve.

"I can get you a wheelchair," JT always said, but Jack growled and complained, saying, "Don't bother me." Sometimes JT would lie awake listening to his father's shallow breathing. He'd hear him moan from the other room, softly, almost like a puppy crying, and wonder how much more pain he could take.

"Rough night?" JT asked bringing water and medication. "What's it like, Dad? The pain."

Jack was lying on the couch, wrapped in blankets, belly as big as a beach ball, wearing thick socks and a stocking cap, His head was a skull, skin as thin and taut as a membrane. And his eyes were sunken so deep in their sockets that they almost disappeared. He looked like he was a prisoner from Auschwitz, JT thought, not his dad.

But his father heard the question and answered weakly. "Son, if you're lucky—you die. If you're not, you live a hundred years."

On the last day his father walked, JT drove him to the steps of the VA. "Why don't you let me get you a chair today?"

"Forget it," Jack said, working hard to get out of the car and stand. His legs were shaky, and he buckled over and almost fell. JT let his dad go and parked the car, uphill from the building. The car idled as he sat looking down at his father, watching him hold the rail and slowly battle up those steep stairs. Jack would pull and step and rest and rest. Then pull and step. It took him over ten minutes to make those thirty stairs. In a final will of strength, he pulled open the heavy wooden doors. As he watched his dad stagger inside, he realized the effort was heroic.

That afternoon, he sat in the lobby looking at the other veterans his father's age in wheelchairs or on vinyl benches sitting close to their overweight wives. They were wearing VFW vests with tiny flags and buttons. Some wore WWII baseball hats and T-shirts that let everyone know they were veterans. JT, though, never felt like one. Even then. How can you be proud when half the country hates you?

When the day was almost done, a nurse brought Jack out in a wheelchair. He looked more spent than ever. His tiny eyes were glassed, and he was shaking.

A few weeks later, JT's dad was gone. He died in the apartment on the bathroom floor. JT lifted him and carried him carefully to his couch. He was buried quietly, in the VA cemetery in May. There was no twenty-one-gun salute or speech about him once fighting for democracy and freedom. JT was given a flag by the government.

In the morning, Evelyn gave JT a green garbage bag with all Jack's possessions. Inside were old photos, hankies, and a yellow and tattered newspaper clipping. The clipping was a picture of his dad as a young soldier, home fresh from the war:

> *Jack Hadley returns to Enid, Oklahoma, after four years of serving heroically in the US Army including tours in Italy, Africa, and Sicily. Mr. Hadley was awarded the Purple Heart, Silver Star, and two Bronze Stars with Oakleaf Clusters.*

It was a stunning thought. JT never knew his father was a hero. It made him cry.

20

The First Patrol

Vietnam, Winter 1969

JT wished Coop hadn't made his stupid joke in the chopper about being his butt boy—not in front of Gurney. It was clear that Gurney was above such shit; he had a special look like he wanted to go places, accomplish something in life. JT wondered if Coop knew how to take anything seriously.

He set his pack down, laid his rifle on top, took off his helmet, and dropped it. He drank from a canteen as Coop spat the last of his chew.

"Jeez!" JT said irritably. "Look what you're doing. You almost spit on my helmet, man." JT punched him in the arm a little harder than playful.

Coop shrugged. "Sorry, man. Have a cow."

JT wiped sweat off his brow with the back of his hand and could feel the heat envelop him as two soldiers walked up. One was white, gangly, shirt off, tanned, cigarette behind his ear. He looked thin, JT thought. Needed a few meals, a shave. His pants were riding low, no hair on his chest or belly.

"So you're the new John Waynes gonna save our ass, huh? Well, I'm Ski, your squad leader, and this here's my main man, Hawkeye."

"Gentlemen," Hawkeye nodded.

JT thought the word *gentlemen* sounded so strange, as if they were about to be seated at a table and Hawkeye was the big black waiter. He shook hands with Ski, then Hawkeye, who was bigger, stronger, and seemed brighter than Ski.

"So where you from?" Hawkeye asked.

"We're both from Oregon. I'm from Portland and Coop's from Joseph, small town other side of the state."

"Another country boy!" Ski exclaimed, looking at Hawkeye like it was unusual. "You ain't into sheep now, are you?"

Hawkeye put his fist to his mouth in a polite gesture and laughed along with JT.

Coop blushed. "Well, I'm not doin' 'em, at least not anymore."

"Guy's a fuckin' comedian. Well, grab your gear, dildos," Ski ordered. "Welcome to the third herd."

Ski and Hawkeye took them around the perimeter toward the command post to meet the LT, but he was gone on patrol. They headed farther along the hill, stopping at shelter halves or sandbagged bunkers and fighting holes. They met Cueball, who was sitting on the side of his hole, boots off, squeezing pus out of a sore on his ankle.

Cueball looked up. "Say, it's Mr. Ski and Mr. Brain. What it is?" he said, squinting against the sun.

JT and Coop pulled out their canteens again.

"Not much," Ski replied, hands shoved in his pockets, scratching.

"Uncle Sam was nice enough to bring us two more for the cauldron," Hawkeye said. "They're from Oregon."

"Or-gone? That's some cowboy country there, boy. Ain't got no brothers in Or-gone." Cueball frowned, then laughed with Hawkeye and they exchanged a little dap. "No shit. Or-gone? That's like chuck dudes ever'where. Am I right or am I right? Wait a second.

Knew this brother once lived in Or-gone. Didn't see another blood for damn near six months. I shit you not! Dude live in some funky little town like Possumville or Porky Pine City. Anyway, some donkey-dick name."

They all laughed at Cueball's description.

"Gotta get these guys situated," Ski finally said. "And you better make sure Doc looks at your foot. That's some nasty-lookin' rot."

"Damn near half the platoon got it," Cueball said, dabbing ointment on the sore. "That or the shits."

"Yeah, well. Talk to Doc," Ski said, scratching.

As they walked along, Ski filled them in on where they were as best he could and what was going down. "Listen, nobody likes new guys. You got that stateside mentality all up in your heads. Next thing you know, you blow someone else away. Last week in First Platoon, new guy dropped a grenade. Blew two dudes away. Understand? So listen up. I don't want no magazines in your rifle 'til we're out of the perimeter or rounds in the chamber 'til I say so. That clear?"

JT and Coop nodded their heads as they walked past guys eating C-rats, cleaning rifles, lying under shelter halves, transistors going, music fading in and out.

"And unzip your flak jackets. If you get gut shot and a round fucks up that zipper, we'll have hell trying to cut it off you. Hawk, can you set these guys in?"

Hawkeye had them drop their gear beside a squad playing back-alley bridge on a Snoopy. They were on the side of the hill that looked directly across rice paddies and up into mountains two thousand yards away.

"This here's Moose, Little Mike, Flowers, and Doc," Hawkeye said. "Chuck dude crashed out over there is Andy." Hawkeye pointed to a poncho stretched with stakes and rope, a Marine sleeping.

"He's the sleepiest son of a bitch I ever seen," Flowers said, nodding toward Andy. He held his cards tight against his chest, looking out for cheaters. "And stinky feet. Whew!" Flowers shook his head and distorted his face. "Them's nasty smellin', bro. He glanced at his cards. "I'm good. Show me the power." Doc was his partner.

Moose was disgusted with his cards. "You been kickin' our butt all day."

"You need ah ass-whippin'," Flowers gleamed.

"Fuck this! I quit." Moose threw down his cards.

Hawkeye explained that JT was the new radioman and that Coop was going to carry extra rounds for his 60.

"But I don't know anything about the radio," JT protested.

"Don't sweat it. You'll learn. You're carrying it until a new guy comes in or you get dead. OK?" Hawkeye waited for a nod of acknowledgment. Then his voice got tense, "Now, where's our Kit Carson? Where's Vuong?"

"Rice snapper's probably walking off our position," Flowers said sarcastically. "Gonna drop artie on us. Fuck us all up."

"Can I get a straight answer out of you guys? Where's Vuong?"

"He left the perimeter about an hour ago," Doc said. "Wanted to get some bananas."

"You know no one's supposed to leave the perimeter." Hawkeye was angry. "He could get blown away."

"Good," Flowers said.

Hawkeye threw a cold stare.

"Don't blame me," Doc said. "I'll sew you up, but I sure as hell ain't babysitting jarheads or rice snappers."

"LT finds out Vuong's gone, it's my ass," Hawkeye snapped. He lectured them, explaining and reprimanding, everybody listening except Flowers, who was lost in himself again.

"Wait a second. Here he comes now." Doc pointed back up the hill behind Hawkeye, who had turned. Vuong was carrying a helmet full of small bananas, looking pleased.

"Where you been, man?" Hawkeye asked pissed off, grabbing a couple of bananas and peeling one. He slipped the thumb-sized fruit in his mouth. "Where were you?"

Vuong tilted his head, confused. He held up the bananas and pointed toward a distant village more than a mile away, answering, "I go bananas." Everyone laughed as if he had just told an outrageously hilarious joke.

"Yeah, and you drivin' Hawk bananas!" Flowers blurted, looking for a squad of laughs, but only got a forced one from JT and Coop.

"He's a damn jackrabbit if ya ask me," Moose said, his huge hand grabbing everything left in Vuong's helmet. "Ain't none ah you guys can hump that fast."

"You're probably right, Moose," Hawkeye replied, turning to JT and Coop who were more relaxed now, less anxious. "So you guys, dig a hole, chow down, and hang tight. In a little while, we'll go over the radio freaks and commiserate. This little guy here is our Kit Carson Scout."

"I Vuong," he said, helmet empty, reaching out to shake their hands. He was wearing tight-fitting camouflage jungles, rifle slung over his shoulder, barrel pointing down, which JT thought was odd.

"Vuong used to be an NVA," Hawkeye said. "In fact, we wounded him a few months ago up in Hue. Life is weird. After he was wounded, he was given an opportunity to come on over to our side. He's a scout now, assigned to Kilo. Walks point most of the time. He's OK." Hawkeye draped a big arm around Vuong. "I'll tell you this much, he's been through hell. A lot of the guys worry about him, and I know what you're thinking. Couldn't Vuong be telling the enemy our plans? Well, the brass don't tell none of us what's happening, so they sure as hell aren't going to tell Vuong. Catch my drift, gentlemen? You guys dig in, make sure the pins on your grenades are bent. I don't want any spoons flying unless we're in a world ah hurt. I'll check back later."

JT and Coop dug a hole, laid out their frags and rifles, then opened some C-rats and waited for night.

"You know the mountains look a lot like eastern Oregon," Coop said, spooning peaches. "Ever been out there?"

"Once," JT said. "When I was just a kid, I went with my dad and uncle up near Enterprise. My dad shot a big buck, and they made me help gut it. Said it'd make a man outta me. I hated it."

The sun dipped behind the mountains. JT's fear rose. Soon the hill full of soldiers disappeared, and even with Coop next to him, he felt alone.

"You squared away?" Hawkeye asked, slipping up next to JT and Coop's hole.

JT could smell peanut butter on Hawkeye's breath. "Yeah, but nervous, I guess," JT said.

"Don't worry. I don't think we'll get hit." He sat next to their hole. "I'll give you the first couple watches 'cause you're cherries. I'll sleep close by. If you have a problem or get spooked, you can shake me. If you have to take a whiz or a dump," Hawkeye continued, "do it before your watch. Use the piss tube we set up or the hole with the wood ammo box covering it. And stay alert. We got claymores strung out there and don't want to get you killed your first day. Make sure to let the guys on either side of you know you're taking a dump. JT, you take the first watch. Coop, you got the second watch. I'll take the third, and Moose and Little Mike will relieve you and ride it out until daylight."

JT sat on the edge of his hole, staring out across the paddies, frags, ammo, and his rifle in front of him. It was blacker than he had ever experienced. The mountains were just another big wave of darkness. He checked the luminous dial on his watch. It was nine o'clock and already he was tired. He thought about enemy coming and being shot in the face or gut-shot like Ski mentioned. How would it feel? He knew he couldn't stand the pain. What if his rifle jammed or gooks snuck up on him? He was afraid and felt like a coward.

Even with the moon bringing the light, JT couldn't see anything and felt a terrible sense of emptiness. Like he was the only one there facing death. Maybe if a group of soldiers were running toward him firing in the daylight he could see them but not now, not in this field of shadows and flatness. He picked up his rifle, waved it, firing in his mind, crushing the night, then set it down, feeling foolish. He grabbed a grenade and pretended to throw it, then ducked. He liked the feel of it in his hand. Like a baseball, it gave him a sense of power.

For a few moments, his thoughts wandered home to Ashley, to when she got pregnant and they got married. He remembered watching her undress for bed, amazed that this was something he got to do every night. Even when he wasn't expecting sex—though they did have sex pretty much all the time—he liked seeing her skin bared, gleaming in the lamplight, liked seeing her body as it changed. He remembered rubbing lotion on her swollen belly, their child kicking. He loved feeling her belly and that internal pad of unborn feet. The rise in her stomach, the fullness of her breasts, and how her long fingers danced when she spoke, as if plucking ideas from the air. He remembered her voice confiding secrets, dreams of the future—how many kids they'd have, the big house by a lake. Then he was playing baseball under the lights with her watching, diving for the ball. He missed her and missed the feel of a baseball in his hands. He wanted to go home.

His eyes grew tired as the first hour crawled. For a moment, JT thought a long swath of blackness near the base of the mountains was moving, an army of crazed enemy in black pajamas about to attack. He heard they weren't afraid and didn't feel pain. They liked to die. Wanted to. They believed they would just keep getting re-born again. What would that be like? Thinking as you checked out that you were on your way back to infancy . . .

He rubbed his eyes, strained, and could tell it was nothing.

In the second hour, he ate a dry chocolate bar, leaving a pasty taste in his mouth. He grabbed his canteen, swirled quietly, and spit to the side of his hole. Then something moved. His heart took off running; his body froze. Ducking in the hole, he held his rifle up and sighted down the long black barrel. His pupils opened as the front and rear sight made a perfect line on the shadows. He could taste vileness in his mouth but nothing moved. It was only a tree. Or shadows cast by the mountain. It was so slight, like the shades in a dark pool of water. His body trembled.

He needed to pee and grabbed himself but was afraid to get out of his hole. He checked his watch again. And again. Finally, it was over. Exhausted, shirt wringing wet, he shook Coop awake.

The night passed.

"OK, gentlemen," Hawkeye said, kicking the bottoms of JT's and Coop's feet, "time to rise and shine."

JT jumped with the kick and his mind cleared instantly. Coop wasn't far behind.

"Eat up," Hawkeye barked. "Your cherry is about to be popped. We're going on patrol, gentlemen."

JT felt a massive wave of dread wash over him. His hands shook as he tied his boots.

"In about thirty minutes, patrol's going out," Hawkeye said. "And in case you geniuses haven't figured it out yet, you lucky bums are with us. Can you dig it?" He smiled. "So chow down, grab your gear, and let's get ready to rock and roll. Oregon, here's the radio," Hawkeye added, setting it at JT's feet.

"Thanks," JT replied.

"You hungry?" Coop asked.

"No, man," JT replied. "Maybe a fruitcake. I'll trade you for a fruitcake?"

"Nah. You can have mine," Coop offered. "I hate it. Makes my dick soft."

JT shook his head. This didn't make sense. He felt too new to go out on patrol. He ate, then nervously checked his weapons and magazines, making sure that the springs were tight and could push the rounds easily.

The sun was up and the heat was coming.

JT brushed a handful of flies away from his fruitcake. He buried his cans with Coop's, threw on his flak jacket, slipped on the radio, and looked out on the paddies and mountains. The mountains seemed closer than yesterday as he turned toward the distant outline of a village. From the top of the knoll he could barely see the thatched roofs. Maybe that was a farmer and his water bull way out there, but it was just too far to tell. He hung the handset on his jacket and reached over his shoulder to see if he could make the radio squawk. He knew nothing about it. What little he learned in training was gone, forgotten. He'd just carry it, hoping Ski or Hawkeye would tell him what to do.

"Hey, fucksticks."

Flowers walked up with the rest of the squad, shades on, do-rag wrapped around his head, no shirt or flak jacket, peace sign dangling from his neck. "How'd it go last night? Get your rocks off?"

He laughed and so did Moose and Little Mike as they gathered around with Hawkeye, Doc, and Andy. Vuong stood by, separate from the others.

"Don't mind Flowers," Hawkeye said. "His mouth and his ass get confused."

Everyone laughed except Flowers, who said, "You can babysit these white boys. I'm gonna get Ski." Before he could leave, Ski walked up with Cueball, Banger, and the rest, including the soldier who came on the chopper with JT and Coop.

"Listen up," Ski ordered. "Our platoon has been short of men and the LT is gone on R&R, so Lieutenant Gurney from Second Platoon is going to hang with us. He'll be leading this patrol."

The red-haired LT stepped forward. JT was amazed. He didn't think Gurney was old enough to be an officer, and he certainly didn't look or act like he thought an officer would. But he had quality and seemed pure and steady.

"There's twenty-two of us, counting Vuong," Gurney said, helmet tucked under his arm, red hair scattered, caught by a breeze.

He stepped over to place a hand on Vuong's shoulder, moving to touch each soldier in a thoughtful way.

"Vuong's on point. Cueball here and Banger will be walking slack. We'll mix it up with Ski, Hawkeye, Flowers, Doc. I'll be with the new guys. Moose and Little Mike, you follow me, then the rest of you guys fall in. Decide who's walking end Charlie. This patrol is nothing fancy. We'll move through the paddies toward the mountains and then sweep toward the ville. I know about the row of shacks near the river," he said, smiling, "but we won't be stopping for dinner." Everyone snickered and laughed. "We lost guys the other day. So make no mistake, Charlie's out there."

The men threw on their helmets and flak jackets, grabbed ammo and canteens, and picked up their rifles, heading off the hill leaving the perimeter. Fields were dry and hard as they crossed in one long line, spread out ten steps apart, eyes focused on the man in front or scanning to the side. Clumps of dirt compressed and flattened under each soldier's boots.

JT felt awkward and unsure of his feet and worried about turning his ankle. In high school, he broke both ankles, once in football and once swinging on the rope in gym, screwing off. So his ankles were tender. He laced his boots tight. His mind was on Ashley and not wanting to die.

Vuong led the patrol at a fast pace that was difficult for most of the men to maintain. As they edged toward the base of the mountains, Gurney yelled, "Slow it down, Vuong."

"Fuckin' rice snapper," Moose puffed.

As the patrol moved, rice paddies became elephant grass and tangles of weeds. The grass was knee deep when Gurney passed the word. "OK, men, stop and rest, have a smoke, easy on the water. Ski, send guys to the side."

JT dropped the radio, sat down, took off his helmet, and poured water on his head. He wasn't tired, but the heat and the flak jacket and radio made his temperature soar. His shirt was soaked.

"Slow down on that water, partner," Gurney said, coming up. He squatted, and JT could see a small black cross on his lapel, no bigger than a dime. "We got a long day ahead of us. You need to hold off on the water." He picked up a blade of grass and chewed on the end of it. "What's your name?"

"Everyone calls me JT, sir."

"JT, that's a good solid name. From Oregon, right?"

"Right."

"Pretty country. Played baseball there once."

"No kidding?" JT was astonished. "I love baseball. Who'd you play for?"

"Used to play for the University of Alabama. We did a West Coast swing and played the University of Oregon."

"Wow! What position?"

"Catcher."

"You don't look like a catcher."

"I know, but then I don't sound like I'm from Alabama either."

Gurney looked at his watch and stood up. "Let's move it out," he said, pulling a map from his flak jacket. He looked at the map, at the mountains, then back to the map. He turned toward the village about a mile away. "Ski," Gurney yelled up ahead. "Get 'em up. Move 'em out."

Vuong led the patrol at a slower pace, even stopping on occasion to let the rear catch up.

SOON THEY WERE CLOSE ENOUGH TO THE village that JT could see huts and a pen with two water bulls. The way the patrol was headed, the village would be on their right and the mountains to their left. They would pass in between.

"LT," Flowers yelled back over his shoulder, smiling underneath his shades. "You sure we can't take a little boom-boom break?"

"Keep moving," Gurney said.

Hawkeye up ahead looked strong, JT thought, carrying a machine gun, biceps knotted in a ball, black skin glistening. With him and Moose, they had tons of firepower. He'd be OK.

Vuong stopped the squad as they began to pass by the village, then motioned them forward. A boy sat on the back of a water bull a hundred yards to the platoon's front and off to the left under a cluster of trees. When he saw the Marines approach, he hurried his bull away from the trees, out of the grass into the paddies, and toward the village two hundred yards away.

The patrol moved lazily now, talking to each other as Vuong forged ahead and disappeared in the grass on the other side of the trees. The back of the patrol was talking about buying a case of beer from the village and maybe scoring some poontang.

Suddenly, just short of the village, an old woman ran out, arms waving, black pants billowing as she ran. She was yelling nonsensically, pointing toward the mountains. Racing up behind her were two younger women and the boy who had been on the water bull. The patrol halted. Gurney spread them out, half of the weapons trained to the right flank, half to the left.

"What's the bullshit?" Flowers yelled loud enough for Ski and Hawkeye to hear.

"That's your old lady," Ski shouted back. "She's pissed off, man. Says you gave her the clap."

"All right, men," Gurney said, walking down the file. "Cut the noise."

JT watched with fascination as the old woman railed, eyes sunk deep in her sockets, face sagged in folds and wrinkles. Her white shirt was frayed and dark-stained, teeth rotten and too large for her mouth. She shouted, danced, waved, pointed to the trees, speaking to Vuong and looking as if she were about to cry. The other women and the boy tried to calm her and finally were able to drag her away.

"What is it, Vuong? What's going on?"

There was an edge in Gurney's voice as he listened carefully to Vuong's clipped English. The patrol had gone well. No one wanted trouble.

"Mamasan *dinky dau*. She crazy."

"Did she say VC? I thought I heard VC?"

"No. No VC," Vuong said emphatically. His face was firm and his voice was full of conviction.

"Why was she pointing toward the trees?"

"She crazy. No VC."

Gurney stood there for a long moment, weighing Vuong's words, then turned and called for the squad to move out. They passed by the village and continued to methodically edge along the base of the mountain, eyes searching the rice paddies on their right, mountains on their left. Soon the village was far behind them.

The sky was blue with only a slash of clouds and floating a huge, glaring sun. The heat was intense, working hard on the men, especially on JT. He felt like he was evaporating. His mouth was dry, and he could feel his lips parch, crack, and start to bleed. He wanted to strip off his uniform and flak jacket, run naked, blasted by a fire hose. Or go swimming in the North Fork of the Santiam River where he used to dive off the railroad trestle. The Santiam was so clean he could see twenty feet deep to the bottom. Just one dive. The radio was heavy, his legs weary, and he stumbled as he daydreamed. The heat had robbed him of his ability to concentrate. He'd do anything to pour all of his canteens on his head and drink freely. Anything.

As the day dragged on, the patrol began to wear down and go slack. Flowers was complaining that the patrol was bullshit, and he wished all the sons of bitches back in the rear would "just fuckin' die."

Whenever there was an elevated voice, though, Gurney would pass the word up front, "Knock it off up there. Cut the crap." They kept moving. Moving through the fields, then high grass, then back to the fields.

An hour more and Gurney signaled the patrol to stop, drink, take a smoke, and eat a can of chow. Helmets off. He ordered Cueball and Banger into the paddies to stand guard. Far off in the open fields were clusters of huts and banana trees, like desert mirages dancing in the distance. He had Ski send a couple of guys as lookouts up into the jungle.

"Hawk, take JT and Flowers," Ski demanded. "Not too far. Just go in, sit down, and come back in about twenty or so."

"Come on, Oregon," Hawkeye said, tugging at JT's radio straps. "You can drop the radio before it drops you."

Hawkeye smiled reassuringly, but JT felt sick. The heat had drained him and the jungle would be cooler, but he sure didn't want to go away from the men. Away from Coop.

Flowers led the way with JT in the middle.

"Fuck this shit," Flowers snapped. "I'm gonna step in the bush, set my black ass down, and ain't no motherfuckin' cracker gonna tell me different."

Gurney didn't hear Flowers's tirade and Hawkeye let it go. The three moved through the tall grass, pushed past some banana trees, and disappeared into the jungle. The temperature dropped quickly as they entered the thicket, and the glare from the sun was obscured by the trees. Soon they were surrounded by dense vegetation.

"JT, go ahead and slip off your flak jacket and helmet if you want," Hawkeye whispered. "I know how hot you are. You too, Flowers. But only 'til I get back. I'm going to do a little recon. Take a look up here a little bit." Hawkeye left his machine gun with JT and took JT's rifle. "Keep your eyes open. And easy on the water, Oregon."

He moved up the hillside slowly through the hanging vines, broadleafs, and evergreens. In a few minutes he was out of sight.

JT sat down in an area soft with sedge and ferns. He was surrounded by small trees, cascading vines, and foliage. His legs welcomed the moss-covered ground. He slipped off his jacket and helmet and felt his body cool. Heat that was trapped lifted; relief was immediate. He took a sip of water, rolling it in his mouth, savoring the wetness; he pursed his cracked lips and felt the water absorb into his skin. He wanted more. Just one more swallow, just a mouthful, but he twisted the cap back on his canteen and put it away. As his body cooled and relaxed, his mind shifted, focusing on his fear. The trees and knots of twisted vines shielding the sun were suddenly more frightening.

"I never fired the 60 before," JT said timidly. "I was in sick bay that day."

"I fired ever' damn thing. Don't worry yer ass," Flowers said, shades on top of his head, easing back, lying flat like he was in a park in the middle of summer.

"Listen, cherry dick," Flowers lamented. "Hawk cut ya some slack. He knew you was gettin' yer ass kicked out there. That's a fact." Flowers shut his eyes, hands clasped behind his head. "Don't wake me less ya have to."

A minute passed, and the stillness heightened JT's fears. Without Hawkeye in sight, he felt lost. In the paddies, he could see the other men, hear them talking, their footsteps scuffing. In the bush, there was only quiet. No sounds of animals or birds or even wind rustling the leaves. Another few minutes passed, his mind racing. Suddenly, he heard the stirring of ferns, brush breaking, and his heart began to pound. He reached for the 60. It must be Hawkeye. It had to be Hawkeye. He pushed Flowers's leg, and Flowers sat up on his elbows, face twisted in a scowl.

"What? Can't you see I'm trying to cop some z's?"

Hawkeye emerged from a cluster of trees and tangle of vines. He was smiling as if he were glad to see them. "OK, guys. We got about three minutes. Don't say squat, just follow me." Hawkeye picked up the gun and led them into the snarls, pushing back vines, sliding through small trees and plants. In a few moments, it thinned and they were in larger trees. They climbed slowly and deliberately.

Then Hawkeye raised his hand to halt and turned to them. "Shush. Do you hear that?" Hawkeye whispered.

JT listened, but all he could hear was his own breathing. His hand gripped his 16 tighter, and he put his thumb on the safety switch and chambered a round. The noise was startling.

"What the hell?"

Hawkeye turned, put his gun down, and stepped back toward JT, grabbed his rifle, popped out the magazine, and rejected the round. "You don't chamber a round until I say so." He popped the magazine in place, picked the round up, and gave it back to JT.

"Fuckin' cherry," Flowers said, smirking.

"Quiet," Hawkeye commanded, no louder than a whisper.

They edged forward a few more feet, stopped. And listened.

"It's water, gentlemen."

Finally, JT recognized the faint sound of water rushing. They moved up on the mountain's slope and reached the edge of a narrow but deep gully. On the other side of the gully and about a hundred yards away was a rock formation molded into the mountain and a white waterfall dropping into a clear pool.

"Damn!" Flowers exclaimed.

"You guys get down, stay here, keep looking. I'll go talk to the LT. He's going to want to scope this out." Hawkeye dropped the gun, switched with Flowers again, then moved down the mountain gracefully like a deer gliding through forest.

Sunlight dappled on the jungle floor and played across the gully. Because of the heavy canopy, the sun was no longer merciless and felt good. Its showered light was soothing. The ground was soft and cool. JT crawled directly behind the machine gun, eased the butt plate into his shoulder, and sighted down over the barrel. The gun was sitting on its bipod, a short belt of copper-colored ammo loaded. The bipod allowed him to swing the barrel easily, scanning across the gully, then to the waterfall and up along the walls of rocks, rolled smooth by water. His cheek rested against the ridges of the heavy plastic stock, both eyes open, firing in his mind. He could hear the water clearly, and the flutter of a bird overhead as a breeze lifted and carried the jungle's smell. His senses had heightened. He could smell the wet rock and moss and feel fine mist hanging in the air. How could this possibly be war?

Bush crackled, and he turned to his side, punching Flowers. The trembling was back. There was movement. Jungle parting. He could see the dark faces of Hawkeye, then Vuong and the rest of the men bent over, traversing the slope, moving up toward his position. He exhaled as they approached quietly, carefully. They stopped and dropped to one knee. Gurney hurried up to Hawkeye.

"What do you think, Hawk?" Lieutenant Gurney asked, kneeling down next to JT and Flowers.

"Could be R&R for Charlie," Hawkeye suggested. "On the other hand, could just be a waterfall we lucked out on. Seen 'em before."

Gurney took off his helmet, set it down, ran his hand though his hair. He pulled out his map and noted the village they passed and the changes in topography, but no hint of the waterfall.

"Either way, we have to check it out. Could be a water source for the enemy. Could be nothing."

He called back to the firebase and made sure he had the right call signs if they needed artillery or air support and rechecked the grid coordinates. He put men out on each flank and pored over his map. "What do you think, Vuong? We got any VC around here?" Gurney asked.

Vuong shook his head, pulling out a blue bandana he had wadded up in his back pocket, wiped his forehead, then tied it around his neck. "No VC. VC go." Vuong pointed east toward the Laotian border. "Village say no VC."

Gurney brought Ski forward and instructed him to take his squad across the gully and secure itself around the waterfall. Ski put JT on point, then Flowers and Hawkeye, his machine gun balanced on one shoulder. Coop was next with the radio, then Ski,

Doc, Moose, Little Mike, Andy, and the others. Each soldier's helmet half covered their look of apprehension.

JT stood silently, a sickening feeling turning inside. He did not want to walk point. Up front, he would be the first one seen, first one shot, first one to hit a booby trap. He had no idea what to look for. Enemy could be anywhere. Why put a new guy on point? He felt frozen again. Unable to move.

"Get your shit together," Ski warned, then he pointed as if JT was a child. "Just lead us down the gully and set in on the other side of the waterfall!"

Slowly, jungle tugging at his feet, JT led the men down the shallow bank, body trembling, boots sliding, his steps unsure. Twenty steps down, he lost his footing and fell. He scrambled up, embarrassed, and moved on. He reached the gully's floor, crossed easily, and climbed the other bank, falling forward, clawing. Finally, he cleared the crest, and the mist hit him in the face. It was more beautiful than he had imagined. The sound and the smell of wet rock and moss was strong, reminding him of the Grotto at Rocky Butte back home with its waterfall coming out of the mountains, dropping like a white horsetail. JT scooped a handful of water as he passed the clear pool, slapping his face and scooping again.

"Keep moving, Oregon." Hawkeye's voice rose above the noise of water splashing.

The pool was maybe ten feet deep and clear to the bottom, like a swimming hole JT knew on the Clackamas River, tucked away in heavy forest. He worked his way to higher ground, lost in longing to dive naked into the pool, feeling the sensation of water comfort him.

Ski and Hawkeye set the men in as the rest of the patrol formed a horseshoe perimeter around the pool and up the mountainside. JT was at the highest point of the horseshoe, resting in a culvert of rocks at the edge of more jungle. Sunlight that made it through the overhang hit the water just right, so that from JT's angle the pool was almost a mirror, reflecting soldiers as they passed. Hungry, he pulled out a tin of fruitcake, took his opener fixed to the chain of his dog tags, and crimped along the edge of the brown can.

"I thought you'd be eating," Coop said, settling in next to him, tucked behind the boulder. "Isn't this place a kick in the butt? We got a zillion places like this in eastern Oregon." Coop's eyes were lit, mouth grinning, stache wet from a face full of water. His enthusiasm was infectious. "Screw the war; this is paradise, man. Plenty of water and a bunch of guys with enough firepower to kick ass big time."

JT shared his fruitcake with Coop, who took a bite and contorted his face in anguish. "Forgot I hate this crap."

There was a flurry of activity below as Gurney walked the perimeter, talking briefly with each Marine and conferring with Vuong, Hawkeye, and Ski. JT finished his food, stuck the empty can back in the side of his flak jacket, licked the white plastic spoon, and looked down across the water. Gurney was standing by the pool, talking on the radio. Hawkeye was sitting on a rock next to him, looking at a map. Ski next to him smoking. Flowers and Doc were not far from the pool while Moose and the others were around and down the hillside, out of sight.

"I could get used to this action," Coop said, pulling out a round tin of chewing tobacco. He placed a pinch in his cheek, put the lid on, and slid it back into a side pocket of his pants.

"Still chewin', huh?" JT asked. "You know that stuff's bad for you."

"Yeah," he replied sarcastically. "It's gonna ruin my health."

JT swirled some water and passed his canteen to Coop. "This place is unreal."

"No shit. Granddad and I used to find places like this. We used to sit up in the trees and watch deer and raccoon. Once saw a bear and a cougar drinking at the same time. They were eyeballin' each other, knowing they were both tough as shit, both thirsty, so they just backed off and let each other go."

Hawkeye came up and told them that Gurney gave the OK to take turns in the water. "You got three minutes, Oregon."

JT and Coop grabbed their rifles and rushed down to the water. They filled their canteens from the fall, took helmets off, laid rifles on top of flak jackets, and neatly stacked bandoliers of ammo and hand grenades. They stripped to dog tags and, bare-ass naked, dove into the water.

JT swam into the waterfall and let it cascade over him. The rush of water and sound was intoxicating. He felt alive, clean, and protected. He swam back through the showering water, splashed at Coop, and dove and floated in an embryonic state.

"You're done," Gurney ordered.

They got out reluctantly as Cueball stripped down to his shorts. One or two at a time the dirty and tired soldiers came and stripped off their crusty clothes, caked from weeks of being in the field. Some were schoolboy shy and jumped in with their pants on. For a moment, the water would turn cloudy before the swirl from the waterfall made it clear again.

Sunlight that had played across the water disappeared into a bank of gray clouds as Gurney, stripped down to his skivvies, dove in. Flowers and Hawkeye and Vuong stood watching as he swam straight into the waterfall.

A few minutes passed. A couple more.

"Dude's been back there a long time," Flowers said. "Prob-ly wackin' off."

Hawkeye gave him a playful shove. "You're a cartoon, man."

A few more minutes passed. Flowers cleaned his shades with the corner of his utility shirt, fired up a smoke.

"What the fuck is he doin' in there?" Flowers asked. "LT?" Flowers shouted. "You doin' the big thing?"

Another minute passed and no Gurney.

"Son of a bitch," Flowers shouted again, agitated. "You fuckin' with us?" His voice carried around part of the perimeter.

Concern reached Hawkeye's face. "Maybe he hit his head," he thought out loud. He slipped off his boots, dove in, and disappeared behind the waterfall. Time slowed.

Finally, the water broke. It was Hawkeye swimming back to the edge. Flowers pulled him up. There was silence.

"He's gone," Hawkeye said. "Gurney's gone."

"What the fuck? Whaddaya mean gone?"

Hawkeye caught his breath as Cueball and Banger approached. "Get back to your positions!" Hawkeye ordered.

"Hawk," Flowers said, grabbing the crook of Hawkeye's arm forcefully. "Hawk, answer me."

Hawkeye composed himself. Panic was not in his voice. "Get Ski. Go get Ski. Now!"

Before Ski could come up to the pool, word had already traveled around the perimeter that Gurney had disappeared. There was terror in the air.

"There's got to be a cave down there," Hawkeye told Ski. "Maybe he's in a cave, messing with us."

"That ain't Gurney," Ski said. "He won't fuck with us. Especially now. Weather's moving in and we got to get out of here. It'll be dark soon."

"Fuck this, man. This ain't right, man. Fuck this." Flowers was riled. "Ask this fuckin' gook," he said, and he shoved Vuong and sent him flying.

"Don't start your shit, Flowers!" Ski flashed a row of teeth, holding back anger.

"Kiss my black ass, fuckin' chuck muther." He started for Ski, but Hawkeye grabbed him.

"Hold on, damn it!" Hawkeye kept them apart. "Look it. There must be a cave, and maybe he's hurt or who the hell knows what happened, but we gotta go down there and check it out. Flowers, you and I can."

"I ain't gonna go down in no fuckin' cave for nobody."

"That's an order!" Ski bellowed.

"Fuck that order and fuck you," Flowers shouted, fists clenched at his side.

Hawkeye pushed Flowers and Ski apart again. He remained calm, taking control. "Cool it. Call the CP. I'll go. Flowers, since you refuse to go, find a volunteer. Get JT."

Hawkeye and Ski talked and figured there was a cave with an air pocket and that they'd need a flashlight and two .45s. They could wrap the light and the .45s in plastic covering the handset and battery on the radio. They passed the word: "Full alert. Lock and load."

"Take off your boots and shirt," Hawkeye said. "Take this .45 and stick it in your pants. Know how to use it?"

JT nodded. His voice was gone.

"Chamber a round, wrap it. Let's go."

The rest was understood. They stuck the .45s in the front of their jungles. Hawkeye dove with the flashlight on and in his hand, protected by the wrap. JT followed. They crossed quickly through the waterfall. On the other side, it was dark as they treaded water. Hawkeye shined the light across the hollowed-out rock ceiling and walls but could find nothing. The water was loud, and it was hard to hear.

"There's probably an underground cave," Hawkeye shouted, holding his flashlight overhead, water at his neck and mouth. They kicked hard, treading. "Let's go."

They dove underwater and followed the wall recess with the flashlight. After a few feet the rock above them disappeared. Hawkeye broke the water first, then JT, his heart thundering. They were in an underwater cave. He handed JT the flashlight, pulled his .45 out, worked to get the plastic off, finger on the trigger. The beam of light danced on the cavern walls as they floated along, head and gun above the water. The ceiling was no more than four feet, and the walls on each side of the channel were maybe ten feet apart. They crawled out of the water onto a shelf, resting on the rough rock, belly down, light searching, guns ready. As the light caught the outline of a tunnel, an explosion ripped through the cave, collapsing the tunnel, knocking them both back into the water. For a moment they were disoriented, panicked, flashlight gone, flailing in circles, swimming toward the sound of the waterfall. They came through the falls gasping, Ski shouting, pulling them from the water.

"What the fuck was that?"

JT was on his hands and knees coughing and shaking.

"Get up. Get up," Ski yelled, helping JT to his feet. Hawkeye was already up, putting on his boots.

"We're in some deep shit," Ski said as the crack of gunfire rang through the trees, biting rock. He got on the radio. "Gurney's missing; we're taking fire. Little Mike spotted a trail. It's got steps carved out in the mountain."

"Secure your position," the radio said. "Tighten your perimeter."

The sky turned black, the temperature dropped, and the smell of a storm was in the air. More incoming cranked the perimeter. Andy took a round in the mouth, teeth smashed, blood and broken bone.

Coop moved down the hillside, level with the pool.

Radio ordered, "You got to check out the trail. You're on your own for now. We're taking rockets and mortars."

"Fuck the trail," Ski said. "There's gooks all over the place and we got wounded."

"Tighten your perimeter."

"We need a medevac. It's almost dark," Ski implored.

"Tighten your perimeter. You need to stay. We're taking fire. Settle down. We'll work this out."

The firing stopped. Doc stuck a tube of morphine into Andy's thigh. JT was back with Coop. The perimeter closed, no higher than the waterfall. Night dropped.

"In an hour we'll move to the other side of the gully," Ski told Hawkeye. "The sound of the water will cover us. This is gookville. There's got to be caves and tunnels everywhere."

Word spread to Flowers and was passed around the horseshoe. Each soldier's eyes riveted. But there was no firing, only the single sound of water splashing.

JT's face felt numb and his body was shaking. He was hidden behind a wall of rocks, Coop next to him. He could smell mint and heard Coop spit. No moon or stars. How would they move in such darkness? An hour or more crawled by, and they were on their feet. Where the hell was Gurney?

The horseshoe straightened. JT and Coop were at the end. Ski had the radio. They moved down the gully blindly, feet tangling, bumping, stumbling in the dark. Rain came. It started heavy, crashing loud and thunderous. The sky pitch dark except for a slash of lighting.

JT struggled to stay upright, his mind bending. Gurney snatched. Gone, like a ghost. Maybe someone else was missing, sucked up by the night. The rain pounded through the darkness, and JT felt like he was in a nightmare or a horror film. Like he, too, could be snatched by a supernatural force.

He slipped and fell, and as he rose, the heaviness of the mud and monsoon rain pulled on him, invisible vines tugged at his feet, and the Marines in front and back disappeared.

He felt alone and could not hear the heavy breathing of the Marines around him. The only thing he could do was trudge forward, try to stay steady, and not lose his weapon.

Once they were down the slope, they crossed the floor and crawled up the ridge, Doc pulling Andy along, his mouth a bandaged bloody hole. The ground was firm. It felt safer to JT. The waterfall was to his back and the noise fading. Fifty yards or so and the new perimeter was formed. A kind of circle, soldiers lying flat, rain gusting at their backsides. Andy weak and bleeding.

The wind picked up strongly and shook the trees, cracking limbs and blowing thick slabs of debris into arms and faces. JT was thinking about Gurney. Doc and Andy next to him. Andy was choking, moaning. Then the wind roared and slammed rain down sideways, soaking everyone. Three days in country and every day a nightmare. He'd never make it home. Lying in mud, JT closed his eyes.

Sometime after midnight, the wind slowed, the rain stopped, and the enemy started firing on where the patrol used to be. They lobbed mortars, fired B-40s and small arms. Ski called in artillery strikes on the waterfall. The shells whined through the night, thudded, exploded, shook the ground, and sent blasts of shooting light. Shrapnel slashed through the enemy troops, bounced off boulders, and blew up in the pool. A short round wounded Ski and killed a kid from New Jersey.

Then it all stopped. And they waited. The whole patrol felt like death row, waiting. A burst of fire, quiet. Waiting.

At 4:00 a.m. the night was still calm. Ski's arm was wrapped with a battle dressing, just below his tattoo of Jesus. Hawkeye crawled around the perimeter telling everyone that at first light they'd move out. Somewhere behind the mountains, B-52s dropped a load. The ground shuttered. Choppers worked, their red tracers sliced down. Quiet again.

As the edges of the horizon turned pink, the perimeter evolved into a single line moving down off the mountain. They took turns carrying the dead and guiding Andy. JT had the radio again. The patrol worked its way through the thick trees and jungle, back to the rice paddies. At first, they hugged the tree line, slowly headed toward the CP. There'd be no chopper for them. Too busy, the radio said, cleaning up big trouble.

The patrol spread out, glad to be out of the jungle. Vuong was back on point carrying his rifle. Flowers was toward the front, Ski and Hawkeye in the middle, JT and Coop following. The CP had been hit during the night, but there would be warm food and rest. They crossed over a meandering dike, closing in on the village. The sun was easing up; clouds hung harmless in the sky. Up ahead, under the same strand of trees, JT noticed the boy on the water bull. As the patrol approached, the boy took a little switch, slapped the side of the bull and drove him in front of the patrol until he disappeared somewhere in the village.

Vuong stepped out, creating distance between himself and the other men.

"Rice snappers on speed," Flowers cracked.

The dead kid from New Jersey was dropped, then picked up again.

JT was fumbling with his canteen when the trees exploded. Cueball and Banger lifted off the ground and came down in pieces. Hawkeye was blown sideways, left arm and leg shattered.

"One-oh-fives in the trees!" Ski screamed. "105s!"

Andy was hit again. Now dead. Small arms fire was pouring. B-40 rockets slamming. JT trembling. Moose and Little Mike raked machine-gun fire through the grass and into the mountainside as the rest of the platoon returned fire.

Flowers was standing, shooting at the tree line, screaming, "Mutherfuckers! Mutherfuckers!" He emptied a magazine, snapped another one in place, took a round in the shoulder. "God!" He staggered and sat down on a toe-popper, erupting his backside.

Ski crawled toward JT as JT fired wildly and rounds kept coming. Ski's helmet was off, his face aged. "Are you hit?" he yelled, but JT couldn't speak. Four men from the back of the patrol stood up and rushed toward the tree line. Another huge explosion blew into them, tearing them into shreds of broken bones. More small arms and B-40s smashed on the patrol.

Ski was lying on his belly a foot from JT, radio next to him. He reached for the handset as a round hit him in the throat. His face changed. He looked at JT like he was sorry, and the light faded from his eyes.

Doc crawled to Hawkeye, put tourniquets and battle dressings on his arm and leg, and stuck him with a tube of morphine. He slid on his belly toward JT as a spray of bullets killed him.

Now there was only JT, Little Mike, Moose, and Coop return-ing fire.

For a moment, the mountainside was quiet. Then trapdoors in the rice paddy opened up and enemy started coming from holes, shooting.

A round caught Little Mike in the back of the head, tearing through his brain, knocking his helmet off, his forehead mush-rooming. Moose turned, firing into them, killing two, then stood up almost casually, his 60 working on his hip, and lumbered toward the trapdoors, gun banging, face crying, and full of snot and spittle. Halfway toward the holes, he was shot in the back and staggered a bit but kept firing before falling to one knee. He had the 60 propped on his knee, belt feeding, barrel smoking. He killed three more as another round hit his arm, a third the back of his neck. Moose stayed on one knee like a bullfighter until a fourth round buried in his face, toppling him back onto Coop, knocking Coop cold. An-other short blast of rounds burrowed into Moose, striking Coop in the hip.

Shots came from the mountainside zinging just above JT's head, ripping into the radio. Another explosion lifted dead Marines and blew them to their backs or sides.

A round took a small chunk from the top of Hawkeye's head. Another creased JT's ear; blood covered his face, flowing into his mouth. A B-40 exploded where Cueball used to be.

Then there was quiet.

JT heard whistles and knew he was going to die. He was not afraid. He thought of Ashley. There was nothing more to do. He was almost at peace when he heard his radio crackle.

"Kilo Three. Kilo Three. Do you read me?"

A series of single shots told him the enemy was killing the wounded. The NVA stepped over the bodies and parts of bodies, sometimes stooping and removing rifles. Two more pops into Little Mike; another into Hawkeye's leg.

JT looked at Ski, prepared to die.

There were more single shots. Then quiet. The enemy soldiers bent over and rummaged next to JT. He could see them squatting, their sandaled feet, a blue bandana.

Vuong.

The radio kept saying, "Kilo Three! Kilo Three! Can you read me?"

21

JT

JT STOOD ALONGSIDE THE HIGHWAY TRYING TO hitch a ride east, up the Columbia River Gorge. He was next to an off-ramp just outside of Troutdale, mountains on both sides of the river. The snow was blowing hard, covering the ramp and highway. In the distance, the river moving, flat and gray, an old tugboat sliding with no current. Big-box trailer-trucks would grumble out of the truck stop, diesel spewing, rumbling down the slick ramp, passing JT. Cars would ignore him, single drivers, eyes averted. Families wouldn't stop, either, kids' faces pressed against steamed-up windows.

He stamped his feet, boots absorbing the shock, legs shaking. He had on his green field jacket, long johns, blue jeans, gloves, and a stocking hat. He'd been there more than two hours. The traffic was slow.

He looked at the river and to the other side at mountains rolling with timber. It reminded him of when his dad had sold Christmas trees from a parking lot. He was just a kid, working in the cold, tying up trees, making tree stands out of two-by-fours. He swore and jumped up and down, knowing he'd be late to work, and the crew boss would grill him. His face was cold, wind and chill coming through his coat.

"Screw this, ten more minutes and I'm getting a ride or getting out of the cold."

The ten minutes passed and another ten when finally a Volkswagen van eased to a stop. It was painted baby blue, windows fogged, right front fender dented, the word "ouch" painted above it, a string of flowers on the door. He got inside.

"Thanks for the ride." He shut the door. The blast of heat felt good.

"Where ya headed?" the young woman asked, bundled in a white ski parka. Blonde hair, nice smile. She pulled out and eased down the ramp and was soon on the freeway, windshield wipers working.

JT looked at her. He was stunned. "I know you," he said. "You're Kendal."

She laughed, astonished, tossing her head back, hair falling across her shoulders.

"From Portland State. JT!" she said, hands gripping the wheel, face breaking back into a smile. "You know I almost never pick up hitchhikers, but I saw you standing there when I was getting gas. You looked familiar and cold. I'm so glad to see you."

JT was excited but tried to stay calm. He had often thought of her, and if his life had been better, he would have looked her up a long time ago.

"So where are you going in this awful weather?" Kendal said.

"Up to Hood River, then over the bridge to White Salmon. Got a job working for Burlington Northern Railroad." He took off his hat and gloves and ran a hand through his hair. It was the longest it had ever been, falling over his ears, touching his collar.

"The railroad, huh? How long have you been doing that?"

Her voice was soothing, and he felt as if she were really interested in him.

"Couple months. I got hired on in Portland as a gandy on a track crew. During the week, I live in a boxcar overlooking the Columbia. On Fridays, I catch a ride to Portland. Monday morning, I hitch back."

"Boy, that must be hard," she said in a way that comforted JT. "I remember you gave me a ride home. Bought me a burger. You had a red Volkswagen."

"You've got a good memory." JT was glad to see Kendal but ashamed not to have a car. "Had to sell my car. Wasn't running very good."

"And remember? We had a couple beers," she said. "You never called back."

JT nodded, and of course he remembered but he was embarrassed. She was so beautiful, he thought.

The snow pelted the window, and they drove for a while not speaking. There was a kind of energy and sexual tension between them. He wanted to start all over again, and this time do it right. But he still had this feeling that he wasn't quite good enough for her. He didn't tell her he had to sell his car because he was broke or that he had been arrested for driving with a suspended license. He remembered the time with her as good and decent.

"The years have zoomed by," he said with a touch of sadness in his voice.

He thought about going from job to job, drinking, getting stoned, sleeping around. Anna was six now.

"So the big question is, what are you doing out in this weather?" he asked.

"Well, I graduated from PSU in June, met a guy, and thought I was in love. But it didn't work out. We broke up before Thanksgiving. So-o-o, I'm going to see a girlfriend who owns a little bookstore in Hood River. She's my best friend. We just lie around, read books, and talk. She babies me while I'm on the mend. There you have it. My recent life in a nutshell."

"How long are you going to be up here?" JT questioned.

"Until just before Christmas, I suppose. I'm on vacation until the first of the year."

"What do you do?"

"Believe it or not, I work at the police station."

"Come on," JT said. "Really?"

"Really. You know that little window when you first walk in to pay traffic and parking fines? That's me."

JT felt embarrassed again because he still had a suspended license and knew he had at least $50 in parking tickets.

"So, if you want to see me again," Kendal joked, "come see me in jail."

They both chuckled and smiled, and the years of not seeing each other dissolved. The van held steady as they moved along, snow covering the road and the surrounding countryside. The river swollen, the mountains quiet.

"Tell me about your work," Kendal said. "You really live in a boxcar?"

"It's just a temporary kind of job. Something to do for a while. I'm going to save some money. I want to go back to school, get a degree. It's a stupid job, really. A no-brainer. I live in a boxcar with a bunch of guys from Montana, Slammer from Arkansas, and a couple from Oregon. We chip ice out of the tunnels in the morning and fix or shore up track along the river." Then he tried to make a joke. "A couple of weeks ago a nut named Montana got drunk and tried to lasso an elk, but that's about it. Nothing mind-bending, that's for sure." As he talked to her, he felt less and less like going to work, but he knew he would already be in trouble for being late. Plus, he was behind in child support payments, and all he needed was for Ashley to have him thrown in jail again.

The engine whined as the road climbed and wound along the river. Traffic was light, and the snow had slowed.

"I can take you across the bridge if you like," Kendal offered. "Save you some time."

"Thanks. If you don't mind, I need to stop in at Penney's and pick up some socks." Their eyes met, and he could sense a mutual attraction.

"No problem. My pleasure, sir." Her smile was all over him.

They took the first exit into Hood River and parked in front of the store across from the Elks Lodge. The town was small and quiet with nothing much to do, not even a movie theater. JT ran in and bought a couple of pairs of thermal socks and a candy bar and hopped back in the van.

"That was quick," Kendal said.

Soon they were crossing the toll bridge into Washington.

"I really appreciate the ride," JT said, wanting to ask her for her phone number, not feeling confident.

"Don't mention it. We're even."

Another long, awkward moment as they both searched for words.

"Well, thanks anyway," JT offered. He was almost ready to ask her for her number when he noticed she was writing something on a notepad. She tore off a small piece of paper and held it out to him.

"If you get bored some night, you can come over and watch TV," she said. "Besides, I still owe you a burger."

She liked him. He knew it, and it felt great.

WHITE SALMON WAS HALF THE SIZE OF Hood River, and businesses were slow or closed for the winter.

They pulled up in front of a rundown tavern, window full of beer signs and advertisements for beef jerky. The front door glass was broken out and plywood slipped in. There was a bulletin board outside with handwritten offers of firewood by the cord, pups for sale, and bingo at the Hood River Elks.

The urge to forget work and be with her could barely be contained, but he needed the job and he could call her soon.

"I'll jump out here," JT said, stepping from the van into ankle-deep snow.

"Where's your boxcar?" Kendal asked. Her voice was lithe and smooth as a field of snow.

"Down the hill. Other side of the railroad tracks. I'll show you sometime."

"I'd like that. Now you call me. I mean . . . if you get bored."

"Thanks," he said, and in that moment he was sure they would be together. He shut the door. And as her van pulled away, JT looked at her phone number and felt better than he had in a long time.

IT WAS JUST BEFORE LUNCH WHEN HE stepped up on the back of the boxcar and pulled open the heavy door. There were two boxcars connected. One was for sleeping and showers; the other held the mess hall, kitchen, and foreman's quarters. The cars were placed on an abandoned section of track that ran parallel to the river.

As he entered the sleeping quarters, he could smell stove oil from the potbelly heating the cabin and grease from the kitchen. The door slammed heavily from a gust of wind, a pile of snow blowing in. There were eight bunks surrounded by tall green metal footlockers and a dozen naked centerfolds. July was riding bareback, December in a stocking cap.

JT took off his coat, gloves, and hat and plunked down on his bed, springs creaking, boots resting on the metal end rail. The crew was chipping ice from tunnels not far away and would be back for lunch.

"Well, kiss my rosy red. You made it back," Benny, said, coughing. Benny was the cook. Thin, barely five foot, he wore thick glasses that perched on his head like oversized goggles. JT thought he looked half dead.

"I couldn't stay away from your fine cuisine," JT said, swinging his boots to the floor, sitting up.

"Crew's due back any minute now," Benny said, wiping his hands on his dirty white apron, tip of a finger missing. "Boss is pissed you didn't make it back this morning."

"Screw him."

Benny coughed, lit a cigarette. "It's your funeral," he said as he left the room.

JT lay back down, shut his eyes, and dozed until the door opened again and men started filing in. They stomped boots, brushed snow off, and moved toward the hot, smelly stove.

"Colder than a witch's tit," Montana said, his front tooth missing. He peeled off his parka, tossed it on his rack.

"JT, I thought you quit. Ya said ya weren't coming back."

"Changed my mind."

Sugarbear and Arkansas and the rest of the gang came in, followed by Railroad Bob, the crew chief. Railroad was pushing fifty-five, belly sagging, hands beat up from pounding rail and knocking out drunks in the bars for years. His nose was flat and off to the side, and his eyebrows were thick and scarred.

"What are ya doin' here?" Railroad said to JT, who was sitting up again. "Work's at 7:00 a.m., not noon."

"Sorry, Railroad. Got turned around, thought I had some wheels. Won't happen again."

Railroad had been in WWII, a ground pounder. "If you don't straighten out, I will fire your ass," Railroad said. "Marine or no Marine. Just don't fuck with my crew. Understood?"

"Understood."

JT went to the head, took a leak in the silver trough, went into the mess, and sat down on the bench at the table. The small room was redolent with the smells of toast, bacon and eggs, and Benny's railroad hash. Stacks of white bread, silver pitchers of hot cocoa, and big silver cans of peanut butter and jam were spread out on the table. There were no windows in the gray wooden walls, so the smells of breakfast and passed gas hung in the air.

Benny came in coughing, a big skillet sizzling, and dished out hash to groans and complaints.

"Tasted better dog squeeze," Arkansas snorted, his odd-shaped head tilted, his fat face sucked in at the cheeks.

"Speaking ah dog squeeze," Sugarbear said, looking mischievous as he poured himself a cup of cocoa, "Arkansas, I saved your life yesterday."

Arkansas looked bewildered as he stuffed toast and jam in his face. "Whatta you talkin' 'bout?"

"I said, I saved your life yesterday. Killed a shit-eatin' dog."

Everyone howled and banged cups except for Arkansas, who didn't quite get it.

They joked and complained, burped loud and on purpose, finished lunch, and loaded up in the back of a canvas-covered truck. JT and the crew were in the back, smoking joints, sipping from thermoses, eating candy bars. Railroad was up front in the cab with Hodge, who was driving. Hodge was the assistant foreman and lived in Hood River, so he didn't sleep or eat with the crew. Didn't work much either.

The truck rolled east into a biting wind that blew and blustered, ruffling up trees and shoving the truck with powerful gusts. The snow had stopped, and the sky was white and endless. As they moved along, JT thought this was just like the Marine Corps. Riding in the back of a truck, bad weather, not knowing where he was going.

The truck hit a dirt road packed with snow and churned along next to the railroad track. They stopped at a section of rail that snaked hard by the river. They'd been there last week and the week before. The track was on a steep bank and whenever the train passed over, the track would slide. The crew's job was to put pry bars under the rail, lift a section up, and shove rock back under it. It was hard and boring.

"Shit," Sugarbear said, jumping down from the truck and sinking nearly to his knees.

JT and the rest of the crew followed. They pulled out picks, shovels and pry bars and slopped over to the track. Railroad got out of the cab banging the door shut; it echoed in the silence. The wind whipped off the river and swirled snow along the tracks. Treetops swayed, and the crew shivered.

"OK, men," Railroad said, slapping deerskin gloves together, then adjusting his red wool hunter hat with ear flaps hanging down. "Same old, same old. We'll start liftin' and shorin' up. JT, you grab the burning barrel."

JT pulled an empty fifty-gallon barrel from off the back of the truck, lifted it to his shoulder, tromped over close to the track, and threw it down. Then he went back to the truck and got newspapers, a burlap bag full of wood chips, lighter fluid, and an ax to split wood. He got a fire going and scrounged for wood nearby.

The crew worked in shifts of three. Two guys lifting, one guy shoveling rock under the rail. The others hung by the barrel, along with Railroad and Hodge, hands over the fire keeping warm.

The crew would heave-ho and lift and shovel slowly, not getting too much done. The cold ate through the layers of coats and sweaters, long underwear, thermal socks, and hobnailed boots. Snot froze, and lips and cheeks cracked in the cold.

An hour into the job, another supervisor pulled up in a pickup and stood by the burning barrel with Railroad and Hodge. He stopped every day wherever they were and checked the crew. He talked to Railroad about hunting and the new mobile home he'd bought, then left to go check on another gang working farther up the track.

By four, the light was changing, and the snow started up again. "Let's call it a day, men," Railroad said. "Just leave the barrel." They put out the fire, with snow, loaded the tools, and left.

Each day seemed colder and longer riding in the back of the truck, working on the track. But at night, JT would walk up to the tavern and call Kendal. Just the sound of her voice made him feel good.

One day, JT was preoccupied with thoughts of Kendal. He imagined her face as he helped clear an old-growth hemlock that had fallen on a section of track. She was decent, he thought, as the whine of a chainsaw tore into the wood. She reminded him of a feeling he used to have back in high school.

Montana was bent over, working the saw, one leg up on the log, cutting through limbs, JT hauling them away. The rest of the crew was farther up the track, two guys working, four at a burning barrel. The snow was new.

JT still had Kendal on his mind when Montana's chainsaw kicked back and ripped into his leg, knocking him to the ground. The saw went flying.

"Oh, Jesus!" Montana screamed. "Ohhhh!"

JT rushed to Montana, who was on his back, trousers torn, blood running in the snow. The saw had cut a gaping gash in his leg clear to the bone, severing an artery.

His howls called the rest of the crew, and they came running, falling in the snow. By the time they reached Montana, they were out of breath and nearly hysterical.

"What the hell! Oh shit. Jesus."

"Goddamn it!"

JT was calm as he hurriedly took off his belt and cinched it tight around Montana's leg just above the wound. Railroad shut off the saw.

"Hang in there, buddy," JT said, and for a moment he thought about Ski, then Gurney.

He took off his coat and sweater, pulled off his thermal shirt, wrapped it around the wound, and tied the arm sleeves.

"You know your shit, man," Sugarbear said as he watched with the others.

"You're going to be fine. You're going to be fine," JT said. But he could see Montana start to fade into shock.

Railroad directed the men to pick up Montana and put him in the back of the truck as he got in the cab with Hodge. But the truck wouldn't start. Railroad worked the key frantically, pumped the gas, but got nothing. The battery was dead. They were miles from a phone. By the time Sugarbear reached a farmhouse, Montana had died in the back of the truck.

The next day, JT told Railroad Bob he was quitting and walked over the bridge into Hood River, looking for Kendal.

"She went back to Portland," her friend said.

22

Hawkeye

HAWKEYE WAS IN AND OUT OF THE hospital for three years and never thought about the patrol, the waterfalls, or all those who died. He never thought about Gurney or Ski and Flowers or Cueball. He couldn't, even if he tried to. Sometimes when he was sitting on his bed in the ward, he'd look at his leg, all scarred and deformed, arm hanging limp and useless, and try to will himself to remember. He'd think so hard about how he was injured that his head would hurt, but it was hopeless. No matter how hard he tried, he couldn't remember what happened. Some mornings when the first light came through the windows, he'd been up all night, lying in his hospital bed, sweating, imagining what he'd been told.

Some doctors thought it was the head wound that caused his loss of memory; others were sure it was psychosomatic. But with budgets being cut and the war winding down, maybe it was best to just forget. After months of care, doctors lost interest and gave up on putting his memory back together again. During his hospital stay, Hawkeye's mother would often visit, bringing pie, and sit by his bed all day and into the night. She'd read and talk to him in an encouraging way.

"Son, you got to get up now. Exercise. Can't stay in bed all day. It'll only make you sicker."

He'd barely respond with a few words before drifting off, thinking about the irony of it all. It was almost funny, this mind of his
that used to work so fine. He could still read a book and recall every
detail, but he couldn't remember anything about being wounded.
There was no picture in his brain of the waterfall or being shot
four times, medevacked for dead, coming back to life trapped in a
body bag. There were no memories of that last patrol, diving in the
waterfall, or tree line exploding. It was erased, forgotten, placed in
a compartment that no one could unlock.

The time in the hospital was long and hard. There were fourteen major operations. Doctors repaired his shattered arm and leg,
removed a lung, and placed a metal plate in his head. His physical
therapy was agonizing: leg brace, learning how to walk and how to
dress with one arm. Sometimes Hawkeye would dream about the
war but not see a face or event he could recognize. Many days he
would read a paper or see footage of the war on TV and be amazed
that he had really been there. Occasionally, he thought he was a
guinea pig in some sick government experiment, and other days he
assumed he had simply gone crazy.

The hospital and the ward became his home. He liked to move
around the wards in his wheelchair, visiting with amputees and
other soldiers with traumatic wounds, more visible and severe.
They'd tell him stories and ask him about what happened.

"Firefight near the DMZ," he lied, ashamed he couldn't remember. Or, "truck got hit doing convoy near Quang Tri." His stories
changed, or he'd say it was "a mistake," and conversation about his
injuries would end.

Ricky was his friend on the burn ward. He had been a pilot, his
chopper shot down at Mutter's Ridge. His whole body had been
burnt except for a small place on his neck about the size of a quarter. This puzzled Hawkeye greatly. He was bandaged from head to
toe, except for the quarter near his throat. He had tubes in his arms
and one running up his nose. Although he couldn't speak or move,

Hawkeye sat with him for hours. Talking about his mother, the changes in his life, how the hospital was trying to get rid of him. Sometimes he'd sit there quietly watching the movement of Ricky's eyes or counting his breaths.

Only once did Hawkeye stay as nurses changed Ricky's bandages and scrubbed down his burned skin. Ricky hardly made a sound, nerves burnt away. Others in the ward cried out in ways Hawkeye never wanted to remember. The last time he went to see Ricky, his bed was empty. Years later, Hawkeye would always look back and wonder about the quarter-piece of healthy skin on Ricky's neck.

The hospital gave him everything—food, attention, and books to read brought by cute girls from the Red Cross and graying grand-mothers, whose grandsons may have served. There were TVs in the recreation room, where guys shot pool from wheelchairs or on crutches, smoking cigarettes. Movies were shown on weekends There were people to talk to or sit with who were far worse off than he was, so Hawkeye never left the hospital. Even when his mother came and tried to take him for the weekend, he'd get nervous, like it would all be gone when he got back.

He'd tell her, "No. I can't leave just yet."

"Son, you have to get out. Come home," she'd say.

But he wouldn't leave. He would read everything he could find and lie awake, sweating.

After over twenty-seven months, Hawkeye was forcibly dis-charged and immediately had severe migraine headaches, so painful he couldn't move. He'd lie in bed at home, curtains drawn, in total silence. Mother would bring him meals or wipe his brow with a cool washcloth and rub his feet, which seemed to help. She'd read to him, too, until he'd fall asleep.

There were no nightmares of monstrous battles or soldiers shoot-ing him again. He just didn't want to leave the room. Light bothered him. Noise was debilitating. He stayed cooped up, rarely speaking, moving only to the toilet, kitchen, or front room.

One morning he woke up hungry and shuffled into the kitchen. His mama was doing a crossword, drinking coffee, sun bursting through the window.

"I'm hungry," Hawkeye said. "Let's go out for breakfast."

His mother was startled, thought it was a miracle, stood up and grabbed him in her arms, and wouldn't stop crying and kissing him.

Over the coming months, Hawkeye walked each day but always took a different route coming home. If he walked to the library down Taylor Street, he'd come back on Grant. If he left by the front door of the apartment building, he'd return through the back door. And if someone walked behind him, he'd cross the street or duck into an entryway and let them pass. He'd try not to walk into the sun, and whenever he walked into a building, he would look at the roof first, step in, scope it out, make sure it was safe. Proceed cautiously. At night he kept his shoes and pants on a chair, ready if he had to go. And before he could go to sleep, he walked around the apartment, checking doors and windows at least twice.

Three years following the war, Hawkeye was walking, limping really, arm hanging loose, like it didn't belong, when he saw a car hit a dog. The dog let out a moan that sounded human and reached into Hawkeye's soul. He watched the dog as it tried to crawl to the side of the road, hip broken, cars screeching. Seeing that dog trying so hard to live triggered something inside of him. He ran as best he could to the dog as it crumbled to its side. For a moment, the dog's eyes seemed to search, as if it knew it was about to die. Then its head turned. It blew air out its nose and was gone. Hawkeye knelt over the dog and started to cry. He cried so hard by the side of the road that the driver who hit the dog tried to comfort him.

That spring, Hawkeye enrolled in school. In three years, he had a degree. His grades were perfect and he was accepted into Northwestern Law School. By the middle of his sophomore year, his teachers and peers were calling him brilliant, a leader. And by the time he finished law school, several major legal firms from the

Midwest and the East Coast were recruiting him. He was offered a great opportunity in New York with an office full of Italian furniture and leather bound books, expense accounts, and promises of future partnerships.

However, other aspects of his life had changed drastically. He was confident, his mother well pleased.

He moved to New York City, where clients and peers called him "Mr. Collins." He bought a brownstone apartment not far from Central Park. In a short time, he joined a successful practice as a criminal attorney and eventually became partner.

He still would walk different routes and watched his back and never sat in a restaurant with his back to a window.

"It's about time you got married, don't you think?" one of his colleagues asked over dinner.

But Hawkeye just smiled. "I'll know when I find her."

During those years, his mind rarely reflected on Vietnam. When people asked about his injuries, he would make up a story.

"It happened a long time ago. I just want to forget." By then, he really did.

At work one day, Joe Kein, who handled real estate for the firm, asked Hawkeye to dinner. "You like Italian?" Joe asked. "I know this great little place with about ten tables on the Westside."

"I appreciate the invitation, but I really want to hit the sack early."

"Come on. My treat, and besides, I want to talk to you about something," Joe pleaded. "You're the only one who will understand."

They caught a taxi after work and by 6:00 were sitting in a booth at Biancones, red wine breathing in their glasses, a basket of bread sticks. They discussed work, drank wine, and dipped bread sticks into melted garlic butter.

"What was it you wanted to talk about?" Hawkeye asked just before he brought his glass back to his lips. The restaurant was quiet, and he could smell tomatoes and garlic.

"I never heard you talk about Vietnam, and I can respect that," Joe said, "but I wanted to tell you about a friend of mine."

Joe drained his glass, filled it. Hawkeye covered the top of his. Hawkeye shifted in his seat. This was the last thing he wanted. He wanted to go home, read a little, and sleep.

"OK," Hawkeye said. "Shoot."

"A friend of mine I went to high school with was killed in Vietnam on this day back in 1968. Every year on September thirteenth, I think about the day Tommy died. We went to high school together, and when the draft came, I was in college and he was working at a truck stop. I got a deferment, and he ended up in the Marines." Joe's voice dropped as Hawkeye listened. "I mean, he was in hell, and I was getting drunk and getting laid." Joe's voice cracked, and his eyes watered. "I just want to say I'm sorry."

Hawkeye knew he should say something, but the words weren't there. He nodded and was quiet.

That night when Hawkeye closed his eyes, he dreamed about Tommy who died and something about a waterfall.

HAWKEYE MARRIED A WRITER FOR *LIFE* MAGAZINE. Linda was intrigued with his intellect, intrigued with his wounds, and lonely. In the beginning, she was kind and interesting, but as time passed, she became self-absorbed and found it difficult to cope with Hawkeye's habits and physical limitations. Before long, it was all she could talk about.

"You never laugh or show any kind of joy. I wish you could play racquetball or go to a Knicks game. Just once I'd like to go dancing."

Hawkeye, though, enjoyed working, reading, or walking quietly alone before first light. Between his work and her work, they were not together much.

By the middle of the second year, it was apparent to both of them that the marriage would not flourish.

"If I see you check the doors and windows one more time, I'll go nuts," she said.

Hawkeye's passion for work waned. Suddenly, there was no meaning anymore. One day he announced he wanted to move back to Chicago. They were eating breakfast on their tiny veranda: poached eggs, toast, black coffee, traffic below.

"Linda," he said, buttering his toast carefully on his plate, "I'm sick of this work. I feel like I'm something I'm not. I sit at my desk and find myself hating my clients. Hating their complaints. Hating the office. I just can't stand it anymore. I want to go back home. Do something meaningful. Something where right or wrong isn't determined by money."

The announcement did not sit well with Linda.

"The war ruined you," she said.

Six months later, they divorced.

Hawkeye moved back to Chicago and bought the three-story, twelve-unit brick apartment house his mother still lived in. He put in new windows, doors, heating, plumbing, and electricity and renovated each unit with thick carpets, tile countertops, paint, and appliances. Did some of the work himself. It was slow but gave him a good feeling. Then he moved in, just above her apartment.

"Mama, you need to take a load off," Hawkeye said one day as he helped her paint her kitchen. He had white on his hands and more paint on his overalls. "Relax a little."

"If I don't work, what am I going to do? Play bingo? Don't worry about me. Worry about giving me a grandson."

Hawkeye laughed and rolled out the rest of the wall.

He practiced law as a court-appointed attorney, read voraciously, and eighteen months later married a nurse named Casey.

They bought a little bookstore not far from the apartments.

They had two children, a girl and a boy, and he was happy.

There were no thoughts of war. His life was good, and his kids grew, but there was still an overwhelming lack of joy.

Hawkeye sat in the waiting room at the veterans hospital, early for his appointment for his annual medical review. He was dressed in slacks and a sweater, holding the *Chicago Tribune* in his good hand, and when he was done reading an article, he set the paper down on his lap, turned the page, folded it, and snapped it on his pant leg.

The room was packed with old soldiers sitting in bucket benches or wheelchairs, their legs battered or missing. Middle-aged men with faces scarred or blind sat waiting patiently. They wore baseball caps and coats or shirts that said they were WWII, Korea, or Vietnam.

They look broken, Hawkeye thought.

Next to Hawkeye was a veteran his age wearing a simple gray sweatshirt with the slogan *1st Cav* in bold blue letters running across his chest. He was slight and sickly-looking, big scar on his throat, but he noticed Hawkeye and spoke to him in a loud, raspy voice.

"You must'a been wounded in the Nam?"

Hawkeye put his paper on the table next to his chair and said, "Yes, yes, I was."

"Me too. B-40. Took out a lung and a hip, caught a chunk just below my kisser." He tilted his head back to reveal the wound. "I was in the First Cav down in the delta. Who were you with?"

Hawkeye thought about it for a moment. "I was in the Marine Corps, Kilo Company."

"An old jarhead, huh?" the guy said in a good-natured way. "You must have been up North in I Corp. How'd you get hit?"

There was the tiniest sensation, but no recollection.

"I had a head wound and can't remember."

"That's bullshit," the guy said, startling Hawkeye. "You can get your records; you've just got post-traumatic stress disorder, man. You got it blocked. I had the same shit for years. It'll come, man. It'll come back, and when it does, it'll be a blessing."

"What are you talking about?" Hawkeye asked, incredulous.

He didn't have PTSD. He just couldn't remember.

"Well, it's like this. I was drunk and miserable for years. Couldn't remember a damn thing about Vietnam, really. Depressed. Wanted to die. And I was mean, kicked my first and second wife's ass. Then when it came back, it was like a flood. Cried for a week. But I felt clean inside. Quit drinking. Straightened up. Problem is, I keep thinking about the guys that were with me. Know what I mean?"

Hawkeye nodded, his mind turning.

"It'll come back. And it will be a blessing."

23

Vuong

BY THE END OF 1973, IT HAD been several years since Vuong led the patrol into the ambush. The war had turned for Vuong that day. He was promoted and given a certificate for his brave and heroic work as a member of the 324b and assigned duty near Hue for a while, then later to a post not far from China Beach. The American troop involvement was over, and his superiors would often tell him soon the war would be, too. By now it hardly mattered to Vuong. The war was inside of him and would be all his life. Neither time nor victory could ease the pain of walking through the village and killing everyone or leading the Marines to their deaths. He thought of that patrol and remembered how he ached inside and wanted to scream and run. Run from the war. From the madness.

And when his comrades had come out of the tree line and killed the wounded soldiers, he felt as if his spirit had died. As if the world had no mercy. Even years later, his dreams were no longer filled with his family or the times that he loved. They were nightmares of the village and the young being shot again and again.

Stories he once cherished about the Fatherland and great ancient dynasties had long faded from his memory. The killing of the Marines still sifted through his conscience and reminded him of his betrayal. All the dead and maimed, the treachery and sorrow, overwhelmed beliefs of seeking benevolence, duty, and faithfulness. None of it mattered anymore. The only thing that did matter was survival.

Vuong's world had become narrow and sad. He trusted no one, had no friends, and had not seen Phung Thu for several years. She, too, had lost her dedication and was known to share herself with men for money. She was hardly a thought anymore. He had heard she was missing and was told she ran away. But news was so unreliable that he just thought of her as dead.

The North was winning the war now; even he was aware of that. Many times there would be celebrations over new ground taken and kept. On those occasions, he had been drunk and with joy girls, but when he was done, he felt empty and alone. His commander said, "That one ambush took something out of you." And it was true. Everything inside of him felt dead. Once the spirit of his father came to him. They were walking, holding hands, but then the dream changed. The redheaded soldier was there, putting his arm around him.

In the spring of 1975 the rout was on. With no US soldiers and no air support for the South, the North was sweeping through the country, tanks rumbling and smashing Quang Tri City.

"Vuong. You are a lieutenant now," his commander had said as the city fell. "One day after we have won, we will get drunk together and be done with this war."

The North controlled Hue, then Da Nang. Dead and wounded scattered the countryside. Victory was coming.

Vuong was sitting on a bridge on the Da Nang River, eating, playing cards, and smoking marijuana with two other officers. The area had been taken weeks ago and was secure and free from trouble. They could bicycle in uniform without fear—because they were the fear. They controlled everything. The raping and looting had long since died, and daily executions of soldiers from the South had waned. It was as if everyone in the countryside was just waiting for a big door to slam.

"We've been at war so long," Vuong said. "I don't know what I will do when it is really over."

A memory surfaced of when he was a Kit Carson and led the Marines into an ambush. He could not kill the wounded Marines. The big black man. He thought of how others chose to shoot not to kill. Some survived, he knew, but shooting the wounded was a nightmare that tortured his soul. He was quickly in the ambush again and how it happened so quickly. And how, after it was done, no one celebrated. He looked straight ahead and let it float away. He'd learned not to let one memory lead to another. Vuong took a drag off the joint and passed it along. He had been smoking for several years and found it helped him sleep.

"Maybe we should grow some of this and ship it to America," one of the officers said, and they all laughed. "We could get rich and have sex with a different American girl every night." More laughter followed.

"What are your dreams, Vuong?" an officer asked, his eyelids heavy from the smoke.

"I have no dreams." Which was not true. He often thought of his parents and brother, who were dead now, and wished them alive. And he thought of Phung Thu.

When the war finally ended in the streets of Saigon, Vuong did not go home. As the last US helicopter left the top of the American Embassy, North Vietnamese flags flew throughout the country. In the basement of Saigon's presidential palace, Southern generals surrendered with a bullet to their heads. The liberation was complete, but the freedom Vuong once talked about never really came. The new leadership created reeducation camps for all former South Vietnamese soldiers or sympathizers. And Vuong was sent to help run a camp up north at Quang Tri City. He had no choice.

"It must be orderly," the leaders said. "Strict and orderly."

FOR SEVERAL YEARS, VUONG WORKED AT A camp and helped oversee the tens of thousands of Southerners who were moved to different parts of the country. Many high-ranking soldiers were shot, thousands more beaten or starved to death. It sickened Vuong, and he twisted into despair. His dead countrymen and the dead Americans were blurring in his mind. Not once was he allowed to go home. He lost all contact with family, friends, and relatives, and the village he once lived in was barely a dream.

He took a lover named Ba Sat. Her hair was long and hung down her back, like Phung Thu's. Whenever they made love, he thought her sweat smelled like rose petals. She had been brought down from the North and worked for the military. Three of her brothers had died in the war, and she was bitter but beautiful.

"I am so tired of working for the government and getting nothing," Ba Sat said.

They were in her room in the city. It had been raining for days, and the fields and streets were flooding. The smell of waste was everywhere. Her room was nearly barren. Their bed was a stack of bamboo mats, and the only light was a candle. There was no electricity, refrigeration, or running water. A bucket by the wall was her shower, and a trench was where she squatted.

"I tell you. I'm tired of living like this, Vuong. Why don't you marry me and get us out of here?"

Vuong knew she was right, but he was tired of hearing her complaints. Complaints only led to ideas of how things could be better, and that was dangerous. Nothing would get better. On the other hand, it was better having Ba Sat than it had been before.

"I could marry you today," he said. "And I would, but I have nothing." He was sitting up, looking down on her slim body. He touched her naked belly, then ran his hand up her thigh to where it was moist.

"Don't," she said irritably. "I'm telling you about something important."

"I'm listening," he said reluctantly. "They keep promising another promotion and more pay, but I don't think it will come." His voice faded.

"You cannot trust them," Ba Sat said, sitting up, hair covering her shoulders like a shawl. "I lost my family and for what? To live like this? So many from the South have fled by boat. And from the North, too. I have heard. They go to America and are given jobs and money and cars and houses."

"Oh, I don't know," Vuong said. Nothing inspired him anymore. Maybe they could go to America? "I, too, hate this way of life," he said. "I want something more out of life than this."

His mind focused on pictures he had seen of California and an American family eating outside at a table, next to a swimming pool. He thought of food in America. Stores and buildings as high as the sky. What it would feel like to ride in an American car.

She softened in the candlelight, lay back, and drew Vuong down to her. Her hand touched where he was warm.

"I love you, Vuong. Take us out of here."

That night Vuong's depression lifted and he planned for a future. When you are in war, the future seems like one day at a time, but now it was different.

For the next two years, they saved what little money they could and bought gold. With gold they could buy passage on a boat that would take them across the China Sea to freedom. They knew they would end up in a refugee camp in the Philippines or Hong Kong, but anywhere would be better than this, they believed. And if they could get to America or Canada, they could build a life.

Stories of the peril and great danger at sea were passed in whispers among the soldiers and military workers. Thousands had escaped, but thousands had also been captured or died, lost at sea. The government was cracking down, and it seemed as though no one could be trusted. But they saved and bought gold and planned.

"We must leave, Vuong," Ba Sat said one night after work, over a bowl of noodles and pork. "I have your child."

When he heard her words, it wasn't joy he felt but a sense of duty and obligation. Maybe this was what he needed. He would have a family again. He could leave and create something good—something to replace the agony in his mind. His father would have been proud to have a grandson.

When the weather turned and the winter storms had gone, they made their final plans.

THEY LEFT WHEN THE MOON WAS SWALLOWED by night and made their way along the coast. They hid in a damp cave for three days, carefully conserving their rations. On the fourth night, a boat could be seen not far off shore. A rowboat picked them up under a sliver of a moon. They boarded an old and crowded ship full of Northerners, its motor chugging and mast sails flapping. When the moon was gone and the sun had come, they were out of Vietnam's waters.

On the fourth day, they were stopped by a ship full of Thai thugs and pirates who boarded Vuong's ship with guns and machetes and robbed and beat the passengers. Those who resisted were shot or hacked or simply thrown overboard screaming. Women were slapped and raped as their men or children watched helplessly. Food was stolen. Vuong was beaten, Ba Sat kicked and spat upon. Many older men were forced to open their mouths, and if gold could be seen, it was pried out with pliers or cut out with a knife. When they left, eleven out of the sixty had been murdered, including the captain and his crew.

The ship drifted under a fierce sun for three weeks as sickness and starvation set in. Soon there was madness. People tearing at their hair, mumbling wildly, eyes bulging, bellies swollen, tongues thick and full of sores. One woman took her infant child, already dead, and jumped into the water. No one could save her. When the woman jumped, Vuong sat complacent, eyes vacant. He huddled with Ba Sat beneath a stretched-out nylon parachute feeling weak and hopeless.

On the thirty-fourth day adrift, seagulls flew above the mast. There was hope. The next day a boat could be seen on the horizon. At first it was thought that it was the pirate ship coming back to torture them. But it was a Vietnamese military freighter. They had drifted into the current, back into Vietnam waters.

24

JT & Coop

JT HITCHHIKED TO JOSEPH IN THE MIDDLE of the night during a snowstorm. An hour or so outside of Pendleton, he got a ride in a blue panel truck from Thomas Laughing Bear. About JT's age, he was worn-out looking and worked for the reservation. The truck was old, and a wiper blade was missing on the passenger side.

"Thanks, bro," JT said. As he closed the door, it creaked loud and sharp, sounding like how a toothache feels. Bear handed him a beer, and they drove in silence, one blade slapping at the snow. The truck hummed through the night past darkened farmhouses and fences buried in rolling fields of snow.

Finally, Bear spoke. His thick, dark hair was long and braided like a rope. His face puffy. His question gentle.

"You were in Nam, weren't you?"

JT finished his beer, put the bottle in the case behind him, and took another. "How'd you know?" JT asked.

"Just a hunch," Bear answered, turning his head toward JT, fat fingers on the wheel. "I was in Airborne, '68–'69. Lost both legs at the knee."

JT was startled and imagined Bear hitting a land mine and being blown in the air. He felt bad, and lucky.

"I had a vision before it happened," Bear said, his voice was deep and resonant, eyes on the road. He slowed just before the headlights caught a doe and buck dancing across the road, slipping into darkness.

JT listened intently, waiting for more. But that was it. They rounded a curve, and the town just sort of popped up without warning. JT barely saw the sign—*Welcome to Joseph*.

"This is Joseph," Bear said, pulling the truck to the side of the road, wiper still slapping. "This is as far as I can take you."

The snow had eased, and they were at the end of the main street. As JT got out of the truck, he thanked Bear for the beer and the ride. "Hang in there, man. Glad you made it home."

"I don't know," Bear said, and drove away.

The air was crisp, and with the morning light JT could see the Wallowa Mountains rising up much larger and more powerful than any he had ever seen. He felt a sense of smallness as they stretched out and seemed to rake the sky. The town was more modest than he envisioned, a Tom Sawyer kind of place where not much happens, not even on Saturday night. He got directions from the attendant at the Texaco who was just opening, moving a rack of snow tires from out of the garage.

"'Bout a mile or so, maybe less," the guy said, cowboy hat pulled low over his eyes, gray coat, collar turned up, red-winged horse stitched on the front.

The sun was warming up as JT found B Street, with four tired houses. The first house he walked past still had on its Christmas lights, with a pickup camper in the driveway and a car next to it up on blocks. The lots were large, with fir trees, apple trees, and berry bushes covered with snow. All four houses had steep roofs and porches that needed fixing.

On the front of the second house in large red letters were the words—

BAA. HUMBUG!

He'd found Coop.

JT stepped on the wooden porch, amused with the greeting, wondering if everything would be the same after two years. He knocked on the door, and after a long minute, Lucy opened it. She was in blue jeans, red socks, a red flannel shirt tucked in. He could smell bacon and incense.

"Come in. Come in," Lucy said, smiling and giving him a modest hug. "Coop will be so excited to see you. He's just getting up. I'll get him."

JT stood in the front room and glanced at the tattered furniture, cheap end tables, cockeyed lamp. A poster covering the crack in the wall was a blown-up photo of Coop in Vietnam, somewhere in heavy jungle. He looked like he was on a recon mission—cammies, bush cover, face painted, carrying his M-16. He had a huge smile, mustache waxed and curled. He looked young, strong, and happy.

"JT, you old piece of shit."

JT heard Coop's voice and the sound of someone hopping across the floor. When he looked into the dining room, he could see Coop in his underwear, shirt off, fat scar on his belly, leg missing.

Coop hopped to the corner of the dining room and grabbed his artificial leg leaning against the wall.

"Just busted the strap on my other leg," Coop explained, twisting in a pirouette, then sitting down in a chair at the dining room table. "This one's a spare."

JT felt sick inside. Coop looked soft, flabby, and much older. It bothered him and reminded him of himself. He, too, was changing, getting heavier, losing the edge. Becoming vulnerable.

They shook hands, and he took off his coat and sat across from Coop, watching him slip a sock on over his stump.

"Kind of looks like the head of a big dick, doesn't it?" Coop cracked, wiggling it up and down as if he were waving bye-bye.

Lucy walked in with a pair of blue jeans draped across her arm. "How 'bout some pancakes?" There was a lightness in her voice that transcended the weight JT was feeling.

"Great," JT said.

A good woman, maybe that's what he needed. Someone who would stick by him even when he wasn't perfect.

Coop pulled on his jeans, strapped on his leg below the knee, and put on some boots. "How the hell you doin', you big turd?" he asked.

His face was rounder and older, his hair thinning. There were bags under his eyes and dark circles. It looked as if he had not shaved for a few days and the stubble had flecks of gray. His mustache was trimmed. He didn't look like the guy on the wall. He looked forty, not thirty.

"I'm cool," JT said. "Thinking about going back to school. Doing something. I'm tired of being a bum."

"Hold on a second." Coop got up and walked into the kitchen, and as he did, JT could see him limp. He came back with two beers.

"Nothing like beer for breakfast," JT said, toasting him, beer cans clinking.

"How's Brad?" Coop asked.

"He's cool. Banging some gal that works for United Airlines. Still flying charters with his dad."

"Tell him I miss his sweet ass."

Lucy brought in two plates of pancakes, bacon, and hash browns. "I told you I don't like you drinking for breakfast," Lucy said, setting the plates down. "You're going to end up an alcoholic." She was angry, fists on the side of her waist. "You promised!"

"You look like a drill instructor," Coop said, and both of them laughed at her.

"You'll think I'm a DI when I get through with you," Lucy snapped, then cuffed the back of Coop's head. "Now, seriously, just 'cuz your buddy's in town is no reason to get drunk out of your mind."

"Can you think of a better reason?" Coop asked.

"Yeah. Maybe if you could keep a job, we could buy a house, and that would be a better reason."

Coop smirked, turned red, and made a face like he was stupid, but it wasn't funny.

"JT, you keep my boy out of trouble if possible. Will ya?"

"You got a cattle prod?" JT joked. "Better yet, I'll hook him up to a twelve-volt and give him a jolt if he gets out of line."

Lucy laughed, "Good. OK, I got a short stack left and some bacon. Any takers?"

"No, thanks, Luce. I'm packed," JT said. "It was really good, thanks."

JT and Coop watched football on TV, drank, joked, ate lunch, napped a little, had a couple more beers with more football. Coop had a great life, JT thought. A home and a wife who loved him and gave him room. She went shopping, came back, and scolded Coop again for drinking. It made JT anxious, reminding him of what he lost and might still lose.

"You ever think about Gurney?" JT asked, beer working on his brain. Just thinking about him tripped some fear inside. A guy just vanishes.

"Fuck, no! He's just dead. Which ain't so bad."

About five o'clock, Coop turned off the TV, and they decided to go down to the bar where Lucy was now manager and part owner. It was her day off.

"Keep out of trouble, boys," Lucy called to them from the doorway as they got into Coop's pickup. "I'll lock the door at twelve!" she warned.

"That fuckin' woman is pure gold," Coop said, reaching under the seat and pulling out a bottle of Johnnie Walker Red. "Want a snort?"

JT declined. Coop took two healthy slugs by the time they got to Main Street.

The bar had changed little over the years. There was still pool and peanut shells on the floor, but the posters of big-titted cowgirls were gone. When Lucy became part owner, she talked her partner into buying a widescreen and bringing in video games. This increased revenue and brought more families during the dinner hour. Her biggest problem was making sure her husband didn't drink the profits and scare off customers.

They watched football for a while, Coop drinking shots of tequila and beers, getting loud and obnoxious. JT didn't try to match him. He wanted to connect with Coop in a different way. He wanted to talk about life and how to straighten it out, how to face the fear and not have to make jokes, get drunk or violent. But it was hard for JT to find the words, and he felt a tension making him nervous and unsure. He didn't want to preach or be an asshole. He didn't want to let go of the pleasure of being with his friend. They played video games. Each time Coop lost, he'd down another tequila, acting a little agitated.

"Don't you think you ought to ease off, buddy?" JT suggested.

"You ain't my fuckin' nanny," Coop charged.

"Come on, settle down. You're drunk on your ass. You've had enough."

"Bull fucking shit!" He slammed back the last shot, grabbed JT's beer, and chugged it. "I can whip my weight in wildcats," Coop shouted to a mostly empty bar. "I was born in a boxcar on a traveling train. Fuckin' and fightin' is my game. Shoot out the lights and bust down the doors and screw all those women for twenty-dollar whores."

JT had heard it before.

"Come here, bitch, and bring me a hot toddy, cause I'm goin' lay right down and fuck everybody."

He staggered, scrambled up, and rushed out the door like a madman. He got in his truck, peeled out in reverse, then started doing circles in the snow in the middle of the street, blowing his horn.

JT wondered why Lucy would put up with any of this. Someone called the sheriff, and a minute or two later, the sheriff's car was turning down the street, chains drumming through the snow, lights

flashing. Coop's truck took two more turns, then sped off past the
Texaco, the sheriff in pursuit. At the end of the street, Coop missed
the turn and his truck started sliding sideways and hit a telephone
pole. By the time JT hoofed it down the road, a crowd had gathered,
and the sheriff was pulling Coop out of his truck. He was mumbling, nose split, blood running, front tooth knocked out.

"Shoot me, you cocksucker," Coop cried. "Just shoot me."

"You frickin' idiot. I should shoot you," the sheriff said angrily,
handcuffing Coop, spinning him around, and yelling in his face.
"You damn near killed yourself! Acting like a drunken asshole! I'm
sick'a yer shit. Yer gonna end up dead. Dead or in the loony bin."

JT stopped the officer as he shoved Coop in the back seat. He
talked to him slowly and said they were friends from the war. He
asked the officer if he could give Coop a break.

"I'm tired of giving this drunk pissant a break. We all know
about his war and all that, but I've had it up to my eyeballs with
his crap."

"Shoot me. Fuckin' shoot me," Coop said again, slumped over
like a boxer on a stool, brain half working.

"Let's take him home," JT pleaded. "He'll just puke all over your
jail. You can write him up tomorrow. He ain't going anywhere anyway. His truck's probably totaled."

The sheriff fumed, swore, and read the riot act to JT. Then he
opened the back door and swore at Coop. When he was done, he
relented.

"It's against my better judgment. I'd just as soon lock his drunk
ass up and throw away the frickin' key." He took a deep breath, got
back in the car, and took them both home.

"Tell Lucy I said she should throw the bum out," the sheriff said.
"Throw him out or get him in a damn hospital." He left, lights still
flashing.

Lucy helped waltz Coop inside, then JT pushed him onto the bed
and stood in the doorway as Coop flopped to his back in the dark.

"Stay there, you shithead."

"I hate myself. I wanta go home."

"You are home."

JT and Lucy went into the front room and sat down. The fire had died, and the room was cold.

"I'm sorry, Lucy. But he wouldn't stop drinking."

"It's not your fault. Coop's been trying to drink himself to death for a long time," Lucy said, sitting back in a rocker.

There was a sadness in her face as she rocked and looked at the fire. He found himself pulled into that sadness, a grief that seemed to have no end. Ashley. Anna. Gurney. Ski. Montana. His dad. How did anyone bear it? They sat there for a long time not speaking. Finally, Lucy stopped rocking and began to weep. JT wanted to comfort her, but he had no comfort to offer. He didn't know if he could help himself, much less Coop.

But he wasn't going to leave him behind. He'd talk to him, once he was sober. Maybe, probably, Coop would just tell him to fuck off, but he'd try.

IN THE MORNING, LUCY SHOOK JT AWAKE. He was on the couch, boots in front of a dead fire. The room had a chill, and the windows were glazed with moisture.

"Coop's gone," Lucy said with a look of loss on her face and urgency in her voice, as if Coop were a missing child.

JT sat up. "What do you mean?"

"I thought I heard him get up an hour or so before dawn, but I figured he was just going to the bathroom and I fell back asleep. When I woke up, he was gone. I found this note on the kitchen table."

JT took the note—

Going on patrol. Love you both.

Coop

Lucy hurriedly put on her jacket. There was anguish on her face and in her voice. "We've got to go," she said. "We've got to find him."

"Try not to worry."

"He took his pistol, JT," she cried. "He took his gun!"

JT grabbed his boots and coat as the crisis became clear. He looked at her directly and tried to calm her. "He probably wanted to shoot a rabbit or something to try and show off. I'll find him. It'll be OK."

"I'm going with you," she said, wiping her eyes. "When I find that son of a bitch…"

The sun was out and reflected hard off the snow as they followed Coop's footprints away from the house and down toward the river. A couple of kids were walking toward them playfully carrying a friend.

"You kids see anyone?"

"No. Nobody," a bundled-up boy said. "We just got outta the house."

When JT could see the river, the prints disappeared.

"Go on back, Lucy. I'll find the goofball," JT said. "Meet you back at the house."

Lucy relented, and JT walked on, a feeling of dread working on him. As he walked along the bank looking down on the clear running river, he thought of their first patrol. It seemed so long ago and as if it happened to someone else. Maybe it was the water, or the trees, or the boys, but when he thought of Coop, it seemed as if he had never known him. All that wildness, craziness, was a big distraction. A feint—look here—while Coop was somewhere else.

Ahead of JT was a cluster of trees, and as he got closer, he started to run. He could see Coop's red plaid coat beneath a tree. He stopped and looked at the coat and then down to the river. Coop was naked from the waist up, standing just off the bank in the water. His head was back, arms raised toward the sun. He had his Johnnie Walker in one hand and his .45 in the other. His shirt and undershirt were floating downstream.

"Coop," JT shouted. "What the hell are you doing?"

Coop dropped his arms and turned toward JT. And in that instant, his face had a look JT had seen before. He looked like he was sorry.

"Don't!" JT screamed.

A DAY AFTER THE FUNERAL, LUCY DROPPED JT at the bus stop, and he caught a Trailways back to Portland. The bus rolled through the countryside, past empty pastures and fields of corn broken down from winter. Snow that fell so heavily in Joseph was miles away, and all that remained were cold, gray patches along the roadside, like soldiers spent or dying.

JT leaned his head on the window. His eyes were empty and his mind troubled, fixed on Coop. He could see him standing in the water and the look on his face just before he died. Farms and barns blurred by, and the bus kept moving.

He thought of their life together, from boot camp to the battlefield and the last moments of Coop's life. He wanted to remember everything as if remembering could somehow keep Coop alive.

When the bus stopped at a gas station in La Grande, JT began to shake with quiet tremors, then his face tightened, eyes welled with tears. *What was happening?* He got off hurriedly, disoriented, staggered into the tiny restroom, and locked the door. He stood at the sink, body shaking, arms braced to hold him up, trying not to cry. Head down, he couldn't fight it anymore and began to weep. At first it was a whimper as he slowly raised his face to the mirror. He looked older than he remembered. Like someone else. He reached up, shut off the light, and was in total darkness, pulling Coop from the water.

He began to hyperventilate and felt like he was shattering inside. As he gripped the sink, tears and memories began to flood him. His body constricted, and he muffled a howl so deep and full of grief that it nearly drove him to the floor. Coop's eyes and the field of wounded and dead lay at his feet. He tried to resist the thoughts, but he saw the VC as they came out of the trees and killed the wounded as he lay helpless. And that's when it happened again. He stood and watched Coop stick a gun to his head. He couldn't save him, couldn't save his dad—he couldn't save any of them.

His body fell back against the wall, and he raised his fists to his temples, moaning and rocking side to side. The room seemed to implode; darkness became untenable. Gunships firing, artillery roaring, and he was trapped in his mind, afraid to die—

A knock on the door.

"Are you OK?" the bus driver asked. "How you doing in there?"

JT took some deep breaths, straightened up, knees weak. He was confused and flipped on the light switch.

The driver banged again, "Bus is leavin'."

JT turned on the water and mumbled but couldn't respond, then splashed his face and the back of his neck.

Outside, a blast of cold wind slapped him as he tried to catch his balance. He walked slowly to the bus, back rigid, chin up, biting down. He sat alone in the back of the bus, sweating. His head was pounding and he wasn't sure what happened. He felt ashamed. Ashamed of what he had become. He knew if he started to cry again, he'd never stop, and then he'd lose his mind.

At Pilot Rock, an old woman boarded, but JT didn't notice. By Pendleton, he was breathing better but exhausted. His shoulders and back ached, and he felt like he had just carried Coop back up the bank and through the snow again.

A busted-up old cowboy got on at Pendleton and sat across the aisle from JT.

"Damn. It's a cold mother," the cowboy said, rubbing his hands together.

JT shifted in his seat as the bus ran through its gears. His own death was hanging over him, traveling with him, as it always had. "When I die, I don't want to look that sorry," he whispered. He had to save himself.

In Umatilla, the bus dropped off twin sisters to their anxious mother, standing beside a station wagon, arms folded, cheeks blushed from the cold. The cowboy was quiet. JT was drained. But his mind was still bouncing from memory to memory.

When the bus turned off the road at The Dalles, it was almost empty, and JT had run through most of his life. None of it too pretty. He remembered his dad drinking and wounded soldiers lying back, eyes open, hoping. He remembered Ashley leaving and Anna's hurt face when he saw her after too long. Coop's body.

On the highway easing up on the Columbia River Gorge, the day was closing. Mountains were round and rocky, but the road straightened some, and the river could be seen. Soon boulders turned to trees, and the trees faded into darkness. The night and the hum of the tires soothed him.

At Hood River, the bus stopped.

"Thirty minutes, folks," the driver said, standing in the aisle. "There's a café open across from the Elks."

JT stayed on the bus and drifted back to White Salmon, living in a boxcar, chipping ice out of tunnels, chainsaw kicking.

Then there was Kendal, filling up his mind.

He closed his eyes and thought of her again.

Tomorrow he'd try to find her.

About the Author

As an 18-year-old Marine, Jack Estes fought in Vietnam in 1968–1969, the bloodiest years of the war. He was wounded and decorated for heroism. After coming home, he attended Portland State University and Southern Illinois University and began writing and speaking about the plight of veterans, about war, and about the mental and physical damage war inflicts on soldiers and their families.

Over the years, his articles and essays have appeared in *Newsweek,* the *Wall Street Journal, Chicago Tribune, Los Angeles Times,* the *Timberline Review*, the *Oregonian*, and others.

In 1993 Jack and his wife, Colleen, traveled to Vietnam to deliver medical and educational supplies and toys to schools, hospitals, and orphanages. He also returned to the village where he once lived, to what Colleen calls his "original point of pain." The purpose was to carry humanitarian goods instead of a machine gun, to replace bad memories with good. He also wanted to try to find a Vietnamese soldier who once helped save his life.

From that trip, Jack and Colleen created the Fallen Warriors Foundation to honor the sacrifices of American soldiers and to help heal the pain of war. Since then, the Fallen Warriors Foundation has delivered hundreds of thousands of dollars in medical and educational goods to the poorest of the poor in tiny Vietnamese villages. In subsequent trips, Jack took doctors and nurses to remote villages and primitive hospitals to give care. He led a group of disabled combat veterans to Vietnam, to their original points of pain, to help them heal. In addition, the foundation has held retreats, events, and theater pieces for veterans and their loved ones.

In 2013 the Fallen Warriors Foundation released a documentary about veterans and post-traumatic stress disorder and co-produced *Mind Zone*, a documentary on how veterans are treated for psychological trauma in current battle zones.

Please visit www.jackestes.com.

Acknowledgments

I am so grateful to Pam Wells for her inspiration, editing, design, and how she could sort through my thoughts and conclusions; and to Alison Cantrell for her invaluable attention to detail. Lastly, I thank my wife, Colleen, for always supporting me.